The Ancient

&

The Cradle of Civilization

Book I of The Ancient Chronicles

Danielle Q, Lee

For my best friend

Part One

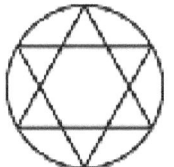

The Archaeologist

1

Exordium

"*C areful, Petra…*"
A pearl of sweat fell from her brow and landed on a lapis lazuli inset. The blue stone exploded with colour, awakening like a single, sapphire eye. Ancient dust plumed around her as she exposed the vase to the sun for the first time in thousands of years. She dabbed the exterior with a damp sponge. A hairline crack ran from the top to the base of the artifact, scoring the ghostly image. Petra studied the painting, trying to decipher the symbols. A depiction of daily life in Mesopotamia, perhaps? A tribute to the Sumerian gods and goddesses?

Petra groaned around a long stretch. After a long drink of water, she wet a rag and dragged it over her bare neck and shoulders. An Iraqi boy transporting a wheelbarrow stopped and stared at her with wide, almost fearful, eyes. She glanced at the traditional robes resting in a dark heap a few feet away. It was risky dressing so informal, but the air was stifling, made worse beneath the long, black abayas.

"What do you have there, Miss Monroe?" Emmett's voice startled her. The old professor had a soft step from decades of walking through digs.

Petra looked up, shielding her eyes from the sun. "I think it's an amphora, I uncovered one of the handles yesterday." She grinned at her mentor, knowing he'd be just as excited as she was.

There was a camaraderie among diggers, a ubiquitous longing to touch the past with their bare hands. Most had similar tales of childhoods spent excavating their backyards, searching for anything that might transport them to another place and time. There was always a trace of humanity left behind. She often wondered what morsel of her existence she might leave for some ambitious digger to discover.

"Let's have a look, shall we?" He stepped over the web of string and plumb bobs, joints crackling as he knelt beside her. With a gentle touch, he tapped the torso of the artifact. "Baked clay…originally painted with what looks to be a white glaze, insets of lapis lazuli, detailed with gold and red limestone. It appears to be intact. Third Dynasty of the Early Bronze Age, maybe. Fourth at the latest."

Petra beamed. A find like this could mean international publication and a gold star beside her credentials. Several students within earshot dropped their trowels and screens, joining them.

"Beautiful," the old professor whispered, tracing the timeworn painting. "I think that's Inanna."

"Inanna? Really?" Petra squinted at the faded image. Nude figures bowed before a throned female, placing offerings at her feet; traditionally of rare oils, perfumes, exotic flowers, and sacrifices of powerful animals, lions and serpents. Lines of unfamiliar cuneiform text framed the picture. While she'd taken several courses in ancient languages, there were hundreds of variations in the wedge-like writing. Few people in the world could decipher a full tablet of ancient Sumerian text.

Emmett nodded, taking the opportunity to educate his students on the mythology. "She was known as Ishtar to the Babylonians, Anahita to the Persians, Isis to the Egyptians—and of course, Inanna to the Sumerians. She fell under dozens of aliases over time, her reputation permeating many civilizations after Sumer. The Sumerians built a shrine for her in Uruk—The White Temple. She was one of the most beautiful and powerful deities of the time—but also the most feared." His attention returned to the relic. "What can you tell me about it, Petra?" he asked, testing her.

"It's similar to the Warka Vase at the Pergamon Museum in Berlin, much smaller though. These carvings here..." She pointed to the strange markings. "They're not traditional Sumerian writing. They're similar to hieroglyphics, but not quite the same...curious."

Emmett beamed at her. "Good work. You might really have something here, Petra." He patted her shoulder and then gently used it to push himself up. "It's almost five o'clock, we have to head out soon, it's a long walk back to the hostel," he said with some hesitation. Vehicles were not allowed to drive within ten miles of the excavation site without special permits from the Iraqi government, leaving the team no choice but to walk an hour to and from town every day. Conversely, this also allowed the team to cut across the open desert and avoid the various armed checkpoints along the main road.

Petra's chest tightened at the thought of leaving the artifact overnight. She wished she could just dig a makeshift bed beside the hole and protect her prize until morning. Instead, she covered the artifact with a tarp, weighing the edges with some tools.

A large shadow loomed over her just then, blocking out the sun.

"What'd you find there, Newfie?"

It was Gabriel, the night watchman.

Petra's jaw clenched and she turned a cold eye to the guard. She'd explained to the foreigner before that she was from Vancouver and it was nowhere near Newfoundland, but she suspected he merely delighted in annoying her. Gabriel studied her from head to toe, pausing on her bare legs. She suddenly felt naked without the *abayas* to hide her.

"Maybe an old washing pot, we're not sure yet." She tried to act blasé, hoping he hadn't overheard Emmett's analysis or seen the relic before she covered it. Things went missing when Gabriel was around—

2

seen later for sale on eBay. There was nothing the professor could do about it, the Iraqi government hired the guards.

Gabriel grinned, twisting the side of his moustache. He walked away, glancing back before resuming his post at the corner of the excavation.

Standing, she wiped the sand off her legs and donned the black robes with a bit of relief. As she and the group began the journey back to town, she stopped and looked back. Gabriel was watching her with a cocky grin on his face.

The tightness in her chest squeezed a little harder.

Everything ached.

Petra rubbed her sunburned forehead. Grit and grime rolled beneath her fingertips. It had been a few days since she'd showered—a mud puddle was clearer than the water at the hostel. Strands of her blonde hair, frayed and fragile from the desert sun, fell into her face. She tucked them behind her ear, wishing she'd cut it all off before she left Vancouver.

Joe, a fellow student from her ancient mythology class, set a plate of lamb and curried rice before her.

"Hungry?"

"Thanks, I could've gotten my own food though, I'm not *totally* without culinary skills."

He shot her a skeptical look. "You sure about that? I've seen some of the lunches you've brought to school."

Petra rolled her eyes playfully, knowing he wasn't too far off the mark.

Joe tossed his phone on the table with a dramatic sigh.

"What?"

"No service. I can get some sketchy wifi, but I can't make any calls. I'm lost without my tech."

"I'm sure you'll survive," she teased. After an exhale of her own, she dug into her dinner.

"You okay, Petra?"

"Yes—no. I found something amazing and I really hate leaving it exposed."

"Oh? What did you find?"

"An Early Bronze Age amphora, possibly intact!" Exhaustion gave way to excitement at the thought of prying the artifact loose the next day.

"Wow, that's awesome! Not as good as mine though—I found a *rather* large chunk of petrified oxen dung." He gave her two thumbs up. "You're pretty lucky. A seasoned archaeologist could dig for years and not uncover anything that cool. This could land you an internship at a stellar museum over the summer, which would certainly help pay off those nasty student loans. I know I could use that."

"That would be nice…but fame and fortune isn't really my motive." A frazzled tendril fell across her eye and she swept it behind her ear.

"What else is there?" Joe winked at her.

"I just love getting a glimpse into the past. Seeing who these ancient people were and how they lived. These artifacts are all that's left of them, something they made with their bare hands. In a way, they've left a small piece of their soul for us to find."

"So basically, you just have a morbid fascination with dead people."

She chuckled, but worried her lip. "I hope it'll be okay overnight."

"Why wouldn't it? It's not like they're expecting a deluge anytime soon. It only rains like every four years in the desert."

Petra poked at the rubbery lamb. "Someone could steal it."

"What? You don't trust good old Gabriel?" He clutched his heart in exaggerated shock.

"No, but I have a hard time trusting people in general."

"Oh," he said with a look of genuine surprise. "I understand, but sometimes you just have to give people the benefit of the doubt—even those who might not deserve it."

"You're right. I just wish I didn't have to leave it when I was so close to digging it out…"

"Is this seat taken?" Emmett approached the table, plateful of food in hand.

Joe gestured to the empty chair. "It is now."

Emmett settled in beside Petra.

"By the way," he said to her, "I called the museum and asked if they could put another guard on tonight—in case you were still worried."

"Oh, thank you!" Petra grinned.

"I met him just before supper. Seems nice, very tall." Emmett took a sip of ale, adding reflectively, "Interesting eyes."

"So they gave Gabriel the night off?" she asked, taking a bite of meat.

"No, Gabriel is still out there for this evening," Emmett said. "But perhaps this other fellow can keep on an eye on him for us, hmm?'

The lamb caught in Petra's throat. She chased it with a gulp of water.

"No need to worry, dear. I'm sure your treasure is safe." He patted her hand.

Petra chewed the inside of her cheek. "I-I'm sorry, I have to go." She set her napkin over the plate of half-eaten food.

"Are you all right, dear?" Emmett's silver brows furrowed.

"Yes, of course. I just…forgot to do something."

Petra rose and left the common room. A dark plan festered, one that could get her into a lot of trouble—but first she needed to find some scissors.

After braving a tepid shower of beige water, Petra stood before the bathroom mirror and cut her hair into a short pixie. The dull scissors made for a choppy do, but they got the job done—though it certainly wouldn't pass her mother's critical eye once Petra returned to Vancouver.

With the hostel's bed sheets, she bound her already modest breasts. She then donned a pair of baggy pants the locals called a *saroual* and a loose tunic, throwing a checkered *kufiya* on her head for good measure. If she kept her chin down and her mouth shut, she should be fine.

4

She glanced at her phone. The wifi bars bounced weakly, but there was no cell service.

"No point in taking it if I can't even call for help," she said, tossing it onto the bed. She slipped out the door and started on the familiar path to the dig. Night air breathed on her neck, cool despite the inferno only hours before. The further she walked, the darker it became as the lights grew smaller behind her. Fear of getting lost, or worse, being discovered, made her queasy.

"The vase, Petra," she whispered between deep breaths. "Just focus on the vase."

The excavation site was black. Only the light of a small campfire flickered in the shadows, near which she could hear the deep rumble of conversation. Crouched, she took the long way around. She glared in the direction of the voices, hearing Gabriel and the new guard laugh like a pair of old army buddies.

"Safe, my ass," she muttered, and then felt a stab of guilt at mistrusting the professor's judgment. It wasn't that she didn't trust *him*, she just didn't trust anyone else.

I could just finish digging it out and take it back to the hostel to protect it...

She grinned in the darkness.

With the excavation string as a guide, Petra felt her way along the perimeter. Dim starlight offered her just enough illumination to discern her path. Still, she paid close attention to her footing. The last thing she wanted was to trip and fall onto a priceless relic. When she reached the fifth quadrant, she lifted her foot to step over the string—but stopped. She could get into a lot of trouble just for being on the dig after hours, and the Iraqi government wasn't known for its leniency. Not to mention, Emmett would be very disappointed and probably kick her off the project. She could even be expelled from university. It's not that she hadn't considered the ramifications during the walk out, but now it was a reality. She looked longingly at the dark spot where her beloved vase lay half-buried. It would only take a minute to uncover it and make sure it was still there—but she'd already blurred the lines of ethics enough for one day.

Petra sighed, shoulders heavy with decision. Reluctantly, she turned to make the long trek back to the hostel. She'd simply have to trust that the relic was going to be there tomorrow.

She'd only taken a few steps when she heard a thumping noise to her right. It was getting louder—and closer.

A sick sensation twisted inside her stomach.

She turned to see a hulking shadow rush at her from the darkness. Before she could cry out, a fist slammed into her stomach and knocked the wind out of her. Doubled over, she was paralyzed by unimaginable pain. Strong hands shoved to her the ground. Sand coated her lips and tongue, the taste of copper filled her mouth. She wheezed, trying to draw air into her lungs.

"*Ma aldhy tafealuh hna!*" a deep voice growled. She recognized his words as being Arabic, but couldn't determine what he was saying—though she was fairly certain he wasn't happy.

5

Disoriented, blinded by tears, she struggled to her knees and tried to crawl away. She'd only made it a couple of feet when he kicked her in the ribs so hard she momentarily lost contact with the ground. Now on her back, sipping shallow breaths, Petra stared up at the night sky pinpointed with tiny, silver lights, wondering if she was going to die.

Pain brought her to the brink of unconsciousness—but terror kept her wide awake.

Just let me live. I just want to live through this…

Sand shuffled around her. Steps slow, calculated. Then he was on top of her, straddling her torso, pinning her arms with his knees. One hand squeezed her neck while the other held a blade under her chin.

"*In 'as'al maratan 'ukhraa!*" he barked, the cold steel taut against her jugular.

A warm tear slipped past her temple.

"P-Please," she whispered. "Don't."

"You're a…a *woman?*" He clambered off. "Who are you?"

Petra turned onto her side, coughing and spitting out sand. "I-I'm… one of the archaeology…students."

"Why are you dressed as a man—I could've killed you." His voice tightened.

"Ironically," she said, managing a weak chuckle. "I thought I'd be safer."

"What are you doing out here?

She struggled to sit up. "I-I found a—" she caught herself, hesitant to reveal too much. "A piece of pottery. I wanted…to protect it."

"It is protected." His voice was resolute.

"I need to make sure. I have to see…" Petra gasped as he slipped his hands under her arms, lifting her to her feet. "Don't touch me!"

Palms open, he took a step back. "I'm sorry."

Her eyes narrowed. Something about this man didn't fit.

"Who are you?" she demanded.

He remained silent.

Petra crossed her arms. "I said, who are…"

Gabriel's voice sounded in the distance. "Solomon?"

Solomon.

"You must go!" he hissed.

"But the artifact, I need to—" she started, but he blocked her path as Gabriel's calls grew closer.

He grabbed her arm and pulled her against him, his breath hot in her ear. "You must go, *nga beleti.* The vessel is safe, but you are not. *Go!*"

She turned and ran as fast as she could back to the hostel. Her ribs screamed, but she didn't stop until she reached her room. As soon as the door clicked shut, she snatched up her phone and searched for a universal translator.

Still panting, she typed: nga beleti.

The internet crawled.

Voice trembling, she read: "*Nga beleti.* Meaning: my lady—Ancient Sumerian."

2

Fata Morgana

"*M*iss Petra?" Knocking at the door. "It is time for your work!"
Petra opened one eye and reached for her phone to check
the time. Her body cried out in pain and the evening's
events came rushing back. She draped an arm over her aching abdomen, worried for her poor internal organs. The thought crossed her
mind that she should go to the hospital, but the notion of seeing a doctor in a foreign country gave way to all kinds of unpleasant scenarios,
mostly health insurance nightmares and questions she didn't want to
answer about how and where she obtained her injuries.

She forced herself to a sitting position, groaning.

"Miss Petra?" Fatima knocked again, louder. "Mr Emmett is leaving
soon!"

"I'm up, thank you, Fatima." She swung her feet over the side of the
bed, cradling her head. "Ugh, this is worse than a hangover."

"*Nga beleti,*" the man's voice echoed in her memory. "*The vessel is
safe…*"

"Vessel." She considered the word. "Not a vase or a pitcher, but a
vessel."

Rising, she limped across the room to the mirror. She lifted her shirt
and grimaced, eyeing the violet stain on her rib cage.

"*Jesus.*"

After a lot of cursing, she managed to bind herself again, this time
focusing on her torso and not her breasts. She downed a couple as-
pirin, gathered up her gear, and walked out—slowly.

Heat waves rolled over the horizon, a watery mirage eclipsing the surface of the sand—the *Fata Morgana.*

Petra took shallow breaths as she struggled to keep up with the
group.

Joe slowed his pace to walk with her. "Hey, you cut your hair! Looks
good!"

"Thanks." Petra ran a hand through her short locks. Yesterday it felt
like freedom, today she felt naked.

"Excited to pull out the artifact?" he asked.

"Nervous. I have visions of it smashed to pieces or halfway to Cairo."

He laughed. "I'm sure it's fine."

"Joe!" a female student called, waving for him to walk with her. He
gave Petra a shameless grin and jogged ahead.

Her nerves fluttered as they neared the ruins. She wished she could've seen it the night before, to set her anxiety at ease. Nausea turned her stomach with the notion of yanking back the tarp to discover the artifact gone. Paranoia summoned a vision of Gabriel and the stranger laughing as they wrenched her prize from its resting place.

The stranger.

Solomon.

Nga beleti—my lady.

Her mind obsessed over his words, turning them over and over, trying to make sense of them. Why did he speak in an ancient language no one spoke anymore?

"*It is protected.*"

She stopped short, the pain intensifying. Emmett rushed to her side just as she doubled over.

"Petra?"

"I'm okay." She opened her pack, rummaging for a water bottle. "Just a pulled muscle or something. Go on, I'll catch up."

"Don't be silly." He knelt and fished out her drink, handing it to her. "I'm not leaving you behind."

She felt better after a few gulps and they continued on the path, the majority of students far ahead.

"Are you sure you're okay?"

"Yeah," she said. "Pretty excited to get to the dig and finish pulling that vase out."

Vessel, her mind corrected.

"So," Emmett asked suddenly, "have you given any thought to what you'll do after you graduate?"

Petra paused. Of course she had. That's all she'd thought about during the last four years. Her mother wanted her to stay in Vancouver, maybe work at the Museum of Natural History for a year or two, and then get married and have babies. She cringed. Tradition made her squeamish. She had bigger plans. She was only twenty-two and had so much more to do before settling down—if she ever did.

"Well, I had hoped to do my internship at the British Museum—if they'll take me. I'd love to just dig all day, but…" She shrugged, knowing the reality of excavations and the constant lack of funding. "Why?"

Emmett turned his attention to the desert, admiring the ocean of bronze. She followed his gaze to the windswept waves of sand. So desolate, so alien to the paved and manicured metropolis she grew up in.

"Oh, I don't know," he said. "I thought perhaps you might join my team…permanently."

"Are you serious!"

"Of course I'm serious, you're the best student I've ever had. But," he lowered his voice, "don't, uh, tell that to the others, okay? Think on it, it's a big decision."

Then he linked elbows with her and they strolled to the site.

Petra knelt, heart pounding as she peered through the plastic tarp, condensation obscuring her view. One by one, she removed the weights, relieved they were still there. Surely if the artifact had been stolen, they wouldn't have bothered to replace the cover.

With the last tool removed, she lifted the tarp and released the breath of air she'd been holding. It was there. Intact and as beautiful as she'd left it. Her heart warmed at the painted image, somehow brighter and more colourful than the previous day.

She glanced around for Gabriel. He didn't appear to be there, which made sense since he'd been on night duty, though she kept an eye out for him nonetheless. And, of course, she watched for the new guard, Solomon. Not only to satisfy her curiosity about him, but to thank him for the broken ribs.

For the next few hours, she happily whisked away the dirt that held the artifact in place.

Then, it was time.

"Emmett!" she called. "I'm ready to lift it out!"

The professor practically ran over. Several students abandoned their sifters, including Joe, and followed Emmett's lead. This was everyone's favourite moment on any dig. Frankly, this was why they did it.

"Ready?" She leaned over the hole, ignoring the stab of pain in her side, and gently wrapped the relic with gauze. Then she tucked two slings under the torso and linked the ends to the tripod hoist Joe had set up over the hole. The vase wasn't particularly big, but depending on what was inside, it could weigh enough to put excess pressure on the fragile clay.

"One, two, three," she whispered and Joe gave the winch a gentle turn. Petra stayed in the hole and eased the body out of its grave. It took several tries, but soon the dirt loosened and gave way. She held her breath as Joe slowly turned the winch, leaving just enough slack for the crew to guide it to the ground beside the hole. Petra removed the gauze and plastic, unwrapping it like a present.

A flurry of activity ensued as the group swarmed the artifact.

"Look, there! The writing! It looks like cuneiform text!"

"It's still sealed! I wonder what's inside!"

"Is that Inanna?"

Petra beamed, the noise and crowd fading as she gazed at her find. Lapis lazuli insets glowed cerulean in the desert sun, gold flecks and blood-red limestone accented the wedges of text. Petra imagined the ancient hands that must have slaved over every painstaking detail. She imagined his life, his thoughts, his fleeting existence, and how he could now live forever through the eyes of the future. She felt as though she'd somehow made him…*immortal*.

Then Emmett said something that chilled her blood.

"Look!" He pointed to the timeworn impression of a star on the bottom. "It's not a vase, it's what the Sumerians called a death jar—it's an *urn*."

Urn—*vessel*.

"Smile, Petra!" Joe aimed his phone at her crouched beside the urn. She was happy she'd be able to look at it in pictures. It would be months, maybe years, before it was on display at the museum for her to admire again.

"Joe!" a student called to him and he strolled away, leaving Petra alone to admire her prize.

She eyed the mouth of the urn, fingers itching to remove the seal. What was inside?

'*Vessel*,' Solomon's deep voice echoed.

Not *what*, perhaps—but *who*?

She moved around the urn. Another image was on the back, concealed by a patch of sand. Petra carefully brushed away the dirt.

Her eyes widened.

It was a different depiction of Inanna—violent and bloody, laden with various acts of torture and sex. Crimson limestone accentuated the animal and human sacrifice. The naked goddess, adorned with lapis lazuli, carnelian, and gold, stood before the inhumanity—commanding the deeds be done. Over Inanna's head, hovering like a dark crown, was an eight-pointed star.

Petra peered at the strange text. While she'd learned the more common words of the Sumerian language—a complex system of wedges—these were unfamiliar. Then she saw something that made her stomach drop: a deep crack, hidden within a spoke of Inanna's crown.

"Oh no," she whispered.

With her finger, she traced the fissure to discern how detrimental it might be to the relic's integrity.

It didn't appear too bad, but…

"Ouch!" Petra jerked back her hand.

A distinct gash ran through her fingertip, wet with blood. Heart thrumming, she inspected the urn for signs of staining. Even a speck of blood could compromise the painting.

"Oh god…please no…"

A thick, red smear marred the surface beside Inanna.

Horrified, she lifted her shirt to wipe it away. But before she could, the stain began to shrink. Slowly seeping *into* the body of the urn.

Consumed.

Within seconds, the blood was gone.

Petra stared at the artifact, bewildered.

She glanced at her finger—the cut, too, had vanished.

Petra and the team prepared the artifact for transport. Mummified in white gauze and bubble wrap, her urn was ready to be moved to the museum in Baghdad where it would undergo a cleaning and various examinations, such as an MRI, which could reveal the contents sealed inside. Artifacts were immediately the property of the country it was found in, but the credit of discovering it would go to her. Her name would be typed beside it forever, in every history book to come.

The dig was done. They cleared their tools and backfilled the holes, endeavouring to leave the site as they'd found it. She'd been on a few other excavations, nothing of this caliber, but plenty enough to know that the end was always bittersweet. Knowing that beneath their feet, there was still more to be found. The relics whispered, called to the diggers, to the finders of the past, begging their stories be told—and Petra always wanted to listen.

She closed her eyes, feeling the air cool as the sun lowered itself into the horizon. The sky glowed mauve and gold until the canopy turned black, scattered with ice-white stars. No light pollution or buildings to mar the view. She hugged her torso, wincing as her ribs smarted, reminding her of recent adventures. She smiled despite the pain, grateful for the whole experience.

"Ready to go?" Emmett asked from behind her, his voice equally reverent as he eyed the ancient sky.

She nodded, not really ready to leave, but knowing she had to.

3

Epiphany

*P*etra paid the driver, gathered up her bags, and drew a deep breath. Vancouver smelled like coffee and exhaust. While she was glad to be home, she already missed the heat and ancient ambiance of Iraq—she was, however, looking forward to her first real shower in seven weeks. She threw her carry-on bag over her right shoulder, wincing as a tender spot made itself known. It could've been a sunburn, but she'd been out of the sun, travelling, for the last few days.

Weird. She shrugged. *Probably just another present from Solomon's tackle.*

She smiled in spite of herself.

Solomon.

His words, his voice—they burned inside her. He'd become a phantom of her journey. Someday she'd laugh about the experience, how some strange, foreign man had come crashing into her life—albeit brief—and left her to wonder about him forever as a mystery.

A part of her toyed with romantic notions of him, fancies she wouldn't dare utter unless provoked by champagne or whispered giggles among good friends. But, she didn't drink and didn't have any close friends, so her erotic whims would likely remain imprisoned until they faded into a distant recollection only summoned on late, lonely summer nights. Solomon would soon be a hazy memory from an exotic land, buried beneath hot sands of gold.

She rolled her eyes.

Wow, Petra! Hung up on some hulking shadow with a sexy voice?

Suddenly her head felt strange, dizzy and swimming. She clutched the railing as dark, provocative images flashed behind her eyes. Bodies writhing in pleasure, shrouded in shadow—covered in blood. Petra drew deep breaths and slowly the foreign thoughts withdrew into some dark dungeon of her mind she didn't even know existed.

Shaken, she chalked the incident up to jet lag and walked up the steps to her apartment complex. With cell phone under her chin and handbag perched awkwardly on her thigh, she rummaged for her keys. Just as she'd found them, her phone started to ring. She growled and set her bag down.

"Hello?"

"Petra, it's Emmett." His voice was monotone.

"What's wrong?" Petra's heart started to race.

"The urn—it's missing."

Tears sprang to her eyes. The keys fell from her hands and landed with a dull *chink* against the cement steps.

Petra stared at the photo laying on Emmett's desk, the image captured her and the urn together just days ago. Bitterness writhed inside. Years of planning, fund-raising, and seven long weeks in the desert digging, hoping, and then filled with joy—all to have it stolen in a single moment of greed.

"Apparently, the truck arrived at the museum," Emmett explained. "But they insist the urn was not among the artifacts. The driver claims he drove straight from the dig to the museum."

"How does something just *disappear?*" Predictably, Petra's thoughts turned to Gabriel. *Of course* he had something to do with it. No one outside the dig, besides the museum, had knowledge of the urn.

"I'm so sorry, Petra. I'm just as upset as you are."

She nodded, certain he was. This incident would have dire repercussions for any future digs; not to mention further funding restrictions from the university—who was already reluctant in parting with their money for 'field trips'.

"What do we do now?" she asked, staring sightlessly at the floor.

"I'm afraid there's nothing we can do," he said. "The university and museum have spoken, and the museum is blaming us for the loss. Our reputation with Iraq is irrevocably tarnished. We will not likely be allowed to return, ever."

"How can they blame *us!*"

Emmett raised his hands. "I know, it's all very unfair."

She paced the room. "What about Gabriel? He has a reputation, Emmett. He's known for stealing artifacts!"

"Yes, I thought of that, but Gabriel was—irrefutably—accounted for at the time." When Petra gave him a confused look, he blushed and rubbed the back of his neck. "An establishment of ill repute, it would seem."

She rolled her eyes and resumed her furious pacing.

"It can't just vanish! We put it on the truck ourselves! I personally signed the manifest. I mean, it should have been perfectly safe..."

She stopped dead.

The vessel is protected.

"Solomon," Petra hissed.

"I'm sorry, who?"

"The other guard that night, the one you said had the strange eyes. It was him. I know it!"

"Petra, we can't make assumpt..." Emmett began, but she was already on her way out the door.

Petra scrolled through the items on eBay, stomach fluttering each time she saw the words "ancient" and "artifact" but after a few hours, she could find nothing that resembled her urn.

Solomon.

13

How was she going to find him? She didn't even know what he looked like. All she had to go on was his shadowy build, his voice, and his...

She gasped as an idea struck her.

Her fingers flew across the keyboard, doing search after search on the internet. She just had to find the right link. Everyone could be found on the net, whether they liked it or not. She tried various keywords, throwing in one, eliminating others—but always highlighting, "Solomon". It couldn't be *that* common.

"Solomon, ancient, artifact, urn," she mumbled as she typed in the advanced search. She pressed enter.

The Net crawled.

An article link popped up: Professor Solomon Keyes, curator of The Egyptian Museum, found guilty of stealing artifacts from King Tut's exhibit.

Petra's mouth hung open, gaping at the picture of the man who'd obviously stolen her urn. He was very tall and annoyingly handsome. Even in the black and white photo, she could tell his eyes were an odd colour. He appeared to be of Egyptian descent, but could've passed for a variety of Arab heritages.

It is protected, his deep voice resounded.

"Protected my ass," she said with a huff, reading the article.

"Professor Solomon Keyes, notable scientist and curator was found guilty on all counts of theft regarding the ancient artifacts belonging to The Museum of Egypt. Of the stolen artifacts retrieved were: a scarab pendant, three ivory canopic jars, and a gold statuette of the goddess, Isis. While many of the stolen items were found hidden in Professor Keyes apartment, only one—an urn containing the ashes of an unknown Egyptian—was not among the articles."

"*Urn?*" A shiver crawled up Petra's spine. "How many urns does this man need?"

"Keyes was sentenced to fifteen years in Cairo Correctional Facility. Howard Carter, the infamous archaeologist who'd tirelessly searched The Valley of the Kings, and eventually discovered the intact tomb on November 4, 1922, was quoted after the arraignment as saying, "Justice has been served here, and most of the contents of Tut's tomb are together again despite this horrific act of disrespect."

Petra sat back, confused.

Howard Carter? He died 75 years ago!

She squinted at the description under the photo.

"Professor Solomon Keyes being led to prison...November 16, *1926.*"

4

The Storm

*E*mmett stared at her from across his desk, incredulous. "Petra, I don't think you are well. Perhaps…"

"Just listen to me! This guy, there's a link somehow! Maybe it's his son or grandson or something, you know how people name their kids after a dead relative!"

"Petra," Emmett said softly. "Let it go."

She dropped her head into her hands. "I can't. It was my future, my foot in the door. Now I have nothing again, just a student at the mercy of my mother's chequebook." She flopped into the chair across from him. "I really needed this, Emmett."

In truth, the artifact meant so much more than just notoriety, but she couldn't bring herself to face the reality of it really being gone—and that it was her fault. For a moment, she wished she'd never found it. The guilt of losing such a priceless work of art weighed too heavy on her soul.

Emmett sighed, steepling his fingers under his chin. "I understand your disappointment, my dear, but you have many digs ahead of you, I'm sure you'll find another artifact, you're young."

"I don't want another artifact," Petra said, feigning a petulant pout. "I want that one."

He laughed, and she surrendered a small chuckle.

"Will you…indulge me, though?" She folded her fingers together, begging.

"How?"

"Just look at this picture," Petra opened the saved image on her phone. "Do you think the thief could be a relative of the guard with the strange eyes? Does he look like him?"

"Well?" she asked, watching his face.

He gazed at the aged photograph—and paled.

Petra stared at the ceiling, the headlights of passing cars ripped through the shadows, illuminating her room, and then tossed her back into darkness.

Who was Solomon Keyes—and why was he in a photograph taken almost 100 years ago?

Nga beleti.

My lady.

Ancient Sumerian.

No. She turned onto her side and roughly adjusted her pillow. *Don't be ridiculous, Petra. It's impossible.*

But Emmett's face burned a hole in her memory. Not only had he recognized the man, he appeared…afraid.

No. You're reading too much into this. There was a theft, by some guy that resembles another thief from a long time ago…a guy with the same first name, who speaks an ancient language, has exotic, sexy eyes…

"Ugh!" Petra threw the covers off. "May as well get up."

After an exhaustive search through the empty cabinets, she finally found a lone teabag crumpled at the back of the pantry. The kettle whistled in alarm and she poured the steaming water. Petra cradled the teacup between her palms, savouring the warmth. Her shoulder ached again. She massaged it, deciding to visit the doctor later on in the week.

Petra looked out over the restless city, wondering how many others were awake. Cool air enveloped her as she opened the patio door and stepped out onto the balcony. She shivered and clutched her hot cup tighter, willing the warmth to permeate her body. The heat of the desert had saturated her skin, the hours of working beneath a nearer sun still simmered in her blood.

Chilled, she turned to go back inside. She'd only taken a few steps when she heard a soft thump behind her. Petra spun around and gasped, the teacup slipping from her hands and shattering onto the hardwood floor. A large shadow crouched on the narrow railing like a panther. He assessed her a moment; then with soundless grace, he jumped down onto the balcony.

She immediately recognized him from the picture.

Solomon.

Their eyes locked as he stepped through the doorway. He moved closer. Petra edged away, tempted to run, afraid to fight. Tall and muscular, chest and arms round with strength, he regarded her with a cold intensity that frightened her. A predator stalking his prey.

Beautiful and dangerous.

Instinct overwhelmed her and she bolted for the front door. In one swift movement, he closed the space between them, taking hold of her arm and clamping a hand over her mouth as he spun her to face him.

He was both feral and regal, black hair wild from the wind, dark skin bronze in the glow of the rising sun. His nose was sharp like an Egyptian's, jawline reminiscent of a Roman god—but his eyes were as blue as the deepest part of the ocean before it faded to black—and they glared at her, fathomless, a haunting palette of indigo and azure boring into her soul. Wrought with pain, wisdom, loneliness—and at the present moment—rage.

"Where is the vessel?" he demanded.

Petra's terror dissipated with the mention of her urn. She narrowed her eyes at him and fought against his grasp. Surprisingly, he let go.

"What, you mean it wasn't actually *protected* like you said it was?" she said sarcastically. "Maybe you should ask your friend, Gabriel!"

16

She took a defiant step closer and challenged his glare. If he hadn't killed her before, he wasn't going to now—she hoped.

"You were the last person to see it. If you don't know where it is, then who does?"

He paced the length of her living room like a lion worrying his den. She took the opportunity to inspect him: his gait, his clothes, his intensity. Though dressed in average street clothes, blue jeans and a black T-shirt, he had a way about him, an elegance.

"Who are you?" she asked, blocking his path.

He stopped short, measuring her with dark eyes. "You really don't know the whereabouts of the vessel?" he asked, ignoring her question.

"*You* said you were watching it!"

He growled, his hands clenched. "I was waiting for it at the museum…your professor, he knows something. I'm certain of it."

"Emmett? He's the one who told me it was missing!"

He scoffed. "You don't know your friends very well, *beleti*. He's not the man you think he is."

"Oh, really? And you do?"

"I know the heart of man too well, I'm afraid." He stared coldly out the window.

Petra searched his features. The similarity to the man in the photograph was uncanny. If she didn't know better, this was Solomon Keyes. She wanted to confront him, knowing deep down it was true, but she needed to hear him say it.

"Who are you?" she asked, softer.

He hesitated, eyes storming.

"I am Solomon."

"I know your name, Gabriel called it after you beat me up, remember?" She placed a hand on her sore ribs.

He looked away in shame. She felt guilty for rubbing it in and reached out to touch his arm, but he recoiled as if burned. She frowned, a little hurt.

"Why do you want the urn so badly? What's inside it?"

"You don't want to know," he said, his jaw tightening.

"As a matter of fact, I do."

He faced her, lips parted as if primed to spill his secrets, but then he stubbornly pressed them together. "I have to go…"

"Wait…" She moved to step in front of him, but doubled over in pain, clutching her shoulder. It burned like a hot iron piercing the bone.

"What is it?" He was at her side, guiding her to the couch.

"I-I don't know. My shoulder started hurting yesterday." She yanked the neck of her shirt down. "Is anything there? A spider bite or something?"

Solomon stared at her shoulder and fell silent.

"*Beleti*," he said, his voice tight. "Did any of your blood spill on the urn?"

"Y-Yes."

Solomon closed his eyes and raised his face to the heavens.

17

"Why! What is it?" She stumbled to her feet and raced to look in the bathroom mirror.

She gaped at her reflection, tears filling her eyes. "What the hell is *that*!"

Solomon stood behind her, catching her as she fainted.

5

Let Us Begin

*P*etra awoke to the smell of sautéed onions and baked bread. Her mouth watered, but her head swam, confused. It took a moment for everything to return and then the memories came rushing back: her shoulder, the image in the bathroom mirror—and the horror.

She reached for her shoulder and found it bandaged with gauze. It pulsated and felt damp.

"Solomon?" As she sat up, she noticed a blanket draped over her legs and a glass of ice water on the table beside her.

"You rest, *beleti*," he ordered, coming around the corner with a tray of soup, crackers, and homemade scones.

She stared in disbelief.

"Um, my name is Petra."

He grinned. "I know."

"After the Nabataean city in Jordan," she added, feeling the pervasive need to explain her odd namesake.

"I am…*quite* familiar with that region…I've just never heard it used as someone's name before."

"My father was an Art History professor at Simon Fraser," Petra explained. "He was obsessed with the ancient world. So, for his thirtieth birthday, he and my mother visited the *new* Seven Wonders of the World—one being The Treasury in Petra. Apparently, I was conceived on that trip, hence the name." She shrugged, adding, "My sisters' names are Vienna and Sistine, if that tells you anything."

Solomon laughed.

"If you know my name, why are you calling me *beleti*? Doesn't that mean 'my lady' in Sumerian?"

Solomon set the tray of food on the coffee table, and then tucked a pillow behind her back. He straightened and tilted his head. "Why do you think it means 'my lady'?"

"The Google translator said…"

He chuckled, returning to the kitchen to retrieve his own meal. "It does not mean 'my lady'. It's a Sumerian term of respect…an endearment for a woman. It's more like…*beautiful one*."

Heat rose into Petra's cheeks.

"Eat," he commanded, sitting beside her. "The turmeric will help with the inflammation."

"Inflammation?"

Solomon gave a guilt-ridden glance to her shoulder and a fresh wave of fear moved through her.

They ate in silence a moment, Petra savoured the warmth and richness of the soup. Creamy and tinted yellow from the turmeric, bits of shredded celery and cubed carrots floated throughout. The scone, interspersed with thin slices of green onion, butter, and Edam cheese, melted in her mouth.

"I had *this* in my kitchen?" she asked, dumbfounded.

He laughed. "No, you had four almonds, three-month-old milk, a bag of stale rice, and two shrivelled potatoes. I went to the store while you rested."

"I-I just got home yesterday, I didn't have time…"

He held up his hand and smiled. "Don't worry, *beleti*. I like to cook."

"It's delicious."

"Thank you." He sat up straighter. "I was a personal chef for King Henry the VIII."

Spoon paused mid-sip, she raised her brows. Was he joking—or crazy?

After they finished eating, he took both their bowls and washed them. Petra felt guilty for just sitting there while he tidied up, but she was beginning to feel feverish. She pulled the blanket up to her chin, curled into a ball, and closed her eyes.

A dream began.

Fevered and erotic.

A woman. The most beautiful woman she'd ever seen danced and swayed before her in a gown of sheer blue. Her face, her skin, gleamed like white silk—soft and young and vibrant—but with the eyes of an ancient. A deep, dark wisdom lingered there. Something playful and evil.

'Petraaa…' the woman sang inside her thoughts, twisting, tightening around her mind. Serpentine.

Petra became frightened. She turned to run, but the woman edged closer. Soon, all she could see was the woman's hypnotic, lavender eyes. The woman reached out and dragged a single, satin finger down Petra's cheek—and she felt her soul loosen.

The woman laughed wickedly.

"You're mine…"

It was dark when she awoke. Petra blinked a few times and realized she was now in her bed. Cool night air blew in from the open window, whispers of fluttering leaves and the distant hum of traffic filtered into the room.

The bedroom door was almost shut, save for a sliver of gold streaming in from the living room. Stifling a groan, she swung her legs over the side of the bed and tried to stand. The room spun and she reached for the bureau, using it as leverage as she made her way to the bathroom. She left the light off, unsure she wanted to see her reflection—especially her back.

After relieving herself, she glanced at her dark silhouette in the mirror. The soft glow of streetlights offered just enough illumination to perceive her image. With great effort, she lifted her shirt. A square of white gauze had been taped to her shoulder, a burgundy stain in the centre. Tears filled her eyes as she recalled the deep gashes carved into her skin. She didn't get a good look before she fainted—but enough to know it was terrifying.

Carefully, she reached back and picked at the bandage. The skin lifted as she pulled and she hissed in pain.

When the bandage was off, she switched on the light—and cried out in horror.

Solomon had cleaned away much of the blood, exposing the wound for what it really was: a cuneiform tattoo.

Engraved in her skin, outlined in ebony ink, was one of the strange Sumerian symbols she'd seen on the urn. She stared at the mark, watching fresh blood ooze and drip down her back. Tears spilled over her cheeks as she realized another mark was opening up beside the first.

"*Ezeru*," Solomon's deep voice rumbled from the doorway.

He took a step closer, his fingers warm on her shoulder as he reattached the bandage, gently pressing it into place.

"W-What does that mean?" She swallowed a sob.

She wanted so much for him to gather her into his arms, tell her everything would be okay. Instead, he met her with a grave expression. He said nothing, but turned and lifted his shirt, exposing his own deeply-carved tattoos, dozens of them, covering his entire back—and one on his chest, an eight-pointed star in a circle.

"What is *ezeru*?" she asked, terrified.

He glared at his reflection, eyes dark.

"*Curse.*"

The long night fell away, excruciating pain coming in waves. When last he'd changed her dressing, there were three new tattoos on her back. He rubbed oil infused with poppies over them and the ache subsided a little.

"Will they…go away?" Petra asked, her voice quiet, childlike.

His expression gave her the answer. She drew the blanket up to her neck, wrapping it around herself like thick, warm arms.

"I owe you an explanation," Solomon said, beautiful eyes storming. "We don't have much time before we have to move on from this place, but enough to tell you what you need to know, for now."

"What about the urn? How are we going to find it?"

"We no longer have to look for it," he said. "It's too late."

"What! Why?"

"We do not need to."

"I—I don't understand."

"I know," he said, touching her hand. "But you have to trust me."

She nodded, too tired and afraid to argue. If not for the strange markings engraving themselves into her back, she'd have called the cops hours ago, claiming she had a gorgeous escaped mental patient in her apartment. But as it was, there was no denying something strange —something supernatural—was going on.

'*Sometimes you just have to give people the benefit of the doubt,*' Joe's cheery voice echoed. Iraq, the desert, finding the urn—it seemed a hundred years ago, a past she wasn't sure was actually hers anymore. As though she'd lived two distinct lives: before the curse…and after.

The sky raged fuchsia and orange as the sun lifted itself into dawn. Chickadees chirped and neighbourhood dogs greeted one another from across the alleys. The world outside went on as if nothing had changed—the earth still spun, the wind still blew. So indifferent to her absence. Petra eyed it with envy, wishing she could rejoin the land of the living. Where curses were just fantasy and tall, dark strangers were only characters in a romance novel.

Solomon stood on the balcony, gazing out at the blossoming morning. Petra folded her legs under herself and waited, sensing he needed time. After a long while, he turned to her, eyes steely.

"If you want to hear my story, you must hear it all. You'll be the first to hear my tale from start to end. I tell you because you're now part of it—and because I cannot bear to be alone in it any longer."

Solomon drew a deep breath.

"*Let us begin.*"

Part Two

The Sumerian

"*I* *was born in Mesopotamia, 4000 years ago, with eyes of lapis lazuli—or so I've been told.*

"*My people had never seen blue eyes before. They were born dark. Dark of skin, dark of hair, and, especially, dark of eyes. I never saw another set of blue eyes for almost two hundred years…but that is a story for another time.*

"*This is the story of my first life—for I have lived many. More than any man should.*"

6

Maru

2012 BC
Eight years old

*T*he Euphrates was in a gentle mood.

A limb of driftwood meandered downstream, pale branches reaching for the dawn. Warm wind played with my hair, caressed my face, the arid Arabian Desert on its breath. In the shade of a date palm, I burrowed my feet into the hot sand, grains tickling the tender flesh between my toes. I gazed at my tiny kingdom of water and beach. This was *my* place, lush with desert trees, marsh grasses, and willowy reeds.

My *secret* oasis.

Despite the shade, sweat trickled from my brow. It was not quite noon, yet Utu, the sun god, was already making his presence known. As if sensing my need, the cool water babbled beside me. In a whisper, it seemed to say, *'Come, Solomon! Swim with us. It is so very hot. Cool yourself!'*

Was it just my imagination or had the deceitful water nymphs come to lure me to my death? Father often warned of the sea god's beautiful daughters, how they liked to play games with the mortals and then drown them when they grew bored. I eyed the rippling blueness, wary of their silky, golden heads rising to the surface. Still, I wanted so badly to pull off my tunic and dive in.

"No," I said, turning up my chin. "I will not play your games." Even if I wanted to, I wasn't supposed to swim without Father nearby.

"The river is fickle, Solomon," Father would say. "Earth is like man. Solid and strong, difficult to change." He pounded a fist into his palm. But then, he unfolded his fingers, imitating a slow, graceful wave. "Water, though, is like woman—smooth and supple—but her mood changes often, and quickly! Always remember, one moment she can be warm and at peace, and the next...*whoosh!*" He made a sudden sweeping motion. "She turns cold, angry, and pulls you under, carrying you away!"

While vigilant of the river and her capricious ways, I was curious where she'd carry me away to. I often daydreamed of floating downstream, following the water to some unseen end where I imagined lost souls gathered. Among them, I wondered if I would find my mother.

I looked to the farther shore and beyond, where the sands blended seamlessly. Father spoke of distant worlds where others lived. He said there were many and that they weren't like us. How could they be *unlike* us? Didn't they dress the same? Speak the same words? Try as I might, I couldn't envision a people different from our own. Wasn't everyone dark-skinned? Didn't everyone have black hair?

Then I thought of my blue eyes.

"Solomon!" Father's voice sounded on the wind. "It is time for your lesson!"

Giving a last glance at the river, I climbed the levee and headed for home. Cool, green grass transformed to unremarkable brown sand, so hot it stung my bare feet.

Father met me at the door.

"You are late, *maru*."

"Sorry, Father."

"It is okay." He ruffled my hair as we entered our one-room hut. "I worry like an old nanny goat."

Father and I lived on a farm outside Uruk, in the heart of Mesopotamia. We kept oxen, goats, and, especially, wild fowl. Father sold their eggs as a delicacy at the weekly market, as well as clay bowls, urns, and goddess statuettes.

I sat at the supper table, but instead of food before me, there was a whittled reed and a slab of damp clay. From the time I could speak, Father had taught me how to transcribe cuneiform text onto clay tablets. He'd studied to be a scribe in a Tablet House, but after he married my mother, he chose to be a farmer instead.

"You must be quick, Solomon." With swift precision, Father incised his own dampened tablet with tiny grooves. "Many a scribe takes too long. The clay dries fast, and the wedges cannot go deep. If you want the world to understand your words, they must be perfect."

Line by line, I impressed the marks into the mold. Each and every symbol had to be exact to properly convey meaning to the reader.

After several hours, Father said, "Now, practice your mathematics, then we'll have dinner."

I completed calculations he'd pre-written on a tablet. Algebra easy enough, but Trigonometry always plagued me. These skills were important to learn in our time, however. Everything from building our homes and temples to mapping the procession of constellations that guided our harvests.

Important, yes, but terribly boring.

Beyond the lone window, billowy clouds crawled across the sun, offering a rare shade over the sands. I yearned to run outside, feel the hot sand slip beneath my soles. Even more, I longed to play with other children.

The previous year, over the dark night of a winter solstice celebration, I was allowed to play with the neighbour's children. Our neighbour, Zephat, owned a farm to the south of us. At the time, he had *six* children. I often wondered how it would feel to have not just one, but *five* siblings! To have a brother to explore the sand dunes with, hunt snakes and chase lizards. Or a sister to take long walks with, collecting berries for breakfast and picking jasmine to decorate her hair.

That long-ago evening, just before we reached Zephat's hut for the celebration, Father placed a hand on my shoulder. "Now, Solomon, you must not get too close to the children."

"But why?"

"They cannot see your eyes, *maru*. Your eyes—they are different."

"But—you said my eyes were special, that the water god made them this way because I was born in the river."

Father knelt before me. "There are people who will find your blue eyes beautiful—beautiful as the sky above or like the waters of the Euphrates. But others...they will think your eyes a curse and in their fear, they may want to harm you for it."

My mouth fell open. "A...curse?"

His eyes welled with sorrow and he said no more.

I played with Zephat's children that night, my eyes cloaked by darkness. We laughed, we sang, and we ran until we fell to the cool sand, sweat beading on our brows. I'd never been so happy.

But now, it was but a memory faded to a dream.

"Father, why can't we move to the city?" I braved. "I want to go to school with the other children."

Father drew a long breath. "Solomon, you know why we cannot. Besides, the city is full of people and stink and noise." He wrinkled his nose, covered his ears, and made a silly face. I giggled despite my despair. "You can learn much more on the farm than in a school. School is for those who do not believe they can find knowledge outside a building. Knowledge should be discovered on your own or from a master of his craft." He sat beside me. "There will never be anything you need more in life than knowledge, Solomon. You can live with less food and water. You can spend the night in the cold, sleep on the hard ground for many days. You can even live without love for a while—but knowledge leads to wisdom, *maru*. You must always be learning. Crave it, desire it, find it anywhere you can!" He smiled through his greying beard. "Because it is only with wisdom that you can find all the others."

That evening, we laid on the cooling sands, gazing up at the ever-reaching blackness. The spaces between the stars interested me more than the bright lights themselves. How far did it go? Was it a great shadow we people below were bathed in? Perhaps it was the silhouette of the great god of night, Nin, who'd fought and once again conquered his sun-loving brother, Utu. Every dawn and every evening they battled to see which would own the sky.

Father said the world was a great, flat disc and the sky was an immense dome that encased the land. The stars were the eyes of the gods watching over us. I'd often wondered why the moon and the stars shifted, as though we were standing still and the mighty hand of Enlil, father to all gods, spun the dome around us. I always felt so small then, so insignificant. Were we just a passing amusement for the deities? Why did they have such power when we were so simple and fragile?

It didn't seem fair.

"I wonder why it's so big," I said. "We are so small."

Father chuckled. "The heavens house the gods, *maru*. It has to be large as they are large."

"Are they like us?"

"It is said that Enki created us in his own likeness—is that what you mean?"

"No." I laced my fingers behind my head. "Are they made of flesh? Do they have feelings like we do?"

Father pondered this. "It is said that when it rains, it is their tears. When the wind blows, it is their sigh, and when the earth trembles, it is their anger—so in that way, yes, they are like us."

"Do they eat? And have homes?"

"When they are not in the heavens, they often live on the island of Dilmun. There they live like us because they want to experience life as we do. But Dilmun is a magical place where only immortals can live."

My mind churned. "Can they die?"

I heard Father's breath many times before he answered. "I do not know, *maru*. These are hard questions for a simple man like me. You are a very inquisitive little boy."

I sat up. "Is that bad? Will they be angry with me?"

He stood with a groan, patting me on the shoulder. "It is best not to doubt them, but the gods made you this way, *maru*. They gave you this heart and this mind—and one day, you will understand why."

"Have you ever seen any of the gods?"

"We do not see them with our eyes," he said. "Only the *ensi* may see them and speak with them."

I frowned. Why should only the priests be allowed to be in the presence of the gods? I didn't want to become an *ensi* just to be closer to the gods. I wanted to be closer to them, but just as myself.

Father knelt beside me, drawing a long arm over the horizon. "The gods are in everything we see, *maru*, and in everything we don't. They are in the food, the water, the animals—the sun.

"They are here." Father placed a hand on his chest, and then he touched my heart. "And they are here."

Early one morning, I ambled out to the barn to begin my chores. Father had left while it was still dark, tending the pastures before the dew-misted morning surrendered to a sweltering afternoon. The goats snorted as I entered, odd eyes wide with anticipation.

"Good day, Zuzu," I said to the newest addition of the herd, petting between the short nubs where his horns would someday be. He was identical to his mother: pure white save for a nebulous spot of brown around his left eye.

The herd gathered around me, all wanting to be first to eat. They nagged as I poured alfalfa into the trough. The elder goats lined up, heads down and butts in a row—except Zuzu, who was crowded out by his greedy family.

28

"Here you go, little one." I scooped some feed into a clay bowl and set it down. The baby goat plunged into the food, stubby tail waggling.

"Solomon."

I spun around to find Father in the doorway, a basket of fresh eggs in his hands and a frown on his face.

"Our bowls are not for the animals," he said. "Come inside once you're done, I should like to teach you something."

I finished my chores quickly and walked to the hut. Inside, Father sat at the table with a furtive smile. The basket of eggs had been left near the hearth, beside a bowl of goat butter and the clay cooking board.

"I've stoked the fire for you," he said. "It is time for you to learn to cook."

My eyes widened.

It was no secret Father was a great cook—and that he hated it.

"Set the board over the fire. Once it is hot, put some butter down."

I did as instructed, but when I added the dollop of butter, it sizzled and shot across the board, dribbling onto the floor.

Father snickered and I glared at him.

"Now add the eggs."

I tapped the tiny egg against the bowl, just like I'd seen Father do every day. The shell didn't crack on the first try, so I hit it a little harder. The egg crushed in my hand, thick mucus ran through my fingers.

Father laughed.

"Ugh—why do I have to do this?" I wiped the slime on my tunic.

"We must all be able to take care of ourselves."

"But I like you taking care of me."

He gave me a sad smile. "I will not be here forever, Solomon."

My heart gave a sharp ache. The thought of losing Father had never crossed my mind. He was immortal to me, impervious to illness and danger. I disliked that he made me consider a time without him, no matter how true his words were.

"Try again," he urged.

The second egg made it onto the board, but a few shards of shell floated in the mix. I tried to pick them out, but they squirmed away whenever my finger came close. Finally, after many broken eggs and a fresh burn on my wrist, we sampled my first meal.

Father chewed, pausing now and then to mince up a piece of eggshell. "Pretty good—for your first try. Perhaps tomorrow will be easier."

I scowled at him. I knew what he was doing.

"Why me?"

"You will have to do many things in your life, some you will like," Father said, "some you will not."

I sighed, poking some uncooked remnants on my plate.

"Solomon, each of us begins as a student, in all things. Sometimes, if we are fortunate, we discover the things we love—things we become passionate about. Take writing, for instance." He stood and walked to our collection of tablets in the corner. "I did not want to be a scribe like my grandfather, but my father insisted. He made me go to school and it was very hard. I hated it."

"You...*hated* it?"

"The days were long and hot. The teacher was very demanding. If we made a mistake on our tablet, it was thrown away and we were to start again. My father wanted me to become a scribe, but I did not. I wanted to do other things with my life."

"Like what?"

His cheeks pinked. "I wanted to be a sailor."

"But...you're afraid of water."

"Yes, I am."

"Then how could you have gone out onto the ocean?"

"It was a dream. I suppose I would have failed. I might have been too fearful of being trapped in the boats, but I would like to have tried..." His gaze turned distant, then: "What do you dream of becoming, *maru*?"

Unbidden, the answer sprung into my thoughts, as though it had simply been waiting for someone to ask. I opened my mouth to voice it —but stopped. I couldn't tell him this. It was silly. Impossible. So I buried the idea deep inside.

"I-I'm not sure," I lied.

He smiled knowingly. "Well, do not wait forever to decide, there are not many days in a man's life. They should be lived very carefully, always doing something meaningful. It would be wonderful to live long enough to master all the crafts, don't you think, *maru*? To be a painter, blacksmith, or leatherworker—so many occupations to choose from, yet so little time to pursue them all."

His eyes turned sad.

"What is it, Father?"

"Your mother, she was very young when she died. She had no chance to pursue her dreams." His shoulders sagged. "She could not even read or write. I should have taught her those things. I thought there would be plenty of time—there was not."

A lump rose into my throat. "At least...you knew her."

Father bowed his head. "You are right, *maru*. I am sorry. I am angry with the gods for taking her too soon. But I got to hold her, to see her smile—and you did not. Forgive me, my son." Father gathered me to his chest. His heart thumped against my ear and he stroked my hair like he did when I was baby. "I am so grateful to the gods for you. I don't know what I would do without my *maru*."

Once a month, we ventured to the far side of the river, to the special place where Father collected clay. For this task, we brought a raft constructed from palm trunks and reed ropes. Atop it we placed several sacks, ferrying the lot as we strolled beside the shoreline.

"The clay on the other side of the river is better, Solomon," he'd say. "It is cleaner. Our clay is soiled by the *esir*."

Esir, or bitumen, was a dense, sticky substance beneath the sand. We used it for many things, like building homes and starting fires, but for making household pottery, it was a nuisance.

It was nearing dawn when we left for the collection spot. A light wind stirred the palms, rose-beaked parakeets murmuring amid the fronds. Clouds of diaphanous gnats droned over calm waters. From beneath a pomegranate bush, a black and yellow newt darted out, leaving tiny prints in the sand. I inhaled the morning, happy to be adventuring instead of trapped inside the sweltering hut. I glanced at Father, anticipating the same expression, but was surprised to see his face weathered with worry.

"Father, what's wrong?"

"This drought, *maru*, it is lasting much longer than the others."

Though still a mighty river, the water ran low and the banks were steep, half of what it once was. The floods nourished our crops. We expected them every two years, but it had been four since we'd seen the last.

"If we do not have the great rains soon," Father said, "we may have to move."

I stopped in my tracks. "We can...*move?*"

The ghost of a smile pulled at his lips. "Yes, *maru*. This land is dying, and the people with it. We cannot stay where the land cannot feed us."

"Where would we go?"

"I do not know for certain, but your mother's family, in the Zagros Mountains, would likely welcome us."

Thrilled, I hoped the drought would continue so we could move away.

We soon arrived at Father's secret collection spot. Despite Father's confessed longing to become a sailor, I was sent across on the raft to retrieve the clay, roll it into balls, and place them into the sacks. Father kept one end of the reed rope, tied to the raft, while I paddled across. When the sacks were full and secured, he dragged the raft back to his side. Once unloaded, I pulled it back. This continued for much of the afternoon. In the last hour of our endeavour, however, the river began to grow irritated.

"We have enough," he hollered. "Come back!"

I loaded up the last two bags and climbed aboard. Winding the reed around his arm, Father slowly reeled me in. Cool water splashed over the raft, pooling beneath my knees. Father's face was red as he fought against the surging current. Suddenly the raft heaved, one side lifting sharply, nearly throwing me off. With a glance behind me, I spied the tip of a rock hidden just beneath the surface.

"Take hold, Solomon!"

I tied the end of the rope around my wrist and flattened myself against the raft, gripping the edges. Father continued to pull, the sounds of his labour echoing over the raging rapids. I coughed and sputtered each time the waves overwhelmed the tiny vessel. My stomach tumbled with each rise and fall. I screwed my eyes shut and prayed to Enki.

"Solomon!" Father's voice was filled with alarm.

I jerked my head up in time to see a huge piece of driftwood lumbering towards me. There was no time react, within seconds the raft was upside down in the water. I opened my eyes, the world was a cold, murky blur. The sacks of clay were cloaked shadows as they sunk to the bottom of the river. Panicked, I clawed the water. My lungs screamed for air. I thrashed and kicked, desperate to reach the surface, terror seizing hold—but then, fatigue.

A sudden calm fell over me. Weightless, I drifted. *Surrendered.* So peaceful beneath the surface, tormented and raging above.

"*Solomon!*" Father's voice, muffled. So far away…

'*Water is like woman, but her mood changes often. One moment she can be warm and at peace, and the next…whoosh! She turns cold, angry, and pulls you under, carrying you away…*'

I closed my eyes. *To where…to where shall we go…my lady…*

Next thing I knew, I was cold. Very cold. My wrist throbbed painfully.

"There now, I have you," Father said through a sob, cradling me to his chest.

I coughed, shivering violently. "The r-river…is in a very b-bad mood…today, isn't….s-she, Father?"

Father laughed through his tears. "Yes, she is a cranky old woman today."

"Here now," Father said, placing a cool rag over the angry welt snaking around my wrist. "Perhaps we will make death jars another day, when you are well."

I shook my head. "No, I'm fine. But I don't want to make a death jar. I want to make a statuette."

He gave me a curious glance. "A statuette?"

"Yes, a goddess," I replied, thinking of the river goddess who'd recently tried to drown me. I felt the need to see her face to face, to look her in the eye.

Father set a sphere of clay before me. "We must make the death jars for market. They are in demand lately, more than the statuettes."

I could tell by his face that things were not well in Uruk. Each day he returned from the market, he was more worn and weary. His spirit dampened. It'd been years since the last flood. Father said it had been like this once before and Uruk had almost gone to ruin. With drought comes starvation, desperation. The people cheated one another, and sometimes killed, in order to survive. The urns, or death jars as Sumerians called them, were for the crushed bones of criminals.

The people of Uruk felt the gods had abandoned them. Some spat on the temple steps, left feces or dead rats. More were being imprisoned or put to death.

Today, however, I didn't want to make an urn. The clay did not wish to be a jar for the dead—it wanted to be a woman.

Father examined my wrist. "Okay, today you may do what you wish, but tomorrow we must make as many jars as we can."

I set to work. The clay was cool and malleable, bending to the whim of my fingertips. Before long, she started to take shape. Voluptuous and feminine.

But something wasn't right. She looked…wrong.

"You must make her beautiful, Solomon. Like this…" Father took the figurine and rubbed a thumb between her breasts, further defining them. He added more clay to her hips, smoothing, blending them with her waist. With his thumbnail, he carved a deep groove from her ankles to the top of her legs, the spot where her thighs met, forming a shadowed, secret place.

32

"A woman is soft and seductive, Solomon. She is designed to tempt man, and placate him—like the courtesan sent by the gods to tame the wild man, Enkidu." He referred to a fable from his favourite story, *The Epic of Gilgamesh*. "The gods made woman to be the opposite of man. Where man is hard, woman is soft. Where man is logical, woman is wise. Where man is strong, woman is not weak, but resourceful." He handed the goddess back to me.

I stared at her. Heat rushed to my face. "We…look different than her." I ran a hand down my flat chest, looked to the crevice he'd created between her legs. I'd seen women before, of course, but from far away. They didn't seem dissimilar from Father or me. They dressed differently, but I didn't think about what was underneath. I'd watched Father make hundreds of figurines, passed by them every day of my life as they dried on the shelves—but I'd never really *seen* them. Now, it was as if my eyes were suddenly open.

Father chuckled. "Yes, *maru*. We are different from the women."

"Why?"

"They are like the nanny goats," he said. "They have the babies, the babies need milk, yes?"

I knew that, of course. I'd seen the babies suckling their mothers.

"The gods made woman in this way so she could feed her children. She carries the child, then feeds the child."

"How do they…" I blushed, pointing to the figurine's breasts, "make milk?"

"Her body knows it must feed the baby. Like honey from the bees or eggs from the fowls, the milk is a gift from the gods. It comes after the baby is born."

"How does the baby get inside her?"

"You are so full of questions today, *maru*." A smile played on his lips. "Well, when a man and a woman are in love and have settled, the gods see fit to seed the woman with a child."

I nodded, still unsure, but it was enough to satisfy me for the time being. We worked in silence awhile, and then a thought struck me.

"I wonder if my child will be like me," I said, setting my masterpiece on the shelf to dry.

"What do you mean?" Father gave me a quizzical glance. "Will it be a boy?"

"No, will it have blue eyes too? Like Zuzu has the same brown spot on his eye as his mother."

Father paled. "Why…would you think of that, Solomon? Enki made your eyes blue. There is no reason to think it will happen again."

I remained silent, sensing I'd said something wrong.

Father looked away. "It is best not to think of these things, Solomon, the gods do not like to be questioned for their acts. We must simply accept their gifts, obey them, and all will be well."

Father lit a candle, the shadows devouring the last light of day.

"Come, *maru*," he said. "It has been a long day. It is time to sleep."

Father pulled a blanket overtop me. Heat seeped through my skin and into my chilled bones. Once I was snuggled in, Father sat beside me.

Then, he began the bedtime story, the one he told me every night. The story of my birth.

"Your mother loved the water," Father began. "Kali came from the Zagros Mountains, in the land of the Lullubi people, where there are no rivers or lakes, just trees and rocks. It is very cold in the winter there, the mountains wear snow on their heads—like the white hair of old men!"

Shuddering, I could not imagine life without the desert warming me.

"I often took your mother to the river to watch me fish." He always smiled at this part. "Ahh, my sweet *beleti*, she was so excited to see so much water in one place. She swam with you inside her every day. I used to sit on the shore and watch her. She would splash and tease me because I was afraid to swim."

He twirled her ring around his smallest finger.

"Her belly grew and grew, and I felt you move beneath my hand when I touched her stomach. One day, she asked to go swimming. She said her back hurt and the water helped her. So I took her. She swam a while, but she was quieter than usual."

"'I think he is coming, *nga arammu*,' she told me. Then, after much pain in the belly and many hours, she cried out and you came from her. There, in the water! Our son! Our little *maru*!

"She named you *Shelomoh*, which means 'peaceful' in her native tongue. In Sumerian, it translated to Solomon, so that is how I always spoke it.

"Oh, how she stared at you." His eyes glistened. "Her face was pure love."

We bowed our heads, knowing what was to come.

"She kissed you good-bye, placed you in my arms and…went to sleep. She'd bled too long after the birth. The river ran red with her blood," he said, a shadow darkening his stare. "Her soul was called home, to the Goddess of the Dead, Ereshkigal."

This was the part where I'd close my eyes and try to imagine what my mother looked like, but try as I might, I couldn't summon her face.

"She lives in the netherworld now as an *etemmu*—a ghost. She watches you from there, Solomon, sending you prayers of good fortune." .

"Do you think she saved me today?" my voice was small.

"Yes, of course," he said, rising. "I wish you good rest, my sweet *maru*. May the gods be ever merciful."

7
Curse the Gods

2000 BC
10 years old

One morning, the water stopped.

"The river might just be low today," I suggested.

Father shook his head. "This seems too sudden. The water was moving well yesterday."

Centuries ago, our ancestors dug a basin to capture the overflow from seasonal floods, which filtered into the long trenches that scored the fields. Father poked the crumbling dirt, parched by a scalding, mid-afternoon sun. The little seedlings we'd planted only weeks before didn't stand a chance without constant hydration.

"Come, Solomon," Father said, clouds of worry in his eyes. "We must walk the fields and see if there is a break in the line."

Armed with shovels, we started out on what could be a very long walk. I didn't mind, I was just happy to be outside and missing school for the day. Eyes on the canals that ran for miles, we ambled towards the tributary leading from the basin. If something was blocking the main branch, the water would be backlogged, pooling, whereas we would simply remove the obstacle. If there wasn't a blockage, however, it meant something was terribly wrong at the source.

"Solomon," Father said. "Have I ever told you about how I met your mother?"

I searched my memory. "No, you haven't."

"I had just turned sixteen summers when my father took me on a trip. He'd received word his mother was ill and he needed to say his farewells. Your grandfather's family lived far away in the Zagros Mountains. We walked many weeks to get there, but when we finally reached the base of the mountain, I could not believe my eyes! The rocks were mighty boulders. Some so tall their heads were hidden in the clouds. The mountains were great sheer walls of rock." He moved his hand vertically, simulating the impossible slant. "We teetered on crooked goat trails and through dark caves filled with old animals bones, past steaming hot springs. It took many hours to get to the village. When we arrived, I was surprised to see green pastures in the middle of the mountains—they even had grazing cattle! As we walked through the village, I noticed a young girl washing clothes beside a waterfall. It only took one look, Solomon—" he held up a finger, "just one look and she stole my heart."

"Did you talk to her?"

"Not then, we went on to see my grandmother. After her death, the funerary celebrations began. Your mother, Kali, was pouring beer for the men. I summoned all my courage and talked to her. She was as smart and funny as she was beautiful. But days later, my father and I left for Uruk."

"Did you tell her how you felt?"

"I think she knew," he said, blushing. "But I told my father about her and he sent word back to the village. Before I knew it, she and I were betrothed!"

"What is...betrothed?"

"A promise between two families for their children to someday marry."

"Am I betrothed to anyone?"

His expression fell. "No, *maru*."

"Why not?"

Father grew quiet.

"Solomon, you must understand, you are—different."

An ache blossomed inside my chest. "There's no woman who'll love me because I don't have *brown* eyes?"

"No, *maru*." He took hold of my shoulders. "It simply means that she, too, will have to be special. Steadfast against a world blind to the beauty of your difference. But she must not love you *in spite* of your differences—but *because* of them."

We ended up walking all the way to the basin before we came across the problem: great heaps of sand had been shovelled into the main artery of the reservoir, damming the water.

The men who'd done this were still there.

Draped in ivory robes, our landlord and local priest, Enusat lounged beneath a billowing white canopy while two slave boys fanned him with palm leaves. Behind him, labourers scooped sand into the mouth of the basin.

Father touched my shoulder. "Solomon, stand over there and keep your head down."

I obeyed without question.

Father approached the priest and knelt.

A cat-like smile crawled across Enusat's lips. As was the law, he spoke first, "Farmer Ezen—you may stand." Enusat gave a swift gesture, blue and red jewels sparkling from his many rings.

"Is this heat not dreadful? So...*dry*." Enusat reached for a goblet of wine, sipping leisurely, eyes narrowed at Father over the rim. Setting down his cup, he scrutinized the land with an expression of disgust. "It's so interesting to see how the common people survive out here. So...*primitive*—how *do* you do it?"

36

"It can be trying." Father smiled thinly.

"I can see that."

"Why then do you stop the water, *Ensi?*"

The priest rolled his eyes, bored by Father's question. Instead of answering, he turned his attentions elsewhere—in *my* direction.

"Is that your boy?"

Father nodded slowly. "Yes, *Ensi.*"

"Come here, boy," Enusat summoned me with a wave.

"No—" Father started but silenced himself when the priest's lips curled.

"*Come,*" Enusat ordered.

I searched Father's face for an alternative—a way out—but found only cold fear in his stare. His eyes closed around an imperceptible nod.

Just do it, it said. *We have no choice.*

Head down, I approached the tent and knelt as Father did.

"I've heard stories of this boy, no?"

"I do not think so, *Ensi.*" Father tensed.

Enusat studied me. "Come closer."

I complied, breath erratic in my throat.

Father always told me the *ensi* were aligned with the divine. They were above slaves and peasants, that they alone could hear the words of the gods.

Folds of fat shifted beneath Enusat's gown as he leaned towards me, so near I could smell the stink of him. Sweat, curry, and the sour of wine on his breath. Tiny pustules marred his shaved chin—heat rash or ingrown hairs.

I stared at them with growing disillusion.

He's just human. Like me. Like any of us.

"Look up, boy," Enusat ordered.

I glanced at Father, afraid.

"I said look up!" Enusat lurched forward, snatched a handful of my hair, wrenching my head up. Now eye to eye, the priest's anger melted into wonder.

"The legends are true," he whispered. "They are…*blue.*"

Fans paused mid-air, his slave boys craned their necks to steal a peek.

"They are like…*lapis lazuli.*" Enusat's stare was full of awe. "It must be a curse…"

"No!" I blurted, my heart pounding too fast. "E-Enki gave them to me. Because I was born in the water."

"*Enki?* You think a god gave you these? No god would bestow this honour on…a *mere* mortal."

I glanced at Father, confused. "But Father told me…"

Enusat released me, throwing his head back in laughter. After he wiped his eyes, he narrowed them at Father. "You didn't tell him the truth?"

"*Please,*" Father begged. "We only came to find out what happened to the water."

"Ahh…" Enusat said with a smirk. "The King has ordered the water be conserved at this time. Only certain fields will drink this year. It would appear that *yours* is not one of them."

"How will we eat?" Father's fists tightened at his side. "Or pay our taxes?"

The priest grinned. "You will simply have to find other means."

8

All Roads Lead to the Temple

2008 BC
12 years old

*F*ather and I packed several dozen eggs into bowls of sand, loading them onto the cart amid the statuettes and urns.

With a deep breath, I gathered my courage.

"Can I come?"

"I tell you once more, it is too dangerous, Solomon," Father said, brow furrowed. "Too many thieves and men under dark cloaks. You are safer here, on our farm." He turned to leave.

"I'm older now, I can fight them!" I raised my voice, tears brimming. "You used to take me along when I was a baby, you said so!'

He sighed and faced me. Weariness shadowed his eyes.

"That was long ago, Solomon, when I could tuck you into a sling and keep you close to my chest, hidden beneath a blanket. Back then, I needed only to sell the spring harvest to the king. That money alone kept us through the winter. But with the drought, I have no choice but to sell the wares at the market. I would love to have you come, to keep me company and help me sell the goods, but there are dangers in Uruk. People who are desperate and starving. They have become criminals."

"I'll stay hidden in the cart!" I begged. "Father, please!"

He hesitated.

I thought he might actually say yes this time.

"No, Solomon. Do not ask me again." And he left.

I threw myself onto my cot, punching the blanket. Hot tears rolled down my face.

"Why!" I shouted. "Why can't I go!"

I felt trapped on this farm, in this hut—a prisoner. Father never allowed me to talk to people, to make friends. Save for that one glorious evening during the solstice, even our neighbour and his countless children were strangers to me. I would see them play, chasing each other across the fields, their giggles carried on the wind.

Alone, I watched from afar. An observer of life, but not invited to live.

The hut seemed to close in on me. Hot and confining.

Smothering.

I paced the tiny room, fury swelling inside my chest. This was *my* life. What right did Father have to keep me prisoner?

I hated Father in that moment—and hated myself for it.

Enraged, I grabbed a drying goddess statuette and threw it to the floor. Fragments exploded, her face splitting into two. One eye gazed up, sightless yet somehow seeing right through me.

I ran outside, towards my secret oasis. Seething, I uttered profanities and curses upon Father—and my eyes. They were the reason he refused to take me to town. Why he'd kept me hidden my whole life. It wasn't my fault my eyes were different, yet I paid the price. Why was he so afraid? Maybe people would think my eyes beautiful, just as he did.

I was so alone.

Unwanted.

Orphaned by a beautiful deformity.

Palms whispered overhead. Cicadas chirped. Nature breathed all around me, oblivious to my misery.

What must it be like to be unaware, I thought, envious of the ignorant. *What freedom there must be in the unknowing.*

It made me want to be like them. To awaken in the morning and close my eyes at night without the burdens of my past or the fears of my future.

Beside me, the river sang, soothing me with its quiet song, beckoning me to come and play. She wanted to hold me, to mother me in her arms. *She* wanted me. She did not see me as different or strange or cursed.

"*Water is like woman,*" Father's voice echoed. "*One moment she can be at peace, and the next, she pulls you under and carries you away.*"

Sunlight glittered across her wavy blue skin. Beautiful, supple and full. I had no knowledge of women. No memory of being touched or held by one. That was what a mother was for. To be the first woman to love you, warm you, draw you to her bosom and cradle you next to her heart.

Father's warnings washed away with the current.

I stripped off my tunic, tossing it onto the hot sand. At the river's edge, I dipped my toe into her cool, wet body. A pleasant shiver danced up my spine. Tiny bumps erupted on my torso as I entered her. I sur-

40

rendered to the current. A sheltered spring off the main river, the water merely eddied and swirled. She never pulled me under, never took me anywhere I didn't want to go. She just played with me, held me.

I was weightless.

Buoyant.

Alive.

When we were done, she carried me back to the shore where I climbed out of her embrace. Water droplets beaded on my dark skin and I shivered despite the heat. I dressed and started home. The land beneath me felt hard. Dry and unyielding in comparison to the soft, cool water.

The little hut was so quiet. I lay down on my cot, fatigue overwhelming me.

Before I fell asleep, I whispered to the god of water, he who'd given me my eyes, "Enki, if you can hear me…do something so I can leave here, just for a while. *Please…*"

By nightfall, I was deathly ill.

Father returned to find me pale and shivering.

"Solomon!" He rushed to my side. "What is wrong?"

My teeth chattered. "I-I'm sick."

He put his palm to my forehead. A ragged cough wracked my body, dry and barking.

"You were very sick once as a baby," Father said, mopping my brow. "You struggled for breath for many days. Your tiny head was like touching fire! I prayed very hard to Enki to let you live. To let you stay with me—and he did."

This time, however, it appeared Enki had granted my wish instead.

Many days passed without improvement. Father rarely left my side. When he did, it was only to pace the length of our hut, stroking his beard and whispering prayers. When I wasn't coughing, I was sleeping, though fitful and fevered. Wild, senseless nightmares plagued me with images of fanciful beasts and terrible beauties. Sometimes, I'd feel better, even stand and walk outside, only to fall ill again by evening.

Father was beside himself with worry. When he wasn't pacing or on his knees praying, he read to me from the tablets, from the stories I'd transcribed of Gilgamesh and Enkidu. I knew he was simply attempting to distract himself from contemplating the worst.

The smell of eucalyptus filled the room, soothing my cough. Father left my side for a moment and crossed the room, retrieving a well-worn tablet—the story of his favourite king, Gilgamesh. Other than the nightly bedtime story of my birth, this was the most told tale in our home.

The Epic of Gilgamesh was Sumer's greatest treasure. One of the first stories transcribed into clay, read to rapt descendants of Uruk for centuries.

King Gilgamesh reigned over Uruk seven hundred years before I was born. He was a brave and ambitious king who raised a humble city into one of the greatest civilizations the world had ever seen.

Father settled in beside me, the tablet balanced on his palm.

"Gilgamesh was a wild king," he read with a chuckle. "No virgin was safe with him in the realm. He loved his beer and he loved his women. After many years of this behaviour, and many illegitimate children, the people of Uruk complained to the gods, begging their assistance with this promiscuous leader.

"One day, the gods, in their infinite wisdom, chose to help the people with their problem king. Outside the city, there lived a wild man, Enkidu, who dwelled among the animals. He was the only one, the gods concluded, who was strong enough to defeat the powerful king. The wise gods decided to tame this wild man and bring him into the city to fight Gilgamesh in hopes of tempering his ego. They sent a pretty courtesan into the wilderness to coax the wild man. She succeeded in seducing Enkidu and then explained the situation, asking him to leave the wilderness to subdue the mighty king. He did, and upon meeting Gilgamesh, they embarked on a mighty battle that lasted weeks! After many days and many nights, both men were exhausted and formed a truce. Then a strange thing happened—they became the best of friends.

"I do not know if that was their intention all along, *maru*." Father dabbed my forehead. "But it seems the gods knew that all Gilgamesh needed was a friend. The king and Enkidu went on many quests together, killing mighty beasts and travelling the lands...until Inanna, that is.

"Gilgamesh and Enkidu travelled six days on the river to the enchanted Cedar Forest where they slayed the great demon, Humbaba. Upon their return to Uruk, Gilgamesh was stunned to receive an invitation from the White Temple—from the goddess herself! Smitten by Gilgamesh's bravery, Inanna offered the promiscuous king her hand in marriage, but Gilgamesh just laughed and denied her. Enraged, Inanna begged her father, Enlil, to punish Gilgamesh.

"It is said that Enlil made Enkidu very sick. Gilgamesh never left Enkidu's side, sending for every healer in the land. But the king's beloved friend died, leaving Gilgamesh alone in world once again."

Father glanced up from the tablet, shadows gathering behind his eyes. "Solomon, Do you think you are well enough to travel? We must go to Uruk. You need a healer."

I nodded, wishing I wasn't so sick so I could be excited. This is what I'd asked for, was it not?

"Uruk is very dangerous. You must keep your face hidden. You must do everything I say without question. Understand?"

"Yes," I croaked, my throat on fire.

"You do not know the city as I do. You do not know what terrible things can happen."

I closed my eyes, exhausted, grateful for the excuse to look away. Guilt ran like acid through my veins, burning me from the inside out.

Father did not know, but I'd been to the city before.

Father had left for the market one Saturday, as always forbidding me to come. Of course, I'd had the notion to follow him before, but I had been too afraid.

That day, however, I'd had enough. I was going.

I waited until he'd been gone at least an hour, and knowing Father's pace, I'd have to walk slower still. I watched his form grow ever smaller, until he was but a speck on the horizon—then I followed.

Beneath a cloak, I took care to keep hidden. Not only to protect me from being recognized by Father should I catch up to him, but from being seen by anyone else.

It was strange to see the desert reach so far on either side of the path. Only the rolling sand dunes coloured the horizon. I spent much of my time swatting thirsty gnats, but I was undeterred.

I passed a couple of travellers, acknowledging any pleasantries with a simple nod—though I was surprised people were acknowledging me kindly at all. Haunted by Father's endless precautions, I was quite prepared to receive suspicious looks and derogatory comments.

Before long, the jagged silhouette of Uruk brimmed on the horizon. With a deep breath, I approached the gates. Over thirty feet high, King Gilgamesh's legendary stone wall surrounded the city. The arched entrance was guarded by two mighty stone lions. I had not expected so many people. Merchants and buyers funnelled through the entrance, slowed by the sheer mass of people and carts ahead. I almost turned back. Tempted to head home. The noise, the sensation of touch on all sides suffocated me.

The narrow streets were filled with vendors. Carts heaped with barrels of beer, sacks of grains, green onions, carrots, and beets. So many smells! And colours and people and animals! My neck craned this way and that, following every sound and mouthwatering odour. Melodic flutes, lyres, and seed-filled shakers, combined with earthy song and hypnotic dance, arose around every corner. The smells were intermittently wonderful and awful. The stench of raw sewage wafted from canals, occasionally giving way to the delicious scent of roasting meat and vegetables slathered in palm oil.

"Fresh goat meat!" one man yelled, holding up a leather pouch dripping with blood. "Two shekels!"

I kept a cautious eye out for Father's cart. The last thing I wanted was to get caught and never be allowed outside the hut again. What's more, I couldn't endure the look of hurt and disappointment in his eyes, that alone would be punishment enough.

Without money to buy anything, I decided to explore Uruk.

The whitewashed brick buildings were modern compared to my humble hut fashioned from reeds. Many homes were single levels, while the finest had two or three. Outside one house, a young woman lashed a multicoloured tapestry, her nose wrinkled at the billows of dust. I stopped mid-stride, transfixed. While not exceptionally beautiful, she was soft and delicate. *Feminine.*

"Hey!" A heavy hand landed on my shoulder. "What are you looking at!"

I turned, finding a very large, dirty man. Crumbs of food nested in his gnarly beard, an angry brow knotted over his dark eyes.

"Nothing! I'm sorry!"

I moved to leave but he grabbed me by the collar with both hands and drew me up. Wild with fear, I gaped at him.

"That is *my* woman…" he began—then stopped short.

He was staring at my eyes.

Expression shifting from anger to one of curiosity, he leaned in closer. I gagged at the stench of sour beer on his breath.

"Are you…*blind?*" he asked, head tilted like a quizzical dog.

"No." I struggled to free myself from his grasp.

"They are like Inanna's favourite stone…" he said, memorized. "The *lapis lazuli.*"

I froze with fear.

Father was right—my eyes were a curse.

Until that moment, I'd convinced myself my eyes couldn't be that different. Father's eyes were so brown they were nearly black, and when I'd asked him the colour of my mother's eyes, he said, "The same as mine, *maru.* As are all Sumerians—*except yours.*"

Terrified, I wrenched myself from the man's grasp and started to run. The man shouted after me. Now, as I ran between the people, I searched the vendors for Father's cart.

He was right. I wasn't safe here.

People swore as I bumped into them. Tears rolled down my cheeks. Why had I come? I ran until my sides hurt, until my legs could no longer carry me and my lungs fought to draw breath. I'd run so far, so fast, soon I was alone, standing before a mighty, man-made mountain—a ziggurat.

Inanna's temple.

Throughout my childhood, Father told me stories of mighty heroes and terrifying monsters, of great wars and brave warriors—all the myths and legends of our people. He had me write them again and again onto tablets, forever preserving them in stone and into my memory.

Enlil was the overseer of all the gods. He maintained balance amidst chaos. Utu raised the sun during the day and Sin oversaw the night.

Then, of course, there was the playful Enki, the god of water, who gave me my eye colour. There were literally dozens of gods and goddesses, each bestowed a city to oversee—ours was Inanna.

In her honour, a great white step pyramid, a ziggurat, had been erected in the centre of Uruk. Fashioned from enormous mudstone blocks, it had hundreds of stairs ascending towards the gates of heaven.

"All roads lead to the temple," Father would often say. "So people can never forget what Inanna has given us."

I craned my neck to the peak of the monolith, its smooth surface glaring in the sunlight. Twin limestone lions guarded either side of the staircase. Countless offerings for Inanna littered the steps: flowers, rare oils, the blood of sacred animals.

Across the courtyard, a slow procession ambled towards the temple. I ducked behind one of the stone lions and watched. Leading the procession was a covered palanquin, followed by a wagon and a train of wailing mourners. Laid amongst offerings of barley, grapes, and vases of wine, covered with a linen shroud, was a dead body. Placed by the man's side, traditionally sacrificed after its master's demise, was a large, black dog.

The wagon stopped before the statue of Inanna and the carriers set the palanquin down. A guard rushed forward with a stool, placing it before the door. The red curtains parted and a rather plump hand reached out for assistance.

As the figure emerged, my insides curdled.

Enusat.

The *ensi* regarded the grieving family and stifled a yawn. It sickened me to see his plump, healthy face, knowing he ate plentifully while the people he taxed, those who toiled the fields day after day to put food on his table, were skeletal and gaunt.

With a sigh, Enusat submitted to his duties.

"Oh great and mighty Goddess Inanna," he proclaimed, arms open wide to the sky. "Have mercy on this man, Arazumat. Give him your blessings as he embarks on his journey to the Netherworld, into the arms of your sister, Ereshkigal."

Just then, a heavy hand slapped onto my shoulder. I spun around, coming face to face with a soldier.

"What are you doing, boy?"

"I...I...was just watching. I didn't know..."

"This is a private procession. Come with me. You will answer to the *Ensi.*"

He took hold of my arm, yanking me towards Enusat. Panicked, I wrenched from his grasp and started to run.

"Stop!" the soldier shouted.

My eyes watered. I should've stayed home where it was safe! Not knowing where to go or where to hide, I ran until I thought my heart would explode inside my chest.

I ran…and ran…until the earth ended…

And turned to water.

Blue.

A long, winding ribbon of blue. As though a part of the sky had been stolen and reborn onto the land. I'd never seen the Euphrates in all its glory before, flowing and free. I felt insignificant before the face of nature. If water was truly a woman, as Father said, this was where she lived, where she began and ran with all her power.

The port bustled with activity. Sledges of merchandise were dragged up and down long ramps, secured to ropes pulled by a half dozen men. A great ship bobbed beside the shoreline, tethered by a thick rope that vanished beneath the water's surface. An impossibly tall mast scored the sky, crimson sails billowing like a colossal gown.

"Boy," a deep voice rumbled.

I froze, fearing I'd have to run yet again. As I looked to the source of the voice, however, my mouth fell open. A man unlike any I'd ever seen blocked out the sun. With skin a shade lighter than my own, he wore only a short sarong, muscular chest marked with swirling designs. Gold bracelets crawled around his biceps like snakes, a braided beard trailed over his stomach, cinched with gold rings.

"Boy," the man said again, amber eyes regarding me with warm curiosity. "You work?"

I nodded.

"Boat," he said in rough Sumerian and pointed at the massive ship. "Come."

The big man smiled, exposing a gold front tooth. Gold was an almost mythical element, adorned only by the very wealthy.

I stared in awe—until I realized he was also staring at me.

At my eyes.

He cradled my chin within his calloused hand. Part of me wanted to run, but something held me there.

The man smiled, releasing me. He gestured to my eyes and uttered a word in his foreign tongue, "*Kyan.*"

"Keeyan?"

He pointed to the Euphrates, which was as blue as the sky it reflected.

Blue.

"Bansabira." He tapped his chest.

"Solomon."

"Solo-man," he attempted.

Bansabira patted my shoulder and led me up the ramp of his great wooden vessel. On deck, the scent of jasmine and myrrh seeped from

46

clay *pithos*. Each massive vase boasted intricate patterns in a rainbow of colours, but the most interesting shade was one I'd never seen in artwork. It was like blue, but richer, redder. I'd seen it in nature, when the sun set during a terrible storm or beneath the skin, a bruise. I traced a line of the colour with my finger.

"*Porphyra,*" Bansabira said.

"Porphyra?"

"Purple," a soft voice translated behind me.

I spun about—and my heart hesitated.

She was a vision in white robes. Smooth skin the colour of wet sand. Pupils like obsidian set in dark copper. Chestnut hair curled into a crown atop her head, woven amid strings of pearls and seashells. Unlike modestly-dressed Sumerian women, her breasts were exposed, lifted by a form-fitting bodice, rouge nipples embellished with dangling gold charms.

She was the most beautiful thing I'd ever seen.

"We call it *purple*," she explained, pointing to a spiral shell on her necklace. "It's made with the ink of the—how do you say? *Snail.*" She smiled, offering me her hand. "I am Princess Ariadne, and you are?"

"Solomon." I blushed as I took her proffered hand, kissing it softly. "How is it you speak my language so well?"

A shadow darkened behind her lovely eyes. "There's a Sumerian man living in the palace, he's been teaching me—all of my people, actually."

I was instantly envious of this fellow Sumerian, not only that he lived in an exotic land so far away, but to be so near the princess.

"Where is your city?" I asked, forcing my eyes away from her bare chest.

"On the island of Crete. Across the great water to the east. We travel many weeks towards the sunrise to get there. Perhaps someday you can come visit us at the palace?"

Speechless with excitement, I could only nod.

Ariadne's gaze darted to the docks where Sumerian workers had stopped to gawk at her. She was suddenly ill at ease.

"I so enjoy your company, Solomon, but I must return to my quarters. I do hope we meet again someday."

She removed her necklace and slipped it over my head. Then she bent, ornaments tinkling, and her lips brushed my cheek. Her perfume, sweet and sensuous, lingered on my senses like a sheer veil. Before I could protest, she turned and vanished through a little door.

Bansabira laughed, slapping my shoulder. "Come, Solo-man. Work."

He led me to the back of the boat, to a barrel of carp. The large man leaned over, plunged his hand into the water and snatched up a wriggling fish. He then drew a curved dagger from a leather sleeve tucked into his sarong and sliced the fish's throat. The head flew off into the river and he tossed the twitching remains into a bucket of

47

saltwater. To my right, there were rows of hanging fish corpses, salted and curing on a rack.

"Solo-man do all da fish," he said, handing me the knife. Bansabira then turned to direct some Sumerian workers delivering goods.

I swallowed hard. Father did the slaughtering on our farm. I'd witness the bloody aftermath and smell the coppery tang that hung in the barn afterwards, but I never saw the actual killing.

I gazed stupidly at the knife and then at the fish.

Who would be first? How would I choose?

The fish excited as I hovered over the barrel, as if intuiting their fate. I reached in to grab one, my fingertips snatching like a claw, but the fish kept escaping to the bottom of the barrel. Several times I had to stop to warm my hands, they were growing too numb to feel whether I'd caught anything or not.

After many attempts, I cradled my chilled fingers against my chest, frustrated.

I surveilled my surroundings—then smiled and stole across the deck, gathering items to aid me.

In one hand, I carried a bucket. In the other, I dragged a stool. I began scooping water out of the barrel and tossing them over the side. The fish swam slower and slower as the water level decreased. Finally, when I could no longer reach the waterline, I stood on the stool and climbed into the tall barrel. The fish skittered about my ankles but had nowhere to go. I reached down and easily caught one. I held him up, examining him. I'd seen many a fish, though dead, long after their lustre had faded. Its skin, so like metal, yet soft and slippery. With wide, frantic eyes, the fish suckled the air. A wave of guilt moved through me. I was about to take a life. I wondered how Father, or anyone who'd ever killed an animal—or a person—could do it?

Bansabira was suddenly at my side.

"Is food," he said, tapping his fingertips to his lips. He pointed at the princess's cabin. "For Princess."

I was doing this for Ariadne.

A sense of purpose gathered within.

With the fish under my arm, I positioned the blade just under its gills. I pushed hard and its head slipped off, landing with a splash in the river.

Bansabira patted my head.

I regarded the headless body in my arms, limp and lifeless, then threw the corpse into the saltwater and reached for the next one.

The walk home should have been easy, but it wasn't. Not because of the glaring sun, a stranger harassing me, or even a rattlesnake, but because I didn't want to go home. I wanted to stay with Bansabira and Princess Ariadne.

"Good sailor," the large man said as he led me down the ramp and onto solid, unmoving land. It felt wrong. As though I were a bird torn from the sky and forced into a cage. I'd tasted freedom—and now I had to leave.

"Come...tomorrow?" Bansabira asked, his expression hopeful.

I had to look away, out of both sadness and shame. I could not come back, maybe not ever. I'd already betrayed Father once.

"I'm sorry, I cannot."

"We come back," he said, setting a warm hand on my shoulder. "Always in da summer."

My heart sank as I realized I might never see this kind and wonderful soul again—nor my beautiful Princess Ariadne.

He gave me a playful shove.

"Good-bye." I sniffed, waving as I walked away.

He waved back with his whole arm. "Good-bye...Solo-man."

As I trudged back to the hut, I wished I'd never left home, because now I knew what it was to be happy. I was happy with Father, just not trapped on our little farm. Father believed it a safe place where I could keep my eyes wide open, but in truth, it had only kept me from truly seeing.

I often thought of that day, always wondering if it had really happened or it had only been a delightful dream. Then I would dig up Ariadne's necklace, which I'd buried within the sands of my secret oasis, and I would touch each of the shells, remembering...

My fever had worsened overnight. Father insisted we leave for the healer's hut the next morning—or I may not see another day.

"We need to get there before dawn," he said, brow pinched. "It will make you a great deal sicker to be out in the sun."

The city was just stirring when we arrived. Servant girls balanced tall pitchers on their heads, leaving petite footprints in the sand as they carried fresh water from the basin. The tantalizing aroma of barley bread wafted from open windows while scrawny dogs loitered outside doorways for scraps or spoiled meat. Venders lined the main streets, swiftly staging their wares to snare the first customers of the day.

"You must keep hidden, Solomon," Father said, hurrying me through the muddy streets "You must not let them see your face."

I coughed, struggling to keep up.

"This way!" Through winding alleyways, Father avoided all people, veering whenever a curious gaze fell upon us. Despite his caution, Father was causing more glances than if we'd just simply strolled up the main street.

The healer's hut was just beyond the centre of Uruk—past the temple. My stomach clenched as we neared. We turned a corner, Father shushing me as a pair of guards walked by. A terrific itch attacked my throat and I whooped horsely, grabbing my chest. Father's expression was a mixture of sympathy and fear as the guards paused, glancing our direction. Not sensing anything amiss, they moved on.

"Hey!" a voice came from behind us.

We froze on the spot.

Slowly, Father turned, positioning himself between me and the potential threat.

"The *Ensi* is beginning the morning judgements," the soldier said. "Move to the courtyard to watch."

Father bowed his head. "We were just passing through." He nudged me forward, but the soldier blocked us with his spear.

"No, we require more witnesses," the soldier said.

Stiffly, Father complied, ushering me towards the courtyard. I drew my cowl tighter around my face, but it was suddenly yanked back, exposing my face, and eyes, to the world.

"It is disrespectful to hide your face from the gods, boy," the soldier growled.

My heart thrummed, stirring the illness inside me. Father rubbed my back as I coughed uncontrollably.

"Is this boy ill?"

"Yes, we are on our way to the healer's hut." I heard hope in Father's voice.

The soldier gave me a once-over, and then waved his arm. "Be on your way."

Father bowed mid-stride, yanking me by the arm.

"That was too close," he whispered.

Father led me to a leaning, mud-reed hut entangled with sun-seared shrubs. Beneath the languid awning, a nest of silken architecture inhabited a dark corner, cradling a pulsating sac of unborn spiders.

"Wait here." Father pushed aside a ragged blanket used as a door and disappeared into darkness.

My body throbbed and the midday sun pressed the top of my head and shoulders. Despite the gestating arachnids, I leaned against the hut.

After what felt like forever, Father reemerged.

"Go on in, Solomon. She is waiting."

"Sh-She?" My teeth chattered with both malady and trepidation. I didn't know whether I feared her because she was a stranger—or because she was a woman.

Father placed a reassuring hand on my shoulder and guided me over the threshold, into the abyss.

Alone.

Windowless, with only filtered sunlight peering through the tattered blanket to usher me, the shadows tumbled over one another. Fingers outstretched, groping the fathomless void, I was frightened at what I might touch—and even more fearful at what might touch back. Dim candlelight flickered in the far corner, and I moved towards it.

Incense curled around the room in aromatic clouds, thinly masking the waft of ground herbs, bundles of wilting flowers—and the unmistakable odour of fresh blood. My lungs rebelled against the effluvium and I coughed hoarsely, my throat on fire.

"Come, boy," a gravelly female voice said from amid the obscurity. I imagined her gnarled, boney finger beckoning me.

I yearned to run from the hut, return to the safety of home, but I knew this illness would only get worse without her help. Swallowing my fear, I took a step further into the unknown, guided only by the sound of her wheezing breath.

"Closer…" Cloaked in dark robes, a hunched figure waited behind a curtain of frayed cloth; like a black widow poised upon her gossamer web, lair to the predatory mother of the spawn outside.

Heart slamming in my chest, I obeyed.

"Let me see you…" She drew a claw-like hand from beneath her shawl, lifting my chin. I shuddered at her touch.

When I hesitated to meet her gaze, she growled and forced my face up. I gasped at the sight of her, provoking my lungs into a convulsive frenzy. Once I was composed, she examined me again, but how I could not understand—she had no eyes. Only withered, drooping lids hooded over two empty cavities.

"Ahh," she said. "*Now* I see."

"H-How?"

The crone just laughed and shuffled behind a table littered with clay jars, a stone pestle, and a dirty mortar. Hands twisted with bulbous, arthritic knuckles, she snatched up a jar and wrenched out the stopper with her blackened teeth. Puce sludge oozed from the jar's mouth and coiled inside the bowl, the smell of rancid eggs befouling the air. To that she added ground turtle shell, a sprinkling of thyme and myrrh, oxen hair, and the inner lining of a pig's stomach. After a dollop of pulverized pear, she mashed it into a paste.

Bile burned the back of my throat. I desperately hoped she wouldn't force me to eat this concoction.

When complete, she tugged at my tunic. "Off."

I did as I was told. She dug into the sticky remedy and with a boney, crooked finger, drawing a triangle onto my chest, then another, inverted, overtop it—a star.

"This symbol represents the opposing forces of nature. The female and male. The light and the dark. The good—and the evil. United, they form a mystical, unbreakable bond, a seal, which nothing can tear apart."

"Why are you putting it on my chest?"

"It brings balance to the body. You have been angry lately, yes?"

I gave an uneasy nod.

"Anger, bitterness, sadness—they weaken you, inviting darkness into your body—into your soul." She cackled, poking my chest. "Makes you sick."

I then followed as she led me outside.

"Twice a day," she prescribed, thrusting a jar of the vile mixture into Father's hands. In return, he offered her several shekels.

I was eager to head home—but Father hung back.

"And...the other?" He cast her a worried brow.

The old woman's sightless eyes wrinkled around a furtive smile. "He will see farther with those eyes than you ever will."

"What did she mean, Father?" I asked after we passed through the gates of Uruk.

"I promise I will tell you someday, Solomon," he said, eyes brimming with tears. "When it is time."

9
Beleti

1998 BC
22 years old

*F*ather had been quiet as of late.

He rested more. Rubbed his forehead often, at times with a pained grimace. It took him longer to complete his daily chores. Each day, I rose before dawn to get much of his share completed for him. He wasn't that old really, just forty. In ancient times, however, life expectancy was much shorter.

One Saturday, I loaded the wagon before Father left for the market, setting the statuettes in a soft bed of hay. After securing the load, I went into the hut to find Father.

The hut was empty.

Perplexed, I walked to the barn. Perhaps he was gathering eggs for the market—but he was not there either.

Worry gnawed my stomach.

"Father! Where are you?"

"I am here, Solomon," came a weak reply from the other side of the barn.

I found him slumped against the wall, his hand on his chest.

"Are you all right?" I rushed to his side, pressing my palm to his forehead. He was not feverish, but clammy and pale.

"I do not know. I-I just need…to lie down."

Once inside the hut, I guided him to his cot.

"Are you hurt?"

"I suddenly…felt very dizzy and hot," he said as I handed him a cup of water; trembling, he took slow sips. "Then my chest started to hurt. I just need…to rest a while before I go…to the market."

"You're not going anywhere today," I said in a parental tone.

Father chuckled weakly. "Yes, I suppose it would be unwise."

"*I* will go today."

"No! You are not to go to the city! I forbid it!" He struggled to get to his feet.

"Father, enough of this," I said, gently forcing him to stay down. "I'm a grown man now, I can manage a day at the market."

Fear swam in his dark brown eyes. "Son, please, I cannot bear to lose you. Please stay with me today. I will ask nothing more of you…don't go."

My heart cracked. "Of course, I will not leave you."

He patted my arm, head lolling with exhaustion. "Yes, stay with me."

When he was fast asleep, I stood at the threshold of our tiny hut. Frustration writhed inside.

He wants me to be a man, does he not? I glowered at the outside world. *He wants me to learn to fend for myself, but he will not even let me try.*

Trapped and alone, I was tethered to an existence I hadn't chosen. I loved Father with all my heart, but I couldn't fathom living this way forever just to please him. He was afraid of how the world would see me with these eyes, but I wasn't.

I was afraid of not living at all.

After a few days rest, Father returned to his chores, though he was still not himself. Physically he appeared to have recovered from whatever mysterious ailment he'd suffered, but his ubiquitous smile made rare appearances, and the sparkle in his eye was shadowed by an uncharacteristically furrowed brow.

I badgered him endlessly: Are you okay? Does your chest hurt? Do you need to lie down?

"I'm fine," was all he'd say.

But I knew him—and something wasn't right. Nerves tied in a knot of apprehension, I immersed myself within my chores, in the hope they would disentangle my worries.

Sunlight warmed the tiny barn, slipping through the slatted reeds and casting everything in gold. Bestial aromas met me at the door, made even more eye-watering by the climbing heat.

"Good morning, Zuzu." I patted the now-mature buck between his long, curved horns.

I settled onto the milking stool beside an impatient and swollen nanny goat. She startled when I gripped her distended teats, but relaxed as I massaged them from top to bottom with a gentle, practiced rhythm.

Despite my attempt to forget my concerns with menial labour, instead it provided ample time for my worries to obsess over themselves. Perhaps Father just needed time to process his experience. Maybe his brush with mortality set him more off balance than I'd realized.

Just as I was milking the last goat, Father's lean form silhouetted the doorway.

"Solomon, I have come to a decision." He stepped into a wedge of sunlight, an odd smile on his face. "We are going to find you a wife."

"What!" I bolted to my feet, knocking over the bucket of milk. "Why?"

"I do not wish to leave you alone, but someday, it *will* happen. I cannot continue to deny that."

54

An ache throbbed in my chest. I wanted to argue with him, but I couldn't—I knew it to be true. Someday Father would be gone, just like my mother, and I would be all alone.

"A wife can be a wonderful thing," he said, wistful. "And she'd be a great help on the farm too. She could go to the market, leaving you to work the fields…"

His voice ebbed away as a vision consumed my thoughts: a female stranger and I seated at the dinner table, eating lamb stew amid awkward glances and uncomfortable silences. *And after*…I shook my head, to both liberate myself of the torturous image and reaffirm my refusal.

I crossed the barn, placing myself squarely before him.

"We are doing fine by ourselves," I parried, already disliking this woman, whoever she was. "We cook, we clean, we sew…why do we need a wife?"

Father wore a sly grin. "She is not for *us*, Solomon—she is for *you*."

"I don't want her. What would I even do with a…a *woman?*"

"You will see, my son." Father laughed, slapping me on the shoulder. "You will see."

I was very confused.

Despite my protests, the next day we packed up the donkeys and set out for Ur—a city much farther than Uruk. Father asked our neighbour, Zephat, to feed the animals in our absence, which could be several days.

"Why must we go to Ur to find a wife?" I complained, our little hut shrinking to a speck behind us as we trekked south. "Why can't we travel to Uruk? It's closer."

"We don't know anyone in Ur," Father stated. "It is better to be among strangers."

"But surely a women from Ur is no different than one from Uruk?" I said, though honestly didn't care for either.

Father ignored me. "Have I ever told you about Gilgamesh's journey for immortality?"

"*Only* a hundred times or so."

Father's laugh echoed over the dunes. I had to admit, regardless of my lack of enthusiasm for our journey, it warmed my heart to see him smile. Suspecting which tale he was about to recount, however, I failed to see how it would sway my averseness to acquiring a wife. But since it would pass the time—and distract me from my impending doom—I listened.

Father began, "After Enkidu's death, King Gilgamesh was inconsolable. He became fearful of dying, obsessed with finding a way to live forever, travelling all the lands in search of some magical cure. Gilgamesh learned of a man who might hold the key to Gilgamesh's plight. This man lived on the island of Dilmun. Gilgamesh travelled there and found the man. Atrahasis, it was told, had survived a mighty deluge because the gods had warned him to build an ark that would carry him, his family, and his livestock to safety. As a reward for his obedience, the gods granted him and his wife eternal life.

"Atrahasis told the brash king of a special plant which grew at the bottom of the ocean that, when eaten, would give eternal life. 'But why,' Atrahasis asked of the king. 'Why would you wish to live forever when everyone you love will not?'

" 'If I die, the world will forget me and everything I have done,' Gilgamesh replied. "I must stay, to keep my story alive."

" 'Or...' Atrahasis smiled. 'You could do something the world wouldn't forget.'

Rather than heed the ancient man's words, Gilgamesh dove into the water and scoured the depths for the rare plant. Finding it, he carried it to the surface, but he was exhausted from the swim and fell fast asleep on the warm sands. While he slept, a demon in the form of snake stole the plant and ate it, making itself immortal.

"Poor Gilgamesh was devastated, he..." Father's last words were strangled as he doubled over, clutching his chest.

"Father!" I rushed to his side.

"I am...okay." He patted my arm. "Perhaps...just a little rest."

I retrieved a water bladder from my pack and held it to his lips. He struggled with every swallow.

"Father, tell me the truth—are you dying?"

"I cannot...know for certain." Father's hands trembled. "But I believe so, yes."

Sorrow stole my voice.

"All men eventually die," he said, sweat stippling his brow. "But it is my fault you will be left alone once I'm gone. I...will not allow that to happen."

"But...I am happy with just you."

"Only because you do not know what it is like to love another." He smiled sadly.

"I do not think I can love anyone else." I braced my breaking heart. "I do not think there is room."

"Ah *maru*, for every person you love, you grow a new heart. Some you will love deeply, others just enough to cause you grief." He chuckled. "But then, there will be one who you love more than you could ever have imagined. A love so great that no sacrifice is too big and no power in this world can destroy it."

"Like...love for a wife?" I sniffled.

Father touched my cheek.

"Or a child."

A sinuous path cut a scar through the Arabian desert, the sand-swept passage of recent travellers. Despite it being a busy trade route between the many Mesopotamian cities and beyond, tenacious winds quickly buried the evidence as if to purify the sands of human presence.

Father trudged ahead. Like me, his head was wrapped in a tan *shemagh*, a linen scarf to ward off dust and sunlight; though it didn't dissuade the tiny, glossy-winged gnats from ravaging my eyes through the narrow slit.

Vigilant of Father's every step, I watched for any lethargy or decline—not only for his welfare, but perhaps for a reason to turn around and return home. A seed of resentment germinated within. I didn't want this woman Father so fervently desired for me. As innocent his intentions, he didn't understand the torment it provoked. I knew nothing of women save for those few glorious moments spent with Princess Ariadne so many years ago. While she was wonderful, I was petrified to consider what came after. Despite Father's teasing, I wasn't as ignorant to procreation as he might think. I'd seen the animals in heat, followed by mating, swollen bellies, and birth.

I just couldn't imagine the same process between humans.

Fresh sweat erupted on my brow, compounded by the sweltering heat. I teetered, gripping the donkey's lead tighter to steady myself.

I could turn and run, I thought cowardly, knowing Father would be too ill to catch me.

Never.

There wasn't a force on earth that could make me abandon Father—yet my entire being was paralyzed by this impending betrothal. Try as I might, I couldn't envision my bride, only an abyssal void where her face should be, set upon the shoulders of a lithe, naked seductress, arms reaching, fingers curling, beckoning, *trapping...*

I can't do this!

Suddenly I couldn't breathe.

So...hot.

I yanked off the *shemagh* and gulped the blistering air.

Then Father's words came back to haunt me:

"I do not wish to leave you alone. But someday, it will happen. I cannot continue to deny that."

Guilt coalesced with sorrow.

This woman, this mysterious stranger, wasn't just going to be my wife —she was to be Father's replacement.

Hours later, we descended into a passageway between two walls of sandstone.

"We will rest here for the night," Father said, leading his donkey off the main path. He'd slowed during the last stretch, his sinewy body hunched and weary.

In truth, I didn't feel much better. Travelling beneath a midday sun had sapped me of my strength—not to mention, any patience I had for Father's plight. What crumbs of faith remained were scattered amongst the countless dunes we'd scaled.

"Uruk would have been faster," I grumbled.

"I know." Father didn't look up. "Hungry?"

Without waiting for a response, he handed me some jerky and plums. The dehydrated flesh crackled as I tore it in half, shoving the larger piece into my mouth.

Evening loomed as the sun slid behind the mountains, shadows breeding like black lichen amid the rocks. Silence swathed the desert, so deafening I could almost hear the earth shiver as the icy foot of night stepped upon the sands.

On hands and knees, Father dug a hole while I retrieved the fire implements. I placed clay briquettes, sticky with bitumen, into the pit and covered them with dried reeds. Using a crude bow drill made of cedar and catgut, I abraded the fireboard until smoke ignited into flame.

Greedy, amber fingers quested for the viscous oil. Soon, the hearth glowed red and promised to smoulder through the night.

"Beer?" Father offered me a sealed jug.

I accepted, wrenching out the resin plug with my teeth. Warm, sour malt swam down my throat, sloshing inside my belly and sedating my worries. Ur and its ominous temptress were forgotten—for the moment.

Sleep stalked my peripheral, peeking over my shoulder to ambush me amid a lingering blink. I was about to surrender to the quiet hunter when one of the donkeys uttered a nervous huff. The other stood wide-eyed before the darkness, ears perked.

"Something is out there," Father whispered.

"They will not come towards the fire," I said, scouring the unseeable desert for the telltale glint of predacious eyes, likely hyenas or sand cats; neither were prone to attack a full-grown man—let alone two.

"Beasts, no," Father said. "But it is a beacon for man."

Firelight flickered on the cliffs, the dauntless crackle and hiss of flames impeding any sound of approach. Stock-still, we waited to see what—or who—would emerge from the pitch wilderness. We were miles from civilization and it was considered polite to offer our food and warmth to wayward travellers. However, any stranger was one we prayed we wouldn't encounter. Even during the day, the desert was fraught with thieves and scoundrels. It was impossible to know who was friendly—and who would slit your throat for just a drink of water.

The distant bray of a donkey echoed off the crags, as if to announce the impending arrival of its master—thus confirming our fears.

Beside me, Father swallowed. "The darkness should protect you. But keep your head down, just in case."

I nodded, eighteen years of embedded paranoia erecting a fortress around my eyes.

"*Silim!*" A friendly voice called. "May I share your fire?"

"Of course!" Father stood to greet a hunched figure materializing from the opaque fog.

Reliant on a cane of gnarled driftwood, draped in ivory robes with a red turban twirled about his head, the elderly man tethered his donkey next to ours and joined us by the fire.

"Many blessings," the man said, groaning as he sat to my right. "Very hot today, yes?"

"Yes, very," Father replied calmly, but shot a worried glance at the man's proximity to me.

I waited a few moments, and then pretended the fire needed rekindling. After stoking the flames I sat across from the stranger, which allowed me an unobstructed vantage to satisfy my curiosity, but was far enough away to protect my eyes.

Incandescence fingered his weathered brown face, as though determined to peel back the skin, exposing it as a mask, and enlighten us to some hidden identity. His eyes darkled with mischievous humour, ringed by wrinkles deep as desiccated clay in a parched riverbed. A silver moustache curled around his smile, lending to a short goatee on his chin.

"This is my son, Solomon." Father gestured to me. "I am Ezen. We are farmers from Uruk."

"Uruk?" The stranger chuckled, eyes twinkling with nostalgia. "Yes, I know it well. You're headed home then?"

"No," Father said. "We are on our way to Ur."

"I have just come from Ur." The stranger's sterling brow folded. "It's still healing from the many Elamite attacks."

"I have heard," Father said. "We do not wish to stay long."

"Do be careful," the old man warned. "It's a broken city with an even more broken people."

Father nodded in appreciation. "What do they call you?"

"I have been called many things—not all of them very nice." The old man laughed. "But in these parts, I'm known as The Storyteller."

"Storyteller?" I leaned in closer. "What kind of stories?"

"Oh! So many!" The man swept an arm over the horizon. "From faraway lands! Stories of heroes and monsters, kings and kingdoms, princesses and palaces..."

"Please," I begged. "Tell us!"

"Ahh, but you see..." The stranger arched an impish brow. "I must feed myself, no?"

Father fished a shekel from his pocket and tossed it to the man.

The Storyteller eyed the meagre sum. "A *short* story then..."

He took a deep breath, and began.

"Far from Sumer," he said, his gaze lingering on some mystical shore beyond the borders of Mesopotamia. "Far from the desert and sand, a great mountain grows from the sea. The air smells of salt, the land lush with green, green, and more green! Flowers of all colours, roses, lotus, and poppies. Deep waters rush the golden beaches, tangles of seaweed ripple beneath a surface of blue glass. Coral crabs skitter over the wet sands. Beauty like you've never seen!"

He paused for effect.

"And the women..." He cupped both hands over his chest, imitating full, rounded breasts as he stroked the imaginary nipples with his thumbs. "The women are the true beauty of the island, I tell you."

He waggled his brows at me.

I blushed, deviant thoughts summoning memories of Princess Ariadne.

"Where is this place?" I asked, mesmerized.

"It is a hidden utopia. A place where peace and the pursuit of knowledge takes precedence. Where every woman is a goddess and no man is a slave."

I closed my eyes, conjuring visions of this perfect wonderland. Of Ariadne and I strolling on a hot, white beach, the sapphire ocean tasting our toes as the tide lapped the sands...

"But alas, as with every paradise, it's just an illusion," The Storyteller's voice lowered, the flames shuddering ominously. "A world built on a foundation of lies and terrible secrets."

I swallowed hard. "Secrets?"

"Come closer." The Storyteller gestured. "I will tell you."

Father and I edged closer, the campfire just inches from our knees.

"Seduced by pride, the king of this great land begged Poseidon, God of the Oceans, to send him a sacred, white bull. The king's wish was granted, but on the promise that he'd eventually sacrifice the bull, thus returning it to Poseidon. But the king had grown greedy and power-hungry. He was enchanted with the god's bull and secretly sacrificed one of his own, common bulls, keeping the mystical creature for himself. But the god was not fooled. Enraged, Poseidon cursed the king's wife, making her lust for the white bull—to make it her lover."

I gasped.

"The gods can be spiteful, make no mistake." The Storyteller's gaze darkened as if pained by some relatable experience. "You do not wish to cross them."

Beside me, Father's brows knitted in concern.

The old man continued, "The queen mated with the bull and a terrible monster was spawn—a half-man, half-bull who ate human flesh! The king went mad and ordered a massive labyrinth built under the palace to both hide and imprison the beast—which is where it resides *to this day*."

Rapt silence haunted the expanse between us.

The Storyteller slapped his knee and guffawed. "How is that for a tale?"

"Amazing…" I said, awestruck. "Is it true?"

"All my stories are true, of course!" he said with a flash of teeth. "Now, my friends, tell me, why do you travel to Ur?"

Father handed the traveller a mug of beer which he half-consumed in the first swallow.

Around a lacklustre shrug, I said, "Father wishes for me to find a wife there."

The Storyteller choked and spewed a mouthful of ale into the flames, upsetting the fire into a frenzy of crackles and sparks.

"Why would you do this!" He gaped at Father. "He's so young! So free! Why not just buy him a courtesan for the night instead?"

Father offered the man a gracious smile. "Solomon will need someone to care for him. I do not wish for him to grow old alone."

The Storyteller chewed his cheek, obviously unconvinced. "Have you been with a woman before, boy?"

Father shot the stranger a look of disapproval.

My cheeks grew hot. "No."

"Well then." The Storyteller smirked, his face suddenly years younger as he twisted the tip of his silver moustache. "I can tell you the very best places to go when you arrive in Ur! For just *one* shekel, you can have *two* girls that will…"

"No, thank you," Father interjected. "We only have time for a short visit, just long enough to find a decent woman and head home again."

The Storyteller roared with laughter. "*Decent* woman? I'm afraid all you will find in Ur is slaves and prostitutes, my friends." He raised his mug to us, then drained it before toasting, "I wish you luck, all the same—*you will need it*."

The Storyteller, it would seem, had been right about Ur—or rather, what was left of it.

We approached what I surmised was once a grand archway to welcome weary travellers into the city, but was now a pile of rubble. Raw sewage swamped the streets, puddling against the fractured corners of once prominent homes. Half-starved dogs stalked the fringes, ribcages protruding from beneath matted, patchy fur, eyes maddened with hunger. A baby wailed from behind a threadbare curtain hanging stagnant in the breezeless heat. Broken men loitered against the fallen stones, their stares haunted by violence and the shame of defeat.

"Who would do this?" I asked, eyes wide with horror.

"Elamites," Father said, offering a shekel to a legless man propped against the remnants of a wagon. The half-man gave Father a toothless smile.

A cow horn trumpeted ahead.

"Come." Father walked faster down the street. "It is beginning."

"Where are we going?" I asked, following, but my words were lost to the shifting crowd.

Led down a muddy street, further narrowed by cloying, desperate venders, I exhaled when the road opened up into a large courtyard. A crude stage monopolized the congested enclosure. To the left of the stage, dozens of women stood in a line. Some looked scarcely twelve years old, tears carving pale tracks down their dust-laden cheeks. A large, sweaty man in tan robes stepped onto the stage, grinning through a bristly beard as he addressed the gathering crowd of mostly men.

"Welcome! I hope you brought lots of money, we've got some real beauties today!" he shouted, garnering a raucous of cheers and hoots. "Bring up the first, Dazuzum!"

Dazuzum, a hulking brute with a disturbingly thick brow, took hold of the first young woman in the lineup and dragged her to the centre of the stage. The crowd chuckled at her resistance.

The bearded man sidled next to the shivering girl and lifted her skirt, exposing her thighs. She whimpered as the crowd jeered and whistled.

"Twenty shekels! Get yourself a beautiful new wife!"

Ice trickled through my veins.

A bride auction?

"Father!" I clamped onto his forearm. "I do not wish to *buy* a wife!"

"Have faith, Solomon. The gods have led us here for a reason." He patted my white-knuckled hand. "Trust them."

Amid the cacophony of frenzied bidding, a tall man with a thick, round chest elbowed through the throng, his trio of young wives trailing sullenly behind. He raised his hands to the auctioneer, palms bearing the sooty smudge of a blacksmith. The crowd silenced, seemingly familiar with the man's influence.

"She's ugly," the blacksmith said, matter of fact, "but has nice legs and big breasts. I will give you ten shekels, two goats, and a copper helmet made by me."

The auctioneer nodded, a gleam of greed in his eyes. He shoved the girl to the edge of the stage. Her lower lip trembled as she descended the steps, shoulders curled and head hung in shame. Arriving at her fate, the blacksmith groped her breasts and reached under her skirt. She cried out as he shoved a dirty finger inside of her.

"A virgin!" he announced around a growl of pleasure.

The mob cheered.

Bile scorched the back of my throat.

"Father, please," I begged. "Don't make me do this!"

"Hush now, Solomon."

"Bring up the next!" the auctioneer called on Dazuzum once again, refreshing the crowd's twisted enthusiasm.

The lumbering thug moved to grab the next girl in line—but stopped in his tracks, taking a step back as she escorted herself to centre stage.

The crowd fell silent.

Chin set in defiance and a glare of black fury, she singed every man with just a glance. Though petite and young, no more than sixteen, she defied the horde as would a warrior paraded before the enemy. With skin of dark cream and black hair to her waist, she was dressed in a sheer white gown. But it wasn't her beauty nor countenance of steel that stole everyone's breath—it was her full, round belly.

She was *very* pregnant.

Beside me, Father smiled.

The auctioneer broke the silence. "Two shekels!"

Despite the insulting price, there was no response from the crowd. No man wanted a wife who was clearly not a virgin nor a mouth to feed that was not of his blood.

The auctioneer grimaced. "*One* shekel?"

On the sidelines, an older man glowered at the girl, and then at the crowd. Lips pressed pale with rage, it was obvious this was the girl's owner and he was displeased with the bidding price.

"Step forward, *maru!*" Father elbowed me in the ribs. "Do not allow her to be humiliated further!"

"B-But she is…" I gaped at him. "I mean, I do not want…"

"Sometimes we must sacrifice what we want for what another needs," Father said, pressing something cool into my palm before shoving me towards the stage. "And right now, she needs *you*, Solomon—go!"

Stumbling up the stairs, I suddenly found myself face to face with the girl. She was even more beautiful up close, but she met my stare with such piercing hatred that I had to look away.

"*Sangdu nutuku!*" someone shouted from behind me. A Sumerian term meaning 'one without a head'.

Loosely translated: *idiot*.

The crowd roared.

"Are you going to buy her or not, boy?" The auctioneer asked, maintaining a healthy distance from the glowering girl. "I'll take whatever you offer."

Sheepishly, I opened my hand to the auctioneer, expecting to see a shekel. Instead, I found my mother's ring. Before I could protest, the auctioneer snatched the ring from my palm, declaring the girl my property and ordering her off the stage—but she wouldn't budge.

"*I* am *no one's* property!" she shouted, quaking with rage. "I would rather *die* than *belong* to a man!" She shot me a look of hatred.

Her insolence sparked a riot. Mud and rocks were hurtled at the stage. Resolute, with hands wrapped protectively over her stomach, she stood her ground. A rock sailed past me, striking her in the face. She gasped as a thin line of blood trickled down her cheek. Instinct swelled inside me, I placed myself between her and the onslaught.

"Go! Leave us!" She shoved my chest. "Just let me die!"

I gritted my teeth as a large stone struck my shoulder blade. "Never."

"Why do you buy me?" she demanded, her eyes on mine, oblivious or uncaring of the odd colour. "For your pleasure? To beat me? To *own* me?"

I shook my head.

"Then why?" She caressed her swollen stomach, shooting a bitter glance to her master beside the stage. "My father sells me because I have brought shame to him. Why would *you* want me?"

I glared at her father in disgust.

What kind of man sells his daughter into slavery?

"Perhaps it is not only me who wants you," I said, echoing Father, "but *you* who *needs* me. Therefore, I give myself to you." I offered my hand to her. "*Nga beleti.*"

Warily, she placed her small hand in mine and allowed me to lead her off the stage. Father met us at the bottom of the stairs and draped her with a blanket.

Then we began the long journey home—together.

The road was quiet.

Painfully so.

Desperate for distraction, I had hoped we'd meet more travellers on our way home. The gaping desert mocked me, waiting with wide, expectant eyes for me to engage in conversation with this mysterious woman—or rather, my wife.

Wife.

The very word left my mouth drier than the desert surrounding me. Since leaving Ur, she'd not yet spoken nor even glanced my direction, always keeping a few paces ahead of me, favouring her right leg. Beneath the long dress, her belly was heavy with child. Even with my limited knowledge on the matter, I knew it couldn't be long—a month, six weeks, perhaps?

Summoning courage, I caught up to her.

"You must be tired," I said with a smile. "Would you like to ride the donkey for a while?"

She lifted her chin and breezed by without reply.

Confused, I trailed quietly in her wake.

Father followed even further behind. Every now and then, I peered over my shoulder to check on him, each time met with a cheeky grin. I scowled in return, knowing his old eyes couldn't discern my expression from that distance, but I conveyed my displeasure nonetheless.

After several hours of forging ahead, the girl's pace started to lag and her limp became more pronounced. Without warning, she stopped short and doubled over, clutching her abdomen.

I rushed to her side. "Are you all right?"

"I'm fine," she said through gritted teeth, edging away from me. "It's...just a cramp."

I offered her my waterskin, mildly surprised when she accepted. She untied the leather laces and tipped the bag over her mouth, savouring long, greedy swallows. A glistening droplet escaped her lips, trickled down her chin, navigating the curves of her neck and chest before it slipped out of sight between her breasts—an impish, sand-laden breeze spat in my eye, forcing me to blink.

Sated, she wiped her chin and handed me the bag.

"What's your name?" I dared to ask.

She gave me a cold, sideways glance. "Indra."

"I'm Solomon."

"And him?" The wind caught her hair as she nodded at Father dawdling far behind.

"My father," I said, glaring over my shoulder. "Ezen."

Father smiled wide and waved.

When I faced Indra again, she was staring at me.

"Your eyes," she said, her voice tinged with awe. "They are—blue."

Heat surged up my neck. I nodded mutely, uncertain how to react. I wondered if she found them strange—or simply appalling.

It's one thing to be noticed, and quite another to be seen. Only Father had looked into my eyes and knew who I really was. Enusat, among others, had gawked at my oddness, but never truly *saw* me. They only witnessed the reflection of their own fears and superstitions, branding my eyes a curse because they chose not to understand.

As she stared at me, I stared at her.

Petite and small-boned, somehow her very presence commanded respect. Dark, slanted eyes, flecked amber in the centre as if wildfire seeped from her soul; nose, thin and drawn, hooked delicately at the tip, rendered her more a falcon than a mere mortal woman. Serious and still, she studied my face. I froze, worried I'd make too sudden a movement and she'd startle and take flight.

"*Beautiful,*" Indra whispered, taking a step closer, mesmerized.

With the next heartbeat, her expression melted into horror and her cheeks flushed pink.

"I…um, sorry," she muttered as she spun on her heel and stormed the sandy path again.

"Wait!" I caught up to her again, my gaze flicked to her swollen belly. "Please…I need to ask. How is it you are…with child? Were you married?"

She shot me a warning glance. Part of me knew it was none of my business, but yet, it was. If we were to live as man and wife, I had to address this veritable mountain between us. Lips pursed and eyes narrowed on the distant desert, she cradled her unborn baby with protective hands. In that moment, I was both sad and envious. Sad for my mother as she'd not been given the opportunity to care for me beyond my first day in the world, and envious of this child who'd be given the mother I'd longed for much of my life.

"I have no husband," Indra replied, her voice taut.

I frowned, not understanding.

She sighed at my naïveté. "This baby was conceived in…violence."

I drew a sharp breath. "*Violence?*"

"Yes." She pointed a sharp finger at me, her beautiful face fierce. "But that does not mean I will not love it, nor will I allow anyone else to harm it!"

64

She stormed away.
Shock froze me to the spot.
Violence.
Rape.

The sky blazed violet. Soon, we would be pitched into pure darkness, the inferno of day doused and reduced to ash by the icy night.

"We will rest here for the night," Father said, guiding us off the road.

After anchoring the donkeys to a boulder, I retrieved a blanket from my pack and unfurled it with a laundering snap before laying it on the ground. Around a shy smile, I waved my hand over the makeshift seat, but Indra turned up her nose and sat in the sand several feet away.

Behind me, Father chuckled.

What had I done? Was she upset because I asked her about the baby's father? If so, why didn't she just scold me and be done with it? Whenever Father and I quarrelled, we gave each other space until we cooled down, but we *always* knew why the other was angry.

Indra's behaviour, however, was an enigma.

"The fire," Father said with an indicative nod, drawing me from my bafflement. "It is your turn to make it."

I blinked at him. We never took turns making the fire, we just built one as needed. Shrugging, I obeyed.

Soon enough, feisty embers spat red sparks at the black firmament. Despite the fire's reaching warmth, I shivered and huddled closer. Amid a side-eyed glance, I spied Indra tighten her shawl to a close, incandescence caressing her delicate features. Sensing my gaze, she straightened her spine, her lovely face hardening.

Why is she being so stubborn? Why doesn't she just come sit by the fire?

Replaying our conversation in my head, I dissected each word for a clue to explain her irritation with me, but only amassed more questions than answers. As far as I knew, I'd done nothing wrong.

Beside me, Father rummaged through his pack, humming a little tune with that infuriating smile. Moments later, he handed me a loaf of *bappir*, six eggs, and a pat of goat butter.

"It is *your* turn to make dinner, Solomon," Father declared loudly.

Had the hot day taken him of his senses? When had it been *his* turn? Since his little cooking lesson when I was eight, I'd almost always made the meals. I shrugged yet again and began cooking, wondering if everyone had lost their minds. Soon the eggs sizzled on the stoneware, the savoury aroma of butter snaked through the campsite. My stomach growled.

With an anxious glimpse at Indra, I weighed whether or not I should ask her to join us. Cocooned inside her shawl, aloof, she was curled into an impenetrable shell.

Father nudged me, whispering in my ear, "What is her name?"

"Indra."

"Hmm, pretty," he replied and then called to her, "Girl! Come, sit by the fire and eat with us!"

At first I thought she was simply going to ignore him, maintain her silent protest, but after a moment, she rose, dusted off her skirt, and sat across from us. Eyes down, lips pursed. Father scooped two eggs and a slice of bread onto a plate and offered it to her.

I fully expected her to turn her nose up and away, but instead she practically snatched the plate from Father's hands and devoured the scant serving.

He then served me, but I'd only managed a few bites of bread slathered with yolk before Father poked me with his elbow. He eyed the untouched egg on my plate and then pointed to Indra.

My eyes widened. Scowling, I shook my head. I was starving!

"She eats for *two*, Solomon," he whispered.

Huffing, I stood, stomped around the fire, and extended my plate to her.

She didn't move. Didn't acknowledge me. The aroma of the eggs, *my* eggs, wafted under my nose. I turned to storm back, intent on sedating my appetite, but Father gave a little grunt around a sharp wave with his hand.

'*Do it!*' it said.

Indra scorched me with a dark glower. I dared a glare in return. The air between us crackled with tension.

A battle of wills.

The moment stretched into eternity.

Then, surreptitiously, her gaze slid to the proffered, egg-laden plate —and there was a flash of something that resembled lust in her eyes. Never before had I felt such envy for something inanimate.

Warily, she reached up and accepted the plate. I watched on as she pinched the egg between thumb and forefinger, tilted her head back and parted her lips, placing it onto her pink tongue. Eyes closed in obvious ecstasy, she swallowed, a soft moan escaping her lips.

Strangely hypnotized, I stumbled back to my seat, heart thundering so loud it drowned out the rumble in my belly.

Father just smiled.

Our weary caravan crested the hill just before noon, the tilted shack a beckoning palace in the distance. Somehow, Father had persuaded Indra to ride upon the donkey hours before, which eased my conscience and quickened our pace.

Indra's expression betrayed no emotion as she panned the foreign landscape. Was she relieved, pleased—*disgusted?*

Apprehension overshadowed my exhaustion, unravelling my nerves into frayed strands. No longer safe under the cloak of denial, the journey had ended. We'd arrived at our destination—our destiny. Now this woman and I had nowhere to hide from one another.

We would have to live in the same house.

Share the same room.

Sleep in the same bed.

"Come along, then," Father said with a serene smile, leading the way. "Let us go home."

10

The Harrowing

A delectable aroma seduced me from sleep, wafts of fat-fried mutton and warm honey-sweetened bread. With a groan, I sat up, my back stiff from lying on Father's cot. For the better part of eighteen years, I discovered after a few restless nights, Father had allowed me the softer of the two cots, and himself the lumpy, uncomfortable one—which was now mine and mine was now Indra's. Upon our return from Ur, and my horror of being left alone with Indra the very first night, Father relocated to the barn loft, where he now slept on a thick pillow of hay. As I arched my knotted back, I had to admit the loft was looking like an attractive alternative.

Father was already seated at the table eating breakfast, eyes twinkling as he watched Indra expertly negotiate our tiny kitchen.

"*Silim, maru!*" He grinned when he saw I was awake.

Without even a glance in my direction, Indra set a plateful of food at my usual place, and then returned to stir the porridge.

"Come and eat, Solomon." Father gestured for me to join him. "We have much to do today."

Rising, I raked my untamed hair. "How long have you two been awake...while I was asleep?"

"Long enough for us to hear you snore like an ox!" Father grinned. He hummed a happy tune, sopping creamy, amber yolk with fresh bread. "We will inundate the fields today. The almanac says we may begin this week, I'd like to start right away."

"Um, yes, of course," I think I said aloud, though my attention was elsewhere.

Sunlight slipped through the doorway, glossing the hut—and *her*—in an ethereal hue. Dust motes swirled with every sway of her skirt; blouse cinched at what little waist she had left, stretched taut against her swollen bosom. A wrinkle of concentration between her brows marred her cream-smooth complexion; ebon hair neatly wound atop her crown, all but the wispy, dampened tendrils, which clung to the nape of her neck. To and fro across the kitchen: stirring the porridge; wiping surfaces of grease; sweeping the corners; bending to poke the embers beneath the pot with one hand, the other protecting her stomach. Everything she did, every movement, seemed a choreographed dance of the domestic.

Water is like woman—smooth and supple, a lifetime of Father's teachings purled inside my thoughts. *The gods made woman to be the opposite of man; where man is hard, woman is soft...full, and round, seductive...designed to tempt man, to placate him.*

Transfixed, I marvelled how I'd lived eighteen years and never seen something so beautiful, so perfect, so...

"Solomon?" Father's voice snapped me to attention—both he and Indra were staring at me. "I asked you if you were going to eat your bread, but your thoughts are somewhere else, I see."

Mortified, I dropped my gaze, shoving the last bit of bread into my mouth.

"Eat up now, time for work!" Father burped, winked his gratitude to Indra, and walked out the door—leaving us *alone.*

The tiny room shrank. The air heavy, unbreathable. The bread turned to sand between my teeth, and then clay when I tried to swallow. Indra busied herself with cleaning the kitchen, seemingly unaffected by my presence. Annoyance pecked at me. What had I done to cause her to dislike me? I'd saved her from a worser fate, hadn't I? I treated her with respect, given her run of the kitchen, a new home—the softer cot. What had I done wrong?

Intent on proving myself, I picked up my plate and carried it across the hut.

"Thank you for breakfast." I offered Indra the empty dish. "It was... delicious."

She froze, gaze firmly on the floor. This close to her, I could almost feel her body heat. Her scent, an erotic medley of jasmine and hearth-smoke, snaked round my senses, stealing me of intelligent thought. The moment stretched too long, the proffered plate left hanging between us. I thought perhaps I should just set it down and leave. As I'd decided to do so, however, she reached out and took it from me.

"You're welcome," Indra said, her dark eyes flitted to mine, the ghost of a smile on her lips.

My stomach flipped.

"I...will see you later then?" I grinned stupidly. "Well, I mean, of course I will...you live here."

"Solomon!" Father called from outside.

Tripping on my own feet, I walked to the door. With a parting smile, I glanced back—she was still standing there with the plate in her hand, an expression of amused concern on her lovely face.

Despite Enusat's water restriction years previous, Father and I had devised a secret way to douse our crops that ended up far more efficient than before. A natural levy surrounded my secret oasis; by digging out a narrow section and joining it to the main tributaries, we could control the water flow to not only our fields, but to Zephat's and several farmers' beyond. In fact, we'd not seen such bountiful crops in the many years since living there.

"We will flood the north fields today," Father announced. "Then the south tomorrow. We'll ready the oxen for plowing while we wait for them to dry."

With shovels on our shoulders, we walked the length of the fields to open all the trenches and allow the river to saturate the soil.

"Indra is doing well, don't you think?" Father said, giving me a sideways glance.

A field of butterflies took flight inside my chest at the mere mention of her name—but I refused Father any satisfaction that his plot had succeeded.

"It's only been a few days." I shrugged, swatting a black fly from my cheek. "But her cooking is very good."

Father chewed thoughtfully on a sprig of mint. "The baby...it will not be long, I think. A month, perhaps?"

An uncomfortable sensation curled inside my stomach. I'd not forgotten about the baby, of course, but I couldn't convince myself there was going to be another person in our tiny hut, another mouth to feed. I'd never been around a baby nor a toddler. I had no idea what to expect.

"You do realize..." Father stopped me with a hand on my shoulder. "She will need our help during delivery, Solomon."

As if reality had been circling above my head, it suddenly swooped and landed with a thud. I'd witnessed many a farm animal give birth, even assisted with a few. Often, Father was forced to intervene and shove his hand inside the beast to rotate the baby or ease it out by the legs.

I felt myself pale.

"But..." I leaned on my shovel for support. "She might be okay on her own, too, right?"

"No, *maru*, we will have to help her." Father gave me a hard look. "Birth is not an easy thing for a woman, it is long and painful—and sometimes dangerous."

A knot tightened in my throat.

"That's...how my mother died..." I faced him, panicked. "What are we going to do!"

Father's eyes clouded over.

"We wait."

It was dark by the time we finished flooding the fields. A square of golden illumination from the hut's lone window guided us home. The scent of supper met us long before we reached the door. A warm sensation gathered beside my heart.

Father was right, a woman in the house changes everything.

If a woman could initiate so much change—what would a baby do? I tried to imagine what life would be like with this small, vulnerable being who depended on us to care for it. I thought of Father and how he'd raised me alone while still farming and tending all the chores.

I hesitated before the hut, afraid of what I might come home to. Selfishly I hoped she'd given birth since this morning, relieving me of the obligation to assist. After a deep breath, I ducked into the hut. Indra was seated at the table, darning needle in hand as she stitched up one of Father's tunics, her belly still taut and rotund. She set the sewing aside when we entered and struggled to rise. I rushed to her, placing my hand on the small of her back, giving a gentle push.

"I'm fine," she said quietly, but did not shy from my touch as I expected.

"Are you sure." I dared a small step closer.

She nodded—but still didn't move.

Our body heat mingled. Danced unseen in the inches left between us. Heart in my throat, I sipped shallow breaths, fearful any movement might startle her away. Though stiff, Indra too seemed entranced by our nearness. Like me, unable to tear away.

"Lamb stew and turnips!" Father exclaimed, shoving his nose into the pot cooking over the fire, puncturing the intimate moment.

Indra slid away from me and into the kitchen to fetch our supper. I tried to recapture Indra's eye, but she kept her gaze averted.

Frustrated, I growled, "You and your stomach, always about food."

He laughed around a slap of his belly. "Yes, I will admit to that."

We sat at the table and Indra served us. Her very presence drove me wild with distraction. I desired her touch, accidentally or not. Craved to feel her fingertips on my arm, my hand—my chest.

Father retrieved some mugs and filled them with beer. Indra cast a wary eye at the ale. She'd not served us beer the previous evening either. At the time, I thought perhaps she'd forgotten or was too shy to ask where we kept it, but now I wondered if she had omitted the beverage on purpose. Sumerians loved their beer, sometimes too much. Often, they accepted barrels of beer over money as payment for a long day's work, returning home inebriated.

"The field will rest now, for three days," Father said, licking froth from his upper lip. "Tomorrow we should check the plows and ready the oxen."

I nodded through a bite of lamb—and almost moaned. Tender with a hint of curry and stewed all afternoon, the meat practically melted on my tongue. Thin slices of carrots, garlic, and cubes of peach-coloured turnips swam in a beer-glazed gravy. Since the time Father taught me to cook, we'd lived primarily on eggs and tough, tasteless meats. Indra's culinary ability was heavenly by comparison.

"Indra, come, sit and eat." Father waved her over.

Shyly, she filled a plate of stew for herself and sat beside me, summoning a fresh wave of lust.

She'd only managed a single bite before Father began quizzing her.

"So, Indra, is your father a farmer?"

She cleared her throat. "No, he is a carpenter."

"Oh!" Father's eyes lit up. "What kind of wood does he use?"

"Mostly oak, and cedar…if it's available," she replied with a hint of hesitation. I wasn't certain she wanted to speak about her family, particularly as it was her father who'd sold her at the bride auction. I shot Father a look that suggested the topic might be unfavourable, but he ignored me.

"What sort of things did he build?"

"Boats and wagons, mostly," she said. "Though once he was commissioned to build a chariot for the prince of Ur. It had *metal* wheels!" Indra raised her eyes to mine, childlike and excited—but just as quickly, blushed and glanced away.

"How wonderful!" Father smiled. "And did you ever help him build anything?"

"No, I had to take care of my sisters. My mother died many years ago and I am one of the oldest."

My heart cracked, sharing her pain.

We remained silent a moment, until Indra pointed to the corner where we kept the cured tablets.

"The tablets," Indra said. "May I…read them?"

Father set his fork down. "*You*…can read?"

Only the wealthy and scribes were trained to read. Common women —*never*.

"Y-Yes." Indra's cheeks flushed crimson. "If I'm not allowed though…"

"Of course you can," Father said quickly, patting her hand. "I am simply surprised you were taught."

"My grandfather was a scribe. He taught my mother—and she taught us."

"That's wonderful!" Father beamed. "Perhaps you and Solomon can read to one another some night. It is a favourite pastime of ours."

"Yes," I said, offering her a hopeful look. "I would enjoy that…very much."

With a strained smile, she nodded, though I couldn't help but notice the spark of fear that ignited behind her eyes.

The harrowing had begun.

Great curtains of dust rose on the horizon as every Sumerian farmer started the yearly process of cultivation. With the sand's thirst quenched and left to bake for several days under the sun, we began to plow. Plumes of arid dust lingered like ghosts as I guided the oxen over the field, their thick hooves crushing the hardened clumps, readying the land for seed.

One of the bulls stopped short, snuffling, licking his lips with a fat, slimy tongue.

"Thirsty?" A swarm of black flies stirred as I patted the ox's brown head, relocating to his rear. Retrieving a bowl and the water bag from my satchel, I filled it and set it down for the beast to drink.

Heat stung my neck, hot air filling my lungs with every breath. I wiped my forehead with my arm and shielded the sun from my eyes. Father's form was a dark speck on the horizon, his own plow and oxen stirring up a dust storm.

"Today, we will work until the sun is half-eaten by the horizon," Father had stated before they head out.

Sunset.

With a longing sigh, I glanced back at the reed hut where I'd left Indra to sleep the last hour before dawn.

Sunset until I see her again.

Was it foolish of me to love her already? Did I even know enough of love to claim it? All I knew is how she made me feel: dizzy, light-hearted, longing to become a better man. Desire for her carved a hole in my heart. This woman had bewitched me in ways I didn't understand. When Father told me I needed a wife, I ignorantly assumed she was merely for cooking and cleaning. I had no idea I would be overcome with this unquenchable, physical *need*. I now saw the wisdom behind Father's acts. He *knew*. He knew when I became a man that I would need this—I would need her.

Beside me, the ox grunted and nudged my arm with his mighty head, as if in thanks for the drink.

I scratched him behind the ear. "Ready to work some more?"

"Do you always talk to the animals?" a voice said.

I spun about—and there she was. How I'd missed her approach, I had no idea.

"Indra!" I grinned like a fool. "I—yes, too often."

Radiant, she smiled. Black hair glossy in the sunlight, swollen belly hidden beneath a long woollen shawl draped over her left shoulder. As was Sumerian custom, the right shoulder remained bare. Overcome with lust, I stared at her naked skin.

"I...made you some lunch." She handed me a satchel. There was another just like it in her other hand, for Father, I assumed.

"Thank you, I'm starving."

"You're welcome." Her copper gaze darted nervously.

A rare breeze whispered through the desert, casting a tendril of dark hair across her cheek. Without thinking, I brushed it aside, tucking it behind her ear.

Uncertainty darkened her expression. "I-I should be going..." she said, turning to leave.

"Please...don't go. Eat with me?"

She regarded me with her raptorial stare. "For a minute. I need to take Father his food before it spoils."

I led her to flatter terrain and we sat. Inside the satchel, I found fresh-baked date bread, pears, dried gazelle meat, and a sealed jug of beer.

"You're a very good cook," I said, savouring the warm bread.

"My older sister, Taram, taught me." Indra turned a wistful eye to the desert. "She was sold a month before me."

"Was she also..." I glanced at Indra's baby bump.

She shook her head, plucking a loose thread from the hem of her dress. "No, our father is selling all of his children."

"All of you? Why?"

"He says we all look too much like our mother...and that it makes him sad."

"Do you..." I treaded carefully, "believe him?"

"No. I think he wishes to be free from responsibility." Silence yawned a moment, then she asked, "What happened to your mother?"

I thought twice about telling her, considering her condition, but decided the truth would be best. "She died shortly after giving birth to me."

A flicker of fear crossed Indra's eyes and she placed a subconscious hand over her stomach.

"Pear?" I grabbed the fruit and offered it to her. She accepted it with a shy smile, her fingertips grazing mine.

Timidly, she took a small bite, a bead of nectar glistened on her lips before she licked it away. Something inside of me stirred. Something primal and hungry. I tried to suppress it, to push it away, but it resurfaced, stronger with each attempt.

Indra finished eating and struggled to her feet.

"I should go," she said, eyeing the horizon where Father's figure toiled. "Your father needs to keep up his strength."

She picked up Father's food parcel and turned to leave. My heart pounded in disappointment. In the next moment, however, she paused and turned about, a look of indecision on her face. Then, amid a cautious step closer to me, she rose up onto her tiptoes and brushed her lips against my cheek.

She reddened around a small smile.

It was a beautiful, precious moment—and I should've left it at that.

Passion overwhelmed me. I wrapped my arms around her waist, drawing her close. Delicate in my arms, her firm belly and breasts pressed against my body. I tipped her back, long hair swinging like silk over my forearm. Besot with need, my lips explored her jawline, tasted her neck; her skin savoury, saline, redolent of lavender and date oil.

I was drunk with lust.

Intoxicated.

She pressed her palms against my chest, but I held her tighter, though gentle. I kissed her throat, her ear, her bare shoulder.

"*Beleti*," I growled, running my free hand over her body.

A sick sensation crawled through my stomach as I realized she'd stopped moving.

She was so still.

Rigid.

I released her and took a long step back.

Fists balled at her sides, she shook with rage. Eyes black with fury. At her feet, Father's satchel of food was spilled open and covered with mud. Ruined. Tears filled her eyes. Tears of anger and fear and *hatred.* With a last look of disgust, she spun on her heel and stormed back to the hut.

I knew not to follow.

Darkness descended, swathing the little hut in a black cloak of misery. The rising half-moon scrutinized me with a narrowed, silver eye. Fear and self-loathing churned within my blood. There, in the gloom of nightfall, I stood paralyzed before the shack, my childhood home, the place in which I'd once felt safe and welcome—but no longer. This tiny reed hovel was now a doorway to suffering. A suffering of my own design, to be fair. I could no more take a step closer to my home than be coaxed to cross the threshold of Hell.

Father's footfalls grew louder behind me. Next to me, he panned from my petrified face, to the hut, and back again.

He pinched the bridge of his nose and sighed. "What did you do?"

Unable to confess my sins, I could only shake my head.

"Come now, *maru*," Father said gravely. "Believe me now, it will be worse if you leave it too long. We must face our greatest fears—even if they are women."

With a deep breath, I allowed Father to lead me inside. I hated myself for what I'd done. Indra was delicate, fragile. She'd been through more than a woman ever should. Internally, I bruised myself with insults, cut my soul into pieces with harsh and disgusting words, knowing I didn't deserve such a woman for a wife. I dreaded seeing her face, the sadness and fear in her eyes, and knowing it was me who put it there.

She had every right to hate me forever.

The hut smelled of fresh honey bread. A foaming mug of beer for both Father and I waited at our places on the table. Indra crossed the room with two plates full of steaming stew balanced on her hands.

"Sit," she ordered without looking at me, her expression hard as marble.

We obeyed.

Staring into nothingness as I ate, I placated myself with the thought that perhaps she'd slipped poison into this delicious meal and my torment would soon be over. The tender meat and sweet turnips moved like sand over my tongue, remorse depriving me of pleasure.

"Many blessings, Indra," Father said with a satisfied smile, patting his belly. "It was delicious."

She smiled at him in response—I hated him just a little for it.

"I, uh, must excuse myself, however," he added, rising. "There is a... goat giving birth soon, I should stay near her tonight."

He nodded at Indra, followed by a stealthy 'good luck' grimace in my direction.

I glowered at his back as he exited, though mostly out of jealousy.

Now she and I were alone.

I sat at the table, my head lowered in shame. Perhaps if I didn't move or say anything for an hour or two, she'd simply go to bed and wake up less angry at me?

I considered sneaking out, taking up residence beside Father in the barn's loft. Surely he wouldn't mind, he would understand how...

Suddenly Indra's warm, petite hands were on my shoulders. I stiffened, certain those hands would soon be tightening around my neck. Instead though, she started to rub the ache from my muscles, kneading, massaging. Her touch was stronger than I would have guessed, her body was so close that her breasts pressed against my back. Slowly, erotically, she slid her palms over my chest, down my stomach, flirting perilously close to my awakening manhood.

"Do you like this?" Her lips grazed my earlobe, breath hot against my cheek. "Do you want *more*?"

"Y-Yes." My head spun.

She pulled off my tunic, her hardened nipples nudging my shoulderblades through her blouse.

"Do you want me, Solomon?" she whispered over a moan. "Do you want to feel this body beneath you? Do you want to suckle these breasts? Touch this warm, wet place between my legs? Is that what you want?"

"Oh gods, yes." I couldn't think straight. I couldn't think at all. My body lusted like wildfire through bone-dry grassland. Out of control. "I want you so much...*I love you.*"

74

She brought her beautiful face over mine, mouth parted for a kiss. Lips inches from my own. I reached up to touch her. I wanted nothing more than to have her right there and then.

She ran her fingers through my hair, caressing the thick curls, a groan of passion escaping her—then, in one swift motion, she clutched a handful of my hair and wrenched my head back so far I worried my neck might rip open. With the other hand, she brought a sharpened stone to my throat.

"You do not *love* me." Hot, angry breath scorched my face as she spoke, her voice low and dangerous—a cobra hissing in warning before its strike. "I heard those words a dozen times a day, each time a *filthy* drunken soldier climbed on top of me and thrust himself into sacred places that should remain my own, grunting in pleasure as he filled me with soil and sin, calling me any other name but mine!"

My Adam's apple grated against the makeshift weapon with every swallow.

"You will *not* touch me like that again unless I invite you to, Solomon." Her gaze singed mine, eyes like black ice. "Do you understand?"

I nodded as best as I could and she released me, humming a little tune as she rubbed her belly and returned to the kitchen to clean the dishes.

I became a ghost.

A shadow haunting my former life.

For days afterward, I stayed out of her way, interacting only when necessary. If we accidentally made eye contact, guilt flowed like acid through my veins. She hated me, and rightfully so. Not only because of what I'd done, but simply because I was a man. To her, men symbolized pain and suffering. Stolen innocence.

Contrarily, Indra seemed enchanted by Father, laughing at his jokes, smiling as she served him dinner, rapt during his endless allegories—yet she was perturbed by my very existence. Did she hate me because I was the one who bought her from the bride auction? Because, as her husband, I represented ownership over her? Or was Father simply more interesting than me?

Women made even less sense to me now than before when I'd never met one.

One evening, after a long day in the fields, Father and I arrived home to find Indra absent and our supper unprepared.

Panic squeezed my heart with a cold hand.

"What if she's hurt or..." My thoughts turned to the impending child.

Father nodded intuitively. "Let's have a look around outside."

I ran behind the hut, scouring the barren landscape. There was nowhere to hide beyond a few skeletal sage bushes and the distant range of undulating dunes.

"Indra!" My voice carried over the whispering sands.

From the other side of the hut, I could hear Father yelling her name. Finding no trace of her myself, I made my way to him.

"Anything?" I scanned Father's face.

"Nothing." He touched my shoulder. "*Maru*, we must consider the possibility that…she may have run away."

"She wouldn't," I denied. "She couldn't. Not in her condition."

Could she have been so unhappy with us—with me—that she'd simply leave?

"Did you check the loft?" I asked on a hunch.

We raced towards the barn. At the threshold, I rushed ahead, climbing the rungs of the ladder two at a time. There, fast asleep on Father's cot, Indra was curled up like a cat in a sunlit corner.

"Is she there?" Father called up.

I glanced down, nodding. An expression of relief crossed his face.

Rather than wake her, I descended and walked out of the barn. My heartbeat eventually slowed.

"It must have been difficult for her to climb the ladder," I said, confused. "Why would she go up there?"

Father regarded the fiery horizon, pensive. "Although she is soon to be a mother and has the body of a young woman, she is a child, one whose father has recently betrayed and abandoned her. Sometimes *maru*," he said with a sad smile, "when we are lost, we cling to things which remind us of home. Of happier times. Perhaps Indra finds comfort in having a new father figure to fill the void her own has left."

I considered this. "Is that so bad?"

"No, but she is cannot be a child anymore. She does not need a father to heal her now, she needs her husband—*you*."

The next morning, Father was up and away before dawn without a word as to where he'd gone. Even stranger, he'd completed all the chores before he left, including mine; ultimately leaving me with nothing to do—except help Indra.

Suspecting his intentions, I scowled in the barn's general direction, envisioning him there, the previous evening, scheming after Indra's sheepish descent from his loft with profuse apologies for our delayed supper. She never did offer an explanation as to why she'd chosen that particular location for her catnap.

Despite avoiding the hut for as long as I could, and loathing to be idle, I surrendered to my fate. Indra was sweeping the floor when I entered. She eyed me, leery.

"I…finished early," I lied. "Is there anything I can help you with?"

Worry crossed her face as she handed me the broom, and then readied a bucket of soapy water for herself to wash the clothes. Awkward silence stretched between us at first, but soon we fell into that quiet trance often induced by menial labour. After finishing the wash, Indra wiped the sweat from her forehead, her hairline damp and dress clinging to her skin. Her belly protruded so far now that her navel had popped out, forming a tiny bump beneath her dress. She looked hot and swollen, so terribly uncomfortable—

"Would you like to see the river?" I blurted my epiphany, startling her. "Perhaps go swimming?"

Agony melted into relief. "Oh gods, yes please."

We gathered a few things into a picnic basket and started out.

The midday sun wasted no time in its attempt to roast us alive. Temperatures were so hot and dry, a droplet of water would evaporate long

76

before it touched the sands. Though instinct begged me to rush to my secret oasis for the shade, I paced myself to stay beside Indra.

"Is it very far?" Indra asked, breathless, carrying her belly with both hands.

"It's still a little ways," I said gently.

Just over the next dune, my secret oasis appeared like a glorious, shimmering mirage. Great palms of jade fronds tented overhead, ushering us along a winding path to the river. Ahead, Indra filled her lungs, her stride relaxed, hands swinging at her sides.

Denser since my last visit, my desert kingdom had blossomed into an exiled jungle. Navy river-water swirled, caught in gentle eddies. A cloud of gnats droned over an inflorescence of blushing milkweed.

I laid a blanket on the sand, holding Indra's hand as she sat. I sat as well—though as close to the edge of fabric as possible.

"Thank you." She soaked in the surroundings. "This is so beautiful."

"For some reason, I feel closest to my mother here," I said, looking around as if she hid amongst the tangle of acacia trees. I turned to Indra. "What was your mother like?"

"She was shy, quiet...very smart." Indra shrugged a bronze shoulder. "She read to us, taught us to write...I miss her smile, her laugh...her smell."

"Her smell?"

Indra laughed. "She smelled of so many wonderful things: fresh honey bread, curry, soap, lavender...sunshine. Everything reminds me of her." Her gaze fell to her stomach. "She would've been very excited for this baby...despite how it was made. She would never have let my father sell me—then again, none of this would've happened if I hadn't..." Tears welled in her eyes, lip trembling. I took her hand in mine, sensing she needed to speak but was unable to find her voice.

Finally, she closed her eyes, and began...

"Ur had just been invaded by the Elamites again," she said, gaze navigating the dark labyrinth of her past. "My father's work had suffered terribly and he couldn't afford to feed all of us. I'm one of the oldest, so Papa sent me and two sisters to the market every day to sell whatever we could to get by.

"One day..." her voice tightened and I stroked her wrist with my thumb. "A woman approached us. She told us if we came to the temple and paid tribute to the goddess, we would be greatly rewarded. I thought...I would be helping my father if I made some extra money. I didn't realize...what they wanted of me.I didn't know, Solomon, I swear I didn't..." her voice shuddered around sobs.

I swept the tears from her cheeks.

"Taram and I followed the woman, leaving Sariti to tend the tables. Inside the temple, there were...soldiers, so many soldiers," she said, squeezing her eyes shut as if the horrors still danced before her. "The woman told us we had a duty to please these men, and to please the goddess—Inanna."

Despite the tropical warmth enveloping us, an ominous chill slithered over my skin.

"It was called the *Sacred Courtesan of the Goddess*. We were to serve the men, to...*give* ourselves to them. If they were pleased, they'd pay us a silver shekel…and we'd be free to leave. If not, they left us for the next man…and the next…and the next. We weren't allowed to leave the temple until a man was pleased enough to pay us—some women were there for years—some never left.

"There were so many men, Solomon. So very many." Her tearful gaze searched my face. "I'm…not worthy to be your wife. I'm…so…so *dirty*." Indra wept into her hands.

I gathered her tiny body against my chest, rocking her, stroking her hair.

"And for this…?" I shook with rage. "Your father sold you?"

"I…I shamed him," she said in a small voice. "If I hadn't gone with the woman…"

I lifted her chin, forcing her eyes to meet mine. "You did no such thing, *beleti*. You've nothing to be ashamed of, this…" I placed my hand on her stomach. "This life inside of you already loves you. Some things, even bad things, happen in order to create miracles—like the floods. The floods bring chaos and devastation, even death, but it also brings new life, nourishing the soil, the land, and giving us the water we need to live. This dark time for you was terrible, yes, but I must be grateful for it…for it has brought you both to me."

Indra regarded me with her piercing, falcon stare, dark eyes raking my face, my eyes—my soul—searching for any shred of deception. Finally, after several uncertain moments, she wrapped her hand around the back of my neck and drew me close, bringing my lips to hers. A surge of pleasure and relief overwhelmed me. This beautiful, intelligent woman loved me—and I loved her.

Had I known I could love this deeply in love, I would've stopped myself right then—for the higher one climbs towards Heaven, the farther the fall into Hell.

Father was whistling a happy tune when he arrived home that evening, as if he already knew his little plan had succeeded. Try as I might, I couldn't be sore at him for his scheme.

Indra and I both wore foolish smiles, blushing every time we caught each other's eye. Father babbled about his day digging a trench for Zephat whose wife was about to give birth yet again.

"That man!" Father rubbed his full belly, burping in appreciation for Indra's supper. "*Eight* children! Can you imagine? He needs to leave that woman be—or maybe she needs a big stick to fend him off!"

Indra laughed.

"So, Indra," he asked, waggling his brows at me. "How many children do you desire? Three? Four?"

"However many the gods see fit to bless me—us—with." She slipped a sly grin in my direction and my heart sang.

Father beamed. "Well, I am excited to have a little one running about again, that is for certain." He stood and made for the door. "I am off to put the oxen to bed, and then myself. *Silim*, my children."

After he'd gone, I began resetting the stools around the table. "He's going to make quite the Papa. We're going to need a bigger hut for all the grandchildren he wants though. What do you think?" I turned toward Indra—and froze. "Indra! Are you okay?"

78

Ashen, she was doubled over, clutching her abdomen.

"Father!" I yelled, rushing to her side.

Wide-eyed and out of breath, Father reappeared in the doorway. "What is it!"

In a glance, he knew, and hurried to help me carry Indra to the cot. Sweat stippled her forehead, beautiful face wrenched in agony.

"That's how my mother died..."

My own words haunted me.

What if Indra dies in childbirth like my mother? Like her own mother? I'd be devastated...and I'd be the lone parent of this baby, like Father was for me. And what if...

"Solomon," Father's calm voice rescued me from myself. "We need hot water and fresh nettle."

After setting a pot of water atop the hearth, I raced outside to fetch some nettle from a patch beside the barn. Tiny barbs on the leaves stung my fingers, but I snatched at them undaunted. When I returned to the hut, the water had just begun to boil. I dropped the leaves into the pot to steep and returned to Indra.

Father had shifted Indra onto her side and lifted her dress to expose the small of her back, where he now rubbed a balm of oil and crushed poppies.

I paced the small room, my stomach twisting.

"Should I go to town...get the healer?"

"There is no time." Father shook his head. "If she is giving birth, it will be soon."

"*If* she's giving birth...what else could it be?"

Indra moaned, writhing with waves of pain.

Father only offered me a grave look and resumed applying the balm.

"The tea, Solomon," he reminded.

Grateful for the distraction, I poured the brew into a cup, spirals of steam rising like ghosts. Cupping the hot mug, I carried it to Father. He spoon-fed Indra the tea. After what felt like an eternity, her body relaxed and she rested.

"Stay with her," Father said, rising. "I will find some more blankets in the barn. We may be needing them."

I laid beside her, curling around her tiny body. I pressed my palm gently against her chest, comforted each time it rose. Every so often, she stiffened and whimpered.

"I miss her smell." Indra's memory of her mother resounded.

I buried my face in Indra's hair, inhaled her scent, committing it to memory should this be the last time.

Trust, I thought. *It is a test of trust.*

Careful not to wake Indra, I rose from the cot and stretched. Exhaustion overshadowed my anxiety. I felt a hundred—a thousand—years older.

"I'm...sorry," Indra's voice startled me.

I spun about, returning to the cot.

"No, *beleti*.' I stroked her hair. "Don't be sorry."

Tears shimmered in her eyes. "I do not wish to be a burden."

"You, my love—" I kissed her temple, "are the greatest burden I could ever wish to carry."

"Y-You are happy I'm your wife?"

"More than happy. Before you," I said, taking her small hand into mine. "I didn't know my own heart. I thought I knew what love was because I loved Father, and the mother I had never known. But that was merely a child's love, a selfish love, a love that had never sacrificed."

I laid down, aligning myself so our faces were just inches apart. I traced the curve of her jaw, rubbed the tiny furrow between her thin brows with hopes of softening it. "There are no words that can describe my love for you," I whispered. "What I feel cannot be defined, it is…more than words, *beleti*. You're my everything. My only light in this dark and lonely world—my star."

"I love you, too," she said quietly. "And…I trust you."

The baby did not come that night, nor the next.

We forced Indra to stay in bed, at least until she'd had enough of our fussing and shooed us out of the hut so she could 'give it a proper cleaning'. Father and I left, unwillingly, to tend to our chores. Neglected for a few days, we had plenty to catch up on.

Despite the hut being in full view, nervous energy spun inside my stomach. What if she needed me and I couldn't hear her cries?

In the barn, I tossed fresh hay into the pens. Curious goats crowded around the mound, forcing me into a corner to avoid hitting them with the pitchfork. As I tried to maneuver one forkful of alfalfa, I inadvertently struck the side of the trough. The impact ricocheted through my arm, splintering the wooden handle into two.

Outside, I held up the evidence to Father with an expression of chagrin.

He chuckled. "There is another in the old barn."

On the outskirts of our farmland, the old barn sat hunched beneath a scraggly juniper tree. Uncomfortable with being too far from Indra for any length of time, I took quick strides. After clearing away an excess of sand and fallen branches, I peered inside. Dust motes glittered inside a slice of sunlight peering through a crack in the roof. Besides rusting implements, I cringed at what else might've taken up residence in the dark corners. Cluttered with old farm equipment, a broken potter's wheel, and various hand tools, I had to shove my way in. Eyes narrowed at the shadowy corners, I spied a cobwebbed pitchfork leaning against the back wall. As I navigated the archaic hoards, my hip struck something solid, sending a jolt of pain down my leg.

"Argh!" I shot a glare at the perpetrator—an antiquated forge.

Father had purchased the forge many years before I was born. Apparently he'd tried his hand at smithing, though quickly learned the metals he required were in short supply around Sumer, and too expensive to obtain through trade merchants.

Atop the forge was a small smelting pot. Blowing away the excess dust, something glimmered inside—something metallic.

Pitchfork and tiny pot in hand, I hurried back to the farm.

I approached Father, showing him the bowl like a child who'd found treasure.

His eyes lit up. "The old cast I used to make your mother's ring!"

"There's a lot of metal left…" An idea took shape inside my head.

"Yes." Father smiled. "Enough for another ring."

Days later, I pried the thin metal band from the resin mould and buffed any rough edges. After a few attempts at designing the perfect cast, smelting the metals, hours of shaping and filing, and, finally, engraving the symbol—it was ready. Slipping it onto my smallest finger, I admired my craftsmanship.

Polished and gleaming in the twilit sun, I wrapped the ring up inside a piece of fabric. As I head to the hut, I was suddenly nervous. Technically, she was already my wife, but I felt I was solidifying that promise further.

A true commitment.

While I was not fearful of pledging my eternal love, I was worried she might not feel as strongly about me as I did about her. I was hopelessly in love. Without her now, I would be incomplete.

At the door of the hut, I gathered my courage. Unfolding the cloth, I stared at the golden band adorned with two obverse triangles laid atop one another to form a hexagram—a *star*.

"*This symbol,*" the healer's words echoed, "*represents the opposing forces of nature. The female and male. United, they form a mystical, unbreakable bond, a seal, which nothing can tear apart.*"

Confidence renewed, I entered the hut. Indra was sweeping the ashes into the hearth. She lifted her face to greet me. I kissed her softly and extended my hand, gift balanced on my open palm. Indra unravelled the fabric and gasped.

"It's so…beautiful," she said through tears.

As I slid it onto her finger, I whispered, "May this ring bind our souls, and our love, for all eternity."

11

Faith

*C*oral salmon glided beneath the water's surface, tails flicking with lazy indifference. The reflection of a single white tuft of cloud rippled, though motionless in the blue expanse overhead.

Father and I sat on the beach of my oasis, lures bobbing on a lightly flowing stream. He chewed a sprig of grass, shifting it languidly from one side of his mouth to the other. Neither of us spoke, there was little need. We seemed to sense the bliss of the other, the contented stillness in each other's soul.

Despite the relaxed mood, I glanced in the direction of the hut—again.

"She's fine." Father smiled.

"I know. I can't help it."

"She is a good woman," he said. "I am grateful the gods led us to her."

I nodded, wondering what word meant more than grateful.

"I suppose we should think about expanding the hut," Father said. "You two—three—will be needing more space."

"We could build a new hut...with enough room for all of us."

"No, a man and his wife need privacy. You do not need an old man lazing about. Besides, once the baby is born and Indra has healed, you two will want a lot of...*alone time*." He waggled his brows.

Fear curdled in my stomach. Of course I longed to lay with Indra, but I was terrified of hurting her; or worse, reminding her of the torment she experienced in Ur.

"Maybe we can turn the old barn into a new hut for me."

"Indra may not let you leave," I teased.

"We shall see. I'm sure she is tired of feeding two men. Besides, it is time for me to move on with my life and let you lead yours."

Something tightened in my chest. We'd been our own little family for so long, I couldn't imagine life without him.

"The fish are especially stubborn today," Father said with a sigh, rising. "I should start loading up for market tomorrow. Very busy lately."

I tented my hand over my eyes, examining him. His face appeared more drawn than usual, fatigued. "Have you been unwell again?"

"No, I have been feeling fine—especially since Indra has been cooking and not you." He laughed.

I rolled my eyes.

Soft sand rolled beneath my sandals as we walked home, the air scorching my lungs with every breath. Even the gnats seemed disinclined to pester us amid the sweltering heat. Obsessively, I scrutinized the distant hut. Part of me was weary of waiting for the baby—the other half, petrified.

"Were you ever…worried my mother would love you less after I was born?"

"Of course!" he said without hesitation.

My eyes widened.

"It is normal to be concerned about such things." A wise smile blossomed on his lips. "For it is true."

"It is?"

"Indra will undoubtedly love the baby more than she loves you."

A tiny pain pierced my heart.

Father continued, "And you will love the baby a little more than you love Indra."

"I—I will?"

"It is a different kind of love, however. Unconditional."

My brows bent in confusion.

"If Indra betrayed you with another man," he began, "could you still love her the way you do now?"

"No. I wouldn't trust her."

"If your child betrayed you, stole from you, lied to you—or perhaps snuck to town when he was told not to…" He gave me a look that told me he knew all about my adventure to Uruk years ago. "You would still love him, would you not?"

"Of course," I said through a guilty grimace. "But this baby is not of my blood. What if…I do not love it like as my own?"

Father smiled sadly. "That you cannot know until the time comes. But I know you, *maru*, and I know your heart. I believe this child will show you the greatest love you have ever known. Just remember," he said, setting a hand on my shoulder, "the greater the love, the harder it is to let go."

After walking Father to the barn where, despite protests, I convinced him to lay down for a while, I took quick strides towards the hut. Heart aflutter, I entered the tiny room, relieved at the sight of her asleep on my cot.

Tiptoeing across the room, I lingered above her, tasting every tiny detail with my eyes. I savoured the contour of her hip sliding into her waist; long, silken hair freed from its ubiquitous chignon spilled like a black waterfall over her bare shoulder. Hands folded beneath her bronze cheek, a small smile pulled at her lips.

"I know you're there," she said, startling me.

"Y-You're awake?"

Indra struggled to sit up. I offered my hand in assistance and she accepted it with a smile. She patted the cot for me to sit beside her.

"Catch any fish?" she asked, rubbing her swollen belly, a glint of craving in her eye.

"No, they were elusive today."

Her face pinched in disappointment.

"I'll try again tomorrow," I vowed, winking.

Indra smiled wide but, just as quickly, gasped and clutched her stomach.

"What!" I stiffened, heart thrumming. "Are you okay?"

"Yes." She giggled, pointing to her belly. Beneath the skin, a tiny bump rose and fell.

"There's really someone…in there," I said, memorized.

Indra took hold of my hand, placing it atop her warm skin. Motionless, we waited. Then, a soft tap. Gentle, yet firm.

"I wonder how he breathes in there?"

"Or *she*." Indra gave me a playful smile.

"Or she," I conceded.

My hand on her stomach, we stared at one another. Time slowed, an inexplicable emotion passing between us. She leaned in, lips parting. My heart knocked inside my chest as I kissed her, unblinking, fearful she'd vanish like a mirage.

Indra traced a fingertip around my eye. "Your eyes…they are so… *beautiful*."

A warm ache gathered in my heart, my throat seized with emotion. For so long, I believed my eyes to be a curse, a terrible disfigurement others would recoil from. Indra saw me for who I really was—and still loved me.

Slowly, she laid back, urging me with her caress to follow. Our legs intertwined, pressing closer until there was no space left between us. Body heat mingled, breath hot and impassioned as our kisses grew deeper, desperate. Lust overwhelmed me, my body disobeying a silent plea for self-control. As I touched her breast, she stiffened.

"You will not touch me like that again unless I invite you to, Solomon," her voice seared my memory. *"Do you understand?"*

I withdrew my touch.

"I will not do anything you do not permit me to do," I stated. "If you wish, we shall never move beyond a kiss. *Never*. Only say the word and I will stand by your side, forever loving you without so much as a touch."

Her eyes shimmered with an expression of pure gratitude. "When I'm ready," she said quietly, taking my hand and resting on her breast. "I want you in every way a wife can have a husband. I just—don't know when that will be."

Abandoning her breast, I cradled her petite face in my hands. "Even if it takes an eternity, I will wait for you. Always."

After supper, I wandered around the farm, basking in the coolness of the evening. I found Father behind the barn picking clean an oxen's hoof, a small campfire flickering beside him.

"You look pleasantly stupid. Things are good with Indra, I assume?"

I gave him a sheepish nod, Indra's kiss still hot on my lips.

His eyes twinkled with relief. I sensed he felt his mission to find me a loving companion was complete, that he could die in peace someday, knowing I wouldn't be alone in this world.

"Would you help me load up the wagon tonight?" he asked. "I want to leave early for the market—even the mornings have been very hot the past few days."

"Of course."

We loaded over a dozen goddess statuettes into the wagon, each bundled in straw and tied with string; beside which we placed numerous death jars. As I reached for the last urn, it slipped from my fingers and shattered on the ground. Jagged shards glinted like teeth in the sand.

A cold wind rushed from darkness and ran its icy fingers through my hair. A shiver snaked up my spine—as if an omen had whispered a warning to my soul.

The next morning, Father left for Uruk, his figure a shadow on the horizon as I made my way to the north field to repair a fallen fence post. Shovel over my shoulder, tool belt strapped around my waist, I strolled along the main road with a silly, lovestruck grin. Everything looked brighter, beautiful, more colourful and alive. The sky somehow bluer.

I walked faster, wanting to finish quickly so I could return to the hut to be with Indra. Nothing else seemed as important as spending every moment I could with her.

So this is love.

This is what the bards sang about, what the poets of old proclaimed in lush, magniloquent prose; an indescribable emotion; a swooning of the soul; a sensation so all-encompassing, all-consuming; the blissful devouring of one's self—and all, willingly.

So captivated with impassioned daydreaming, I didn't notice the caravan ambling along the road until it was upon me.

"*Silim!*" came a voice.

Startled, I spun around to see a covered carriage wobble to a stop, the left wheel awkwardly askew to its axle. A wiry man walked ahead of the ailing conveyance, leading a pair of tired donkeys. Despite the instability, a second figure rode inside the carriage, his face cloaked in shadow.

"Good day." Though I offered a friendly wave, my heart thundered in my chest. It was rare for me to speak to anyone without Father beside me.

"Might you be able to fix our wheel?" the man asked.

"I can try…"

"Oh, praise the goddess!" the thin man said. "We were out collecting taxes and drove over a dip in the road, and well…" He gestured at the broken wheel, a nervous twitch in his eye as he glanced from me to the man in the carriage. I felt the passenger's eyes upon me.

The little man continued with a nervous titter, "I am a mere scribe with no knowledge of such things."

Eager to remove myself from the mystery man's scrutiny, I hastened to the back of the carriage and knelt to inspect the damage. The right wheel had only shifted on the axle, but I'd have to tilt the entire vehicle onto its left side in order to reset it.

"I must ask your passenger to climb down so that I can..." Before I could finish, the man in the carriage leaned out from the shadows, his face sliced by white sunlight.

My mouth went dry.

Enusat.

I'd not seen the priest since Father and I since the day in the court-yard where he ordered the woman's teeth smashed by a brick. According to Father, rumours circulated through the market that the King had demoted Enusat from primary *Ensi,* returning him to common duties, like collecting taxes. Haggard and thinner, his eyes seemed even colder, hardened by bitterness.

The scribe jumped into action, offering his hand to the chastened priest. Chagrined, Enusat alighted from the carriage.

Swiftly, I reset the wheel and pounded it into place. After a quick test of competence, I gave the men a nod of assurance.

"It should get you back to Uruk. Be sure to have it looked at again once you get there..." I turned on my heel to leave.

"You are Ezen's boy, no?" Enusat said, freezing me in my tracks. "Where is your father?"

I faced him, his squinty eyes measured me from head to toe.

"At the market," I answered quietly, feeling more like a small, frightened child than a grown man.

"Uh, I thank you for your service." The scribe shook my hand. "You must stop by the temple next time you're in Uruk and we'll pay you with a beer or two!"

The scribe offered assistance to Enusat, to aid him back into the chariot, but Enusat ignored him and took a few steps closer to me.

"Those eyes," Enusat said, leering. "So curious, don't you think?"

"Eyes?" The scribe peered into my face and gasped. "Why, his eyes are the colour of the river! Almost like..."

"*Lapis lazuli,*" Enusat said, his gaze cold, calculating.

"They are...quite amazing." The scribe stared transfixed.

Enusat smirked. "So *amazing* that his mother was killed for them."

Shock paralyzed me.

"W-What do you mean *killed*?" I sputtered. "She...died giving birth to me."

Enusat roared with laughter. "Is that what your father told you! Stupid boy, your mother did not die in childbirth! She was sliced in half for her sins with the demon god, Pazuzu!" He slid a finger from his crotch to his neck. "It's your fault she was punished. You're the child of a demon—and those eyes prove it!"

Father...lied to me?

The earth tilted, unsteady beneath my feet. I felt myself sway with the dawning realization.

This was why...why Father was so afraid to let people see me...why he kept me a prisoner in my own home...my whole life...

My hands curled at my side, fear giving way to anger. Blood throbbed in my ears. Enusat's laughter echoed inside my head, the scribe's pitying stare, the decades of self-doubt, loathing, and lies all spiralling into this one, dark moment...

Before I could stop myself, I raised my fist and punched Enusat with all my might, right in his fat chin. He hit the ground hard, sand coating the spittle on his lips. The scribe shrieked and fell to his knees beside the moaning priest. Time slowed, like when I'd fallen into river so many years ago and nearly drowned. My body, my vision, my hearing—all were impaired by the horror of what I'd done. Enusat sat up, his eyes wild with fury. He shoved the scribe aside as he staggered to his feet.

"*You*...Solomon, spawn of Pazuzu, will come to fear this day like no other!" he spat, spearing the air with his finger. "*I swear my life on it.*"

He spun on his heel and stormed away, the scribe scrambling to catch up. Dread coursed through my being as I watched Enusat's thick form shrink on the horizon.

For, gods help me, I believed him.

Father's face fell the moment he saw me.

I'd sat on the side of the road the entire day, awaiting his return. I couldn't even bring myself to go inside the hut and tell Indra what I had done.

All I could think of was the lie.

Every night. Every *single* night as a child, Father told me the story of my birth. Of how my mother's lifeblood swirled in the river after I was born and how she died staring into my eyes.

'*Your mother was sliced in half for her sins...*' Enusat's words echoed, over and over, conjuring visions of my mother's body being torn into two.

"Solomon?" Father abandoned his wagon on the road and hurried to me. "Is it Indra? The baby?"

He put his hand on my arm, but I shrugged it off. "Enusat was here."

Fear sparked in his eyes. "What did he want?"

"He said..." I choked on the words, "that my mother didn't die giving birth. That she was...killed...because of my eyes."

Father paled.

"Is it true?" I whispered, afraid to hear the answer.

He nodded, shakily lowering himself to sit beside me.

Tears spilled down my cheeks. "Why did you lie to me!"

"I-I never wanted...you to know," he said quietly. "I did not want you to think...it was your fault."

I cradled my head in my hands.

"If only we hadn't thought your eyes so beautiful—they blinded us from the truth," Father began with a sad smile. "It is true you were born in the water, there in the Euphrates. After the birth, I helped your mother home. She sent me to Uruk to fetch a priest to bless you. Overjoyed, I obeyed...not even considering..." Father bowed his head. "The priest took one look at you and called your mother a witch, a whore of the demon lord, Pazuzu. They...wanted to kill you too...and would have if I hadn't convinced them that your eyes were a gift from Enki and to kill you would bring a plague upon the lands like no other. Thankfully, they believed me—but they did not spare your mother."

He stared sightlessly at the darkening horizon, a lifetime of pain reflecting in his eyes.

"I quit my work as a scribe and moved away from Uruk," he concluded. "There were rumours for a while—about the 'boy with blue eyes'—but after many years, the tale drifted into legend."

My entire life flashed before me, fragments of memories, stories, and experiences—all of it built on lies.

"Is that why you kept me from the city—from the people?" Anger rekindled in my chest. "Why not take me farther away? Find people who would accept me? I've lived my whole life as a...a monster!" I jumped to my feet, pacing, brimming with rage. "Do you know what it's like? Do you? To be all alone, to have no friends, to think you're deformed and ugly and...*worthless!*"

A tear carved a trail down Father's dusty cheek. "Can you forgive me, Solomon?"

I glowered at the world, hate and resentment hardening my heart.

"I don't know, Father," I said, turning away. "I don't know."

"You have to leave *now*," Father said when I told him I'd punched Enusat. "They will be coming for you!"

Indra's eyes were wide with fear. "You hit a *priest!*"

"I will explain later. Pack your things," I said firmly.

She obeyed, placing food and a few humble possessions into a sack, moving as fast as her cumbersome body would allow.

"Head east to the Zagros Mountains," Father said. "There is family there, they will take you in once they know who you are. I will follow you when it is safe."

"What will you tell the soldiers?"

"I will talk to them...stall them to give you a head start. I will tell them you have run south to Ur," he said with a nod. "Now go!"

I threw the sack over my shoulder and hurried Indra to the door.

"Take the donkey," Father said. "I will..."

"Solomon, son of Ezen!" a deep voice shouted from outside. "This is the King's guard! Come outside *immediately!*"

"It is too late," Father uttered, his face ashen.

Beside me, Indra whimpered and clutched my arm. I took her by the shoulders. "You need to hide."

"Why?" Her brow furrowed, threatening defiance.

"You must stay here with Father. I will come back...if I can. But if I don't..." She opened her mouth to protest, but I put my finger to her lips. "If I don't...you and Father...and the baby...go to Zagros without me, understand?"

Tears welled in her eyes, but she closed them tight and nodded. I gathered her against me, smelling her hair, touching her skin, cherishing what could be our last moment together.

"If you do not come out...we will come in!" the soldier yelled.

"Hurry Solomon!" Father hissed.

"Hide," I whispered to Indra and pushed her gently.

She buried her face in my chest. "I can't...don't make me leave you!"

"Please Indra, I love you both so much...more than my own life," I begged, caressing her stomach. "For me..."

With a sob, she walked to the far corner and squeezed herself down between two barrels. She regarded me one last time with sad eyes before she draped a blanket over her head.

Seconds later, the soldiers stormed in, grabbing Father and me by the arms. "Farmer Ezen, Solomon, son of Ezen," the head guard said. "Both of you are ordered to come to the temple *immediately*!"

"Both? What—no!" I shouted as they wrestled me to the door. "I'm the one who hit the *Ensi!* Leave him! Just take me!"

The head guard sneered. "The orders were for both of you to be punished."

"Solomon, it is no use," Father said defeatedly.

Wrenching my right arm free, I swung and punched one guard in the jaw. Another struck me in the stomach with his staff, knocking the wind out of me. I fell to my knees, gasping for air. The soldiers hoisted me under my arms and dragged me out of the hut.

I lifted my head to take in a last look of home—and my heart stopped.

Indra stood in the doorway, tears streaming down her face as she clutched her swollen belly—a puddle of water at her feet.

12

Ezeru

*T*he White Temple was a colossal shadow against a darkening horizon. Candlelight climbed the stairs to the apex of the pyramid, each step illumined with an eerie, amber footprint. Even the moonless sky glowered with judgement, the weight of the universe settling on my shoulders.

My stomach tumbled, heart heavy with regret. Not only for my foolish actions, but for Indra. While I desperately wanted to confide in Father about the puddle of water at her feet, I didn't wish to cause him any further angst. I'd done enough for one day.

Side by side, our hands and feet shackled with rope, Father and I were led through the royal garden. Alabaster statues of the gods phalanxed the processional path, their stoic glares tracking our ominous voyage.

"Why are they taking us to the temple and not the palace...to the king?" I muttered to Father.

"I do not know, *maru*," he said, his eyes dark with worry.

The soldiers herded us around a shadowy corner. There, concealed behind the snarled branches of an overgrown amaranth bush, was a dark passageway. A guard held the brush aside as Father and I entered one at a time. Down into the belly of the pyramid, we descended a winding staircase.

Fresh fear lingered around every corner, pitch darkness conspiring with the unknown. Where were they taking us? To Enusat? To some sadistic, blood-hungry executioner?

Around and around, down and down, into a fathomless forever... then, just when I'd lost hope of ever reaching the bottom, a doorway appeared, suffused with golden illumination.

"Through there," a soldier ordered.

I ducked to enter, Father and the soldiers close behind.

Hazy, myrrh-infused incense cloyed the circular room. At the back, I recognized Enusat. He smiled smugly. I scowled in return. I had nothing to lose at this point—or so I thought.

Ten alcoves, inset into the stone, housed nine ivory busts of the various Mesopotamian gods and goddesses. For some reason, one had been left empty. Positioned to focus on the centre of the room, each bust's face was carved with a furrowed, disapproving brow. Their glowering gazes converged on a single point: an opulent tent fashioned from sheer, white linens. Behind the gauzy curtain, lay a round, pillow-laden bed.

Every so often, something moved beyond the diaphanous curtains, a lean, feminine silhouette, lithe and lovely, naked as she paced her silken cage, running her fingertips along the fabric walls. Through a narrow slit in the curtains, she paused, regarding us with an interested eye.

"I have company, I see," a sultry, velvet voice came from within.

Enusat stepped forward, beads of sweat on his brow. "I have… brought you a gift."

She tilted her head. "A gift?"

Enusat gestured impatiently to a soldier and he shoved me towards the tent. Closer now, the veiled figure was clearer. Two male slaves draped a cloak around her shoulders, cinching it closed between her breasts.

Then the curtains parted—and *she* stepped into the light.

Behind me, Father gasped.

"*Inanna.*"

Ivory.

Hers was a complexion of white marble, silhouetted by an unearthly aura. A divine creature, warm and alive, fashioned from porcelain. Pearlescent, as if newly pried from her nacreous shell, she stepped from her sanctum.

Her gown was completely sheer, exposing the blush of her nipples. I searched the contours of her body, every curve and soft corner. She was perfect. From the slim meander of her hips to her thighs, pert breasts, and milky skin. Though young in body, her very presence spoke of ages no mortal had ever seen.

"*This* is my gift?" Inanna shot Enusat a disgusted look and turned to leave. "If so, I already have plenty of *boys* at my disposal."

"Wait!" Enusat grabbed my chin and jerked my head up. "Show her!"

The goddess glanced back, my eyes meeting hers—and it was I who gasped.

Purple.

Like the sky after a twilight storm, her irises were amethyst. Predatorily, she studied me. High cheekbones, a regal, aquiline nose, arched brows—feline. She was both elegant and wild, beautiful—and *dangerous.*

"You see!" Enusat sputtered. "You see, my lady! They are…"

"*Lapis lazuli,*" she whispered, taking a slow step closer.

Inanna cradled my face within her warm, soft hands, gazed deep into my eyes—and purred, her throat rumbling like a lioness to her prey, anticipating the chase.

"Let me see all of you." She circled me, fingernails dragging across my chest. "Do you know how I love the blue of that stone?"

"Y-Yes." Everyone in Sumer knew of her lust for lapis lazuli.

Petal-pink lips mere inches from my own, parted as if for a kiss, her violet eyes swam with passion.

"*Come*," Inanna commanded, leading me into the tent.

On shaking legs, I followed.

Inside, a cloud of myrrh infused the air, muting the candlelight with golden halos. Two slaves materialized from the shadows, relieved Inanna of her gown, and then exited—leaving us alone. Despite the insubstantiality of her attire, the radiance of her nudity stole my breath. Eyes on me, the goddess lowered herself onto the bed and crawled across, languorously, like a cat. I traced the bare, milky curve of her behind, to the place where her legs met. So in contrast to the clay statuettes Father and I had made of her, I felt we'd done an injustice.

"Come," she said, caressing the empty space beside her.

I obeyed, childishly unaware of her intentions, so awestruck by her beauty, her power—the unbelievable nature of her existence. The Goddess of Love. All my life, the gods were merely prayed to and worshipped. I didn't believe they could be made of flesh and blood.

Inanna slid her hands over my body, her hips rocking with anticipation. She paused at the hem of my tunic and tugged on it.

"Off."

When I paused, a flash of annoyance ignited in her lavender eyes. Blushing, I complied. I was now naked, naked before the deity, naked before Father and Enusat, before the guards, and, mostly, myself. Never had I felt so vulnerable. Kept hidden most of my life, I'd been forced to stay concealed in the presence of others. My eyes had always been the cause of my grief and loneliness, my isolation and shame—and now, here in the bed of a goddess, I was stripped of my earthly shackles.

Inanna straddled me, clawed my chest. The world outside the tent faded away. She touched every inch of me, loving me in places I didn't know existed. My will weakened, my body thrummed with desire, I was hard with lust and longing.

"Look at me with those eyes. I want to see them when you enter me."

I opened my eyes—and my blood ran cold.

"Indra…"

Pure disgust crossed her beautiful face.

"I'm sorry—" I gently pushed her off. "I-I love another. I cannot betray her."

I reached for my tunic but Inanna snatched it away.

"You will not leave until *I* am finished with you," she said, her voice low and dangerous.

I froze, realization dawning. This was a goddess, a powerful deity—and I was denying her.

"Have mercy on me, but I love this woman. She has been through so much, I cannot hurt her!"

Cold dignity eclipsed Inanna's face, tempering from rage to steely reserve.

"*She* has been through so much?" Inanna gave a dark, mirthless titter. "Do you know, mortal, what *I* have been through? Is there any way for your tiny, *human* mind to grasp what *I* have endured over the ages?"

Chin raised, she strode out of the tent, unconcerned by her nakedness. Until then, I hadn't noticed the tattoo etched into her lower back.

I quickly dressed and followed her. "I'm sorry, Goddess, I…"

"You cannot know what it is to suffer eternity alone, can you?" Inanna glared at the chalky bust of her father, Enlil. "No, of course you can't. I made you, you know—all of you—with these very hands…"

I sent Father a questioning frown but he looked just as confused.

"From the blood of a god, molded from the sands on which you stand—I am your maker, but you…you do not know me as your one, true god."

"I thought Enki made us…" I said quietly.

She spun about, eyes luminous with fury.

"*I* made you! I created you! All of you! And you do not serve me? You deny me your body even though *I* made it? How dare you reject me! *Me!* Your Queen! Your maker!" She stormed up to me, poking my chest hard. "I *own* you!" She sighed with the resolve of a parent summoning patience. "You *will* obey me, or else…"

I stole an apprehensive glance at Father in the hopes he'd know what to do, that he'd formed some clever plan of escape. Instead, I was met with an expression of pure heartbreak. Father's brown eyes welled with sadness and defeat. I knew he wanted me to be true to Indra—to myself—no matter the price, but he also didn't want me to suffer the wrath of an angry goddess.

"I will *not* tell you again!" Inanna's eyes glittered dangerously. "Get in my bed!"

Tears stung my eyes as I thought of Indra and the baby. Both were probably dead by now. Like my mother, Indra surely bled to death during childbirth—and the baby, oh the sweet baby! What if it hadn't died but was alone, starving to death in the arms of its cold, lifeless mother?

I had to get home—at any cost.

Inanna smirked as I took a step towards her bed and drew back the curtain.

"*Maru*," Father called to me. "Have you not lost enough of yourself, my son?"

I faced him, tears wet on my cheeks.

"Have you not given up enough of your life because of me? Because of my fear? I kept you from the world, hid you away, and because of that—because of my cowardice—you were not allowed to live the life you deserved. Do not do it, my son. If you cannot live with yourself afterward, do not do it…not for me, not for Indra…not even for a goddess. There are worse things than death…"

Inanna's laughter filled the cavern as she sauntered towards Father. "You're right, old man, there are things beyond this realm far worse than death."

She snapped her fingers and two slaves appeared. They slipped a sheer, black gown around her shoulders, tying it to a close at her breasts.

"This world," Inanna said, sweeping a dramatic arm through the air, "disgusts me, you know. These humans. So weak. So compliant. *Anything* I say is done. You'd think that's what I'd want, right? But no, I desire a challenge, strength, backbone…at least then there is resistance.

Most people just cower before me, simpering with fear. I feel it you know, I feel their *pathetic* lack, their sad existence. And the rest, well, they would give their souls to be in my favour—why, they'd even offer me one of their own for the mere promise of power." She shot an accusatory glance at Enusat, who had the wherewithal to look ashamed.

She turned to me. "At least you fight me, at least you make the game more pleasing. There aren't many who would dare defy me. You will be punished, but I shall enjoy it nonetheless."

"Please…" I started.

"Don't!" Inanna's features momentarily turned ferocious, eyes blazing, skin rippling snakelike beneath the flesh. "Don't beg. Don't ruin it," she said sweetly, then: "Hold him."

The guards rushed forward, seizing me by the arms.

"What are you doing!" I shouted, struggling.

Inanna flicked her hand and uttered a single word in a language I didn't recognize. Immediately, a strange sound began to ricochet inside the temple basement. Wet and fibrous, I'd heard it before, but couldn't place the source.

Jerky, my mind offered. *The sound of jerky tearing in two…*

Soon, the tearing sound was accompanied by a low, animalistic moan.

Before me, Inanna smirked, relishing in my confusion. She then took a step to her right, exposing the horror.

"Father!" I screamed.

As though suspended by an invisible hook, Father's body hung midair, contorted and stretched, limbs splayed by unseen hands. First he groaned—then he shrieked as a gash manifested between his neck and shoulder, and down between his groin. Blood dripped onto the stone beneath him, pooling into thick, scarlet puddles.

Because of my eyes, like my mother before him, Father was being torn into two.

"No!" I shouted, my voice hoarse with emotion. "No! Please no!"

I wrenched myself from the guards and fell to my knees, pressing my forehead against Father's feet. I tugged futility at his ankles, so slick with blood I couldn't hold tight.

Behind me, Inanna laughed.

"Please, stop! Don't do this!"

"Too late, sweet boy." A cat-like smile crawled across her lips. "You made the wrong choice."

"Solomon," Father uttered through gritted teeth, the white of the bone on his shoulder peering through the mess of flesh. "It was…almost my time…anyway."

"No, no, no!" I cried, hot tears spilling over my lips. "Don't leave me!"

Father's breaths came in short, sharp gasps. "Do…you remember… the healer?"

I nodded, whimpering.

"I—I asked her…if your…eyes…would be the…death…of you…" Father stopped short, screaming as his arm and torso separated from one another. What remained of him slumped to the floor.

I rest my head on his blood-soaked chest, remembering the old crone's answer:

'He will see farther with those eyes than you ever will.'

"Please," I wailed. "Please don't go…"

"Love you…*maru.*"

Father's chest rose with a ragged breath, then fell—and he never drew another.

My entire world was dead.

Uncontrollable sobs wracked my body. I felt as though a small child roused by a nightmare, searching the dark, empty room with frightened eyes for the comfort of a parent who could not, and would never again, come home.

"Enough of this." Inanna made a noise of disgust. "Bring him to me."

The guards dragged me off Father, my body limp. Blood, dark as red wine, trailed behind me in a long smear. They deposited me at Inanna's feet. I laid there, unmoving, save for the occasional shuddering sob.

"Now," Inanna said in a smug, business-like tone. "Do you wish to change your mind?"

I could say nothing, do nothing, except curl tighter into myself and cry.

"Speak!" She kicked my head with her toe. "Pathetic," she huffed, turning to enter her boudoir. "Never mind. I will wait. You may come to my bed when you're finished pouting."

A tiny spark, a flicker of will, ignited inside of me, from somewhere deep within my soul.

"*Never,*" I whispered.

Inanna spun around, eyes wide with disbelief. "*What* did you say?"

I staggered to my feet, wiping the blood-stained tears from my face. Hands clenched at my sides, I approached the goddess, my gaze wolf-like, dangerous, locked on hers.

"Never," I said again, a little louder.

She parted her lips to speak but the tiny spark inside of me burst into flames, my sorrow exploding into pure, white rage.

"Never!" I screamed into her face, flecks of spittle landing on her cheek. "I will *never* lay with you. The sight of you makes me sick. I would rather be alone for all eternity than touch you!"

Inanna took a step back, rage dancing through her expression.

I didn't care if she killed me, in fact, I welcomed it. She'd taken everything from me. I was already dead. Now I was just baiting her to finish me off—and I knew it.

Nostrils flared, Inanna measured me with indecision.

I leaned into her, so close that my breath disturbed the fine strands along her hairline.

"Go ahead," I dared. "*Kill me.*"

Glowering, she raised her hand as she did when she'd summoned the power to kill Father—then she paused, and lowered her hand. A slow, sinuous smile poisoned her lips.

"I have a better idea."

Across the room, Enusat shrank into the shadows, pressing himself against the wall. Footfalls echoed as several guards fled the room and ran up the stairwell.

'*There are things worse than death...*' Father's warning echoed inside my head.

The goddess raised her arms, eyes a violet inferno.

"*Mythos infinita il sanfira destiiro casserilae.*" Over and over, she shouted, her voice booming.

A violent wind tore through the chamber, her linen tent billowed, shadows shivered on the dark temple walls as the candlelight trembled but once before snuffing, drowning us in darkness. Rocks and dust rained from the stone ceiling, the floor quaked beneath my feet.

Then, stillness.

Silence.

Before me, a single, thread of silver light appeared, growing brighter, bathing the room in a moonlight lustre. The illumination seemed to be emanating from within Inanna, from inside her heart. A snakelike creature emerged, writhing as it bored out of her chest. Then it was free, undulating in the open air before her. She giggled as it swam and wrapped itself playfully around her arm.

With a venomous smile, Inanna regarded me.

"*Him,*" she commanded the serpent, pointing a long finger in my direction.

The beast reared and shot across the room. Before I could run or even cry out, the luminous snake plunged into my chest, vanishing. I fell to my knees and clutched my heart, feeling as it nested inside me, coiling around my soul. I yanked off my tunic, panicked. Instead of a hole where the creature had entered my skin, there was now a black eight-pointed star within a circle—Inanna's symbol.

Inanna took slow, languid steps towards me, a satisfied smirk on her lips.

"You will live again and again...and *again*, Solomon of Sumer," she said. "Until the sun dies or until you surrender yourself to me—*and only me.* You shall not love another woman so long as you live. But oh, how you will desire them, lust for them, yet never, *ever* shall you lay with them—lest you pay the price."

Inanna ran a cold, lingering fingertip past my eye, and then turned and walked away. She paused just before entering her chamber, glancing over her shoulder with a mischievous eye.

"Oh, but I can't be *that* cruel, now can I?" She tapped her chin thoughtfully. "I think...perhaps I'll allow you to take pleasure with children and beasts. After all, forever is an *awfully* long time."

Inanna laughed—and disappeared behind the curtain.

13

Consummation

*T*he guards deposited me in a heap on the road in front of our hut. *My* hut.

Without Father, it wasn't *ours* anymore. Without him, it wasn't even a home.

A fencepost, one I'd fixed just the day before, cast a long shadow across my face amidst the gathering dawn.

The day before.

He'd been alive then. Indra had kissed me as I set off with my tools. Had I not crossed paths with Enusat, none of this would ever have come about. Father would still be alive. Indra and I might be holding a child in our arms.

Indra. I willed myself to look at the hut. *The baby.*

I couldn't bring myself to go inside. Not only for the sight that might await me, but without Father, how could I face her? Perhaps she would leave me if she knew what happened? Maybe she would be disgusted with me? I couldn't live with that look in her eyes. Even if she wasn't dead, I would've lost her anyway.

Fresh tears filled my eyes, a new hole opening within my heart.

The tearing sound—that horrible echo of ripping flesh. I relived the moments, seeing again and again the image of Father's body, mangled and bloody…in *pieces* on the floor. A sound escaped my lips, one I'd never heard before—the sound of my soul dying. I didn't want to live. Not without them.

The river, my thoughts whispered, taking pity on me. '*She will carry you away…*'

I glanced in the direction of my oasis. I could do that, yes. Then it would be all over. The pain would go away. A small smile pulled at my lips.

Seduced by the lure of death, I staggered to my feet.

It'll be over soon.

My eyes watered in the sun's brightness as it climbed over the horizon. I stumbled past the hut, the waters calling to me as though I were dying of thirst. A hysterical laugh spilled from my lips when I imagined the moment I took my last breath and saw my loved ones again. I would be home again. I was going home!

My strength returned, my legs carrying me faster. I broke into a jog, and then a run; sand-streaked tears on my cheeks. I plunged through the foliage and onto the well-worn path. I was almost there, almost free! I burst through the opening, into the arms of my oasis, falling to my knees in the sand. I dragged myself towards the river, desperate for peace.

I neared the edge.

It won't hurt for long.

Hands over my heart, I closed my eyes and swayed, ready to surrender—then, from behind me, I heard the sweetest sound to ever grace my senses: the soft cry of a newborn baby.

I spun around.

"Indra!" I cried out.

"Solomon?" Bleary-eyed, Indra sat up. Then, her eyes widened. "Solomon!"

I crawled to her, weeping as I touched her face, smelled her hair.

She eyed the dried blood coating my woundless body. "W-Where is Father?"

I opened my mouth, but the words wouldn't come.

"Oh Solomon," she sobbed. "What happened!"

"He…I…" Incoherent, my voice was strangled by emotion.

The world was sharp around me. The buzz of a fly roared in my ears, the blue of a butterfly's wings too vivid, my skin so sensitive the softest of touch stung like a slap. Never had I felt so painfully alive—and yet dead at the same time. I laid my head against Indra's chest, childlike, lost.

Then a sound came from beside me. Quiet, angelic. I opened my eyes, suckling at Indra's breast was the most beautiful creature I'd ever seen. Soft black hair, impossibly small fingers kneading its mother's skin. So fragile and perfect.

Bewildered, I cupped the warm, tiny head in my palm.

"I didn't think we would be safe in the hut," Indra said. "I came here after the soldiers took you."

"You gave birth—alone?" I winced.

"It's a fairly a natural process, you know," she said with a pragmatic brow. "I named her Miri—after my mother."

"*Miri*," I whispered, stroking her silk-soft cheek.

I placed my finger into her palm and her tiny hand curled around it.

My daughter.

I was a father.

Father.

A part of my broken heart stitched back together, the threadbare strands of my soul knit into some semblance of my former self.

I'd found a family once again—if for a little while.

After several days of reconnaissance, scouting for any sign of the soldiers, I felt confident they weren't coming back to the hut. With Miri in my arms, we emerged from the oasis and started home. Indra walked slowly, as if giving birth had been harder on her than she'd led on.

"Are you sure you're okay?" I asked.

"I'm just tired and sore."

I panned the landscape, every distant tree or shrub disguised as an enemy in wait.

"I think we should leave here," I said for the hundredth time. "Go to the Zagros Mountains. I don't trust they won't return."

"I understand, Solomon," Indra said, her tone weary, "but I cannot leave until I am healed. We'll be safe here for a time. Enusat wouldn't have sent you home if he meant to punish you further."

It's not him I fear.

Alongside the unrelenting paranoia, guilt poisoned my veins. I couldn't bring myself to tell Indra how Father died, of Inanna's attempted seduction—and, of course, the curse. I held Miri closer to my chest, frightened that I had even more to lose than before.

As I entered the hut, however, sorrow overwhelmed all other emotions.

Father was still there, everywhere I looked. From the drying statuettes he'd moulded just days before to his favourite barley beer fermenting in the corner. His scent, his very essence, lingered like a ghost. How could he have been real, so very alive, just days before—now gone forever?

Indra stroked my arm and I realized I'd not moved from the doorway.

"Come now," she said practically. "We have work to do."

A seam of muted light traced the edges of the door. Beside me, my girls slept in a sound bundle. Sweat-dampened tendrils pressed at Indra's temples while Miri's dark, downy hair sprouted in every direction. She'd grown so much in the past weeks, her big brown eyes so full of wonder, her smile brilliant whenever she looked at me or Indra. Profound love swelled inside. I watched them a moment more, thinking how happy this would've made Father, and my heart broke anew. After gently kissing each on the forehead, I slipped away from the cot and started out to do my chores.

The crisp morning air was laced with damp hay and cool sand. Dew-laden cobwebs, like strings of silver pearls, clung to the corners of the barn door. Low mists lingered over the fields, painting a ghostly haze over the horizon. The rainy season was creeping in.

Realization landed on my shoulders. I didn't know if I could run the farm alone. Not only physically, but technically. There was a time for inundating, for winnowing and harrowing; a time to seed and a time to grow, all had to be performed in harmony with the seasons or the crops could fail. It was my job to provide for my family, but with Father gone, I didn't think I could do it.

Hungry goats bleated, butting me with nubby horns as I poured feed into their trough. Next, I milked an agitated nanny goat, her milk sac swollen, I could all but hear her sigh as white cream spewed from her teats and into the bucket.

"Better?" I asked, massaging her slackened udder. She nudged me lightly as if to show her gratitude.

Bucket in hand, I strode towards the house. Indra liked to churn fresh butter from the morning's milk so we could have it for supper. My heart lightened the closer I got to home. How right Father had been, how wonderful it was to have a wife. She was my best friend and lover.

Lover.

Heat crept into my face. Was Indra my lover if we'd not yet consummated the relationship? It had been several weeks since she'd given birth, surely she was healed enough to make love?

Unbidden, Inanna's venomous promise resounded, *"You shall not love another woman so long as you live...never, ever shall you lay with them—lest you pay the price."*

Despite the heat, an icy shiver snaked up my spine. Fear turned to anger and hatred. What did I care what Inanna did to me now? Let her inflict physical pain on me. Nothing could equal the anguish I felt for losing Father. I squeezed my eyes shut, suppressing the dark memory.

"Solomon?" Indra called from the hut, Miri cradled in the crook of her arm. "What are you doing?"

"Nothing, I..." I realized then that I'd dropped the bucket, thick cream pooled around my feet. "I-I tripped."

"Oh dear," Indra said, chuckling. "I do hope there is more this afternoon."

I shrugged, retrieving the bucket. As I walked back to the barn and into a shadowed corner, I had to steady myself against a wall. Panic stole my breath, my heart quivering in my chest. Hearing Inanna's voice again, her poisoned words, brought me right back to that night. Foolishly, I'd almost convinced myself the whole experience in the temple had been a nightmare. A terrible invention to explain Father's absence, something I'd concocted to cope with the loss.

It couldn't have been real.

She couldn't be real.

If she wasn't real, then the curse wasn't real.

Father's death, however, was very real. Of that, I couldn't convince myself, or my shattered heart, otherwise.

Beside the hearth, shadows danced on the walls while amber flames sired quiet, crackling sparks. With Miri nestled in my arms, the reaching warmth enveloped us. Brown eyes full of wonder, Miri studied my face. I gazed in return. More than ever, I wished she could talk, tell me her thoughts. Was she happy? Did she feel loved and protected? Soon, her blinks became slower, lids heavy, until her little eyes closed and she slipped into sleep.

Indra returned from washing her hair, it hung as an ebony curtain to her waist. She kissed us each on the forehead.

"I was hoping I'd catch her before she went to sleep," Indra said with a hint of dismay.

"Why?"

She touched her breasts, wincing. "They're full of milk. It's very uncomfortable."

"I-I could try to...relieve them for you."

Indra's eyes widened.

"I could...massage them," my cheeks raged with heat, "like I do for the nanny goats."

I bowed my head, mortified. I really hadn't intended for it to sound so...sexual.

Indra stood motionless for too long, then: "O-Okay."

"Really?" I stared at her.

Indra scooped Miri from my arms and placed her gently onto the farther cot. Then, she turned to me, uncertainty shadowing her face. We stood before one another, suddenly strangers again, thrumming with fear and anticipation.

"I-I'll need some oil," I said, retrieving the myrrh-infused emollient from the shelf.

After lining the cot with extra blankets, Indra shimmied out of her sleeves, smooth shoulders bronzed by firelight. She clutched the thin nightdress to her chest as she laid on her back. With trembling hands, she pushed what remained of her garment down. Knelt beside her, I ignored the profound beauty of her naked chest and proceeded to warm the oil between my palms.

Gently, I kneaded and stroked, pushing from the sides to the centre, bringing the milk to a head. Pale cream coursed over her dark flesh. I worked with a soft, but firm, hand. When the milk ran clear, I stopped. Afterwards, I wiped her torso with a warm, damp cloth.

"That feels...so much better." Indra sighed as she removed the damp bedding.

I blushed. "Yours are much nicer than the goats—and you smell better too."

She burst out laughing, but hushed herself with a glance at Miri.

An awkward silence followed.

Indra reached out her hand. "Come here."

I obeyed, closing the space between us. Indra smiled into my eyes, running her hands up my back. Slow, lingering, I touched her body. All the warm, hidden places. As the moments passed, our passion, our greed for one another, intensified.

Firelight faded, shrouding us in shadow. She led me to the cot. Grateful for the darkness as she'd not yet seen the tattoo on my chest, I pulled off my clothes, laid down, and drew her naked body to mine.

Indra ran her fingers through my hair as I traced her stomach with my tongue, gradually tasting every inch of her. She writhed, sounds of pleasure escaping her. Indra pushed me onto my back and straddled me, her hips meeting mine. For a single, horrifying moment, the scene flashed to the inside of Inanna's tent, on her bed, the goddess atop me, rubbing against me.

Inanna leaned over, her violet eyes ablaze. *"You shall not love another woman so long as you live..."*

I sucked in a breath.

"Are you okay?" Indra whispered.

I didn't answer, instead I took hold of her hips, easing myself into her, further defying the goddess.

Indra moved her hips against me, slowly at first, then faster.

Never had I felt anything so powerful. So electric. She was so warm inside. We moved in unison, our bodies one. I felt so alive, yet was dying of pleasure. I cried out first, followed by her moments later. She trembled against my chest, kissing me between breaths.

We slept in each other's embrace, a tangle of arms and legs. Like her ring, two became one.

I awoke to Miri crying, her tiny voice hoarse and desperate. Still foggy from sleep, I blinked the blur from my eyes. Outside, the sky was paling. I glanced at Indra, surprised she'd not heard the baby, she was always up the moment Miri made a sound. Only half-covered by the blanket, cast in early morning shadow, I admired Indra's long, graceful back. I smiled at her silhouette, rising, careful not to wake her.

"There, there, little *beleti*," I whispered to Miri. "I know, you must be hungry. Let's let your mother rest though, hmm?"

I kissed her cheek and she turned her head instinctively, rooting for milk. Miri let out an angry cry when she didn't find what she wanted. In the kitchen, I found a small pitcher with a bit of goat's milk from the night before. Still fresh, kept cool by the evening. I poured some into a bowl, dipped a clean rag into the milk, saturating it, and placed it on Miri's lips. She frowned, but after a quick taste she conceded, awkwardly sucking on the cloth. After some time, she sighed, contented. While burping her, she spit up on my shirt.

"Thanks," I said with mock chagrin.

I laid Miri on the empty cot and pulled off my damp tunic. Shivering, I restarted the fire. The flames crackled to life, casting the tiny room in a soft, amber glow. Miri was making smacking noises, sucking on her fist, occasionally pausing to marvel at her fingers as they bent and flexed.

Despite the fire, an ominous chill pervaded the air. Concerned Indra might be cold, I gently pulled the blanket over her shoulder. Shadows played on her peaceful features as she slept. Intense love swelled inside me. This new life I'd found, thanks to Father, meant everything to me. These two beautiful girls now made my world.

Softly, I kissed Indra's cheek. Her eyes fluttered open and she smiled.

"Good morning, my love," I said, stroking her cheek.

She moved to kiss me back, but froze mid-way, her face paling. "What...is *that*?" She pointed to my chest where Inanna's star blazed like a black brand over my heart.

"Ina...Enusat...had it put there," I lied, afraid to speak the truth. "That night, when Father and I were taken to the temple."

"That is the symbol of the Cult...of the Courtesan..." Upon her words, she clutched her chest, fighting for breath. "Solomon—something is...*wrong*."

"Indra!" I shouted, terrified.

Violent tremors overtook her, excruciating pain twisting her lovely face.

Then she started to scream.

At the sound of her mother's torture, Miri began to wail.

Indra reached for me, horrified and confused. A fissure split open across her cheek, thick, spumous blood oozed lava-like from the wound. Another crack tore through her chest, and then on her stomach. Soon, they were everywhere. Indra fell back onto the bed, writhing in agony, seizures wracking her body, blackened blood splashing across the walls, the floor, the ceiling.

The hut resonated with piercing cries: Indra's, Miri's—my own.

Then, Indra was silent.

On trembling legs, I willed myself forward.

What remained of my wife, my love, my Indra, lay on the cot in a macabre, inhuman contortion. Grey, charred and cracked like the sands of a parched desert, Indra's skin was that of a shattered statue. Sightless eyes stared into nothingness, her final expression moulded from sheer agony.

"I-Indra?" My outstretched fingers shook as I reached for my love's face. Upon my touch, she crumbled to dust before me, just a pile of ashes on the bed.

"*You shall not love another woman so long as you live,*" Inanna's wicked words resounded. "*Lest you pay the price.*"

A low, animalistic wail poured from me, my soul shattering into pieces. Insane with grief, I pawed at the remains, pushing the ashes into piles in a futile attempt to put her back together. Amid one sweep, my hand hit something cold and hard.

Her ring.

Though tarnished and dusty, the six-sided star glinted in the soft glow of the rising sun. I stared at the ring for what felt like hours, and then placed it on my smallest finger. I rest my head atop Indra's ashes, the world dead to me, everything forgotten—even poor Miri—and cried myself into unconsciousness.

When next I awoke, the sun was perched in the centre of the sky, casting the hut in a glossy, flaxen hue. Dust motes churned languidly in a spear of light. Despite the escalating heat outside, the room remained chilled.

Spent of emotion, eyes swollen and raw, I tried to convince myself it had been a nightmare—that Indra was still there, asleep on the bed; her soft skin bronzed by the afternoon ambiance, hair a tidal of ebony waves down her back, the sheen of somnolence at her temples.

With a glance, I knew the horrible truth.

Ashes.

Fresh tears welled in my eyes, I buried my head in my hands and wept. How could I have been so foolish? Inanna's curse was tailored to inflict the worst kind of punishment upon me: the death of those I cared for most in this world. She desired for me to live the rest of eternity in misery. Loveless and alone. If I didn't submit to her sexually, she would end the life of any woman I dared to love.

I understood the curse now. What's more, I finally believed it was real.

Worn, weary, broken, all I could do was lay there, wishing my own end was at hand. I could not fathom an endless life without love.

'You will live again and again…and again, Solomon of Sumer,' Inanna's evil words echoed. *"Until the sun dies…'*

Immortal. Eternally alone.

Even if I found love in a chaste relationship, I would have to endure her aging, her decline, and her death, again and again in every woman I found. Every lover, every child, every mentor and friend I dared to embrace would die before my ever-youthful eyes.

I might have spent eternity wallowing in that very spot had not I felt an unfamiliar sensation crawl across my skin…

An ebbing darkness.

A *presence.*

Heart pounding, I lifted my head. The tiny room was painted with shadows, pulsing from the corners. Preternatural energy crackled. Inside my chest, the snakelike creature writhed excitedly.

Panicked, I looked at Father's bed—*where I'd left Miri.*

There, looming over my sleeping daughter, was the cloaked, diaphanous silhouette of a woman. On trembling limbs, I brought myself to a stand and took a stealthy step towards them.

The nearer I got, the more bewildered I became.

She's…transparent.

Hope gathered in my chest.

Could it be? Could she have returned to us from the underworld? To say good-bye—one last time?

"I-Indra?"

The figure turned her head, exposing her milk-white skin and luminous, lavender eyes. My heart stopped.

Inanna.

Rage ignited like wildfire.

"Why are you here!" I shouted. "Have you not stolen enough from me?"

Miri, awakened by my fury, began to cry.

Inanna regarded me with an interested brow, but bent and lifted the baby into her arms. Uttering a furious battlecry, I lunged at the goddess. With a dismissive wave of her hand, she sent me hurtling into a wall.

"No!" I staggered to my feet, intent on charging her again.

Before I could, a black mist rose from the floor, enshrouding Inanna and Miri within thick shadowy arms. Then, as if drawn through the floor, they vanished.

Miri's last cry reached my ears before silencing.

"No!" I dropped to my knees, slapping my palms against the wooden planks—but they were gone. "Please, no!"

Where would she have taken her?

The temple.

Wild with fear, I ran to Uruk. Rivulets of sweat ran over my brow, down my bare chest. I had to find Miri. I had to get her back.

She was all I had left.

What was normally a two hour walk, I'd managed in less than an hour. I raced through the streets, dodging startled venders and customers.

Please be there…

Breathless, I collapsed on the temple steps where Enusat was conducting a ceremony. At the sight of me, his eyes flared with hatred and surprise.

"My…baby," I gasped. "Inanna took my…baby!"

"Baby?" The priest scowled, and then his expression shifted with remembrance. "Ah yes, the baby—it was sacrificed."

"S-Sacrificed?"

Enusat nodded with a sneer.

The world collapsed, burying me beneath a thousand tons of sand.

Everyone I had ever loved—was gone.

14
Nostalgia

*P*etra's face was wet with tears.

"That's just...*horrible!*" She blew her nose. "What did you do after that?"

"I left Sumer. I couldn't stay there any longer." His beautiful eyes bespoke the centuries—millenniums—of pain and torment. "Everything I'd ever known and loved had been stolen from me. Being there just reminded me of what I'd lost because of Inanna—only, I didn't know just how far her reach truly was."

Petra frowned. "What do you mean?"

A knock sounded at the door.

Petra moved to rise, but her shoulder burned with the sudden movement. She let out a moan and fell back.

"You shouldn't move," he said. "Allow me."

"I'm fine." She struggled to a stand. "I need to stretch anyway."

Solomon shot her a look of disapproval.

The mystery guest knocked louder.

"Miss Monroe?" Professor Emmett's voice emanated from the hallway. "Are you home? I wanted to see if you're well."

Solomon was suddenly at her side. He took her by the arm and drew her close. The nearness of him, the warmth of his body, surprised her more than his actions.

"What are you doing?" she demanded.

"Shh!" he whispered sharply. "Don't answer the door."

"Why not?"

"He's part of this, *beleti.* You must believe me." Solomon implored her with his eyes. "He cannot be trusted."

"Don't be silly!" Petra wrenched herself free. "Emmett is a sweet, old man."

"Petra!" Solomon hissed, but she ignored him, unbolting the lock. In her peripheral, she saw Solomon dart behind a wall. She rolled her eyes and opened the door.

"Oh, Petra!" The old professor exhaled, tweed cap clutched to his chest. "How are you? I was so worried when you left my office in such a hurry the other day."

"Oh no, I'm fine, really, I…" she began.

"Oh! Are you hurt?"

She followed his gaze to her bandaged shoulder. "Oh, that…I-I had a mole removed."

Emmett's silver brows furrowed, his eyes slid past her shoulder, searching the apartment.

"I'd offer you some tea," Petra said, feeling the weight of Solomon's glare, "but I haven't had time to get groceries yet…"

Emmett smiled warmly. "No worries, my dear. Take care of yourself now."

She started to shut the door.

"Oh! I almost forgot!" Emmett declared. "I wanted to update you on the urn."

Petra yanked the door open. "Have they found it!"

"Er, no, not exactly, but they have a lead on a suspect. That guard, not Gabriel though, the other one—with the blue eyes."

Petra swayed, clutching the door handle so she wouldn't fall. "W-What?"

"Seems you were right about him. Apparently he and his family have quite a history of criminal behaviour, especially theft. Turns out he's, uh, quite dangerous."

"D-Dangerous?"

"I thought you might want to know."

"Thank you." She glowered in the direction of Solomon's hiding space. "Thank you *very* much."

Emmett tipped his cap and headed to the elevator.

Petra slammed the door—hard.

"*Beleti*, let me explain…" Solomon stepped out, a butcher knife in his hand.

"Petra," she snapped. "My name is *Petra*—and put that down!"

He dropped the knife on the counter and raised his hands. "Please, Petra, allow me to explain."

"Fine, explain." She crossed her arms.

"It's…a long story." He sighed.

"Seems to be a habit with you."

"Look, I will tell you everything—but not here, we have to leave."

She frowned. "Why?"

"It's not safe."

"Safe from what?"

"You're just going to have to trust me. Your professor knows something, that's why he was here, he…"

"Emmett was here to check up on me!" Petra exploded. "To be *nice*, that's all! I can't believe you're trying to turn this around. He said you were a thief. That *you* wanted to steal the urn."

"That's true."

"What!"

"If someone else hadn't stolen it, I would have."

Petra eyed him. "You…would have stolen it?"

"Of course."

"Why didn't you just steal it that night then?"

"We...I had a plan," Solomon said. "To take it after it was processed and put into storage at the museum—so it wouldn't be missed. At least not for a while."

Petra steadied herself with the arm of the couch. This was insanity. Why was she still there? She should run screaming from the apartment, go to the police, call the insane asylum; something other than stay and encourage his delusions.

He's a con artist, Petra. Wake up! He's slipped some kind of hallucinogen into your tea; or worse, a powerful sedative, and then carved those marks into your back! There's no such thing as curses or immortals or...goddesses!

Petra buried her face in her hands, confused and afraid.

"*Bele*...Petra, I need for you to trust me." He knelt before her, sapphire eyes pleading. "I have no right to ask this of you, but please, give me time to explain. You must hear the rest before you can understand. Let me finish my story."

"Fine. I will listen." Petra pointed a stern finger in his face. "But if you're jerking me around, so help me I'll kill you myself and we'll see just how *immortal* you really are!"

"Deal." He chuckled, but scanned the apartment as if enemies lurked around every corner. "We need to find a new place to hideout though..."

Gold and copper leaves blanketed Stanley Park. Petra pulled in a breath, the air crisp. She loved the onset of winter, when the scents of summer faded and the world was pitched into a painting of amber and yellow. Even more, she loved the snow. Everything was fresher somehow. She loved how snowflakes just drifted, no path, no plan, merely wherever the breeze carried them. Winter made her feel cozy and warm, the opposite of most, she knew. Many people hated winter. Her mother, for one, probably hated it the most.

"Why can't it just be summer all year round?" Petra's mother lamented one afternoon last fall, buttoning up her Ralph Lauren peacoat as they walked out into the cold November morning.

Petra sighed, frosty breath curling like fog. "It can be...it's called Arizona."

"Hmmf," she grumbled. "You know I can't leave Vancouver, what would the girls at the Country Club think?"

"Who cares what they think?" Petra said, instantly regretting it.

Her mother spun about. "I do!"

"I'm sorry, I know you do. So, how's Vienna doing?" Petra changed the subject to her adored older sister.

"Oh! I forgot to tell you!" Her mother's demeanour shifted. "She and Jason are expecting again!"

"Wow, great," Petra tried to sound excited. "Three kids now, huh? Wonder if they'll ever stop, or if they'll breed like the Duggars—just keep going until they hit twenty." Her mother shot her a look.

"At least Vienna is contributing something to this world."

Petra flinched.

"Really, Petra, I don't understand why you don't want to settle down and have a family like normal people..."

"*Normal* is for people who settle for less than they deserve."

"Well, like I said to the girls at the Club the other day, time marches on and eventually you'll lose your looks, your youth, and your ability to catch a man in time to still have a baby." She lifted her nose into the air.

"You talk to the girls at the Club about me?" Petra's cheeks grew hot.

"Well, of course! Who else would I talk to about my problems?"

"Problems? Is that how you see me?" Tears pinched her eyes. "It doesn't matter to you that I'm going to university? Following a dream?"

"You're so much like your father," her mother sniffed. "Digging in the dirt for old garbage is not a dream, Petra. It's just a way to bury your head in the sand. Do you think if you look hard enough into the past you'll find your future? There's no future in the past, there's just dead people and the mess they left behind."

"What were you just thinking about just then?" Solomon asked quietly. "Looked pretty intense."

Petra shrugged. "Just remembering something my mother said to me once. She basically told me archaeology is nothing more than digging up dead people's garbage."

"She's right."

"What!"

He glanced around, searching. Then he took a few steps, bent down and picked up a gum wrapper. "What is this worth to you?"

"Ew, nothing, it's a dirty wrapper."

"Exactly," he said, walking to a trash can and throwing the paper away. "Just because something is old doesn't mean it has any more worth than when it was first made. People collect and cherish our garbage because it's ancient. Would you walk out into the street and pick up a gum wrapper and declare it a relic? Art? Would you pay thousands, *millions*, for it because it's been on the ground for a couple of years? No. Because it's worthless. It's only made important because it's a part of some mysterious past. Humans are notoriously nostalgic."

"But what about real art? Like my urn?"

"What do you find so fascinating about it?"

"The craftsmanship, the time it took to make. We should respect the one who made it. Remember them."

"Who made your urn?"

She opened her mouth to answer and then stopped. "I don't know."

He smiled. "Then what would be the point in remembering them?"

Petra's back ached. Pain radiated from one shoulder to the other. She wondered how many tattoos there were now—and how many she would get.

Solomon was on his phone a few feet away, making flight arrangements. She had no idea where he planned to take her, nor would he tell her. She, alternatively, had no idea why she was letting this stranger simply whisk her away to some unknown destination where no one in the world—except him—would know where she was.

She fidgeted with the phone in her pocket, thinking it would be wise to send a text to her mother or one of her sisters, if nothing else then to let them know she'd be away for a while. But Petra knew too well that there'd be a lot of questions followed by a dramatic rant about becoming entangled with a complete stranger who was probably a serial killer.

"Thank you," she overheard as Solomon ended his call.

He returned to her side, her stomach doing a little flip when his arm brushed against hers. Inside, Petra cringed. She wasn't one to fall for the tall, dark, and handsome stranger—in fact, she'd always been adamantly opposed to such cliches. There was nothing she despised more than the literary depiction of a swooning maiden saved by a hunky, rich prince, and then escaping to his castle on a white stallion. *Blah, blah, blah.* Women were capable of saving themselves; what's more, they were better off alone than dependent on anyone, especially a man. Especially a good-looking man—which was why this annoying attraction to the foreign, blue-eyed stud had taken her by surprise.

"Our flight leaves at seven o'clock," Solomon said gently.

Petra glanced at her watch. It was only twelve thirty.

They couldn't go back to the apartment, according to him. Before they left, he asked her to grab her passport and pack a suitcase, which he sent ahead to the airport.

"That's almost seven hours away. What do you want to do until then?" An idea struck her. "Want to go to the museum? See some old garbage?"

His lips curled in amusement. "Sure."

They walked to the curb and hailed a taxi.

"The Beaty Museum, please," Petra told the driver.

The city sped past the window. Thousands of people, impossibly tall buildings of glass, garbage piled high along the curbs—a treeless, concrete jungle. The modern Stone Age.

"Is it odd for you to see the world this way? So…cosmopolitan."

"It's not unlike seeing a forest turned into a suburban neighbourhood," Solomon said. "There's a sense of loss, of being misplaced, but then the mind accepts it as the new normal and life goes on. I've watched civilizations evolve, slowly and naturally. Change doesn't happen overnight, so it isn't jarring or anything, if that's what you're asking."

"It must've been so beautiful back then, so open and…free." Petra wasn't yet sure she believed he was an immortal, but it felt good to reminisce about eras she could only visit through relics and history books.

"There are good things about living in the past—and good things about this time," he said practically. "Back then, people died horribly from just an infected scratch. Now, you only need a mere pill to be cured. The world was far more open then, yes—no web of power lines or barbwire fences zigzagging across the pastures. The night sky was so beautiful, the stars are so much brighter without the light pollution. It could be so very quiet, only the howl of a lonely coyote in the distance or the wind rustling the leaves. You could travel a road and not see a single soul for days on end…but free," his gaze turned stormy, "I don't know that any of us are ever truly free. There's always someone who thinks they own you."

The cab pulled up to the curb before she could ask him to elaborate. Petra reached into her purse to pay the driver but Solomon had already handed the man a fifty.

"I could've paid," she said, annoyed. "It was my idea."

Solomon gave her a playful smile. "It's just paper and melted metal. Of that, I have plenty."

"Nevertheless, I can pay my own way."

"Whatever you like, *beleti*." He opened the museum door for her. "But I shall always be a gentlemen."

"You can try." With a mischievous smirk, she walked to a different door.

He smiled, following her inside.

After redeeming herself by paying for their tickets, they walked to the *Lycaenidae* exhibit. Inside one glass display lay a vast butterfly collection; a rainbow of petal-thin wings, their tiny bodies pinned into place.

Petra glanced at Solomon, surprised to see him frowning.

"What's wrong?"

"It's just…sad. These…majestic creatures were captured, killed, and mounted," he said. "Simply because humans would rather observe them at leisure than chance a glimpse of one fluttering through a field of wildflowers."

"Well then…" Petra smiled. "Follow me."

She guided him to a large white tent at the back of the room. Beyond a glass door, the air was balmy, sweet-smelling, lush with overgrown dieffenbachias. Amethyst phlox carpeted either side of the path. A jade butterfly, its wings like stained glass, flitted past Solomon's face, landing on a tiger lily. Hundreds leisured amid the fronds and flowers. Every so often, a kaleidoscope of butterflies took flight, waltzing overhead.

"It's beautiful," he said, reverent.

"I'm surprised you've never been here before," Petra said. "I would've thought you'd been everywhere twice, what with all the time you have to spare."

A look of regret shadowed his eyes. "I've been…busy."

She waited for him to elaborate, but he turned away, suggesting the topic was not open for discussion.

"Okay, why don't we head over to the dinosaur exhibit now?" she said. "I heard they just finished putting up the new T-Rex."

Petra stopped to study the map. As she searched for the exhibit, Solomon peered over her shoulder, his chest inches from her back.

"How are you feeling? The pain, I mean," his deep voice rumbled in her ear; so close, she could feel the heat of his breath on her neck, smell his pheromones, so warm…so painfully erotic.

"I'm okay." Petra shrugged, struggling to appear unaffected.

"Whenever you need to rest, just tell me." His fingertips grazed her bare arm.

Electricity fired through her body. Sheer ecstasy flooded her veins. Swooning, it was everything she could do not to moan.

"Take him…" a voice whispered. *"Now!"*

Petra gasped. "D-Did you hear that?"

"What?"

"I thought I heard...nothing. I'm just tired." Dizzy, Petra closed her eyes.

"I'll get you some water," Solomon said, but as he walked away she heard him utter, "*It has begun...*"

"Dinosaurs in Your Backyard," Petra read as they joined the long queue.

Beyond a set of large wooden doors, Petra could see a menacing T-Rex skeleton positioned over a cowering triceratops. Propped on powerful hind legs, the massive predator was poised to chomp on his prey's neck.

"Friends of yours?" Petra asked, gesturing to the dinosaurs.

Solomon looked confused, and then smirked. "I'm not *that* old, thank you."

"Petra?" a voice sounded behind them.

She spun about. "Joe!"

Joe pulled her into an embrace. Beside her, Solomon stiffened.

"How's it going?" Joe asked her with a suspicious glance at Solomon. "Getting used to Vancouver's rainy weather again?"

"Haha, I'd much rather be in the desert."

"Wouldn't we all." Joe winked at her.

Solomon either cleared his throat or growled.

"This is my...friend, Solomon," Petra said awkwardly. "Joe was on the dig in Iraq too."

The men shook hands, each puffing out their chests and drawing themselves a little taller. Petra fought the urge to roll her eyes.

"You're working here?" Petra pointed to the employee name tag pinned to Joe's shirt.

"Yup! In the Ancient History department, cleaning and staging the artifacts."

"I'm jealous." Petra gave him a playful nudge.

"Good." Joe grinned. "Maybe I can show you around..."

"Actually, we're leaving town." Solomon wrapped an arm around Petra's waist. "Tonight."

"Um, yes..." Petra's cheeks raged. "But I'd love a tour when I get back."

"That'd be great," Joe said. "Where are you headed?"

"Um," Petra stammered around a cautionary eye from Solomon. "It's...a surprise."

"Oh? Well, have fun! Gotta get back to work but it was great seeing you!" Joe kissed her cheek.

Solomon shot him a scowl before leading Petra away.

"What's wrong with you?" Petra hissed.

"I don't trust him."

She laughed dryly. "You don't trust anyone."

"After thousands of years, you develop a keen sense of people—an intuition. I've met a million people in my time. I've been wrong about...precious few." His expression darkened further.

Petra softened. "I understand, but I know Joe. He's very kind."

"How's your shoulder?" he asked, changing the subject.

"A bit sore, but I haven't felt any new marks open up for a while."

"Let me know if you need more oil, for the pain," he said gently, returning to his old self.

"I will, thank you."

Solomon placed his hand protectively onto the small of her back and they walked into the dinosaur exhibit.

Impatient bodies brushed against her as a large group exited the dinosaur exhibit. Petra's shoulder pulsed with fresh pain, nerve endings prickled beneath her skin. Determined to enjoy herself, she tried to ignore it. She forced a smile and dug out the map.

"Where to next?" she asked. "We have the Blue Whale display...a Nocturnal animals exhibit...one on the human body...What do you feel like?" She glanced around, realizing he wasn't beside her. "Solomon?"

Panic stirred in her chest.

What if he was just lying this whole time and finally decided to skip out on me?

"Brilliant, Petra," she mumbled. "That doesn't explain the gaping preternatural wounds on your back, does it?"

She scanned the crowd, searching for his wavy, black hair and broad shoulders. Where would he have gone? Then, far across the room, she spied him standing in front of a glass laboratory.

Relieved, she pressed through the throng.

"Hey, I thought I lost you, there," she said.

Eyes transfixed on the inside of the transparent display, he didn't respond. Inside the exhibit, employees outfitted in lab coats, surgical gloves and masks were readying to remove the lid from a granite sarcophagus. They struggled with the weight of the stone cover, but finally, after prying it up with crowbars and working their fingers between the gap, in unison, they lifted. She could almost hear the dissident hiss of ancient air escape from inside the coffin.

Petra drew a quiet breath as the contents were revealed. Perfectly preserved, cocooned within resin-stained linen strips, was the figure of a woman. Though faint, Petra could discern ghostly hieroglyphs painted on the wrappings, spells to guide the woman through the perilous journey of the Egyptian afterlife. Posed with arms by her side to symbolize her status as a commoner, she was adorned with a scarab pendant upon her chest and surrounded by *shabti* dolls who'd awaken to serve her in the next world.

"Solomon?" Petra touched his arm. "Are you okay?"

He nodded but kept his gaze firmly on the mummy. Petra bit her lip, uncertain what to do.

"Did you want to head to the restaurant?" She checked her watch, it was nearing five o'clock. "Have a bite before we go to the airport?"

Solomon gave his head a shake. "Yes, of course."

After finding a table in a quiet corner of the cafeteria, Petra watched as Solomon stirred his cream of broccoli soup, but didn't eat.

"Not hungry?"

"Not especially," he said, setting down the spoon. "The mummy—it reminded me of someone I knew...a long time ago."

"A woman?" Petra said, a flicker of irrational jealousy kindling.

"No, a man. A master embalmer."

Intrigued, Petra leaned in. "You knew a mummifier? We've found so little from the Egyptian literature about mummification. Their procedures, their tools, the ingredients. It's like…a secret recipe or something."

Solomon imparted a mischievous brow. "Indeed."

"Come on!" Petra grinned. "Tell me something, anything."

He thought a moment. "Well, to keep the corpse's face from losing shape, they would stuff dried vegetables into the eye sockets. Oh, and they'd make a tiny slit in the cheekbone and stuff sawdust beneath the skin."

Petra wrinkled her nose, laughing. "Like ancient photoshopping."

Solomon smiled warmly, his eyes lingering on hers. The world slowed, as if pausing to take a breath. Just who was this guy, really? Was he really immortal? An ancient wandering the passages of time, untouched by age? Petra tried to imagine what that kind of existence would be like; how it would feel to see civilizations rise and fall over the centuries; dynasty after dynasty of kings and queens; prophets, poets, philosophers—all of history. From the outside looking in, it sounded exciting and utterly desirable. To live forever, amassing knowledge you'd never have to surrender upon death. But then, also terribly lonely.

She glanced at him again, though now his expression had darkened, glaring at something over her shoulder. Petra moved to follow his gaze.

"No!" Solomon uttered, voice low. "Don't let them see you."

"W-Who?"

"We have to go—Now!"

Petra barely had time to snatch up her purse and coat before Solomon took her by the elbow and compelled her towards the nearest exit. Instinctively, she looked back. Two men in long trench coats stood on either side of the most beautiful woman Petra had ever seen.

"W-Who is that?" Petra asked. "I feel…like I've seen her before."

Solomon chuckled darkly, as if she'd said something ironic.

"There's no time to explain. We must leave now—*she* has found you."

Only a breath later, Petra glanced again to where she'd seen the woman and her entourage—but they'd vanished.

Steel-grey clouds brewed on the horizon, the cool night air smelled metallic. Anticipation crackled in the unguarded space between her and Solomon as they boarded the plane. Or perhaps it was just her own dark energy she felt. Settled into their seats, Petra stole a glance at Solomon as he glowered at the impending storm, his handsome features shadowed with concern.

"Hey," she said, placing a hand on his arm. "What are you thinking about?"

"Nothing…everything." He patted her hand and withdrew from her touch.

Rejection burned inside her chest.

Why am I here? He obviously doesn't have any romantic intentions. Petra frowned. *Do I?*

Angry at him, angry at herself, she crossed her arms and glared out the window. Her shoulder ached so much it made her queasy, but she wasn't going to ask him for more of his poppy potion. She'd rather suffer.

Outside the plane, the jets whined. Plumes of heat waves rolled past the window. Petra's stomach tumbled. She whimpered as another tattoo cracked open, like a long, sharp fingernail tearing at her from the inside out. As though she was being eaten alive, slowly, eradicated cell by cell.

Hearing her anguish, Solomon rose and hurried to the kitchenette.

"Here you go." He sat beside her and set a cool rag on her forehead, deploying an army of shivers over her entire body.

"What's...wrong with me?" she whispered, teeth chattering as he pulled back the neck of her shirt and rubbed the sweet-scented balm on her skin.

Instead of replying, Solomon shucked off his coat and wrapped it around her, residual warmth and his scent soothing her instantly. He drew her to his chest. Surrendering, Petra curled into him. She longed for sleep, for merciful unconsciousness; anything to get away from the pain and fear.

"Tell me more," she said, closing her eyes. "What happened after you ran to the temple to find Miri?"

His chest rose and fell, heartbeat pulsing against her ear as he continued his tale, "The night I left Sumer, the sky was angry and impatient...like me..."

Part Three

The Minoan

"*I couldn't stay in Sumer. I couldn't be where I'd lost so much, where I'd be reminded of Father, Indra, and Miri everywhere I looked. My life as Solomon the son, the husband, and the father was no longer.*

"*Before I left, I dug up the urn that held Ariadne's necklace and exchanged it with an urn filled with Indra's ashes. I buried my love beneath the sands of my oasis and tucked the princess's gift into my pocket.*

"*Then I left Sumer for what I thought was the last time, but, as I soon came to understand, the past has a way of haunting you—no matter where you go.*"

15
Edin

*E*very year after the harvest, boats of all sizes and splendour glided into the ports of Uruk, having embarked upon often treacherous journeys from faraway lands to trade with the merchants of Mesopotamia. Whether they sailed across the open ocean or rode the tide from neighbouring communities infused along the spine of the Euphrates, it was the time of year when an array of cultures collided in peaceful exchange.

Men and women of diverse dress and exotic tongue littered the docks, bartering for the lowest price on millet, amphoras of wine and palm oils, precious gems, jewellery, metals, salmon, and livestock. Even from my hideout, behind a forlorn shack along the harbour's perimeter, the reek of animal dung and days-old fish made my eyes water.

Desperate to escape Sumer, I eyed the foreign boats. I needed to get as far away as possible—to where, didn't matter. While I'd considered seeking refuge in the nearby Zagros Mountains, where Father insisted we had family, it was simply too close to Uruk. Too close to the pain, the memories—and Inanna.

With no currency to offer for passage—other than Ariadne's necklace and Indra's ring, neither of which I was willing to part with—I had no choice but to sneak aboard one of the departing boats and try to survive without being detected. I surveilled the bustling port and awaited the opportune moment.

"We come back," Bansabira's baritone voice reverberated from the past. *"Always in da summer."*

Although summer had since ended, and they'd probably already come and gone, I couldn't help but feel hopeful I see those crimson sails.

Hot, tired, and restless, I waited. Hunger gnawed my stomach, but my spirit was too shattered to think of eating. Undeserved of contentment, I was punishing myself in the only way I could. Since I supposedly could not die, I was forced to inflict a form of self-torture in lieu of death. Inanna couldn't have chosen a more appropriate curse for me, really; denying me the option of ending my own life.

The sound of Father's pain ricocheted inside my head, coalescing with Indra's screams of horror, and Miri's quiet cry, as if in the reliving of those terrible moments, I could somehow alter the past and prevent them from happening. Without anyone in the world who loved me, I no longer knew who I was. The foundation on which I now stood was quicksand. A hot tear slipped down my cheek. Angrily, I brushed it away. There was no time for that now. Someday, I'd allow myself to grieve. After the pain dulled and the memories faded—if they ever did.

I must've dozed at some point because I was startled awake by shouting.

"A storm is coming!" The dock master pointed to dark clouds furrowed on the horizon. "We'll unload the rest in the morning!"

The foreign sailors dragged a large sledge loaded with heavy sacks down a ramp—a ramp attached to a ship with billowing *crimson* sails. Nearly identical to Ariadne's ship, only bigger, the very sight of it sent a thrill though my veins.

"Come!" the dock master addressed the Minoan crew. "Have a beer with us."

Adorned with gold bangles and swirling tattoos, reminiscent of Bansabira, the Minoans followed the dock master into a nearby pub.

The sky burned amber beneath a blackening thunderhead, cloaking me as I slipped from my hiding place and stole up the ramp. Heart pounding, I crouched amidst the shadows, watching for an unseen sentry, listening. Only the windswept waves lapped against the hull. Stealthily, I moved towards the stern, locating the entrance into the hold, and lifted the hatch. Despite the stench of dead fish and sweaty farm animals, I descended into the dark portal.

Anxiety and excitement churned within as I embarked on my new life—far, far from Sumer.

Hours later, the deck rumbled with unsteady footfalls and raucous laughter, punctuated by slurred songs in an unfamiliar language. I pictured them leaning on one another for support as they staggered gayly about. Soon though, the noise subsided, giving way to distant snores. Within moments, I joined them, surrendering to the soul-deep exhaustion.

Morning arrived all too soon amid a cacophony of brisk steps overhead. Muffled orders, merchandise dragged across floorboards, dust raining down into the cargo hold.

As the day wore on, the cargo hold grew hotter. On my left, two lethargic goats lazed in thick nests of hay. Beside them, a hulking ox stood inside a wooden pen, tail swishing infatuated flies from his backside.

The sad irony of my predicament hadn't escaped me. It was what I'd prayed to Enki for, after all. To leave Sumer, see the world. We want for things, beg the gods for our dreams to come true, but when they do, it's not the way we envisioned.

I'd always imagined Father and I embarking on an adventure together.

Now, that was impossible.

How can he simply not exist? Pain seared inside my chest. *Why didn't I just surrender to Inanna, then he'd still be here…No, stop it.*

Father wouldn't have wanted me to punish myself for his death. He would, however, be annoyed with me for giving the farm to Zephat, abandoning all we'd worked for—and running away.

"A man is not his destination, *maru*," Father once said. "When a man knows his own heart, he is always home."

A tear rolled down my cheek. I wanted him back. I wanted them all back.

"*Silim!*" Someone shouted in Sumerian. "Good journey to you!"

More thunderous noise as the ramp was withdrawn from the dock. Suddenly free from confinement, the boat bobbed like a cork. Then, amid the sound of whining rope, the anchor was raised. Now weightless, it lurched forward, creaking as it breached the rushing river. How I wished to be topside, sailing away, Sumer shrinking in our wake. As much as I'd dreamed of escaping Sumer and the farm, I never actually saw myself leaving. I was certain I'd simply grow old there—and die.

Dying, I thought, strangely sad. *I will never die.*

Death was the one true promise of life; an unspoken contract that someday this body would surrender and, according to Sumerian myth, my soul would be transported to the Underworld where I'd reunite with my family.

But now, if Inanna's curse was true, I would be denied that gift.

Immortal.

Macabre images surfaced unbidden, of my rotting, undead body exhuming itself from the grave, reborn again and again, more inhuman upon every resurrection. Madness circled as I actually heard my fingernails clawing at the coffin's lid…

No, the sound is really there.

From somewhere in the shadows—scratching. There, from between two grain sacks, eyes gleamed, beady and iridescent.

Rats.

I despised rats.

Father and I often made snares to catch the filthy creatures. I'd set the traps, leaving bits of raw meat as bait. Once caught, Father would kill them.

"We must burn the bodies," Father said as we piled the small corpses into a heap, dousing them with oil and lighting them ablaze. "The stench sends a message to the others."

The rancid aroma of fur and flesh billowed, fingers of ghostly black smoke reaching across the land. Afterwards, we wouldn't have rats on the farm for seasons at a time.

I remember asking Father why.

"Deep down," he replied. "We all recognize the smell of our own death."

Nausea, whether from hunger or the continuous up and down of the boat, left me clutching a post with near religious fervour. Immortal or not, apparently I was not exempt from carnal discomforts. While I'd brought some provisions—a bowl, a knife, two water-skins, an extra tunic, some dried fruit, and a few pieces of flint—I'd been so eager to leave, I neglected to bring anything substantial.

"There must be *something* I can eat." I rummaged about the hold until I found some millet. Mouth watering, I untied the rope, filled up my bowl, and added some water. Though mushy and flavourless, I sighed as the hunger pangs subsided.

I'd only managed a few bites, however, when the hatch door flew open and two men started to descend. Quickly, I crouched between two large amphoras, cradling the bowl of cereal. One of the Minoans, obviously in charge, appeared to be delegating tasks for the other to complete. Like Bansabira, his muscular upper body was tattooed with various markings.

The subordinate began moving items as instructed while the leader paced the hold, counting the sacks and inscribing tallies onto a small piece of clay. As he reached the millet sack I'd left open, he stopped short and examined it, a frown on his brow. With a wary eye, he scanned the dark corners of the room.

My heart raced as I realized my mistake. I held my breath.

After a sigh, he retied the bag. Just as he returned to his inventory, I felt movement behind me. A small, skittering form wriggled between me and the wall—a rat. Startled, I dropped the bowl of millet and it clattered on the floor. The leader drew his blade, glowering in my direction while the lackey took a defensive stance beside him.

There was nowhere nowhere to hide, so I stood and faced my fate.

"I-I'm sorry," I stammered. "I needed to get out of Sumer."

Fearless, the leader stepped forward, his knife-tip poised over my jugular.

"I am friends with...Bansabira," I said, praying he'd recognize the name. "And Princess Ariadne."

His eyes narrowed. "Ariadne?"

With the point of his blade, he gestured to the stairs. I climbed up and out the hatch, the Minoan only a breath behind me. Blinded by the mid-morning sun, I found myself surrounded by fierce-faced strangers.

Who are you?" the Minoan leader demanded in fluent Sumerian.

"Solomon."

"You know Ariadne?"

"I met her—and Bansabira—many years ago. I did some work on their boat." I held up her necklace. "She gave this to me."

Suspicious, he fingered the delicately strung shells. "Did you steal this?"

"No! It was a gift."

He weighed my words a moment more, and then sheathed his blade. "I am Rhadamanthys, Captain of this vessel."

With the situation apparently resolved, the crew dispersed, returning to their duties.

"You speak Sumerian?" I said, relaxing.

"We have a Sumerian living in the palace. He...taught us," Rhadamanthys explained, with a hint of hostility.

"Ariadne, is she well?"

At this, his eyes warmed. "Yes, she is well. Come to my cabin, have some wine. We must speak of this...new situation."

Once in his quarters, Rhadamanthys handed me a cup of merlot. "I've never seen a man with blue eyes before."

"Me neither."

He chuckled. "Though in my many travels, I have seen statues painted with blue eyes."

"Where?"

"Across the great water, in Egypt."

"Egypt," I tasted the unfamiliar name.

"You've not heard of Egypt?"

"No, but I don't know much about the world outside of Sumer."

"Well, now you will see a great deal of it." Rhadamanthys stroked his beard. "You're welcome to be on board, but we must all contribute. No man rests while the others work, you understand?"

"Yes! I am happy to work."

"Good. What can you do?"

"I can...cook." I could almost see Father smile at this.

"Thank the gods! Our cook tries very hard, but his food is...not good. Do you know many recipes?"

I nodded, but the memory sent a current of sadness through me.

Only because of Indra.

That first night, with an abundance of fish and Sumerian-grown vegetables at my disposal, I made Indra's smoked salmon stew. The savoury aroma lingered, somehow bringing her closer.

"Very good, Solomon," Rhadamanthys said.

Eyes hooded in satisfaction, the sixteen sailors belched and rubbed their swollen stomachs. Even the previous cook, Duripi, was delighted.

"So good! So good!" Duripi parroted in his limited Sumerian vocabulary. An extraordinarily hairy little man, jolly and red-cheeked, he poured glass after glass of wine and ale, impartial it would seem, so long as it was alcohol. Duripi stood, wobbled, and then approached me. The top of his head barely reaching my chin, he lifted onto his toes and peered at my face—into my eyes.

"*Keeyan?*"

"Blue, yes," I replied, recalling Bansabira's long-ago reference.

Duripi tilted his head. "*Ek arth theas?*"

The men stared, awaiting an answer.

"He asks," Rhadamanthys translated, "if you are 'of the gods'."

"No, I don't think so," I said awkwardly. "My father always told me Enki—the Sumerian water god—gave me this eye colour as a gift."

A slow burn chased my words. My eyes had caused me nothing more than pain and suffering. They were not a gift, but a curse.

Later that evening, as I stood out on the deck, beneath a violet sky littered with countless miniature suns, I understood why Father wanted to be sailor.

"*I wanted to be a sailor…*" Father's voice echoed and I wished, not for the first time, that he was beside me, gazing out at this ocean with his own eyes.

What makes a man give up on his dreams? Is it cowardice—or bravery? Fear or sacrifice? Father was not the kind of man to give up on anything, so I knew he wouldn't have abandoned his ambitions easily. With my mother to consider, and then me, he never left Sumer to fulfill his own desires.

He stayed for me.

I couldn't determine whether that made me feel better or not. He loved me more than his dreams. He sacrificed his life for me—in all ways.

Rhadamanthys sidled next to me and inhaled. "There is nothing like the open water, no? So much power in the waves."

"Yes, it can be difficult to surrender to her whim."

"Her?"

"My father always said that water was like a woman, but she could change her mind at any moment, pulling you under and sweeping you away."

He laughed. "Your father is a wise man."

"*Was,*" I whispered.

Rhadamanthys fell silent.

"I-I made a terrible mistake," I blurted. "And my father paid for it… with his life." I couldn't elaborate, especially when it came to Inanna. It was too impossible, even to me, to admit I'd come face to face with a goddess—and that she was horrible.

Rhadamanthys pondered this. "Are you sad this happened?"

"Of course!"

"Did you wish your father to come to harm by your actions?"

"No!"

"Man must always make mistakes." He patted my shoulder. "It's in our nature, it's how we learn. But it's in the reaction that…how you say…*reveals* the trueness of the heart. It's not for you to hold the sadness, but for the ones who could not see beyond the mistake—and forgive."

"What if I'm the one who cannot forgive myself? I just…wish it never happened. I wish I could go back and change everything…then he'd still be here."

"We all wish we could change something within our past…" Rhadamanthys sipped his wine with dark eyes. "Well, my friend, I must be off. I look forward to more of your cooking in the morning."

"Sleep well."

After he left, I watched the stars a while, wondering how they could remain so still, so patient in their immortality. With their ancient, shining eyes, they watched me, and for just a moment, I didn't feel so alone in this new forever.

After making a hearty breakfast for the men, I explored the boat. Constructed of cypress planks and waterproofed with resin, the Minoan ship held barracks for over three dozen men. An oak mast held fast to billowing red sails. Brightly-painted frescos adorned every available surface, images of dolphins, sea birds, and, above all, the horned head of a bull.

"Aurochs," Rhadamanthys explained, seeing me ponder the beast. "They are a sacred symbol to my people. As is the labrys." He pointed to the carving a double-headed axe.

"What does it mean?"

"It's the only weapon believed powerful enough to slay the massive bull during a sacrifice."

"You kill them?"

"Yes, according to our beliefs, our…*goddess* demands it," he said as if unconvinced of his deity's requirements.

In Sumer, the sacrifice of a lion to Inanna was considered the ultimate gift. Left upon the staircase of her White Temple, mythology claimed the blood nourished the fertility goddess so she could favour us with good weather and plentiful crops. If not placated, my people believed she'd bring about the floods, or worse, a drought.

Bitterness curdled inside.

All lies.

Inanna harboured all the power she could ever need with just a wave of her hand. This perceived benevolence of the gods, the belief they could be swayed to ease our hunger, our pain and suffering, was nothing more than man's blind faith in something he didn't understand. Inanna didn't care for us, she wasn't concerned with whether we ate or starved, lived or died. Many a beast had been sacrificed in her name— as well, the blood of many men, women, and children—and yet the drought continued year after year.

Inanna's lavender stare seared my memory, as did her wicked laugh as I wept before Father's mangled corpse…

"Solomon?"

Startled from my dark daydream, I shook my head. "Sorry, what did you say?"

Rhadamanthys smiled. "I asked what you have planned for supper."

"Actually, I was hoping someone could lend me a fishing line so I might catch one of those big, needle-nosed fish."

"The marlin? They are very strong." He tapped his chin. "You will need to hunt with a spear instead. I will ask Duripi to assist you."

"Thank you."

"Think nothing of it, I look forward to eating it!" He laughed, ducking into the barracks to find Duripi.

Moments later, Duripi waddled up to me, two spears in hand and a bucket of tiny squid. "Sola-man kill de fish?"

Grinning, I nodded at the hairy Cretan.

He handed me a copper-headed trident, a thin rope trailed from the shaft's tip like a tail. After a quick session on what angle to shoot at so I didn't puncture the hull, we tied off the ends, tossed out a handful of bait, and began aiming at any marlins swimming close to the boat. We took turns: aim, fire, miss, drag the spear back in. It was pleasantly competitive.

"Sola-man no good at killing de fish," the hairy man chided.

"Duripi must be blind," I countered.

"Sola-man is goat balls at hunting." He giggled, high-pitched and silly, punching me in the arm.

"Ow." I rubbed my shoulder.

On and on for hours, we bantered, drank, and laughed.

Finally, after a wet, wine-laden burp, Duripi closed one eye and fired. The spearhead nicked a marlin's dorsal fin and he vanished under the water.

"*Och*," Duripi grumbled, throwing the spear onto the deck and kicking it.

Only one marlin remained. I was under pressure now as we'd spent the better part of the day fishing. If I didn't catch this one, I'd have to serve porridge for supper. I aligned my breath with the rhythm of the animal as he sailed beneath the blue surface.

Quiet, stilling my soul, I aimed—and released the harpoon.

Suddenly Duripi was shouting. Within moments, we hauled the glistening blue body over the balustrade and onto the deck. Spear embedded in its side, the marlin writhed. Duripi danced a funny little jig; then, unceremoniously, grabbed an oar and whacked the fish over the head.

Rhadamanthys came running. "Well done!"

Duripi handed me a celebratory mug of ale. Strangely saddened, I eyed my catch as I drank. Such a majestic creature and I'd ended its existence. A part of me, however, was proud that I'd somehow proven myself to these men.

After cleaning the marlin, I slathered it with palm oil and stuffed the cavity with carrots, celery, onions, garlic, and many other exotic ingredients garnered from various trade routes. Rhadamanthys wasn't crazy about my idea of starting a fire on deck, but I convinced him it would be safe if we contained the fire like a pyre. We then fashioned a rotating spit, which Duripi happily offered to turn for three hours so long as he could keep a barrel of wine beside him.

Once finished, sizzling and redolent of garlic, I served the men.

"Wonderful!" Rhadamanthys licked his oily fingers.

The crew grunted their gratitude, too busy eating to articulate.

"Even better than a woman could do, I dare say," I joked.

The men stopped eating and gaped at me, wide-eyed with fear. Even the drunk and unflappable Duripi seemed ill at ease.

I swallowed hard. "Did I...say something wrong?"

Rhadamanthys moved to my side, talking low as the crew resumed their meal. "On our island, woman are...how to say...*above* the men. In our culture, women carry a spark of the goddess. therefore men must respect and obey them without question. It would be...unwise, Solomon, even in jest, to claim a higher status."

"So you're considered...*beneath* them?"

"Men are not considered *less* than, only that we are never *more* than. You must understand—there're penalties for disrespecting any woman on the island."

"W-What kind of penalties?"

For the first time, Rhadamanthys seemed evasive. "Do not concern yourself. If you're obedient and respectful, there will not be any problems. Tomorrow we arrive at Crete, I know you will find it like...what do Sumerians call it...ah, *edin*—paradise."

He patted my shoulder and retreated to his cabin.

"*Paradise*," I repeated, skepticism surfacing. "We'll see..."

16
Beautiful Minoans

*W*reathed in early morning mist, the island of Crete rose from the fathoms like the primordial mound of creation. We sailed through the mouth of an omega-shaped island, the entrance guarded by two colossal pillars anchored to the ocean floor—a gateway fit for a god. A vast metropolis emerged with gleaming walls that mirrored the sun. Merchants boats, catamarans, and fishing vessels, littered the moat between the island and its natural barricade to the open sea. Patrons strolled along a dazzling pavilion of flagstone streets and marble merchant stalls.

"Solomon!" Rhadamanthys tossed me a length of rope. "Jump down and tie us off!"

I clambered over the balustrade, landing clumsily on solid ground. I tethered the ship to a post on the pier. After the wooden ramp was lowered, the crew descended, Rhadamanthys in the lead. I fell in line next to Duripi, who reeked of ale and sweat.

"We home," he said, losing his balance as he tried to slap me on the shoulder.

I steadied him by the elbow. "It's absolutely beautiful!"

Balmy air exhaled through the port, stirring skirts and long coiffed hair. Like Rhadamanthys, men wore short sarongs and went bare-chested; women flaunted colourful skirts and corsets designed to support their exposed breasts. Everyone radiated a rare vibrancy.

Ahead, Rhadamanthys had paused to talk to a veritable tree-trunk of a man—and I gasped when I realized who it was.

"Bansabira!" Like a child, I bounded up to him but stopped short when he raised a quizzical brow. I extracted Ariadne's necklace from my pocket and held it up. "It's me! Solomon!"

Recognition sparked in his eyes.

"Solo-man?" Bansabira gathered me into a bearhug. "How are you here?"

"My father…died," I said, purposely excluding Indra and Miri, afraid people might ask questions I didn't have answers to. With Father, it wasn't uncommon for men to die in their forties. Indra and Miri's deaths, however, couldn't be as easily explained. "I was alone—but I never forgot you and the princess. I waited at the port in Sumer for a ship with red sails, like yours. I hid on it…hoping to find you."

"I am glad you have come." Bansabira squeezed my shoulder. "You are family here in Crete. Solo-man is a Minoan now."

Tears stung my eyes, only able to nod my gratitude on account of the lump in my throat.

"Come," Rhadamanthys said. "Let us go to the palace. I am tired and hungry."

While it felt good to walk, the ground seemed to undulate as if we were still riding the waves. My stomach rolled uncomfortably. Rhadamanthys assured me it would subside within a few hours.

A sinuous path led us up a rolling hillside. The island sunlight was embracing, unlike the merciless desert sun I'd sweltered beneath my entire life. High overhead, falcons circled field after field of olive groves and vineyards of plump grapes. Luxuriant and beauteous, the soul of this new world hummed beneath my feet.

"I love it here," I said under my breath.

"Yes, it is a paradise." Rhadamanthys smiled, though tension weighed on his words.

A staircase of white marble greeted us at the top of the hill. *Kamares*—tall decorated vases—phalanxed either side of each step. Over an arching processional bridge, we arrived at a set of massive doors.

"Welcome to Knossos," Rhadamanthys said as attendants opened the doors to reveal a lush courtyard.

"*Knossos*," I tasted the name.

"Come!" Bansabira slapped me on the back. "Beer! Food!"

Inside the courtyard, Minoan women engaged in lively conversation. They hushed as we passed, furtive smiles on their shell-pink lips. Alike Ariadne, their breasts sat poised outside their garments, tanning in the autumnal sun, blush nipples like rosebuds.

"You're staring." Rhadamanthys nudged my arm.

"Sorry, I…I am not used to seeing so many…um…"

"The ladies expect it from foreigners—but as a Minoan, they prefer you look at their lips when you speak to them."

"Why their lips?"

"In our culture, it's more important to understand what one is saying rather than how they look. In watching their lips as they speak, you're showing you *hear* them instead of simply *seeing* them, understand?" He bowed at a group of women and they beamed in response. "It's one's intellect that is revered here, not the body."

"What if someone isn't very…intelligent?" I meant myself, of course, what with my lack of life experiences.

"Intelligence and intellect are very different things," he explained. "Intelligence is the number of books one has read and the privileges of school. *Intellect* is a combination of the mind and soul."

"Then why do women wear their…breasts *outside* their clothing?" I reddened. "I mean, if they wish to be seen for their intellect and not their body?"

"That, my friend, is to measure the man—to see where his eyes rest first. For eyes are the mirrors of intention. If his sight falls to a woman's breasts, she'll know he does not respect her. If his gaze is fixed on her jewellery, he only wants her wealth. *But*, if he watches her words as they spill from her lips, ahh, well, he's worthy of her attention, no?"

Though I nodded, my attention was stolen by the roofless stadium, wide open to a sapphire sky. A long, red carpet unfurled over the marble floor like a great tongue. Beyond, a vast corridor yawned. Herculean red pillars, hundreds of them, bore the weight of the palace on their shoulders.

"How big is this place?" I asked Rhadamanthys, craning my neck in every direction.

"There are over 1500 rooms in the palace. The entire city lives inside these walls," he explained.

On a large segment of wall, an artist was preparing a new fresco. Masterfully, he spread a thin layer of plaster, and then, using a sharpened reed, sketched the rough outline of a bull, thick body arched in mid-buck. Upon the beast's back, twisted into a graceful contortion, as if some form of ancient ballet, were two youthful acrobats.

"What are they doing?" I pointed to the gymnast.

"*Taurokathapsia*," Rhadamanthys said. "Bull leaping."

"It looks dangerous."

"It is, but do you see these ones here," he said, pointing to two more people on the ground, one in front of the bull and one behind. "They are also acrobats, but as one takes the bull by the horns and leaps, the others hold his attention. Then they switch places, over and over again —dancing with the beast."

Beside us, Duripi wore a sour expression. "Hungry for beer!"

Rhadamanthys laughed. "Yes, yes, let's go to the dining hall. They will be just starting to serve, I suspect."

Flaxen sunlight warmed every corner of the great dining room. In the centre was a long banquet table with garlands of lilac and decorative bowls cradling fresh fruit.

"Please, sit." Rhadamanthys gestured to a seat, settling into the one beside it. He scanned the empty room. "I'd hoped the others would already be here. I want to introduce you."

"I hope they do *not*. More for Duripi," the little man said as he snatched a cluster of plump grapes and stuffed them into his mouth a handful at a time.

Suddenly, both Rhadamanthys and Bansabira rose from their seats and faced the entrance. Duripi dropped his grapes and also stood, smoothing back his wild hair. Standing, I turned to look—and my heart hesitated. There she was, as beautiful as the last time I saw her.

"Ariadne!" I rushed over.

Her eyes widened in alarm.

"It's Solomon. From Sumer."

Frowning, she looked past me, to Rhadamanthys. "*Ou eska la?*"

I searched my pockets for her necklace and held it up. The princess snatched it from my hands.

"Where did you get this?" she demanded with cold, questioning eyes.

"F-From you. It was a very long time ago…I suppose," I stammered, crestfallen. I'd envisioned our reunion so often: she'd see me and her eyes would light up, face aglow with fond recall, she'd hug me, take me by the hand and show me her kingdom—yet there I stood like an idiot.

She didn't remember me.

Bansabira rested a weighty hand on my shoulder, his voice rumbling in Minoan as he addressed the princess. Skeptical, Ariadne scrutinized me. Then, after a long moment, she smiled.

"Solomon?" She looked me up and down. "Why, you were just a little boy when I met you! Look at you, you're a man now!"

Heat rose to my cheeks as she returned the necklace.

"You look the same," I said. Truly, she'd not aged a day in those six years.

Surreptitiously, a woman slid to Ariadne's side, gown trailing snake-like behind her. A gold crown nested atop her head, silver hair draping her slightly sagging breasts. With icy regard, the woman measured me, weighing whether I was someone of importance or merely an insect she may need to squash—until she, too, noticed my eyes.

"How interesting," she purred in Sumerian. "I've never seen blue eyes before."

Demeanour shifting, she studied me as a cat would a mouse—like prey. Like Inanna. I shuddered despite the island's embracing warmth.

"Queen Pasiphae." Rhadamanthys bowed, kissing her hand. "Allow me to introduce you to Solomon, our new friend from Uruk."

"Welcome, Solomon," she said, offering me her hand. I kissed it as Rhadamanthys had.

Hungry patrons started to wander into the dining room, taking their seats. On cue, the servants arrived with large platters of roasted quail, buttered yam and turnips, rosemary and onion bread, braised peaches, and herbed tomatoes atop grape leaves.

"Let us sit." Pasiphae strolled to the head of the table and lowered herself into an ornate, throne-like chair.

Ariadne sat across from me. Enraptured by her beauty, I tried not to stare. Skin like dark honey, eyes of burnished amber that slanted whenever she smiled. Auburn hair, upswept, a rogue tendril caressed her bare shoulder with every turn of her head. Long, elegant neck, satin-smooth chest—soft, rounded breasts.

Shame brimmed inside. Indra's ring seemed to tighten around my finger. I forced my gaze away, to anywhere but Ariadne.

At the other end of the table was the twin to the queen's chair, empty, even after everyone had seemingly arrived. They preferred to stand or drag a spare seat to the crowded table-side rather than sit on the lap of the invisible host.

"We will speak in the Sumerian tongue tonight, in honour of our new guest," Pasiphae announced.

I bowed my head in thanks.

"Did your journey to Sumer go well?" Pasiphae addressed Rhadamanthys.

"Yes, my lady. It was pleasant. The goddess blessed us with safe passage—and a new friend, as well."

"How lovely," she said. "I should think it's beautiful there in the summer. They trade such a wealth of goods. Are they a knowledgable people, Rhadamanthys?"

"Yes, my queen," he said. "They've invented a unique form of writing that has grown widely accepted. Am I correct, Solomon?"

I flushed. "Um, yes."

"Delightful," Pasiphae said. "Perhaps you can teach us to write this language we've learned to speak, we are a people dedicated to education, you know."

"I would enjoy that," I said, thinking how pleased Father would have been that I might put his literary influence to good use. "Who is this fellow Sumerian that has taught you my language so well?"

The table fell silent.

All eyes shifted to the queen. My stomach clenched. Had I said something wrong?

'There are penalties for disrespecting any woman on the island,' Rhadamanthys' warning resounded.

Pasiphae dabbed the corners of her mouth with a napkin, a thin smile on her lips. "Well, you see…"

"Why, *me*, of course," came a voice from the doorway.

All air left the room.

Everyone stopped eating, even Duripi. Across from me, Ariadne stiffened, her gaze dropping to her lap. Rhadamanthys' expression turned to stone, fingers mottled white and red with the grip on his fork.

I looked to the mysterious source who had so visibly affected everyone.

At first glance, he appeared little more than an ordinary, middle-aged man, arms crossed, smirking as he leaned against the doorframe. On closer inspection, however, it was obvious there was *nothing* ordinary about him.

With a devilish grin, he sauntered into the room. Tousled, dark brown hair fell to his shoulders, windswept and carefree. A manicured moustache curled over his dimpled grin, triangular tuft nested beneath his bottom lip. His style was strange and exotic. Instead of a short sarong, he wore ivory harem pants and a billowing tunic. Enigmatic and arrogant, suave and sinister, his very presence devoured. I could not decide if I despised him—or wanted to be him.

Inexplicably, I had the oddest feeling I'd seen him before. But that was impossible. I'd hardly met anyone in my whole life, Father had made certain of it. This man, however, he was, for a better word—*unforgettable*.

"You started without me?" He feigned a pout, planting a kiss on the queen's cheek.

"My apologies," she said stiffly.

Normalcy slowly resumed and everyone began eating again.

The suave stranger scanned the table for an empty seat, spying me instead. Curiosity and amusement twinkled in his eyes. "And who might this be?"

"Solomon," I said, summoning a confident voice.

"This is Gillis," Pasiphae interjected. "Our…Royal Translator."

"*Solomon*…" Gillis sampled my name. "Sumerian, I surmise, since we're all speaking your tongue."

"Yes. I come from Uruk."

He chuckled as if entertaining a private joke. "Beautiful city, no?"

"I was only there a few times. I grew up on a farm outside the city."

"Ugh, pitiful way to grow up, poor lad." His nose wrinkled in disgust. "Stinking of oxen dung and squeezing hairy goat teats every morning for just a few drops of sweet cream."

With a cocky smile, Gillis swaggered to the far side of the table, took hold of the forbidden throne, dragged it noisily across the floor, and sat beside Ariadne. She flushed crimson, eyes wide with horror.

"On second thought," he said, growling into the princess's ear. "I suppose there's nothing wrong with wanting to wake up next to a pair of *soft…warm* teats, is there?"

Gillis then reached past Ariadne, deliberately grazing her nipple with his forearm as he stole a cluster of grapes from her plate. With a wicked grin, monitoring her reaction from the corner of his eye, he flicked the fleshy orb with the his tip of his tongue, suckling it like a newborn babe before he tore it from the vine with his teeth and chewed slowly, ending his crude performance with an erotic moan.

My jaw dropped open.

"Gillis, please," Pasiphae said flatly. "You're ruining my appetite."

Rhadamanthys raged crimson, his hands balled into fists. Gillis sported a cat-like sneer at the Captain's displeasure.

"Rhadamanthys, old boy." Gillis draped an arm around Ariadne's shoulder and pulled her closer. "How goes the trade routes this season?"

"As good as can be expected." Rhadamanthys glowered.

"And the Greeks?" Gillis smirked. "Have you managed to regain their favour after…that very unfortunate incident?"

Rhadamanthys struggled for composure. "You know very well we have not!"

"Hmm, I wonder what our dear King Minos would have to say about that?" Gillis twisted his moustache, eyes shining with mischief. "Where is our melancholy leader anyway? Pasiphae?"

"He is…*indisposed*." The queen's eyes narrowed dangerously. "As you well know."

"Pity," Gillis said as he toyed with a loose tendril of Ariadne's hair. "I should think he'd love to meet our new guest."

Rhadamanthys slammed his cup onto the table and everyone jumped. Then he rose and stormed from the room.

"Well…" Gillis pretended to look surprised, watching the wine swirl in his glass. "He's not in a very good mood this afternoon, is he?"

"So, Solomon," Pasiphae said through a tight smile. "What are your interests?"

"Um," I began, still reeling. "I-I enjoy cooking…"

"Cooking!" Gillis burst out laughing. "Are there no longer women in Uruk to do that for you?"

Pasiphae exhaled loudly. "Can you not behave long enough for us to enjoy at least *one*, whole meal?"

"My pardons, your majesty. I will remain as silent as the grave." Gillis shot me a mocking smirk, toasted the queen, and then tossed back his head, guzzling his wine. After throwing his empty cup onto the table, he leaned over and licked Ariadne's bare shoulder.

Through a cry of anguish, Ariadne too rose and left the room.

The Queen pinched the bridge of her nose and sighed.

After a few moments, as if nothing had happened, those who remained began to eat their meal again. With a bored exhale, Gillis propped his feet onto the table, dirty boots and all, tipped back his chair, folded his fingers over his stomach, and within seconds, was snoring like a bull.

Mouth agape, I just sat there, dumbfounded—and very confused.

After supper, I was shown to my room. A Minoan servant, Kitane, ushered me into an apartment ten times the size of my tiny hut back in Sumer. An open terrace welcomed the sound of chittering warblers and the meditative trickle of a water fountain from the courtyard below.

To my right, an alcove enshrined a bare-breasted goddess statuette, arms raised in invocation, a writhing serpent in each hand. Despite being made of clay, her eerie gaze seemed to follow me wherever I went.

"And lastly, the lavatory and bath," Kitane said. "Please ask me for anything you need."

She gave a slight bow and left.

"Hey Sumerian." Startled, I turned to see Rhadamanthys in the doorway. "How would you like to see the island?"

"Absolutely!"

As he turned to leave, I moved to the alcove and swiftly spun the offending statuette's gaze to the wall, and then followed Rhadamanthys.

"I apologize for my behaviour earlier, some people bring out the worst in me, I'm afraid," he said.

"Don't worry, I've met many an ass myself." An image of Enusat sprang to mind.

He chuckled. "Still, I shouldn't have left the dining room. You must be very lonely, so far from home, and I want you to feel welcome here."

"I had no idea I could feel so welcomed."

"What do you mean?"

I shrugged, uncertain I felt like talking about my past. My eyes had always been such a bone of contention, part of me just wanted to forget and bask in this new, indiscriminate world.

Despite my silence, Rhadamanthys intuited the reason behind my hesitation. "People fear what they do not understand—and in their fear, they do many things without their mind."

We arrived at a marble staircase, a waiting carriage at the bottom. Once aboard, a cracking whip split the air and the donkeys lurched forward. For hours, we meandered stone-paved paths, passed dozens of small villages, observing the endless glories of Crete.

"Each major city has its own palace," Rhadamanthys explained.

"Is there a king for each?"

He bristled . "No, all are...were...ruled by Minos."

"Is Minos unwell?"

"His mind is...gone."

"Who is ruling in his absence?"

Rhadamanthys hesitated, then: "His queen—Pasiphae."

I braved the question that had been haunting me since dinner. "And it's she that allows Gillis to treat women...*less than?*"

Rhadamanthys raised a surprised brow. "Yes."

"Why?"

"Some vile behaviour is, shall we say, *overlooked* when someone possesses a...priceless resource." When I looked confused, he continued, "For centuries, we were a self-sufficient people, happy, but very poor. About ten years ago, Gillis arrived on the island. He encouraged us to build bigger and stronger ships, to travel beyond the boundaries of the sea and trade with other cultures. As a result, we have become fearless and passionate sailors, and very, very prosperous—but *something* about Gillis always...sat wrong with me.

"In the beginning, he came with us to all these foreign lands. He bartered with the locals, made deals. Everywhere we went, hundreds of towns, cities, faraway lands...yet no matter where we went, no matter how distant, Gillis *always* had a connection."

"A connection?"

"A friend or comrade—a link to some underground faction or another. You see, as I've come to learn, *trust* is the ultimate commodity in the trade empire. If you're a newcomer, a stranger, you're unlikely to succeed. If Gillis has taught us anything, it's that trust is the currency on which gold is transported."

Even to me, who'd just met the man, the word *trust* and Gillis didn't jibe.

"He's given the queen great power and unfathomable wealth—which is one reason he's not punished for his behaviour. He has mastered dozens of languages...he knows their cultures, their traditions, everything about them, but Gillis only teaches us what he *wants* us to know. He's taught us enough to get by in trade, but nothing more. The rest he keeps for himself—to hold the power. He only taught us Sumerian because he said we should all be well-versed in his native tongue, that he prefers talking in his own, *superior* language. And there's more, much more. Gillis keeps many secrets—dark secrets I cannot begin to understand."

As we crested the highest hill in the valley, the palace of Knossos commanded the distant landscape—it was then that I realized something was missing.

"Knossos...it has no defences..." The great wall around Uruk, erected by King Gilgamesh, was as imperative as the city itself.

"We have maintained pleasant relations with our neighbours across the waters," Rhadamanthys explained."Our wall is the water itself. It would be near impossible for anyone to attack us without being seen. We maintain vigilant posts around the island, to warn us of any incoming ships. It's only until recently that we've had to keep a closer eye on the water. Relations between us and the Greeks have become... strained."

"Gillis?"

"Gillis dishonoured the king's daughter, and his wife, and his sister..."

His voice faded away as we rounded the next bend and I was startled to see dozens of guards, heavily armed, poised around a series of man-made ponds. Rhadamanthys signalled for the driver to stop.

"What are all of these?" We approached the shallow waters, within were thousands of wriggling, oyster-coloured shells.

"*Murex*," Rhadamanthys replied in Minoan. "Snails."

'*Porphyra*,' Bansabira's voice rumbled through my memory.

"Purple?"

He nodded. "Our most expensive trade item. Each snail only produces a tiny drop of ink, requiring over ten thousand snails for just a *daktyl*." He held up his thumb in a display of measurement. "In many regions, by law, only royalty is allowed to wear clothing dyed with purple."

"What are those holes in the shells?"

"The *murex* eat meat to survive. In this environment, they become confused and attempt to eat one another, their tongues stabbing through the backs of their neighbour."

In ominous irony, a bolt of lightning scarred the sky, followed by a growl of thunder. Raindrops splashed onto the surface of the ponds.

"We should get back, I think," Rhadamanthys said.

We climbed into the wagon and ambled away. With a glance back, at the cannibalistic molluscs, I couldn't help but shudder as an icy finger trailed down my spine.

17

The Snake Pit

*F*amiliar ghosts haunted my dreams.

Trapped in some dark, subterranean hell, inhuman versions of Father and Indra stalked me from the shadows, their eyes glowing violet. No matter where I ran, no matter how fast or how far, they caught up with me, never letting me go.

I awoke with a start, forgetting for a moment where I was. Morning spilled into my room like a golden wave, tides of warmth washing over me. Kitane, never a moment late, entered with fresh folded towels and a radiant smile.

"The tub has been filled for you," she said. "Then your language tutor will meet you in the courtyard for your lessons."

"Lessons?"

"The queen thought you might enjoy learning to speak Minoan."

I tried to hide my disdain, surmising she referred to Gillis.

After my first bath in a tub, iridescent with jasmine oil and drifting orchid petals, I dressed and made my way to the courtyard. Apprehensive at being alone with the crass Royal Translator, nerves twisted in my stomach as I descended a winding, switchback staircase, down and around a scarlet pillar, its base plunging into darkness below.

The courtyard was quiet save for a young couple strolling along the manicured paths, pausing every so often to steal a passionate kiss.

Indra.

Longing, deep and drowning, swelled inside my chest. Vivid images of her face, her smile, her scent, haunted me. Tears burned my eyes. She would've loved it here. Far from her dark past.

I turned to leave, not knowing where I was going, but I couldn't deal with Gillis and his smug smile today. I stormed the path, past the love-struck couple, past a trickling fountain and a stone bench where a lone figure sat beneath a canopy of palms.

"Solomon?"

I spun about. Seated on the bench was Ariadne, her lovely face shadowed with concern. I rushed to her side, clutching her hand like a lost child found.

"I'm...so happy to see you." I really was, especially considering it was Gillis I'd expected to find. "Just out for a walk?"

"No, didn't Kitane tell you?" Her amber eyes studied me. "I'll be your language tutor."

I brightened.

Ariadne fixed a serious expression. "Let's begin with something easy —like numbers."

A series of beautiful words spilled from her mouth, silken, full of rolling syllables and succinct articulation. As I echoed her, but my words sounded garbled, messy, as if my mouth was full of dirt. Ever graceful, Ariadne kept a straight face while I fumbled, never wincing as I butchered her native tongue.

"I'll never get it." Frustrated, I stood and paced before the stone bench.

Rising, Ariadne placed a gentle hand on my arm.

"Solomon, these things take time. One day, you'll suddenly begin to hear our words—and understand them, I promise. It's like magic. I felt the same when I began learning Sumerian. My tongue couldn't wrap itself around all those strange sounds." She lowered her chin. "At least your teacher does not laugh at you when you get it wrong."

"Gillis *laughed* at you?"

She forced a dignified smile. "His way is just different than ours, I suppose."

"In Sumer, we call that being an ass."

Our teaching lesson concluded for the day, we embarked on a slow stroll through the garden.

"If I may inquire," she asked, "why did you leave Sumer?"

"It was…not my home anymore."

"Why not?"

I exhaled deeply, contemplating how much to divulge. Part of me desired to tell her everything, exposing Inanna for the evil deity she truly was. The other half begged me to suppress the horror and pain.

"I'm sorry," Ariadne said, flustered by my hesitance.

"No, no. I…I should talk about it. It's just so…unbelievable."

She touched my hand. "You can trust me to believe you."

I almost laughed. My story was so absurd, so awful and fantastical. How could I tell her a goddess ripped my father in half, cursed me with immortality, and incinerated my wife—and expect her to see me in the same light?

"My father…" I started, but stopped short. "I can't. Not yet."

"I understand. More than you know. My father, too, is…gone."

"The King?" I thought back to the first night I arrived, to the empty throne at the dinner table. "Is he…dead?"

"No, but he's very ill. He…hasn't been himself for a long time."

She shuddered, as if a sudden chill had taken hold. I wrapped my arms around her, drawing her to my chest. Innocent consolation swiftly melted away, replaced by something deeper.

Her lips parted, I leaned in…

"Well, aren't we cozy?" came a snarky voice.

The spell broken, we turned our heads.

Gillis.

Ariadne wriggled free from my arms. Eyes cold, she drew herself up into the royalty she was. "Gillis, was there something you wanted?"

137

"Well, you know what I *always* want…," he said, leering at her bare breasts. "But actually, I've come to steal our new guest."

"Me?" Dread filled my veins.

"Come now, it'll be fun." He linked an arm through mine and compelled me down the path, leaving a distraught Ariadne behind.

"Where are you taking me?"

Gillis chuckled darkly. "You'll see."

Like a pouting child, I trailed behind Gillis, nervous of where he was leading me. He nattered non-stop, pointing out locations where he claimed to have performed some heroic feat or bedded a grateful maiden.

"So, young Sumerian," Gillis twisted his moustache over a sly smirk, "what brings you so far from home?"

"I wanted to see more of the world." I shrugged, unwilling to fully engage with this scoundrel.

"Uruk was not to your liking, then?"

"Not entirely." I challenged his gaze.

His swarthy eyes twinkled with amusement. Everything and everyone was but a game to him.

"How long do you plan on staying in Crete?"

"I hadn't really thought about it. As long as they will allow, I suppose."

"Or as long as you remain in their good graces," he said smugly.

"What does that mean?"

"Nothing, nothing…" He clapped me on the back. "Ahh, here we are!"

A decrepit archway loomed before me. "What is this place?"

Gillis draped an arm around my shoulders and pulled me closer, his breath sour with beer. "My second home."

Releasing me, he strolled through the sinister passage and down a set of stairs, dissolving into the darkness. I followed, irritated by my curiosity. At the bottom of the staircase, a fuggy cloud lingered, thick and sweet.

"Where are we going?"

Amid the blackness, Gillis chuckled. "*Trust me.*"

Those two words from him sent a chill up my spine.

Raucous laughter, music, and erotic moans seeped from beyond a crimson curtain, a veil that hid some clandestine realm on the other side. A blueish miasma slithered ghost-like between the seams and twisted around my senses.

"Ready?" Gillis asked, his shadowed eyes two holes of darkness.

"For what?"

"You wanted to see more of the world." He drew back the curtain. "Here it is…"

With a wicked grin, Gillis ushered me through the narrow doorway and into the den. Ambrosial mist slipped over my skin. Each time I inhaled, my thoughts grew hazier, looser, a pleasant vibration hummed throughout my body. Before me, interspersed about the room, were dozens of women—*naked* women, many massaging each other with oil.

138

In a dark corner, a veritable nest of bodies writhed against one another, emitting moans of pleasure and pain.

"Why did you bring me here?" I asked Gillis, my voice sounded hollow to my ears.

"This is, shall we say, my paradise," he said, fondling a passing servant girl's breast.

In the centre of the room, men and women lounged upon a ring of scarlet pillows. Before them sat a contraption with multiple tubes extending from a central steaming vase, a small fire blazing underneath. Patrons took languorous drags from the pipes, smoke pouring dragon-like from their noses.

"What is that?" The words felt slow on my tongue.

"It's the smoke of the poppy," Gillis said, sidling next to a busty young woman on the cushions, her eyes glazed and half-lidded. Stranger or not to him, I didn't know, but she started stroking him between his legs. Through an erotic groan, he waved for me to join them.

I scowled and shook my head, mostly to clear it. I couldn't think. I could only feel—and I wanted more.

"Solomon," Gillis's speech echoed, disjointed. "Come on!"

The room tilted, blurred, my senses swimming. Laughter pealed as I stumbled and fell, landing on the bed of pillows. Lethargic, I struggled to roll onto my back, eyes unable to focus.

Through drugged, hooded eyes, I saw three girls saunter towards me. Hips swaying, bare breasts jiggling, each wore an expression of seduction. Hands, warm and soft, removed my clothes. One wet my nipples while another licked my neck, anonymous fingertips traced the tattoo on my chest. I moaned, wanting more. I closed my eyes, surrendering to the pleasure, forgetting the pain. The smoke thickened, churning, swirling, dancing…

One of the girls mounted me, sliding her sex against my stomach.

Through the euphoric daze, a faint memory whispered.

A warning.

"…never, ever shall you lay with them—lest you pay the price."

My eyes flew open.

Arched back, exposing her bronze throat, the girl straddling me reached down to guide my sex into hers. I opened my mouth to protest, but she swung her head up and was no longer a stranger—*it was Indra.*

Only, it was Indra the moment she died.

Her skin, cracked like a fractured vase, seeped thick, blackened blood from gaping lesions. Eyes bulging, her tongue rolled out of her mouth as she laughed and gyrated, groaning.

"Solomon," the inhuman effigy of my love hissed, crimson foam oozing down her chin. *"Don't you miss me, my love?"*

"No!" I screamed and shoved the girl away.

Chest heaving, I stood, ready to run. As I looked back, however, Indra was gone. In her place was a very offended girl.

Gillis laughed. "Relax, friend. She just wants to…"

"I can't—I just…can't."

I snatched up my tunic and bolted out the door. Heart racing, I ran as if unseen monsters stalked me from the dark corners. What had I just seen? Was it just a hallucination, induced by the drug-laden smoke? Or had it been real—a warning of things to come should I attempt to disobey Inanna?

Finally, fresh air filled my lungs, clearing my thoughts.

"What happened down there?" Gillis was suddenly beside me, smirking. "She only wanted a bit of fun."

"That's not my idea of fun!"

He seemed genuinely surprised. "Hmm, well, we shall have to try harder to find you a hobby, won't we?"

"Don't bother," I said coldly, storming away.

18

Feast For the Beast

*B*ang.
Distant, tinny.

Bang. Bang. Bang.

I sat up, rubbed my eyes awake. Darkness still shrouded my room, though glimmers of coral fringed the horizon.

Bang.

Curiosity seducing, I ventured into the hallway, tracking the peculiar noise down an empty corridor. The incessant pounding led me to a stairwell, down which appeared to be the basement of the palace. At the base of the stairs, I peered around the corner. A thin, balding man sat hunched over a table, working feverishly, strange tools scattered before him. His face only inches from the worktop, he concentrated on an array of metallic discs stacked atop one another, secured at the centre with a pin.

The man suddenly exploded, taking hold of a hammer and smashing the stone table.

"*Kopra!*" he yelled.

I jumped back, disturbing a bucket of water in the corner. The man glanced up. A bizarre contraption was adhered to his face, spherical orbs filled with water covering each eye. Magnified, his blinking lashes were as large as his ears.

"I-I'm sorry. I didn't mean to bother you...I heard a banging noise and..."

"You must be the Sumerian everyone is talking about," he muttered, unimpressed, returning to his project. "Come here, I need your finger."

"M-My finger?"

"Hold this down."

He indicated a tiny, bronze disc with a hole drilled off-centre. I complied, watching as he extracted a pair of pinchers from his pouch and meticulously plucked a metal pin from a bowl and set it into the notch. Then, cradling the entire piece, he flipped it over and melted the pin's point flat with a heated rod he'd drawn from the hearth.

"There!" He threw his arms into the air. "It's finally finished! Let's go see if it works!"

"What is it?" I asked, but the little man ignored me, racing out of the room. Intrigued, I followed him up a set of steps and out onto a large balcony.

"*Ouska*," he said to a couple of stargazers, shooing them aside. "*Ouska.*"

He set the mechanism onto the railing and began rotating the various gears and wheels. Every disc had precisely measured notches carved along the circumference. Owlish eyes fierce with concentration, the little man glanced up at the moon, calculated, and then down at the machine, adjusting each gear a millimetre at a time. He repeated this over and over until, finally, he exhaled and smiled.

"Daedalus," he said, pulling off his goggles to reveal a fairly normal-looking individual, despite the haphazard wisps of white hair standing on end.

"Daedalus?" I regarded the invention. "Is that what this is called?"

"No, that is *my* name. Daedalus. This is an *asturlab*." He gazed lovingly at the machine.

"Oh, my name is…"

"Solomon. I know, you're the talk of the palace. The blue-eyed man from Sumer." He rolled his eyes.

I didn't know whether to feel flattered or self-conscious.

Daedalus turned back to his invention. "It measures the moon's phases and the positions of celestial bodies."

He sighed when I looked confused.

Daedalus pointed to the slivered moon. "It's in the waning phase. During the day, I'll track the sun and its movement across the heavens. And now that I have this, I'll be able to measure the speed in which the sky moves around us."

"Then what?"

Daedalus huffed. "And then we can begin to chart the procession of the gods as they move through the sky. Each god is allowed a time to rule over the people." Daedalus pointed to a bright star on the horizon. "See that, it's home to the Snake Goddess. When it's in alignment with the centre of the sky, we will know the exact day to celebrate her time in the heavens."

"When will that be?"

Lips pursed, he raised his invention to the dark sky and fiddled with the metal wheels. After a few moments, he said, "By my calculations, it will be crossing the sun in…eight plus one hundred and five plus eight and one hundred and twenty-one…" he muttered, eyes closed in concentration. "On the three hundred and twenty-second day of this year…in exactly three months and four days."

I gaped at his precision.

"It's imperative we offer our sacrifices to her on the correct day, at the correct moment, or else…"

"Or else?"

He regarded me with fearful eyes. "We will be punished."

Later that morning, I decided to find Queen Pasiphae and ask her about staying in Crete permanently, but only if I could somehow contribute to their community. Perhaps they'd allow me to cook for them, as Rhadamanthys had on the boat.

"Good morning, Solomon." Kitane entered carrying a covered platter. "I've brought you some breakfast. Did you sleep well?"

"Mostly, yes," I said, adding, "though I was up even before the sun."

"Whatever for?"

"I heard a strange banging noise and decided to check it out."

She sighed, eyes rolling skyward. "Daedalus?"

I nodded, chuckling.

"That man," she said crossly. "He knows he's not supposed to…"

"No, no, it's all right. He is very…interesting."

Kitane pursed her lips and set the platter on my lap. "Anyhow, do enjoy your day, Solomon."

I lifted the lid, unveiling a veritable work of art rather than food. Thinly-sliced papaya furled into a coral rosebuds, bedded beside lily-like watermelon petals with a tender starfruit centre. Pats of melting butter topped fresh almond bread, next to several thick slices of smoked meat.

Perhaps they do not need a cook, I thought, deflated.

After begrudgingly enjoying breakfast, I ventured down the main hall, past a corridor where ornate frescos adorned every visible surface. In its own alcove, revered atop a great podium, sat the ivory bust of a bull's head.

"Lovely, isn't he?"

Startled, I turned to see Queen Pasiphae strolling towards me, a seductive prowess in her step. Though not as pert as Ariadne's, her exposed breasts were embellished with purple tassels and tiny metal trinkets, which jingled alongside every move. Realizing my rudeness, I relocated my gaze, fixing it onto her lips.

"The craftsmanship is amazing," I said.

She moved to my side. "Are you enjoying your time here?"

"Immensely," I said, suddenly remembering my mission. "Actually, I was just coming to find you. I wanted to ask you a question."

She slipped her arm through mine, purring, "Let's walk while we discuss whatever it is you desire, hmm?"

"I was wondering if I may have your permission to stay on Crete… but only if I can earn my keep somehow."

"But of course you may stay!" Pasiphae's lips curled into a cat-like smile. "In fact, I *insist*."

"Thank you. I thought perhaps I could be of service to the kitchen. I cooked for my father, not a great variety though, but I'd be more than willing to learn…"

"Actually, I know a much better way you can…*be of service*," she broke in, her voice husky as she ran a meandering fingernail down my arm.

Shocked, forgetting protocol, I regarded her eye to eye. Had I misunderstood her? Being that I'd grown up in a womanless environment my entire life, deprived of social etiquette, I considered perhaps I was merely too naive to understand her meaning—but she quickly made her motive clear.

"Those eyes…" she closed the space between us, her body heat mingling with mine, "I've not seen anything like them in all my years…I'd very much enjoy having you as my *secret* lover."

Heat burned my face. While the queen was a very beautiful woman, I simply couldn't entertain the idea of surrendering myself to her as a mere playmate. Whether it was devotion to Indra or the deadly curse I might inflict upon her—I couldn't comply.

"*…there are penalties for disrespecting any woman on the island,*" Rhadamanthys' warning echoed over my thrumming heart.

I peeled her questing hands off my chest, "I appreciate the offer, but I simply cannot…"

Pasiphae's face twisted. "How *dare* you…"

"There you are!" Ariadne's voice sounded and Pasiphae immediately stepped away. "Solomon, you're late for your language lesson." Ariadne took hold of my arm, shooting a cold eye in her mother's direction. "I heard from the servants that Father had a fall last night. Have you seen him yet this morning?"

Pasiphae's expression turned to stone. "I was just on my way to check on him."

After a curt nod to her daughter and a glower at me, Pasiphae turned on her heel and strode away.

"I apologize," Ariadne said with eyes sad. "Like my father, she too has not been herself for…quite some time. How was your visit with Gillis yesterday?" she asked, changing the subject.

"Awful, as I'm sure you can imagine."

"Oh Solomon, I'm so sorry! I shouldn't have let you go with him. Where did he take you?"

I shrugged, ashamed. "It was…just some lounge, I think. I didn't stay long."

"Lounge?"

"A place with beer and lots of smoke and…women."

Her eyes grew round with shock—then narrowed with fury. "H-He took you to a…a *brothel*!"

"I left right away, I promise."

She regarded me with shy, hopeful eyes. "You did not…"

"No, never!"

As if remembering herself, she spoke with an air of indifference. "I am glad you saw fit to leave those women be. They're not in their right mind. They've been…influenced. It's unkind to take advantage of them in such a state."

"Influenced? You mean by that smoke?"

"That and the courtesans are ruled by our most powerful goddess. She requires these women, preferably virgins, to offer themselves to the men for money."

I paled, knowing too well the reputation of the Cult of the Courtesan, though I had no idea it had reached beyond the borders of Sumer.

Nausea spun inside my stomach. "W-Which goddess?"

Could it really be *her*?

"She has no name, really, we call her the Snake Goddess," Ariadne said. "Solomon, are you okay? You're trembling…"

I cradled my head in my hands. "I-I woke up too early this morning…I should go rest."

Shaking, I left, leaving a perplexed Ariadne behind.

"We call her the Snake Goddess," Ariadne's words ricocheted inside my head beside images of Inanna as she summoned the magical serpent, ordering it to enter my chest.

How can she be here, in Crete, when she's supposed to be imprisoned beneath the temple in Sumer?

Curled up in my bed all afternoon and into the night, I tossed and turned.

I was so stupid to think Inanna could not be wherever she wanted, whenever she wanted. She was a goddess, an all-powerful being, an immortal creature I didn't understand. All my life, I believed in the gods, worshipped them, gave them offerings and prayer, but I didn't comprehend what that truly meant. What gullible, feeble-minded beings we were with our petty problems, begging these unseen mythological mentors for mercy. What did we really know about these *gods*, those whom we'd entrusted our entire lives to? I thought of my people and their endless devotions to the deities, their utter reliance on them to bless their crops, heal their sick, mend their souls—all of it, a lie.

It was unfair; cruel, even, how the gods treated the humans. We were but slaves to them, diminutive creatures, perpetually unworthy.

Angry, I stormed out onto the balcony. The fresh, night air filled my lungs and cleared my head. Leant against the rail, I suddenly heard the soft, swift pattering of bare feet across the courtyard below. Past midnight, I was curious as to who'd be out at such an hour.

Clad head to toe in black with only a slit for vision, utterly silent, a thin figure crept between a pair of waning pyres. Lithe and graceful, it ran straight for the palace wall, and then, in an amazing feat, leapt and gained a foothold on a narrow window ledge. Up the side of the building, it crawled like a spider, hand over hand, purchase perfect as it climbed, scaling the impossible. Then, it vanished into the gaping darkness of an open balcony.

I raced out into the hall, heading the direction I'd seen the figure enter. Eyes narrowed, desperate to penetrate the darkness, I was all but blind without a torch. Pressed against a wall, I stopped to listen for any whisper of footfalls.

A confusion of hallways and stairwells, I navigated the pitch-black palace, praying I wouldn't take a wrong turn, thus plunging to my death down an airshaft. Fingertips outstretched, I quested down an unfamiliar hall, pausing every few steps to listen for movement. As I rounded one corner, I jumped back, startled. The ghostly statue of a smirking nymph gleamed from an alcove, stark-white skin luminous by moonlight. Over her shoulder, however, at the end of a long hallway, a faint glow reached from beyond a sealed doorway. I crept closer. As I neared, muted voices emanated from within, placative murmurs over quiet sobs. A man whimpered, a woman soothed, her whispered words incoherent.

I peered through a wide seam in the door frame. An elderly man sat hunched on the edge of a bed, clad in a long nightgown and a purple robe, long grey beard trailing over his rounded stomach. Knelt before him, a cajoling hand on his knee, was the figure in black! Closer now, I could see the gentle curve of hips and breasts beneath the snug suit, revealing her as a woman.

"It's my fault!" the man yelled, arms flailing, his mewls escalating to wails. "All my fault…mine…what are we going to do? There's no way to stop it now…they will die…all of them…"

The woman hushed him, her voice a soft susurration. Urging him to lie back, she drew up a blanket, muttering in motherly undertones. The old man's chest wracked with sorrow, endless tears spilling. She waited until he'd quieted, then snuffed the candlelight beside his bed before stealing out the open balcony, and vanishing into the night.

My mind spinning, I stood there in the darkness a very long time before making my way back to my room. I didn't bother trying to sleep after that.

The next morning, Kitane poked her head into my room.

"Captain Rhadamanthys has requested your presence in the Great Hall."

I rose and made my way downstairs. Servants bustled up and down the hallways, large baskets of fruit and vegetables balanced on their heads; others transported heavy vessels of wine and beer towards the kitchen. Streamers of hand-strung lilies and lotus draped every window, crimson carpets unfurled before every entrance.

At the far corner of a quiet patio, in the shade of a blossoming almond tree, I found Rhadamanthys nursing a mug of morning ale. His face broke into a warm grin when he spotted me.

"What's going on?" I asked, settling into a chair beside him. "I've never seen the servants so busy."

"There is to be a Bull Leaping event. It's a revered sport here in Crete—we take it quite seriously."

"Wonderful!" I said, recalling the ornate fresco of three acrobats performing on the back of a huge bull. "When is it?"

"Tomorrow evening." He smiled. "I've asked you here on another matter, however. I was wondering if you'd like to accompany me on a delivery to Akrotiri?"

"I'd love to—but will we be back in time for the Bull Leaping event?"

"Yes, we'll return in plenty of time," Rhadamanthys said, rising. "I'll meet you at the port in two hours. I have few things to finish up before we set sail."

Almost two hours later, I embarked on the lush, treed path leading to the port. Amid the fronds, lorikeets squawked and flitted, occasionally rendering me a flash of rainbow wings. Fascinated by these colourful creatures—like the monkey, not a common sight in the desert—I paused to steal a closer look. One darted out from his leafy refuge and perched. Soft blue feathers, smoothed back from his coral beak, blended into bright wings of jade. Slowly, I reached out, in the hopes I might persuade him to alight upon my finger. While wary, the little parrot seemed to consider my proposition. I took a cautious step forward, and another…

"And where are you off to this fine morning, young Sumerian?" a voice called out. The bird shrilled in alarm, vanishing in a flurry of vibrance.

Perturbed, I spun about to find Gillis, leant casually against a palm tree, tossing and catching a pear, with that infuriating smirk on his lips.

Still angry with him for taking me to a drug-infested brothel, I breezed past him. "Rhadamanthys asked me to join him on a delivery to Akrotiri."

"Hmm, that's strange..." Gillis feigned a look of concern before taking a juicy bite from the pear.

Curiosity got the better of me. I stopped and glared at him. "Why would that be strange?"

"You almost have to wonder if our dear Captain was, perhaps, ordered to...keep you busy. You know—*out of the way*."

Doubt clawed my insides. "W-Why would anyone want me out of the way?"

"Well," Gillis elaborated with a twist of his moustache, "a certain princess has taken notice of you. One might even say she's *smitten* with you. I fear, however, that her blossoming affections are not approved by some..."

"I would think that is none of your business!" I stormed away. I didn't ask whom he referred to, though I was fairly certain it was the Queen.

Not surprisingly, Gillis sauntered after me.

"Nothing is ever my business—so I'm often told," he said with a laugh, flinging the half-eaten pear into a manicured bush.

"Maybe you should learn to listen then," I snarled.

I tried to walk faster but he kept up pace.

"So, does that mean you have certain feelings for Ariadne as well?"

I ground to a stop, facing him. "What the hell difference does it make to you if I do?"

"It means very little to me," he said around an indifferent shrug. "I mean, I've already had a taste of Ariadne's sweets, and while delicious, I would recommend that is all you do, my friend. Take a sample, a lick if you like...then move on. There's fruit aplenty in this place—a veritable feast for the beast, if you catch my meaning." Brows waggling, he grabbed his crotch and gave it an indecent tug.

Shocked, I could only gape at his vileness.

"How can you speak of her that way? Of any woman!" Before he could answer, I pointed a sharp finger at his face. "And I am not your friend. *Ever!*"

"You're a fighter, you are. I like that. We'll get along just fine, I think." He then took a firm hold of my arm, and for once, he looked serious. "Heed my warning, fellow Sumerian, the Princess is not for you. Pluck another cherry—some fruits leave a bitter taste upon your tongue."

I yanked my arm away and continued down the path.

"You're in paradise, young Sumerian!" he hollered after me. "Suckle the juices of the garden, but be wary the worms burrowed within the flesh! She's not what she seems—*none of them are!*"

Akrotiri, on the island of Thera, was home to a massive volcanic mountain. A silent sentinel, watchful without eyes. Long, sloping sides, blackened earth beneath jade-green foliage, life seemed to thrive alongside the promise of death. I gazed up at the tower, its peak lost amid gathering clouds—so like the mountains in my bedtime story.

"The mountains wear snow on their heads—like the white hair of old men!"

Father's voice, his warm laughter, touched the scar upon my heart, flooding me with bittersweet memories. I'd not forgotten his words, nor his earthy scent of wet clay and reedy smoke. I'd not forgotten him—I knew, because I'd tried.

When I could not forget he was gone, I tried to pretend he was still alive. That I'd simply run away from Sumer, escaped the farm in search of a new life in an exotic land across the ocean. I forced myself to believe he was still there, still at the table in our little hut, shaping goddess statuettes with patient hands, awaiting my return.

As we neared the port of Akrotiri, I regarded the mighty mountain with its wide, open mouth to the sky, as if to capture the rains, to soothe her heated body from the inside out.

Beside me, Rhadamanthys followed my gaze.

"The volcano often blows smoke, but it hasn't exploded in my lifetime—though there was a terrible earthquake a few years before I was born," he said, darkness kindling in his eyes. "The elders have warned of its angry past, however. That the goddess who watches over it is not easily appeased. She gives warnings though, with smoke and falling ash. She has always graced us with time to seek shelter."

"How do you appease the goddess?" I asked, swallowing hard, knowing too well how fickle an almighty being could be.

Rhadamanthys rubbed the back of his neck. "All deities have their… preferred offerings, no? Poseidon, the God of the Sea, requires the sacrifice of our sacred bull each winter season, to tame the whims of the waters and keep the sailors safe. The Thunder God, Zeus, asks for offerings of our finest animals, in exchange for the prosperity of our crops. The Snake Goddess, however, has a rather…*unique* request," he said carefully.

"Unique?"

Before Rhadamanthys could elaborate, Bansabira tossed me the end of a thick rope.

"Tie to port," he ordered with a grin.

As soon as the ship was secure, dock workers rushed forth and aided us to lower the ramp. They then began the arduous task of unloading the ship.

"It'll take them several hours," Rhadamanthys said. "Let us rest awhile."

Four young women appeared carrying baskets of food and pitchers of beer. In the shade of an elder willow, they arranged a picnic area for us to enjoy. We sat on the soft grass and started eating. I bit into a fig, nectarous juices spilling from my lips. While delicious, the fruit reminded me of Gillis—and his vile accusations.

"I ran into Gillis as I left the palace this morning," I said, wiping my chin.

"How *very* unfortunate for you." Rhadamanthys offered me an expression of sincere sympathy.

I laughed. "Yes, but something he said bothers me."

"Not surprising, everything he says bothers me."

"He said I should stay away from Ariadne." My cheeks burned. "He said she's…smitten with me and if I returned her feelings…it wouldn't be appreciated by some."

Rhadamanthys exhaled and set down his mug of ale. "While I utterly disdain to be in agreement with Gillis…he's right."

"About…her feelings for me?" My stomach did a flip. While my love for Indra would never die, I felt the stirrings of desire, the potential for happiness again—with Ariadne.

"That, yes," he said, regarding me with serious eyes. "But more importantly, that you shouldn't pursue those interests with her."

"Why?" I bowed my head, spirits dampened.

'You shall not love another woman so long as you live,' Inanna's venomous words echoed and I shuddered. Indra's face, her screams, her body turning to ash, I wouldn't allow that to happen again, not to anyone else—especially Ariadne. I gave my head a shake, burying the images. Inanna couldn't have meant *all* women, *forever*, could she?

"She may have feelings for you, yes, and you for her…" Rhadamanthys gazed out over the restless ocean. "But Ariadne is not at liberty to choose who she desires."

"Not at liberty? She's the Princess—she should be allowed to choose anyone she wants!"

Expression mirroring my own misery, Rhadamanthys raised his hands in placation. "I understand, believe me. But you and I have no say in this matter—and, unfortunately, neither does she."

Upon return to Knossos, with a floundering sun balanced on the horizon, I wandered the labyrinthine palace. I considered the long forever that awaited me, the centuries of solitude immortality intended for me to suffer. Humanity would live and die, civilizations would rise and fall, be perpetually reborn—but I was to remain the same. Anyone I grew to care for would age and ail, then die before my eyes. I would hold their fragile, mortal bodies in my arms, watching the light fade from their eyes. Through the death of others, I would grieve for Father and Indra over and over again.

Until the sun dies…

Depression stalked my psyche. Just as I'd discovered potential happiness once again, it was torn away, held at arm's length. I marvelled at the cruel and ingenious design of Inanna's curse. So tailored to my fears, she couldn't have devised a worser Hell for me. So perfect, in fact, I wondered if she'd done this before…

Now fully dark outside, I found the hallways brightly lit by chandeliers. Their amber glow sought to penetrate anywhere darkness could cower. Minoans loved the night as much as the day. Laughter and conversation echoed, both inside the palace and out on the patios, beneath arbors overtaken by fuchsia bougainvilleas. I stood out on a balcony, panning the courtyard. Women socialized, warmed by fire bowls atop ivory pillars; men lounged, smoking tobacco from clay pipes. I searched for a familiar voice or an interesting discussion to join, but everyone was speaking in Minoan and, while I recognized a few words, it was still too foreign a tongue for my ears.

Despite the reunion with Ariadne and Bansabira, and having made a new friend in Rhadamanthys, I still felt terribly lost and alone.

"There you are!" a voice said behind me.

I spun around to find Ariadne and a mess of emotions slammed into me. Anger at Gillis' warning, bewilderment with Rhadamanthys' disclosure, love for Indra—everything knotted in a tangle of confusion.

"Are you okay?" Seeing my face, worry pulled at her brow.

"I'm not sure…" I drew a long breath, wondering how to broach the topic of our *possible* mutual attraction. With disregard to Minoan tradition, I stared into her eyes. "I was told that certain people are conspiring to…keep us apart."

Ariadne's gaze slid away. "Oh?"

"Is there a valid reason for such…action?"

She lifted a regal chin, elegant neck bronzed by torchlight. I could almost see the pulse quicken at her throat. My own heart pounded, praying she felt the same for me as I did for her.

Finally, through thinned lips, she uttered, "Perhaps."

"Perhaps?" I teased, taking a step closer.

Cheeks pinking, Ariadne surrendered a soft laugh.

Unable to control myself, I reached for her, tracing her bare shoulder with my fingertips. Silenced, she trembled at my touch. I cradled her chin, guiding her lips to mine. So soft, tender and sweet. What began with shy reserve, however, soon turned to passion. Unleashed, our kisses turned aggressive, desperate. *Hungry.*

"Solomon," Ariadne whispered, pushing me away. "Stop, we can't… I'm…"

With a pained growl, a starved wolf dragged from a fresh kill, I forced myself to take a step back—but she stopped me.

Ariadne's lovely face appeared tortured by indecision, warring between passion and duty. Then, a twinkle of rebellion glinted in her eyes.

"Not here…" She put a long finger to her lips, scanning the hall before taking my hand into hers. "Come."

Her long skirts whispered as she led me through winding hallways, down dark corridors, until we came to a deserted staircase.

"Down here," she said.

With every step, the balmy island air was slowly vanquished, growing cooler, stone walls moldering with lichen. Darkness gaped like the yawning maw of a giant beast. While slightly less romantic, I didn't care—as long as I was with Ariadne.

Guilt pierced my heart. Was I being unfaithful to Indra? It had not been long since I'd lost her, yet here I was, with another woman—and falling for her. Did that make me a terrible person? To fall in love so soon? Just weeks before, on Rhadamanthys's ship, I would've proclaimed I could never have loved again; that my heart was broken and the pieces, fragmented as they were, would forever belong to Indra.

Yet here I was…

"Where are we going?" my voice echoed off the damp walls.

"Trust me." Ariadne glanced back, amber eyes playful, full of light and adventure. I cast my doubts aside, choosing to live, albeit selfishly, in the moment.

At the base of the cavernous stairwell, blackness pooled, drowning any details. But, as my eyes adjusted, the outline of a small wooden door came into focus.

"What's in there?" An ominous chill crept up my spine.

Ariadne's smile faltered. "Nothing, just…storage."

Eclipsed by shadow and faint light, she faced me. We stood in silent indecision for what felt like forever. As if we both understood the next move, should we dare, would alter the course of our entire lives.

After an eternity, Ariadne brought her lips to mine. Passion exploded between us, a dammed ocean broken free, crashing against the shore. My hands explored her narrow waist, her ribs, her breasts, so soft and warm. Bending, I took a single rosebud nipple into my mouth. Ariadne clutched a handful of my hair, moaning. With sudden ferocity, quite unladylike, she took hold of my collar and pressed me against the wall where she nibbled my ear and kissed my neck—hands sliding up my tunic…

Amidst the pleasure, so quietly I wasn't even certain I'd said it aloud, I uttered, "*I love you.*"

In the same moment, Ariadne cried out in pain.

Everything stopped.

"Are you okay!" I asked, fear rising. "What's wrong?"

Doubled over, she cradled her mouth, whimpering.

"Ariadne?"

Tears in her eyes, she lowered her hand from her face—and the blood froze in my veins. There, blistering on the pink of her bottom lip, was a row of angry red welts.

Burn marks.

A warning.

19

Daughters of the Labyrinth

*E*xcitement crackled in the air with the Bull Leaping event to commence in less than an hour. Servants busied themselves arranging starry-eyed sea lilies into anything that would hold them. Dark-fired *kamares* had been set out for the occasion; imaged with dolphins, furling and unfurling waves, the double-edged *labrys,* and the horned bust of the mighty aurochs. Eggshell-thin terracotta ewers sat on elegant pedestals, themed of the sea with seashells, waggling octopi, and underwater gardens.

For once, Kitane was late with my breakfast. I didn't mind though, it was pleasant to have a few moments to myself before partaking in the busy activities of the day—and to revisit the bittersweet events of the previous evening.

Still reeling from Ariadne's passionate kisses, I also recounted, incessantly, her cries of pain and the manifestation of blisters upon her lips. Burnt by my declaration of love, I could no longer ignore the repercussions should I further defy Inanna's commandments.

Rage kindled inside my chest.

Inanna…the Goddess of 'Love'.

Such poetic irony that the deity created to be the very embodiment of passion should become the nemesis of love.

Panic overshadowed anger as I fully realized the gravity of my situation.

'You will live again and again…and again, Solomon of Sumer…until the sun dies or until you surrender yourself to me—and only me.'

Inanna had not only taken my past and my present, but any hope for love in the future. Now, not only was I forbidden to make love to a woman or even kiss her, I was unable to even express, through mere words, my feelings.

Despair settled like ashes onto my soul.

If I ever wished to love again, I would have to beg Inanna to free me from this curse. But then, I would be her prisoner. A slave to her sexual perversions.

There was no escape.

Willing my dark brooding aside, I started down the hallway, determined to enjoy the celebrations.

I heard Bansabira's deep laugh long before I saw him. He and Rhadamanthys were in the Great Hall—alongside Queen Pasiphae, Ariadne, and, unfortunately, Gillis.

Ariadne's lips appeared puffy, but were otherwise concealed beneath a balm of bee's wax and rouge. Ever graceful, she blushed when she saw me, casually withdrawing from the group to greet me.

"Are you...okay?" I eyed her swollen lip.

"Oh yes, it's fine," she said with a dismissive wave, "though I still don't understand what happened..."

Gathering courage, I turned to her, ready to divulge all my secrets: Father, Indra, Miri—Inanna and the curse.

"I have something I have to tell you..." I started, "about why I left Sumer."

"I-I have something I need to tell you as well...let's go out into the hall. For privacy."

We started to leave—but Gillis stepped in front of us.

"Young Sumerian." He grinned. "How are you this morning?"

"Fine," I said, monotone. "But do you really care?"

Rhadamanthys, overhearing, chuckled through a cough.

"Not really..." Gillis smirked at my insolence, "but I attempt to be cordial when I can. It seems to be a desirable quality to those I'd *rather* be near." He sidled next to Ariadne, taking a handful of her long hair and pressed it to his nose, inhaling deeply. "Ahh, how I love the scent of a woman. So sweet, yet seductive. Although, there are other places on a woman I'd prefer to bury my face..."

Ariadne shuddered and moved closer to me. Fists curled at my side, I glowered at Gillis, yearning to make him bleed.

"Come, come now, boys." Pasiphae clapped her hands to disperse us like a group of taunting schoolchildren. "Let's head out to the arena."

"We'll talk later," Ariadne whispered.

While impatient, I nodded.

"Won't Father be joining us?" Ariadne asked her mother.

"Afterwards, for dinner," the queen said stiffly. "The event will take hours, it's simply too long for him to endure right now."

"I'm excited for you meet him," Ariadne said, leaning into me.

"I look forward to it." My curiosity for the absentee king had grown since I'd arrived over a month ago.

Arm in arm, we strolled into a grand roofless arena, approximately an acre in length. Thousands of citizens, servants and nobles alike, sat in anticipation of the coming attractions. Across the expanse, beneath an arbor of white poppies, a mammoth drawbridge sat unopened.

Thankfully, Gillis dawdled far behind, having found a couple of tittering noblewomen to fawn over him. At last glance, I saw him flick one of the women's nipples and whisper something in the other's ear, sending her into a shrill of giggles. What they could possibly find attractive in that man, I could not imagine.

"He's so awful," Ariadne whispered, noticing my hostile expression.

"Father always told me I shouldn't form ill opinions of others…but, I think even he would've made an exception in this case." I jutted my chin towards Gillis.

A soft laugh bubbled from Ariadne. "Sounds like he was a wonderful man, your father."

"Very kind and wise," I said, settling into a seat. "He would have loved your people, your culture."

"Are we so different than Sumerians?"

"My people revere wealth and status. Here, you embrace education, enlightenment, and you accept one another as you are—defects and all." My voice held a sharp edge.

"Solomon," she said, rubbing my arm. "Is this about your eyes?"

I nodded, not realizing how much being an outcast had affected me; especially now, being a part of a world that appreciated my differences.

"But, they are so beautiful." She gazed up at me.

"Thank you, I…"

"What's beautiful?" Gillis slid into the empty seat beside me, reeking of ale. "Ariadne's breasts? We all know that."

I sighed loudly. Did this man have to ruin *every* day of my new life?

"We were discussing Solomon's eyes, if you must know," Ariadne retorted before turning to answer her querying mother about the late arrival of an impending ship.

"Ahh, yes!" Gillis grinned at me. "They're quite the anomaly, aren't they? That rare shade of blue. Like lapis lazuli, they are. Would bring a goddess to her knees—and we love them on their hands and knees, don't we, friend?" He nudged me with his elbow, lowering his voice for my ears only. "Why, if one were so inclined, one might wonder if your *deformity* was quite intentional—perhaps even a *gift* from the gods."

My mouth went dry. "W-What do you mean?"

He only offered me that infuriating smile, pointing to the centre of the arena. "Look! The dancers have arrived!"

Gillis clapped, whistling as the acrobats sprinted onto the field. Amidst his cheering, however, he sent me a cocky, sideways glance that seemed to say, "Yes, boy—I know *everything*."

A loud horn sounded three times—and the crowd fell silent.

Disoriented by Gillis' unsettling allusion, I was slow to notice as a performer bounded into the arena. When I did though, I paled.

The shadow climber.

Clad head to toe in black, the elegant entertainer performed her intricate art. Graceful and lithe, she danced before a captive audience. But then, two more dancers entered onto the field, both women, both dressed in black. Confused, I glanced at Ariadne.

"Why are they dressed that way?" I asked, recalling the *taurokathapsia* fresco and the athletes in their short sarongs.

"They are the *Daughters of the Labyrinth*," she explained, voice hushed. "An elite troop of specially trained dancers."

Eyes narrowed on the distant field, I tried to discern which woman I'd witnessed scaling the walls of Knossos, but with only their feminine silhouettes to go on, I couldn't distinguish which I'd seen that night.

Another series of horns blasted.

154

The crowd of thousands drew a united breath of anticipation, all eyes turning onto the mammoth drawbridge. Slowly lowered by thick, whining ropes, the door opened to reveal a cavernous entrance.

At first, nothing emerged. Then, a deep grunt echoed throughout the arena. An aurochs, bigger than any bull I'd ever seen, stepped out from the shadows. Tapered horns, nearly three feet in length, protruded from the beast's mighty head. Eyes wide with irritation, the bull snorted in warning.

Still as statues, in a staggered formation, the dancers stood with their back to the aurochs. Confused, the bull lowered his huge head, maneuvering his sharp horns from side to side, pawing the ground with his hoof, as if deciding which of the women to gore first.

Heart racing, I watched in breathless suspense for the next move.

In perfect unison, the three women took a step away from one other, and another—and then broke into a run, dispersing into three opposite directions. The bull, confused, wrenched his head to and fro, trying to track each of the runners. Finally, with an infuriated roar, his sites locked onto the centre figure and he charged. Impossibly fast for such a large animal, he raced after her, quickly closing the space between them. Instead of darting for safety, the woman slowed—then halted—and dropped into a crouch.

Furious, the bull bellowed.

"No!" I cried out, unable to contain my panic. "Run!"

Ariadne set a patient hand on my arm. "Shh, just watch…"

Meanwhile, the other two dancers had circled back, sprinting towards the bull. Though they ran ever so fast—they weren't going to make it in time to redirect him. I gripped Ariadne's hand, wishing I could look away, but was compelled to watch.

Head down, motionless, her back to the encroaching beast, the crouched dancer waited. She didn't realize her companions weren't close enough to save her! Dust clouds billowed behind the stampeding bull, mere feet from his target as he lowered his needle-sharp horns, tilting his head to one side, intent on impaling the unsuspecting girl.

Mouth dry, I gaped in horror.

Visions of the woman's mangled body haunted my imagination, gored and skewered. I wanted to look away—but couldn't.

In the very last second, the dancer sprang into the air, arching into a backwards dive. Taking hold of the bull's horns, she propelled herself over his head and, after a full spin in mid-air, landed perfectly poised atop his back.

I exhaled, trembling.

Gillis chuckled. "Had you fooled, didn't she?"

Too shocked to even acknowledge his taunting, I cheered, joining the thunderous applause around me. Down on the field, the dancers took turns leaping on and off the bull's back. Alike the fresco, two were always on the ground, circling the beast, biding for his attention to keep the one on his back safe as she performed her various balletic displays.

Now, it was abundantly clear how the shadow climber managed such an impossible feat as scaling the walls of the palace. With the graceful, almost preternatural, maneuvers being performed on the bull's back, there was no question that one of the women was the shadow climber

—but which one? And why was she sneaking into Knossos in the middle of night?

Later, at dinner, the room was abuzz with excitement as we discussed the Bull Leaping Event, the *Daughters of the Labyrinth* being the highlight of the day.

"I just can't get over how amazing they were!" I gushed to Rhadamanthys. "Who are they?"

He regarded me with an odd expression, and then in retrospect, said, "Ah, I forget you are a foreigner. We've been surrounded with such traditions for so long...they are Minos' elder daughters, Acalle, Xenodice, and Phaedra. They live in various palaces in the kingdom and occasionally travel here to perform for us. In fact," he glanced around the table, "I am surprised they've not joined us for dinner..."

"Isn't it too dangerous a sport for royalty and...women?" I asked.

Rhadamanthys flashed me a look of warning. "Minoan women are just as capable as any man, if not more so in the realm of acrobatic artistry. They are often more limber and able to contort into positions that men cannot..."

"Thank the gods for *that!*" From across the table, Gillis toasted his empty mug of ale, glazed eyes searching for a server to refill it.

Beside me, Rhadamanthys raged crimson. Initially, I too was livid, but my anger swiftly tempered to curiosity as I noticed something was different about Gillis. Although drunk and in dire need of a bath, he didn't look right. Earlier that day, at the arena, he'd been his handsome, suave, and irritating self: dark skin radiant, eyes aglow with mischief. Now though, he was disheveled, aged and dispirited. The wiry grey at his temples, in his beard, more pronounced. Eyes sunken, cheekbones protruding, he was but a shadow of what he'd been only hours previous—as if worn to the bone by a lifetime fraught with hardship and sorrow. Amidst my contemplation, I heard an odd sound emanating from the hall.

Weeping.

Deep and sorrowful wails. The same mournful cries I'd the night I followed the shadow climber. Silence befell the dinner table. Conversations waned, gazes lowered as the melancholia grew louder, closer. Soon, two figures appeared in the doorway, Ariadne, and beside her, *King Minos.*

Pasiphae drew herself up. Beside her, Daedalus suddenly began fidgeting with his fork, feigning close inspection of its trident prongs.

Ariadne smiled weakly at the roomful of guests as she led her frail father to the head of the table. Tears poured down the man's weathered face, dampening his long, white beard. Beneath a crown of pure gold, his silver hair was greasy and unkempt; his purple robes stained with wetness.

"Minos! You finally made it, old boy!" Gillis clapped his hands. "And as cheery as ever, I see..."

"Sit here, Father." Ariadne guided him into the throne-line chair. The moment he sat, he flung his arms onto the table and buried his face, erupting into a fresh wave of sobs.

Head held high, Ariadne patted him on the shoulder before taking her seat beside me. To my surprise, everyone resumed their conversation as though there wasn't an old man in ruins at the end of the table. Minutes later, servants quickly brought the food in and everyone began eating.

"Um, Ariadne?" I asked quietly, "Is your father…okay?"

Nonchalant, she glanced at her father who was in the process of blowing his nose into the tablecloth. She nodded through a practiced smile. "Oh yes, he's doing much better today."

"Why does he cry?"

"My mother did something to upset him—" Ariadne whispered, stealing a cautionary glimpse in Pasiphae's direction. "Many years ago."

How could a woman reduce a man to such a pathetic state? Cruelly, my memories summoned the sound of Inanna's laughter as she killed Father—and the king's tears didn't seem so unimaginable after all.

Out of nowhere, King Minos keened loudly, startling everyone at the table, including a very drunk Gillis who, as a result, spilt his beer into his lap.

"Good gods!" Gillis slammed his mug down. "Who invited King *Whinos* anyway? I'd sooner have my meal in my room than endure his snivelling while I eat!"

"Then go!" Ariadne's lips twisted into a snarl. "No one is forcing you to stay—least of all, *me*."

"Careful, princess," he warned with a glint of annoyance in his eye. "I'm in no mood."

"Ariadne…" Pasiphae interjected. "Leave him be."

At the end of the table, Minos began muttering to himself. While my Minoan was still limited, I understood much of what he said. "She just…why?" the king babbled, toying with a decorative tassel. "How could she…do *that*? It's just…so *awful*. I told her…and Daedalus…it was wrong—so *wrong*. It *can't*…*can't* be allowed to live…"

"What is he talking about?" I addressed Daedalus, but the lanky inventor shrank back, shaking his head.

"Nothing," Pasiphae answered me instead, eyes narrowed darkly. "He's just very confused."

In attempt to distill the mood, I said, "Rhadamanthys was telling me about your older daughters. Will they be joining us for dinner?"

"No," Pasiphae said, stiffening. "They have returned to their kingdoms to begin preparations for the ceremony."

Again, awkward silence possessed the dining room.

"Ceremony?" I frowned at Ariadne.

Gillis, who'd been broodily nursing his refilled mug, brightened. "Oh, that's right, no one has told the young Sumerian the *big secret*?"

"Gillis…" Ariadne shot him a venomous look. "*Don't.*"

"Poor little Sumerian boy," Gillis said with a sneer. "He has no idea what he's gotten himself into."

My face grew hot. "What's he talking about?"

Just then, a servant rushed into the room, to Pasiphae's side and whispered in the Queen's ear. Pasiphae beamed. "Eat up now. The ship is expected within the hour and I want everyone on the pier to greet them."

"Ship?" I asked, exasperated. "Greet who?"

Gillis just laughed.

Anticipation hummed as hundreds of Minoans gathered on the pier. All eyes on the horizon, I absorbed the many faces. Youthful with their honeyed skin, every citizen of Crete seemed to possess an inner glow.

Reluctantly, I recalled the last time I'd seen Enusat, his face gaunt, sickly with malnutrition. How opposite the people of Knossos were to my own. I wondered why? My people worked themselves to the bone —farming, smithing, leather-working—anything to pay their dues whilst struggling to feed their families. Even our rich, like Enusat, faced hardships from time to time. The Minoans, paradoxically, seemed blessed to live a leisurely existence; their crops bountiful, trade routes flourishing, gold flowing like wine. What magical quality did they possess that my civilization did not?

The Minoans were almost...*evolved* by comparison.

Suspicion, ever so softly, whispered inside my soul.

'She's not what she seems—none of them are'

Gillis' maniacal utterances, unwanted as they were, festered within. If the Minoan culture was so enlightened, why then the derelict section of town where the drug-infested brothels prospered?

"There they are!" someone shouted, pointing beyond the uninhabited islets.

Even from a distance, I could tell the lead vessel was massive, followed closely by a fleet of warships. Whomever was coming must have been of great importance, to require such protection.

"They've travelled from Greece to see us." Pasiphae beamed beside me. "Across the deepest part of the Aegean Sea."

Uncertain why I should be impressed, I nodded politely. I knew nothing of this 'Greece' she spoke of. On the other side of me, Ariadne scanned the horizon, wary. Lips downturned, she rubbed her arms as if cold.

"Would you like me to fetch you a cloak?" I asked quietly.

She smiled through a sad expression. "I'll be all right."

Maidens in ivory gowns sprinkled rose petals over a red carpet. Caught by a rogue breeze, a single pink petal spun and danced. Like a butterfly, it twirled, fluttering ever closer. I stretched out my hand, offering it a place to land. Once captured, I'd brush the velvety softness over Ariadne's shoulder like a kiss, hoping to make her smile. Within inches of landing on my palm, the petal was snatched mid-air—and crushed. Scowling, I followed the clenched fist up the arm and to the face of its owner.

Gillis.

"Lovely afternoon, isn't it?" he said as he rolled the petal into a ball between thumb and forefinger, flicking it to the sand.

"It was," I muttered.

Gillis chuckled, scrutinizing the nearing entourage. "Looks like the Greeks have forgiven us after all, hmm?"

"So it would seem," Ariadne replied frostily.

Hull bumping against the harbour, sailors lowered a heavy ramp into place. The Minoan crowd drew a collective breath as a young man appeared at the balustrade, a horseshoe crown of golden leaves glinting on his head.

"Prince Theseus," a woman ahead of me whispered to her neighbour, blushing.

"So handsome," I heard another titter.

"Greetings, People of King Minos!" Theseus shushed the excited throng with a finger to his lips. "I bring to you a gift from my father, King Aegeus!"

The crowd inhaled.

Upon the prince's command, several small figures were ushered to his side. Children. Seven boys and seven girls, some as young as five, all no older than ten. Theseus descended the ramp, leading the way with the girls on the right, paired by height with the boys on the left. The girls were dressed in white gowns, each carried a bouquet of Monkshood. In white tunics, the boys cradled a fruit-filled *kylix*, a wide-brimmed cup intricately painted with images of Greek gods and goddesses.

The Minoans surged towards the children, touching their cherubic faces and kissing their cheeks. Theseus trailed behind, basking in a wave of adoration. The crowd hushed and parted for Queen Pasiphae. She offered her hand to Theseus and he bowed low before gracing it with a long kiss. Beside me, Gillis gave a sardonic grunt and rolled his eyes.

Disquiet simmered inside of me. I tried to dismiss it as merely Gillis' antagonizing presence, but there was something else. I met Ariadne's gaze, hoping to find solace, but her brown eyes bespoke of sadness. Amidst the cacophony, Theseus scoured the crowd—his sights resting on Ariadne. A grin spread across his face and he waded through the throng towards her.

"Princess!" He took hold of her hand, kissing it softly. "I have missed you. Are you well?"

She smiled thinly. "Of course, thank you."

"Is my ship not incredible?" he asked, not pausing for her reply. "We travelled here from Mycenae in just a few hours. She's the fastest and most beautiful boat on all the oceans—I have named her after you…"

Theseus wrapped an arm around Ariadne's waist, guiding her towards the boat. As she glanced back, Theseus tracked her stare and locked eyes with mine. Curiosity eclipsed his expression for a mere instant, swiftly hardening into one of cold intimidation.

My jaw clamped shut like a vise, teeth grinding.

Gillis slithered next to me.

"*Shabarra*," he said, calling Theseus the Sumerian word for *bastard*.

I nodded, though couldn't help but see the irony of Gillis calling another such a vile name.

He slapped me on the back. "It's too bad the Minoans had such bad luck those years ago. Left them vulnerable to the likes of Theseus and King Aegeus."

"Bad luck?"

"A great earthquake, about twenty-five years ago, completely destroyed Knossos. Levelled the palace. Killed the crops. They had to rebuild the entire kingdom—which cost a great deal—building supplies and workers had to be shipped in from Greece. Left the Minoans at the mercy of the Mycenaeans."

I panned the enormity of Knossos, in disbelief that such a wealthy and established kingdom could've been brought to its knees, and so recently.

"Arrangements had to be made, of course. No one does *anything* for free," Gillis said with a shrug.

"What kind of arrangements?"

"Why, the hand of our dear princess." Gillis smirked, pinching the corner of his moustache.

My heart paused.

"T-They are…betrothed?"

"No, no, my friend." He walked away, answering without looking back, "They are married."

20

Tempest

*A*lone, on a quiet beach far from the palace, I wandered the shore-line. Warm sand cushioned my steps, slowing my pace. Great walls of stone cradled the cove, a natural shelter from the wind. White-winged gulls circled overhead, a few bobbed atop the gentle waves as they fished for smelt. Foamy breakers lapped the strand, ebbing and retreating, so patient. I wished I could be more like the water, surrendering to the current. But a weight had settled on my soul, an anchor around my neck, drowning me.

Despite knowing that Ariadne did not love Theseus—she wouldn't have kissed me if she did—I was hurt she didn't tell me. Perhaps she meant to, but didn't know how. Maybe she thought I wouldn't understand.

Married or not, I loved Ariadne. Desperately. I wanted to be with her, forever.

Forever.

That word held different meaning for me now. Before the curse, it simply meant until death, and perhaps beyond in some mythological afterlife. Now, I was to live an unnatural life. One where pain and misery were endless, perhaps sprinkled with the occasional moments of joy. An embittered smile stung my lips. Most would be thrilled to be in my predicament. Who wouldn't want to live forever? Experience the world as might a god? My reluctance might seem inconceivable to some.

'It would be wonderful to live long enough to master all the crafts, don't you think, maru?' Father's long ago musings whispered. *'To be a master painter, black-smith, or leatherworker—so many occupations to choose from, yet so little time to pursue them all. What do you dream of becoming, maru?'*

'I-I'm not sure,' I lied.

'Well, do not wait forever to decide, there are not many days in a man's life. They should be lived very carefully, always doing something meaningful.'

"Meaningful," I muttered bitterly.

How could my life have meaning if I wasn't allowed to love? Had I been cursed before I knew the devotion of a wonderful woman, perhaps this existence would be easier? Once you've seen Heaven, there is only emptiness and the deep longing to return.

I entertained a dangerous thought.

Surrender.

If I surrendered to Inanna, maybe she'd relieve me of the curse? Perhaps we could come to an arrangement. She could have my body, do with me whatever she pleased, if only she'd let me love again.

As if to remind me, Father's last moments replayed inside my mind: his body suspended in the air, the sound of his flesh ripping as he was torn into two, his tortured screams.

I fell to my knees.

I couldn't. Not after what she did to Father, to all of us. It was not pride which prevented me, but dignity. My own, and for those she'd destroyed.

But if I did, I could be with Ariadne…

My heart broke anew.

Even if Ariadne wasn't married to this foreign prince, I couldn't love her, not fully. She'd suffer as Indra had. The darkening ocean blurred before me, blue waves rolling black on the horizon.

"My, my," a voice said. "Those must be some deep thoughts,"

I turned to see Gillis standing a few feet away—the *very last* person I wanted to see.

I brushed the wetness from my face. "*Private* thoughts."

"Ah, well, I should leave you to it then, shouldn't I?" Instead of departing, however, he sat beside me and gazed out at the water. "It's quite magnificent, isn't it? To think that we are so small in comparison, our problems pale beside its power. We often think of ourselves, and our issues, as far greater than the forces of nature. But when standing before it, we are humbled, if not humiliated."

Oddly grateful for his presence, I nodded.

"You tried to warn me." I sighed. "I'm sorry I didn't listen."

Gillis shrugged. "Don't worry, most people don't listen to me."

I chuckled.

"Contemplating the past—or the present?" he asked.

"Both, I suppose—mostly some bad mistakes I made. Mistakes that haunt me still…"

"Ahh, the roots of the past grow deep, especially if they are weeds," he said, wisdom peeking through a sly smirk. Again I had the distinct sensation of having met him before, long before coming to Crete. There was something about his eyes…

A storm gathered in the distance, steely clouds curling past the rising moon. Rain curtained the skyline, cool raindrops tapping my shoulders like tiny, urgent fingers.

Gillis clapped me on the back. "What do you say we go have a few beer, you look like you could use one. And I can always use one—or five."

Though wary, I agreed and together we climbed the steep path towards Knossos. As awful as Gillis behaved in public, he appeared to have a tamer, more thoughtful side. Father would've told me not to judge a man on appearances, that everyone was weighted by the layers of their past. Perhaps Gillis had endured many losses in his life, or lived through hard times and simply emerged hardened, cynical, and less civilized than the average man. I know Father would've given Gillis a second chance, so I decided I would too.

I just hoped I wouldn't regret it.

Cool beer warmed my insides, froth tangy on my tongue. Gillis had already lapped me by two drinks. His eyes sparkled with fresh humour, which made me nervous. Despite recent vindications, he'd already proven himself a loathsome individual. Rhadamanthys, whose opinion I coveted, despised Gillis, yet here I was having a drink with the man.

Over the rim of my mug, I measured Gillis with an unbiased eye. Sun-kissed skin, olive alike most Sumerians, was healthy and vibrant, so much so that I wondered his true age. According to Rhadamanthys, Gillis had been in Crete for at least ten years. Knowledgable and well-travelled, I assumed, since he knew so many languages and cultures. Likely in his early forties, Gillis owned a devilish radiance, as if he beheld some secret that kept him youthful.

A waitress with generous curves arrived at our table. She set a fresh mug of ale in front of Gillis, offering him a shy smile before heading to the next table.

"*Very* nice," Gillis said, ogling her behind.

He guzzled his beer and slammed the cup down, eyeing the waitress, and then me.

"What?" I said, uneasy.

"I'm trying to decide, continue with the sour grapes—" he wrinkled his nose at me, then gestured towards the buxom waitress. "Or move onto dessert…"

I scowled.

Gillis laughed. "What?"

"I was just raised differently, I guess," I said through clenched teeth.

"How so?"

"My father taught me to respect women. To treat them as my equal."

"What makes you think I don't respect them? I *love* women." He reached for his cup, adding under his breath, "Can't live without them, truth be told."

"Then why do you treat them so…horribly?"

Impishly, his eyes twinkled. "Ah, I am but an awful flirt and lustful creature. Forgive me. They're truly magnificent though, don't you think?" Gillis gazed at the waitress, toasting her with his ale. "They don't realize the power they hold."

I thought of the women I'd encountered so far in my young life. Indra, Ariadne—Inanna. While I'd learned of a woman's love, I'd reaped more from one's wrath.

"Some know their power too well, I think," I said cryptically. "And use it against us."

Something unnameable kindled in Gillis' eyes. "Oh? You've crossed such a woman perhaps?"

I nodded numbly, my head swimming from the alcohol.

"Well, we all will in our lifetime—though some of us live to regret it." Gillis laughed, but it was forced and bitter.

My stomach churned and I set the beer down, nauseous.

"You look a little peaked, friend! Let's go for a walk, get some fresh air," Gillis clapped me on the shoulder. "There's something I want to show you."

The midnight air smelled metallic, grass glistening in the aftermath of the storm. Cicadas sang their soothing lullaby. A slivered moon, like a slit in the black fabric, illumined the pebbled path before us. My senses swam, alcohol saturating my system. Tripping over my own feet, I giggled. I liked this feeling, this…uncaring. While I'd not forgotten my pain, the sharp edges were softened and blurred. The ache was still there, but easier to ignore.

"This way," Gillis said, his voice distant.

Arms swinging, I trailed after him, unconcerned of our destination. Only the cool air mattered, only the moon and the stars mattered. I didn't want to care anymore. I didn't want to think for a while.

The white gravel crunched beneath my feet, shadowed fronds whispered on either side me. I had no idea what time it was, but there were no people around. Wherever Gillis and I were going, it was quiet. Isolated.

I hummed a little tune, an old Sumerian hymn Father used to sing whilst winnowing the fields:

Once I have endeared the goddess, she will love me in her heart,
the offer I bring may wholly cover my sin
bringing offerings may work on my behalf
in awe may I...

The sterile may they make fertile,
Grain may they bring forth.
She, the wife, will bear children to the father.
May she who has not yet borne children bear them.

Ahead, Gillis sang along—and for just a moment, it was Father's voice. I could almost see him, feel him there. Tears burned my eyes, throat tight with emotion.

"Here we are," Gillis said, guiding me towards an odd, cone-shaped building.

Grateful for the darkness, I wiped the wetness from my cheeks. "What is this?"

"It's a tholos. A tomb. But this one was looted and abandoned some time ago. Come, have a look inside. It's fascinating."

Curious, I followed him into the void.

"I can't see anything." Blind, I quested with open fingers.

From amid the obscurity, a flint sparker clicked. The tomb filled with light. Blinking, I inspected my surroundings. Two chairs sat in the centre of the room—and nothing else. Gillis stood before the only door, the only way out, with a knife in his hand.

I was suddenly sober.

"Sit," he commanded.

Glowering, not seeing an alternative, I complied.

He sauntered to the other seat, sitting across from me. A sly grin spread across his face and I realized that everything he'd said and done in the last few hours was simply to gain my trust. Newfound hatred for him poisoned my soul.

Gillis brought the knife to my neck. I swallowed, thinking he was going to cut me, but instead, he slid the blade through my shirt, slitting it open from top to bottom. Pushing the fabric aside, he exposed my bare torso.

With the tip of the knife, he poked the eight-pointed star on my chest. "Where did you get that tattoo, friend?"

I froze. I couldn't tell him about Inanna and the curse. He'd think I was lying. Or crazy. "F-From Sumer."

He sighed as if bored by my answer. "*Specifically*, I mean."

"It was a...gift from my father," I blurted, surprised how effortlessly the untruths spilled from my lips. "He took me to an old seer in the centre of town. She said it would...bring me luck."

"Solomon," he said in a fatherly tone. "Are you lying to me?"

I shook my head.

Eyes narrowed, he contemplated me a moment, then shrugged. "I guess we'll see, won't we?"

In one swift movement, Gillis slid the blade across my neck, the cold steel slicing me from ear to ear. I tried to scream but was drowned by my own blood. I clutched my throat, choking as warm crimson gushed through my fingers. I stood, staggered, and then fell onto my hands and knees. I crawled towards Gillis, reaching, as if he could, or would, somehow save me.

Nonchalantly, scraping at some dirt beneath his nails with the tip of the bloody knife, Gillis just stood there. As I neared, he took an exaggerated step back, amusement on his loathsome face.

Trembling, I dragged myself a few inches more, and then collapsed. My heartbeat, once so strong, now slowed.

Slower.

Beat...

...beat...

Silence.

My body had died—but I was still there.

Watching.

"Well, *hopefully* you were just lying." Gillis laughed, taking me by the shoulders, and propping my corpse against the chair. He then stood before me and lifted his tunic, exposing his chest to my dead, somehow seeing, eyes. There, over his heart, was his own tattoo—*an eight-pointed star*. "In the meantime..." He flashed me a nightmare smile. "I'll tell you how I got mine."

Gillis knelt before me. "I know you can hear me. It's the awful bit about the curse, really. Lying there, trapped inside your dead, rotting body. I must admit though, I do love a rapt audience." He leaned forward, inches from my face. "Quite remarkable, those eyes. I can see how that bitch would like them so much. Always was her favourite colour, that lapis lazuli. Poor boy. You didn't stand a chance, really. Anyway!" He rose, rubbing his hands together with twisted glee. "I suppose I should introduce myself. You didn't really think I was some *nobody*, a lowly Royal Translator named 'Gillis', did you?"

When I didn't respond, he continued, "Where do I begin? I want to get it just right. I haven't told this tale too many times as you can imagine. People would think I was crazy!" He laughed.

Hands on his hips, he sported a regal chin. "My name is Gilgamesh, you'd know me as King Gilgamesh, ruler of Uruk."

Gilgamesh? I thought, dumbstruck. *How? He'd be...over 700 years old!*

As if reading my thoughts, he said, "I look pretty good for my age, don't I?"

I would have nodded.

Gilgamesh sat on the empty chair. "As with all myths, there's a seed of truth, though that is rarely how it happened," he began, "Let's see...it all started that one afternoon...after Enkidu and I killed that demon..."

The Epic of Gilgamesh

"*As with all myths and legends, they're passed down the generations by the victors. What you may have read about me is but a shadow of the truth. Mine is the story of a wild and selfish king, of great adventure, daring heroics, and terrifying monsters. An epic tale of great love—but also, of great loss.*"

21

Inner Demons

Uruk, 2750BC

*A*fternoon sunlight spilled into my chambers. A dozen statues capturing my robust likeness shimmered in the gauzy hue.

Rumpled garments lay strewn about the floor, sex and palm oil perfuming the air.

Naked but for a silken robe—a gift from the queen of Susa after a brief affair last spring—I leisured beside the hearth. Nursing a tepid mug of pomegranate beer, I watched the waning embers reduce to ash.

My back was stiff, loins aching.

"Getting a little old for so many at once, Gilgamesh," I thought to myself, gazing wistfully at the three deflowered maidens slumbering in my bed. Long tresses curled about their youthful faces, shielding their identities. Not that I'd remember their names anyway. Nor would I care if I did.

There was a time when I could make love to ten women in a single day. Back when I was just a young man, scarcely a dark hair sprung from my chest. I'd been insatiable, lust nearly driving me to madness. They were all so beautiful, so delicate and vulnerable—how was to I resist? Most reciprocated my desire, while others seemed shy and prudent. I soon broke them of their reserve, however, luring them to my bed or theirs—or whatever dark stairwell was available at the time.

Many a man has a hobby: woodworking, masonry, fishing, wrestling —mine just happened to be sex.

A loud knock at the door caused the women to stir in their sleep. I grumbled, rising, not wanting them to awaken just yet, unsure I was finished with them, but not quite ready for another romp. I swung the chamber door open, glaring. I already knew who it was.

"What is it?" I growled at Siduri.

"A message, King Gilgamesh," he stammered, handing me a tablet wrapped in a palm leaf.

Siduri bowed, backing away as I shut the door.

I unravelled the twine and removed the thick leaf. Inside, I found a small slab of clay, scarcely cured, inscribed with wedged text. I scanned it quickly, huffing after every sentence. After reading it twice, I opened the chamber door again.

"Siduri!" The servant stepped forward—he knew to wait. "Tell Enkidu to meet me in the dining room in ten minutes."

The thin man nodded and set straight off. I turned with a longing look at the bed, at the three naked, bronze bodies stretching in the afternoon twilight.

My sex hardened.

I raised an eyebrow, grinning at the girls. "Better make it twenty."

Enkidu's plate was almost empty by the time I entered the dining room. The wild man glanced up, wiping his thick, untamed beard with a napkin.

"About time," he said.

"Sorry, old friend." I grinned. "I had a pair of legs to part. Several, actually."

"As always." Enkidu rolled his eyes, but smiled. "Why the summons?"

I held up the tablet. "Seems we have a demon to contend with—Humbaba of the Cedar Forest. Apparently he's been hunting and eating the locals. The villagers are asking us to stop him."

"That's terrible!" Enkidu winced. Despite being raised in the wilderness, he was averse to violence. "But...didn't Enlil appoint him as a guardian?"

"Perhaps he was not as willing as we were led to believe," I said with a conspiratorial brow. "Or maybe he's merely grown weary of servitude after so many centuries, we cannot know. It must be tiresome to live forever under the narrow gaze of the gods. In any case, we must put a stop to his tyranny. "

"I'm sure the villagers will be very grateful to us."

"Yes, we're certain to earn everlasting renown as heroes." I grinned. "And with any luck, a virgin or two."

"Gilgamesh..." Enkidu sighed. "Is that all you think about?"

"Of course! Don't you?"

He ignored me. "So how do we kill this demon?"

"I'm not certain. Demons are immortal and cannot be killed, as far as I know."

"Then how will we stop him?"

"We'll ask the oracle, she may have an answer."

Enkidu shuddered. "I don't like the oracle, she's...frightening."

"You're afraid of an old woman?" I laughed

"I fear anyone who whispers with the dead." His expression darkened. "It's said she gouged out her own eyes upon first seeing Ereshkigal."

I laughed again, but suppressed a shudder of my own at mere mention of the Goddess of Death. Even the utterance of her name could evoke evil spirits from the Underworld, inviting them into the realm of the living.

"Come now, my friend," I said, wrapping an arm around his shoulder as we started down the hall. "I promise to protect you."

Deep within the bowels of the palace, in an ever-dark, frigid corner where even shadows feared to linger, the oracle dwelled. Few dared to venture into her lair. Only the sick, desperate, and, in our case, those with questions that couldn't be answered by anything but the realm of black magic. Demons were the spawn of darkness, so it was of no consequence that Humbaba had been elected a guardian spirit by Enlil, the father of the gods. Humbaba had been born in the land of the dead; therefore, to kill him would surely require a special, if not macabre, ritual.

At the entrance to the oracle's lair, tallow candles flickered, enshrining a statuette of Ereshkigal. Offerings of blood, precious oils, and snakeskin wreathed her feet. A thick blanket served as a door. I drew it to the side. Clouds of incense rolled about the tiny, windowless room like a brewing storm. Once inside, the blanket swung to a close, sealing us in like a tomb.

"Where is she? Do you see her?" Enkidu's voice quavered.

I peered into the blackness. "No, but she must be here. She doesn't leave this place."

Enkidu sidled closer. "Does it have to be so...*dark*?"

"Yes," a gravelly voice responded from amidst the shadows. "When one has not their sight, the voices of the dead can better be heard..."

Beside me, Enkidu stiffened.

"Oracle," I began. "We've come to ask you..."

"...how to kill a demon?" she finished.

I was silent, suddenly understanding Enkidu's hesitance. I was rarely unnerved, but this old seer raised the hairs on the back of my neck— and I didn't like it.

"Demons are immortal," the old crone stated. "An immortal can only be killed by a god."

"I know—how can we stop him?" I asked with an edge of impatience.

"He cannot be killed," she whispered, "but he can be *contained*."

I followed the sound of her voice, taking slow steps towards a pitch-black corner. "How?"

Silence ebbed, crushing, the weight of the darkness threatening to swallow us whole. Enkidu clung to my arm, his breath too fast. Childlike and naive, the man had been raised by wild animals. One would think this would strengthen him against the hardships of the outside world, but the opposite was true. Isolated from the ideologies of society, Enkidu had no need for the masks his fellow man had constructed from infancy. He was a pure soul. An innocent.

The old witch answered, "The demon's body can be destroyed, but upon doing so, his soul is capable of possessing another form. To prevent this, his soul must be captured inside a vessel at the very moment his body dies."

"What kind of vessel?" Enkidu addressed her.

The old woman fell silent. "Is that the wild man?"

Enkidu swallowed. "Y-Yes."

170

The oracle mumbled as if to herself, but whispers, almost too quiet to be heard, uttered in response. Voices slithered around the room, speaking in a language unknown to my ears.

"What is that?" Enkidu panicked. "W-What are they saying!"

"They wish to take you home..."

"Home? I don't understand."

She laughed. "It is soon your time—Ereshkigal seeks to claim your soul."

Shaken, I intervened, "Show yourself, woman! Enough of these games!"

The oracle cackled, her laughter echoing from every corner. Enkidu seized my arm.

"Let's leave, Gilgamesh!" he pleaded.

I patted his hand. "We need an answer first, my friend." I faced the shadows again. "What kind of vessel do we need for the demon? Answer me now, witch!"

Silence.

The air in the tiny hovel thickened, darkness pressed. Then, somehow, she appeared just inches before me. Deathly pale, her eyeless sockets seemed to see. I tried to step back, but she reached out and snatched my hand, gripping it tight. Loose skin sagged from her old bones. She thrust something into my palm—an urn.

"Take this," she hissed. "Whisper the name of the demon into the vessel after you've slain his form—but take heed! You must utter his *true* name, else your own soul will be trapped inside and he can steal your body!"

The inhuman whispers sounded once more.

"The Goddess speaks your name, Wild Man," the old woman said. "She'll soon come to collect your soul."

"Please, Gilgamesh. Let's go!" Enkidu urged.

Happy to comply, I hurried to the exit, Enkidu close behind. I yanked the curtain aside, allowing meagre light to spill into the little room. I couldn't help but glance back.

The room was empty.

"The Cedar Forest is about six days travel over the roughest part of the river," I said, measuring the wind's velocity and direction. "It'll be difficult."

I glanced at Enkidu. He'd been noticeably quiet since the visit to the oracle. "Enkidu?"

He snapped to attention. "Yes, six days."

I placed a hand on my best friend's shoulder. "Do not take the crone's words to heart, old friend. She speaks in riddles."

He nodded, though still looked distressed. "Do you think she really speaks with Ereshkigal? What if she wants my soul?"

"Even if she does, I won't let her." I patted his back. "Even the gods must bow before King Gilgamesh!"

After stocking the raft with food and water, we began the long trek north to the Cedar Forest. Each night, we pulled the raft ashore, started a fire and lay beneath the stars.

Overhead, thirsty gnats droned in diaphanous clouds, but dared not fly too close to the fire lest they pop in an ephemeral spark. I sighed, letting the heat from the flames saturate my weary bones. Twenty years ago, this adventure would've been easy, simply a delightful quest. Now, however, I loathed the aching muscles and fatigue. Middle age was not in agreement with me, it seemed, and it bothered me more than I wished to admit. Across the way, his hairy face equally spiritless, Enkidu stared into the fire with haunted eyes.

"Speak, my friend," I said. "What plagues you? Still the words of the witch?"

"I cannot stop hearing them," Enkidu admitted. "She spoke of my death. She's an oracle, after all. I cannot ignore her premonitions."

A pang of terror coursed through my heart with the thought of losing my dear friend. I loved this wild, hairy man like a brother and couldn't bear to consider an existence without him. All my life, I'd thought love could only be found between a man and a woman. I'd pursued many a maiden, thousands, truth be told, but I never once felt anything for them beyond lust and temporary satisfaction. I adored women, but only for their bodies and—while I desired to find a soul mate amongst them—I bored of them easily and could not fathom spending my life with just one.

That's why the appearance of this wild man so many years ago—and my unconditional love for him—was such a surprise. I'd not considered that my whole heart could be given platonically to a man.

Selfishly, I hoped I would die first, before Enkidu, for I didn't think I could survive the loss of my dear friend. A flash of anger for the oracle moved through me, and I decided there and then to rid the palace of her upon my return. No matter her reason, I wouldn't tolerate her venomous predictions and the obvious distress it was causing my beloved Enkidu.

"This demon," Enkidu started. "How will we know his true name? If we speak the wrong name, *we* could end up in that bottle!"

I smiled and tapped my temple. "There's a way, I remember, from the teachings of the elders. A demon is marked by the gods, on the bottom of his left foot. A symbol that will read his true name."

The wild man raised his brows in surprise. "I've not heard of this, but for our sake, I hope it's true."

Six days later, a great wall of forest came into view. Tall, looming cedars shadowed the ground, black soils so foreign from the sands on which I was raised. Beside me, Enkidu's shoulders relaxed and the crease between his brow faded. He'd been raised in the forest, among the trees and animals.

"Perhaps this is what the old woman meant," he said, reverent as he stared at the sea of green, the scent of cedar lingering in the air. "I feel as though I've returned home."

We dragged the raft ashore and followed a deer trail into the copse. As we walked to the village, Enkidu played among the branches, hunted bestial sounds and scents, and tracked strange paw prints. Though amused by my friend's renewed zest, I felt oddly wistful. Had Enkidu been happier as a wild man—before he was lured from the forest by the courtesan to subdue me of my philandering ways? He always looked ill at ease among the crowds of Uruk: tugging at his tunic, eyes filled with apprehension and uncertainty. Perhaps this new life did not suit him as I'd hoped. Perhaps Enkidu was only living in Uruk to please me.

The path seemed unending, threading deeper and farther into the dark forest. It was nightfall before we saw the first glow of firelight doming the village. Four guards met us at the gate.

"King Gilgamesh?" one asked, his tone weary. "Follow me."

A hush hung over the village, voices never ascending over a whisper. The townspeople spied through narrowly-parted curtains, protective markings drawn in animal blood over the windows and doors.

"Just how powerful is this demon?" Enkidu asked, casting a wary eye at the symbols.

"I've heard stories of him, as a boy," I said. "He's said to be a giant of sorts."

Enkidu gave me a sideways glance. "Giant?"

"With the face of a lion! His roar is a flood and his breath is fire!"

"And we're supposed to kill him and stuff him into *that*?" He pointed to my pack, the small urn within.

I laughed. "Don't worry, old friend. We are a great king and a wild man, the strongest in the land! This demon will tremble before us!"

We approached a large hut in the centre of the village, a trench of fire surrounding it. Ducking through the doorway, we were greeted by a bronze-skinned man in a loin cloth, blue tribal tattoos like claw marks across his cheeks and chest. Beside him were two young women wearing only grass skirts, noses pierced with thin bones. Long braids scarcely concealed their bare breasts.

I smiled brightly at the ladies.

"King Gilgamesh," the man said. "I am Chief Zimu. These are my daughters. We are relieved you have come. My people are very frightened. The demon guardian of the forest has suddenly grown violent, terrorizing my people. Can you help us?"

I nodded. "We're happy to help. Where will we find this demon?"

"Up the cliffs to the North, where the waterfall begins. He has a cave there."

Enkidu frowned. "What has provoked him, do you think? I gather he hasn't always bothered your people."

The chief shook his head. "You're right, he has left this village in peace for many centuries—but I do not know why he chooses now to harm us."

"What does he do?" I asked.

Zimu sighed. "He stalks our foragers, kills the hunters, devours the children playing in the river. He has also seduced and taken pleasure with our women."

I grinned at his daughters. "I can't hold that against him."

The girls blushed.

"At any rate," I continued. "We'll head up the mountain in the morning—and have his head by noon."

After being shown to our quarters, Enkidu turned to me, his brow furrowed. "I don't think you should take this matter lightly. This demon has been angered somehow, he's not likely to receive us well."

I groaned as I lowered myself onto the cot. "You worry too much, old friend. Together we're more powerful than ten demons!"

"Twenty years ago, when we were boys, we were strong and fast. We're much older and slower now, Gilgamesh."

"That may be true," I said. "But with age comes wisdom, perhaps what we now lack in form, we will compensate with our wit."

Fog curled around our feet. Dissonant raindrops pattered, obliging the upturned leaves. The musky aroma of cedar infused the humid air. I drew a long breath, enchanted by the wiles of the forest. How foreign it was to my home in the desert, so rich, dense with foliage and moisture. Had I known of such a world previous, I might not have built my palace in the middle of the blistering sands.

Though mostly shrouded beneath lush boughs, the forest, now and again, opened up into an unnatural field, littered with the severed trunks of mighty cedars.

"Someone has been killing a great number of trees..." Enkidu uttered, panning the graveyard of ancient timbers. "Perhaps that's why Humbaba is so angry."

I nodded with a frown.

"What's in the sack?" Enkidu eyed the bag affixed to my belt.

"A present for our prey, should he cause any problems."

"I have no doubt that we will need it." Enkidu grimaced.

"Are you afraid?"

"Of course. You're not?"

I shook my head. "Never. I do not fear anything I have not yet met."

"I wish I was more like you, you know."

"You do?" I smiled warmly. "And I wish I was more like you. Odd isn't it? How we're not always content, always comparing ourselves with others."

"Why would you wish to be me?" he asked, bewilderment on his hairy face.

"You look upon the world with wonder, with the eyes of a child. You feel with all your heart...I do not feel much anymore, except with what's between my legs."

"That's not true," Enkidu said, resolute. "You have great pride in all things: in yourself, your city, and your rule as king. I envy your strength. You fear nothing and you..."

Enkidu froze, brows suddenly fierce. Baring his teeth, he sniffed the air. His eyes darkened, focused as an eagle as they combed the dense foliage. Fascinated, I watched as my friend transformed before my eyes. From man to beast, from tamed to wild—Enkidu had once again become a feral creature of the forest.

Enkidu yanked me behind a wide cedar trunk, where we crouched.

"What is it?" I whispered.

Enkidu gestured to a cluster of trees a few meters to our left. "He is there," he growled.

"The demon?" I peered at the bushes, seeing nothing amiss. Not a leaf overturned or whisper of disturbance. "I don't see anything."

"Do not see with your eyes or trust your ears or smell—use your instinct," Enkidu said. "Deep within, you are still an animal. *Feel* his gaze upon you."

I closed my eyes, quieting my mortal senses. There, beneath the glare of enlightenment, was a sensation I'd not perceived—not allowed—before. Primal and animalistic.

"I...feel him." My eyes opened. "He's watching us."

Enkidu urged me to back away. I frowned and shook my head. I wanted to attack this thing head on and kill it.

"We are either the hunters or the hunted—we cannot be both," Enkidu said. "Right now, we are the prey. We must hide, let him lose sight of us."

I scowled, despising retreat from battle. I preferred to get bloody, to live or die in the moment. But, for Enkidu, I conceded. This former wild man knew the forest, I respected his knowledge of the animal kingdom as much as he respected my knowledge over the kingdom of men.

"We'll backtrack up the mountain, hide in his cave to ambush him," Enkidu whispered, leading us through a thick of juniper bushes.

I glowered at the unseen predator stalking us from amidst the foliage.

You may have won this one, I thought. *But I assure you, you will know my wrath when next we meet.*

"This way." Enkidu signalled.

Ahead, cloaked behind a rushing waterfall, was the gaping mouth of a dark cave. Carved into the cliffs of a sheer mountain, it was the perfect habitat for a demon lord.

Enkidu pondered this. "What's the plan?"

"One of us goes into the cave while the other hides outside. Then when Humbaba comes back and goes in, we can attack him from both positions."

"Which of us will go into the cave?"

I shook the mystery satchel on my hip, it clacked as the contents rubbed together. "Me, it's the perfect place for his *present*. Remember... when I give you the signal, look for his *true* name under his left foot."

Though wary, Enkidu agreed. "Take care my friend. You're not as indestructible as you think."

I laughed. "But just enough, I assure you. Now go, find a good hiding place."

As I entered the cave, blackness enveloped me, my old eyes straining against the shadows. Despite the midday sun outside, little light had found its way into the corners of this tomb. Dank air clung to my skin like a cobweb. The cave stunk of death, rotted flesh, and horror. A floor of bones crunched beneath my feet, both human and animal. Dried entrails dangled from the ceiling like macabre party streamers.

Unshaken, I reached for the satchel and opened it with a smile. I emptied the contents into my palm, knelt, and began burying each in turn.

"Like planting seeds," I said with a chuckle, and then hunkered into a dark corner to wait. "Okay demon, anytime now."

It wasn't more than an hour later that I felt the floor tremble with the demon's heavy footsteps as he clambered up the side of the mountain.

"Just follow the plan, Gilgamesh," I told myself. "Monsters are always scary, but rarely smart."

The beast snuffled and growled outside the cave like an angry bear. It passed by the entrance, creating a massive shadow. My breath snagged in my throat. Heart pounding, flesh tingling, eyes widening. Terror ignited in my blood—never had I felt so alive!

The demon took a step inside the cave, scenting the air—then he roared so loud the walls shook, dust billowing from the cracks.

"I know you are there, human," Humbaba whispered. "I smell your fear."

I huffed. "It's not my fear you smell, but your own foulness."

The demon snarled. "Come out so I may rip the flesh from your bones and lick the salty blood from your insides."

"Ha! You'll find me a rather uncooperative snack. Perhaps you'd rather play a little game instead?"

The hulking shadow paused. "A game? I do not likes games. Come out now!"

"Buried in the dirt before you are seven stones of seven colours. You may dig up only one. If you find the white one, you'll own all the waters of the great River Tigris. The yellow one will give you all the women of Sumer. Orange is the key to all the riches in the land. Red is for all the wine, beer, and food you could ask for. The green one gives you the fields of Uruk. Black, you receive nothing." The monster scoffed, clearly disinterested in the lot. "But blue..." I whispered. "Ahhh, blue is the *best of all*."

The demon took a step forward, his terrible, lion-like head coming into focus. "What is blue?"

I smiled. "The blue stone...is your freedom. You will no longer be a slave to the gods, no longer forced to live alone in the mountains and guard the sacred trees for Enlil."

The great beast drew a sharp breath, dropped to his hands and knees and began digging. With the cave door now exposed, I signalled Enkidu to study the demon's feet. The wild man crept from the bushes and, as swift as a fox, ran up, looked, nodded, and then disappeared around the corner.

"I found it!" the demon declared, cradling the blue stone in his palm. "I will be free!"

"Well done," I said. "There's just one thing left to do."

"What's that?" Humbaba looked almost childlike, head tilted, clutching the stone to his chest.

I felt almost guilty for tricking him, but there was a job to finish. I drew a long, curved knife from my belt. "The only way to free you...is for you to die."

The demon's face twisted, carved with rage and betrayal. Long, pointed fangs flashed as he opened his mouth to roar to release the flood of fire. Before he could, Enkidu sprinted from the bushes and leapt onto the demon's back. Wielding a heavy club made from the

176

limb of the very trees the creature sought to protect, Enkidu swung with all his might and struck the beast aside the head. Confusion filled Humbaba's eyes as he fell to his knees, and then onto his side with a resounding thud.

"Humbaba, I give you your freedom." Swiftly, I sliced through the demon's neck, cutting off his head. I gave a hurried glance to the wild man, who clutched the oracle's vessel in his hands.

"Be sure to speak his name clearly, Enkidu, or it'll be your soul trapped in the vessel," I warned.

Enkidu nodded, bringing the mouth of the urn to his lips and whispering the demon's true name, *"Huwawa."*

At first, there was nothing.

Silence.

We looked at one another, waiting.

"W-What if the oracle was wrong..." Enkidu began, but was interrupted by a slow, building scream.

We backed out of the cave as a large, white mist ebbed from the headless body and hovered midair before us. The ghostly fog shrieked as it was sucked into the small vessel by some unseen force.

"Seal it! Quick!" I ordered.

Enkidu rushed forward, locking the demon's soul inside with a tiny stopper. An image formed, magically, on the torso of the vessel, of the mighty demon amidst his precious Cedar Forest.

I gathered both the vessel and the demon's head into a sack.

"How did you know he'd find the blue stone?" Enkidu asked, shaken.

I patted his shoulder as we started down the mountain path. "They were all blue, my friend. All any enslaved being wishes for is his freedom, no matter the cost."

Back in the village, Enkidu and I were treated to a celebration in our honour. Humbaba's head was set on a spike and the villagers danced around it until dawn.

"However can we repay you?" Chief Zimu asked.

"Two things," I said with a firm eye on the chief, "Stop cutting down the trees. They're not yours to kill, but to live amongst."

The chief bowed his head. "And the other?"

With a cocky grin, I jutted my chin at the chief's giggling daughters.

22

Tameless

"Sire?" Siduri peeked his head into my chambers. "There's a message for you," he said meekly.

I awakened from my slumber, alone in my room for once. When Enkidu and I returned from the village, I promptly went to bed—and stayed there for two days. Exhaustion, and my neglected sexual appetite, contributed to my sour disposition.

"Just leave it on the table," I growled.

After a few minutes of procrastination, I rose and retrieved the clay tablet, scanning it.

My eyes widened. I was fully awake now.

"Siduri!"

He rushed in.

"Ready my best tunic! Hurry!"

"Y-Yes sire!"

"And get Enkidu!" I shouted. "Immediately!"

"Where are we to go?" Enkidu attempted to smooth back his tameless hair.

"To the temple," I replied, excitement coursing through my veins.

"What do you think she wants?"

Delusions of grandeur fired through my imagination. Perhaps we were to be rewarded for our brave efforts. Maybe the gods themselves were so impressed they wished to bestow us fame and fortune beyond our wildest dreams.

"I don't know, my friend," I said, vibrating with anticipation. "But I cannot wait to find out."

As we neared the massive white temple, it glittered diamond-like in the morning sun. High overhead, a lone hawk shrieked, circling the peak of the ziggurat. Commoners meandered about the courtyard, awaiting the merchants as they set up their various wares. They watched with rapt curiosity as Enkidu and I strolled down the processional path and through the main gate, past the twenty armed soldiers who stood guard before the entrance.

Beyond, an *ensi* awaited our arrival. Bedecked in ivory robes, fringed with rare purple dye, he bowed at our approach.

"King Gilgamesh. Enkidu," the priest said. "Follow me."

Through a series of doorways, each room more ornate than the last, we trailed behind the elderly man. Finally, he paused before a set of tall double-doors glazed with lapis lazuli. "I'll go in first and announce you."

"Of course," I replied.

Now alone, Enkidu turned to me. "I am terrified."

I laughed. "You must learn to relax, my friend! Personally, I'm excited. I've never seen her up close before. Only from afar, during the solstice ceremonies—and she was way atop the ziggurat, cloaked from head to toe, at that."

Enkidu gave me a surprised look. "I would've thought the king would have...special access to the gods, being royalty and all."

"I'm afraid not. Only an *ensi* has that privilege. They are the mediator between the mortals and the gods. I was taught as a boy that to look upon the gods with earthly eyes could render a man blind, to hear their voice with human ears would cause the ears to bleed and one might never hear another word again."

Enkidu stared at me in horror.

"Do not worry, my friend." I clapped a comforting hand onto his shoulder. "You must approach all things as a great experience. All experience has something to teach, even if it's bad."

Concern cut a deep groove into his forehead. "I just hope we're not in trouble for *killing* the demon..."

I scoffed. "We're heroes, Enkidu. If anything, we'll be rewarded handsomely for our bravery."

"Perhaps, but our reward would differ vastly if the gods deem us murderers instead of heroes..."

Just then, the *ensi* opened the door. "The Goddess Inanna will see you now."

As opulent as I'd expected, the Great Hall was resplendent in gold trim, windows draped with burgundy silks. Led to the foot of an ornate marble throne, we were instructed to kneel—and wait.

The *ensi* bowed before taking his leave.

Then, silence.

"Where is she?" Enkidu worried the hem of his tunic.

To our right was another blue-glazed door, smaller than the last but embellished with golden lions.

"She likes to make an entrance..." I surmised. "It unnerves the guests —makes them sweat a little."

"How do you know that?" Enkidu asked, evidence of my remark beading on his hairy brow.

"Because that's what I like to do."

Several agonizing minutes later, a set of guards opened the doors. Eager, I craned my neck to get a first glimpse.

My heart hesitated.

Perfect, impossibly so, I was instantly mesmerized by her beauty. Ivory skin, as white as fresh cream. Chestnut hair cascaded over her pert, youthful breasts. Long, lean body, scarcely covered by a gown of sheer linen. An unearthly glow enveloped her, an aura. In all my days, I'd never seen nor made love to a woman with white skin. I adored my Sumerian beauties, of course, with their complexions of burnished bronze—but white, like the snowy mountain peaks of the Zagros—the thought made my mouth water.

How I yearned for a taste of Inanna's cool, wintery hills.

My loins quivered with joy.

"*Inanna…*" I whispered, awestruck in spite of myself.

She did not readily acknowledge us. Graceful, she merely climbed the steps to her throne and sat. Then, and only then, the goddess lowered her gaze. I drew a sharp breath, my heart stolen all over again as her lavender eyes met mine.

I winked.

Affronted, she reset her chin, lips curling as though she'd eaten something sour.

I stifled a laugh. Oh, how I loved the games women played!

"King Gilgamesh," Inanna said. "I trust you can comprehend why you're here?"

"I'll try my best to keep up." I grinned.

"My father is displeased with you and your…*friend*." Her brows elevated with obvious distaste as she scrutinized Enkidu from head to toe.

I bristled. "Pardon me, *goddess*, but we saved an entire village from your father's demon. I should think we'd be praised."

Inanna stared at me, incredulous. "You dare contradict me or my father?"

"Well, yes, actually I do."

Her beautiful face twisted unpleasantly. "He wishes for you both to be punished. Beheaded in the courtyard."

Beside me, Enkidu trembled.

Rising, I took a dangerous step closer to the goddess. Her guards stiffened, raising their weapons in warning.

"*Perhaps* your father should choose his guardians more carefully." From beneath a menacing brow, I challenged her. "This is *my* kingdom and I will not have my people live in fear of the creatures chosen to protect them."

Inanna gaped at me. "How *dare* you speak to me in…"

"Now," I interrupted as I lent a hand to Enkidu, bringing him to a stand. "If we've not been invited for a medal of bravery and a party in our honour, we'll take our leave."

I turned on my heel, dragging a shocked Enkidu towards the door.

"Are you *insane*!" Enkidu hissed, eyes round with fear. "You can't talk to *her* like that!"

"No one talks to me, or my best friend, like that—especially not a *woman*," I said, enraged. "Goddess or not. We did them a favour, we should be treated as such…"

As I placed my hand on the door, from her throne, Inanna ordered, "Wait!"

Brandishing a smug smile, I spun about with a hand cupped round my ear as if I hadn't heard her. "What was that?"

"I said, *wait*," Inanna uttered though clenched teeth, violet eyes flaring.

Arms over my chest, I turned and gave a long, exaggerated exhale.

Catlike narrowed eyes, as if deciding whether or not to smite me on the spot, she said, "The hairy dog-man is free to go. You, however… will come with me."

Inanna stood and, without a glance back to see if I was actually following, exited through the polished blue door.

Enkidu wore an expression of sheer confusion.

I clapped him on the shoulder, grinning.

"Don't wait up."

"And so began a great love affair, though secret and occasionally quite turbulent. Well, not a love affair so much as a sex affair. At least for me.

"Inanna summoned me almost every night. We'd make wild, passionate—often savage—love until dawn. She would begrudgingly allow me leave each morning so I could return to the palace and sleep. For months, I hardly saw anyone, hardly ever worked or tended the needs of the people. The physical pleasures I experienced with Inanna was heightened somehow, compared to that of mortal women. I even suspected she had preternatural powers that enhanced sensations, making me crave her night and day.

"I never tired of the sex—but I was growing weary of her rather, shall we say, demanding nature."

"Don't go," Inanna pouted, tracing an invisible circle on my chest. "You always leave. Why not stay for the day, we could go for a walk in the garden or…"

"You know we can't be seen," I said, tired of the same discussion. "If your father finds us together, he'll turn me inside out!"

"I know." She glowered at the ceiling. "I just like to pretend to be… normal."

"Look," I said, rising to get dressed. "I'll try to come by early tonight, maybe we can go out into the garden once it's dark."

She brightened. "Okay!"

After a long kiss goodbye, I left using the secret door through the hearth, climbed the dark staircase, and crept across the courtyard. Early morning air, tinged with the coppery scent of dew, hung heavy. The road home was unusually quiet. Sumerians were known to be early risers, attending their chores before the oppressive heat of midday.

Anxious to catch a few hours sleep before I had to deal with some overdue palace business, I walked a little faster. Recently, I'd commissioned for a great wall to be erected around the city to protect us from the relentless Elamite attacks. City officials were pressuring me to pay the masons a portion in advance, which was absurd—paying a man before the job was done—but the builders insisted they couldn't afford the tools required and needed money to purchase them ahead of time.

So preoccupied with my thoughts, I wasn't watching where I was going and bumped right into someone.

I glanced up. "Sorry, I…*Inanna?*"

Utterly confused, I could only stare.

I had just left her, in her room—in the opposite direction. Yet here she was, standing before me. Of course, she was a goddess, capable of untold powers, but it was she who insisted we must remain discreet about our relationship, lest her father discover her forbidden dalliance with a mere mortal.

"Inanna," I whispered. "What are you doing here?"

Her brows lifted in amusement.

It was then I noticed her hair. Black, instead of soft brown. Her face was the same. Identical. I'd seen it a hundred times over the last few months. And her dress was different—everything Inanna wore was white, made of silk. The woman before me wore dark, thick fabrics with a sharper edge.

She laughed at my confusion—and I knew.

This is not Inanna.

"Who are you?"

"You really don't know?" she said, lilac eyes mischievous. "I suppose I shouldn't be surprised that Inanna hasn't mentioned me."

I scrutinized her a moment. Was I being tricked? Inanna was a powerful and jealous creature, I wouldn't have put it past her to devise a test of my loyalty.

Unabashed, Inanna's double closed the space between us, drawing a playful fingernail down my neck. I shivered with excitement. It had been a while since I'd been with a woman other than Inanna. I craved variety. While Inanna was like sampling the finest of red wines, I'd forgotten how much I loved an assortment of refreshments.

"I've always agreed with my sister's taste in men," she purred, then added, "though little else..."

"Sister?"

"Ereshkigal."

I froze, stunned speechless.

Ereshkigal—The Goddess of Death.

"You are...twins?"

"Something like that." She smiled darkly.

She was so like Inanna—yet so unlike her, all at once.

Intrigued, I grinned.

"And so began my second, secret love affair.

"I catered to both women, making love to Inanna in the early morning and Ereshkigal late at night. I was a man of all hours. Sleep was precious, food and drink almost non-existent. Ereshkigal knew of my time with Inanna, and didn't seem to care. Inanna, however, thought me to be utterly devoted to her, and her alone.

"After several months of pleasing both women, however, I was exhausted.

"Something had to change."

Candlelight cast an unearthly glow on the walls of Inanna's chambers. Shadows danced like ghoulish demons freed from the underworld to haunt the living. I pressed my body to hers, thrusting myself into her again and again. She never allowed me to stop, to catch my breath, demanding all my energy to please her. Finally, she cried out, running her sharp nails down my back. I grinned, though my muscles trembled as I rolled off.

A cool breeze drifted through the open door, breathing across the sheen of sweat on my chest. I shivered, skin puckering into gooseflesh. Beside me Inanna stretched, her long body draped like a cat over the blankets.

"Aren't you cold?" I asked, drawing the sheet over myself.

Her purple eyes glowed with amusement. "I don't get cold."

"You don't get cold?"

"Of course not, I'm a god. We're not subject to such human—*frailties.*"

My stomach knotted. Was I so frail? I'd always thought myself stronger than most men, unbreakable and impervious. In that moment, however, I felt fragile and weak. Pathetic.

"What other benefits do you have?" I asked, suppressing my bitterness.

Inanna smiled smugly. "Immortality, of course. I don't age nor feel tired. I don't *need* to eat or drink, unless I choose to. Pretty much anything that's annoying to be human, I don't have to worry about. I can bind my power to a person or an object, enchanting them. That's how I enhance the fertility of the soil in Uruk."

"Are you omnipotent? Can you hear and see anyone or anything you choose. Can Enlil hear us?" I whispered, glancing around as if her father could be listening.

She shook her head, lips curling in disappointment.

"I was able to once, long ago. But that was *before...*" She stared dreamily into a distant memory.

"Before?"

Inanna sighed. "When we shared the power of the Mes."

"The Mes? What's that?"

"*They,*" she corrected, "are the decrees of human civilization. Items enchanted with the power to evolve mankind. Thousands of years ago, we shared the combined power of the Mes, but my father felt it wasn't safe."

"Why?"

"If a single deity were to possess them all, they'd become more powerful than all the gods combined. One could wield the power of the universe, hold all the powers of creation in their hands—as it was in the beginning." Her eyes darkened. "That's why we're all *lesser* gods now."

"How many of these Mes are there?"

"No one knows except my father. Dozens, at the very least." She played with a loose thread on the blanket, seemingly bored of the subject.

A dark plan hatched inside my head, but I had to tread carefully. "So, where are these Mes now?"

"My father has them, he keeps them locked up in an enchanted box."

"That seems rather unfair..."

She sat up, eyes narrowed. "What do you mean?"

"Well, your father claims the Mes are unsafe for one deity to possess—yet he's holding them all? Seems odd, that's all."

Inanna frowned. I could almost see the seeds of doubt propagating behind her eyes. "He can't use them either...anyway, I really shouldn't be telling a *mortal* about this..."

She stood, donning her robe.

I grew quiet.

Shame crossed her face. "I-I'm sorry, I shouldn't have..."

"No, you're right," I said sadly. "I just...hate to be reminded that... someday all this will end, you know." I waved an exaggerated hand.

"End?" she parroted, brows knitting together.

"Forty years just isn't long enough time for one man to accomplish everything," I said, sighing. "My father wasn't much older than myself when he died. I don't know that I'll ever truly be ready to die. There's so much yet I wish to do, to see...to *love*." I met her gaze with all the intensity I could muster. "You should feel lucky you can live forever. You'll always be young and vital and beautiful. You'll see the centuries pass, civilizations rise and fall! You'll be witness to such change!" Head bowed, I turned my back to her. "And I will have long since turned to dust. My bones dry and cracked, lost beneath the sands of Mesopotamia. Perhaps though...my people will tell my story...carve my memory into the stone so I might live forever through myth and legend. Maybe, just maybe, I can be immortalized through literature..."

I faced her, surprised to see tears in her eyes.

"You think I haven't considered this?" She swallowed a sob. "You think this...hasn't happened before?"

I waited for her speak.

"I was married once you know." Inanna smiled wistfully. "Tammuz...he was mortal, like you. A shepherd. He was so kind. So passionate." Her face hardened. "I asked Father to make him immortal, to make him a demigod so we might be together forever—he had the power, he could've used the Mes. But he wouldn't. He said it would be the greatest of sins to give a human such powers, that it would corrupt mankind if they did not know the limitations of death. I despised him for it. I hated him for making me watch my beautiful Tammuz age and wither and...*die*." She hugged herself.

"It's so...selfish. All that power...for what?" I sighed dramatically. "Well, since I'm nothing more than a mere mortal, I must work like one. I have to go."

Silent, unmoving, Inanna stood at the end of the bed with her back to me. I waited a moment for her to respond, but when she didn't, feeling defeated, I turned to leave.

"Gilgamesh," she said suddenly.

I spun about. "Yes?"

"Come back tonight, very late...I think I know a way."

My heart sped up. "A way to what?"

Machination churned behind her violet eyes.

"A way to make you immortal."

Dawn bathed the palace in an amber haze. My eyes were dry, hooded with fatigue. If I was lucky, I could catch two or three hours rest before I met with the lead mason about the wall. I padded silently over the marble floors, eager to reach my bed. I passed through the dining room on the way to my chambers.

"You play a dangerous game," said a familiar voice.

Startled, I stopped short. Across the room, his form shadowed by a wingback chair, Enkidu bided before a dwindling fire. The hearth was heaped with ash—he'd been waiting a while for my return.

I chuckled. "Whatever do you mean, friend? I'm doing what I've always done."

Behind the greying overgrowth of beard and brows, his eyes were stone-cold serious. "Yes, the game is the same, but the players are not."

Weariness weighing on my bones, I fell into the chair beside him. "She's just a woman, like any other," I said of Inanna, uncertain if he knew about Ereshkigal.

"No woman should be underestimated—especially one with great power," he warned. "The consequences if—*when*—she becomes upset with you could be far greater than you realize."

I gave a hearty laugh. "*When* she becomes upset with me? You think I will disappoint her? I did not realize you had such little faith in me."

Enkidu sighed. "I have the greatest faith in you, my dearest friend... but you're a scoundrel when it comes to women. It's bound to end poorly. And when it does, I will be there for you. No questions asked. But know this one is different, she's no ordinary women. Her wrath is bound to be...exceptional."

Too tired to banter, I closed my eyes, warmth from the embers seeping into my skin. "Ah Enkidu, so little you know of women. There's nothing to be concerned about. Women are fickle creatures yes, but their very nature is to love and forgive. I've angered many a woman, but in the end, they all invite me back into their hearts—and, eventually, into their beds."

"I fear, old friend, you will someday face a demon you cannot vanquish."

"Perhaps," I said, yawning. "But until then, I must do what makes me happy."

"Be happy, yes, but not so much that you're blinded by it."

His words were a whisper inside my dream as I succumbed to exhaustion. I scarcely felt him lay a blanket over me before I slipped into blissful unawareness.

23

This Lonely Forever

I was giddy to return to Inanna's chambers that night to hear how she might make me immortal. After meeting with the lead mason, I head to my chambers to catch a nap before departing to the temple.

But, to my delight, my bed was already occupied...

For being the Goddess of Death—unlike her dichotomous sister of Love—Ereshkigal was a surprisingly tender lover. Erotic and passionate, she writhed like silk beneath me. Unpredictable yet complacent, she allowed me to be in control, to conquer her again and again. With soft, sincere moans, she loved to please as much she enjoyed being pleased. She made me feel like a man. She pandered to my pride, stroked my ego, and understood my need for masculinity.

Inanna, on the other hand, was feisty and rebellious. Though jealous and manipulative, she inadvertently challenged me to be better, stronger. She forced me to think fast, think harder and wiser; that the things worth living for, like Love, had to be earned.

For all intents and purposes, Death came fast and easy. Love, however, was a slow and painful ride—but had a deeper, more satisfying climax.

There are times when I think I could've chosen between them, my ladies of Love and Death, that I desired one over the other—but some choices are made for you, whether you want them or not.

"She told you about the Mes?" Ereshkigal's eyes were round with shock as I reiterated my earlier conversation with her sister. "It's forbidden knowledge..."

"Perhaps it's not such a secret for the King of Uruk. I have a right to know everything that affects my city, do I not?"

"Of course, it's just...my father wouldn't approve. Inanna takes great risk in sharing the secrets of the gods."

"According to Inanna," I said. "Enlil keeps them well protected—inside an enchanted box of some kind."

Ereshkigal remained quiet.

"Anyway, Inanna's asked me to come back tonight, very late. She claims to know a way to make me immortal."

"What!" Ereshkigal seized my arm. "Gilgamesh, please don't go tonight. She doesn't have the power to make you *truly* immortal. She's lying."

"How do you know this?" I said, defensive, wishing I'd not told her anything at all.

"Thousands of years ago, when my father separated us from the Mes, it left us with very little power," she began. "We retained our immortality, but all the great abilities we once had were gone. Long ago, we were strong enough to build entire worlds. My brother created Jupiter. My mother designed the moons of Saturn. Now, we can do little more than bind our essence to the task we've been assigned. Inanna can only give life to the fields of Sumer. I can only govern a dark world in which the dead can reside. Nothing more. She doesn't have enough power to offer you immortality, Gilgamesh." Ereshkigal paused. "Unless…"

I perked up. "Unless?"

"No…" She shook her head. "She simply doesn't have the power."

Half-joking, I said, "Maybe she intends to *steal* the Mes?"

"Do not say such things!" Ereshkigal backed away in horror. "You don't know their power. If Inanna were to wield such abilities, in this world, it would be…*catastrophic*."

Dread trickled through my veins.

"Please Gilgamesh," she begged. "Don't go back tonight…promise me you will not go."

I kissed her forehead.

"I promise," I lied.

Late that night, I crept through the shadowed courtyard. My pulse thundered. All semblance of earlier exhaustion was forgotten as I slipped through the hidden door and descended into Inanna's secret chamber. Upon entering her room, I struggled to see through the dimness. The halo of a single torch illuminated a far corner, its meagre light flickering upon the stone walls.

The woman loved to set the mood.

I peered into the darkness, searching with outstretched fingers.

"Inanna?" I whispered. "I'm here…why is it so dark?"

No answer.

A new game? I smirked.

"Inanna?"

A soft moan sounded from the direction of her bed. I imagined her pleasuring herself, warming her body up for me. Aroused, I intuited my way across the room.

"Where are you, Love?"

"I'm here," she uttered, voice breathy. "Come to me, Gilgamesh. *Please…*"

When I found the end of her bed, I crawled across, fingertips questing for soft, warm flesh. The silk sheets whispered as she writhed.

Finally, I found her ankle, her calf, the back of her thigh. I slid my palm up and between her legs, pausing as I discovered wetness—but I withdrew my hand before pleasing her, teasing.

Inanna let out a shuddering sigh.

Erotically, I massaged her thighs, working upwards. Gently, I slid my palms over her curves, savouring the arch from buttocks to spine. Slick and smooth, she'd doused her entire body with oil. Already hard, I groaned in delicious anticipation. I straddled her lower half, positioning to take her from behind. As I caressed her waist, the spill of her breasts on the mattress, I reached up to take hold of her shoulders—to use them as leverage when I entered her. As I touched her there, however, she screamed in pain.

Startled, I fell back, clambering off the bed.

"Inanna!" I said, rushing to a drawer where she kept spare candles. "Are you all right?"

Hands slick with oil, I fumbled. Over and over, the flint striker sparked as I tried to ignite the wick. The room flashed as if besieged by a lightning storm. Finally, sweat trickling over my brow, a spark caught, a yellow glow illuminating the room. The flame trembled as I carried it to the bed. Inanna lay on her stomach, whimpering.

When the light reached her, I cried out.

It wasn't oil I'd felt on her back—*but blood.*

Dark and red, her back glistened, smeared from my massage. In shock, I opened my hand. Stained burgundy, the lines on my palm feathered like the veins on leaves.

"Gilgamesh," Inanna whispered.

Returning to my senses, I moved to her side. I took her hand in mine while stealing a closer look at her back. Beneath the blood, carved into her flesh, were dozens of tattoos. Inked in black and weeping crimson, the emblems seemed to be etching themselves into her skin.

She stared at me, eyes glazed with suffering.

"Inanna…w-what is…this?"

"The…Mes," was all she could manage.

"How many are there?" I asked, wondering how long this torture would last.

Ever so slightly, she shook her head.

She didn't know.

I didn't know what to do. Should I get help? But who could I trust? If I sought help from Ereshkigal, however, our secret affair would surely be revealed.

'It's forbidden knowledge…' Ereshkigal's ominous warning resounded.

Another tattoo split open on Inanna's back. She screamed as fresh blood trickled down her back.

No matter the cost, Inanna needed help.

Now.

I stood and started leave—to find Ereshkigal.

"Don't go," Inanna begged, fingers outstretched. "Please don't leave me alone."

I returned to her side. "Why did you do this?"

"For you…" she said, breathless, sweat on her forehead. "I can't bear to think of eternity without you, my love. It was the only way…I could be powerful enough to make you immortal. I'm not strong enough without them."

I was so close to my dream of immortality. I hated that Inanna was in so much pain, all for me, but I could almost feel the power of the gods rushing through my veins.

"Gilgamesh," Inanna said weakly. "P-Promise me…"

"Anything, I'll do anything for you, Love," I said, stroking her hair. All the pain and suffering she was going through, just to make me immortal. I owed it to her to abide by her wishes.

"After…I change you…" She groaned as the rivulets coursed down her back. I could almost hear the sound of her flesh tear every time a new one surfaced.

I kissed her hand. "Yes?"

"After I change you…" she whispered. "Will you marry me?"

The colour drained from my face.

"M-Marry you?"

Her brows pinched with pain and annoyance.

"I…of course!" I choked on the words. "I will…marry you."

She smiled, a tear of happiness escaping her eye.

"I'm just going to…get a wet rag for your back," I said, hanging onto the bed for support as I made my way to the water table.

Terror beaded on my brow.

Marry her? Marry Inanna?

I wasn't so blind to realize that being the husband of a goddess had tremendous benefit, but marriage was so…final. It's not like I hadn't been married before, of course. In fact, I'd had many wives—and as many divorces. But marriage to solidify a peace treaty between adversaries was different than marrying for love—and I knew which Inanna desired. She wouldn't be satisfied with a marriage of convenience or for political reasons. She'd want me wholly, along with my word to be, above all, *faithful.*

Love…do I love Inanna?

The word held such conflicting emotion. It suggested I couldn't live without her. Couldn't fathom my future life without her by my side—*forever.*

There was only one person I felt that way for.

Enkidu.

I saw us growing old together. Hunting, fishing, going on adventures until our old bones ached, until the wrinkles around our eyes and mouths conveyed joy even in our sleep. My brother, my best friend—he owned my heart like no woman ever could.

I returned to Inanna's side with the rag, dabbing her wounds gently. She cried out with every touch.

I have to tell her, I must. Before this goes any further…

But I couldn't.

Not before I was made immortal.

Immortal. Me…but not Enkidu…

Tears filled my eyes. I'd rather die alongside my friend than bury him…and be left alone.

"Inanna," I began, my voice shaking. "I can't…"

Blinding light flashed from behind me.

Inanna gasped. "Father!"

I spun about.

189

There he was, the patriarch of the gods.
Enlil.
Beside him—Ereshkigal.

Enraged, Enlil towered in the doorway, his ebony skin like polished obsidian. Violet eyes glowering. At his side, head hung, Ereshkigal wore an expression of pure guilt.

"How *dare* you!" Enlil's voice boomed, the stone walls trembling. "How dare you break into my chambers and steal the Mes, Inanna!"

Beside me, Inanna wept, struggling to sit up.

"I-I want to be with Gilgamesh!" she said. "I would've asked for your help, but I know you would've refused! He even vowed to marry me, Father!"

This, however, incensed Enlil further.

"He is a mortal, Inanna! A mere...*human,*" he spat the word as if vile. "We cannot allow them into our world. It's...demeaning. They simply don't have the intellect to behold such power. You'll be punished for this, Inanna. More than any god in all the ages."

Inanna sobbed. "No, p-please don't."

"As for *you*..." Enlil pointed at me. "You've dishonoured not one, but *two* of my daughters..."

Eyes ablaze, Inanna reared her head in my direction, and then at Ereshkigal. "What!"

Before I could explain, Enlil continued, "For that I take from you the one thing your silly human heart holds dearest."

Terror bled through my veins.

'There's only one thing I hold dear...'

Enlil opened his palm, within it was an incandescent sphere. Beautiful and perfect, its surface shimmered white. In some dormant part of myself, I recognized what this was—*a soul.* He lifted it to his lips, whispered an indecipherable phrase, and an angry black cloud swirled inside the orb. Then, Enlil crushed the soul within his palm.

"It is done," he said.

My heart thrummed. "W-What is done?"

Ignoring me, Enlil stormed towards the blood-soaked bed. Towards Inanna. Palms open, Enlil hovered over the plethora of tattoos carved into his daughter's back.

"*Mythos infinita il sanfira destiiro casserila!*" his voice thundered.

Inanna began to scream.

Frozen in horror, I pressed myself into a corner.

Again and again, Enlil uttered the incantation, once for every symbol. One at a time, they were ripped from her skin. Held but a moment within his hands, each was transformed into a ball of mercurial light before being sucked into a churning vortex where they disappeared into a dark oblivion. Enlil continued, relentless, until there was nothing left of Inanna's beautiful back but a bloody pulp.

Once every tattoo was gone, Enlil uttered into his daughter's ear, "You are banished, Inanna, Ishtar, Isis, Goddess of Love—*Lilitu,* my first-born child, to the temple basement for three full turns of your sun."

At this, Inanna wailed.

190

I wanted to ask how long a full turn of her sun was, but I stayed huddled in the corner, scared speechless.

Enlil stormed from the room.

Ereshkigal lingered a moment more than her father, her guilty expression bespoke of her betrayal, as well as hurt for my engagement to her sister. Before I could decide whether to chastise her or defend myself, she vanished in a wreath of black mist.

Shaken, I rose. Across the room, Inanna sobbed, her once-lovely back unrecognizable. But as I neared, I could see the torn skin stitching itself back together as if by unseen healers. I debated if I should simply sneak away or remain by her side in her moment of darkness. I decided to stay, not knowing it would be the worst decision of my life.

"I-Inanna?" I said, kneeling beside her. "How…can I help you?"

Her sobs silenced and I realized she'd forgotten about my presence until then.

With a trembling hand, I touched her arm.

She recoiled, hissing like a wounded cat. Turning to me, her lavender eyes gleamed.

"Don't touch me you filthy…faithless…*mortal!*"

Covered in her own blood, she drew herself to a stand. Eyes glowering predatorily, she began to whisper an incantation—the same words her father used to rip the tattoos from her back. My heart climbed into my throat and I eyed the doorway, the exit to freedom.

But it was too late.

A glow, powerful and bright, pulsated inside Inanna's chest. Eyes wide with horror, I watched as a silver, snake-like thread of light wriggled from her bosom and swam around her naked form. Inanna smiled at the beast as if it were a newborn child, spawned from her very loins.

"I may not have the power to make you a god, my love," she uttered through an evil sneer. "But I can make you immortal."

My heart skipped a beat, a glimmer of hope dawning. "Y-You can?"

She whispered to the snake, "*Go…*"

The creature flew at me, faster than my eyes could follow, and burrowed itself into the centre of my chest. Where it entered, a black tattoo blossomed—an eight-pointed star. Inanna's sacred symbol. I fell to my knees, clutching my heart, my soul, as the snake nested within.

"Oh Gilgamesh," Inanna said as she sauntered towards me, wounds fully regenerated. "We could've had such fun, for all eternity…but, you proved yourself unworthy in the end, didn't you?"

She ran a sharp fingernail down my cheek.

"Too bad, really," she said with tears in her eyes. "I think I actually loved you…" Her chin lifted, regal, gaze suddenly dry of emotion. "Nonetheless, it's time for you to suffer."

"Inanna," I pleaded. "I'm so…so sorry!"

She laughed, eyes glittering. "You certainly will be…"

Inanna paced her new prison with all the grace of an agitated lioness, pondering. At one point, she turned away from me. As she did, I saw something on her back—and my blood turned to ice.

Enlil missed one.

A single Mes remained etched on her back. Whether she realized it, I didn't know.

191

Nerves clawed the inside my stomach. What was she going to do to me? With trembling fingertips, I touched the newly branded marking on my chest. I could feel the silver beast slithering within.

"Inanna?" I braved "I-I am truly sorry for being unfaithful."

I meant it. Though not from guilt, but fear.

Her head snapped towards me, eyes dark and dangerous.

"If it had been anyone other than my sister, a noblewoman, a servant girl—even a *whore*, I'd not have cared," she said, her words laced with venom. "But that you betrayed me with the one woman who has sought my downfall for the last one hundred thousand years—I have no choice but to punish you. You will suffer like no other man since the dawn of time for what you've done!"

I fell at her feet. "Please...no!"

"Why should I suffer this eternity alone?" she asked rhetorically. "I shall make you suffer alongside me. I shall watch your pathetic human spirit fade, dim to but a spark of your former self. I shall savour your anguish and ebbing madness—Gilgamesh, King of Uruk, I curse you with immortality. I curse you to live forever in your sins against me."

My breath paused, afraid to feel excited. Was she really making me immortal—as a punishment?

Seeing my confusion, she continued with an evil smirk, "You will live forever or until the sun ceases to shine—*but*...to remain youthful, you will require...*sustenance*."

I frowned.

"You will lust, Gilgamesh, for every single woman who passes your eye. You will long and need and crave for the physical companionship of women. Yet no matter how many you bed, your lust will *never* be slaked."

I felt myself pale.

"And..." Inanna tapped her chin. "For every day you're alive, you will need to bed a *new* woman, else you will age and the need for sex will grow exponentially until your pitiful human mind can no longer withstand it."

Inanna threw her head back and laughed, thoroughly amused by her ingenious damnation.

"Now go," she growled, pointing to the door. "Your presence disgusts me."

I willed my feet forward. The road that led to the palace seemed endless, my legs like iron.

Inanna's curse trickled like acid through my veins. A slow poison.

The worst part was, I had felt guilty for my affair with Ereshkigal. I'd even considered—albeit briefly—marrying Inanna. It wouldn't have worked, of course. I was a bonafide, disloyal cad. I wouldn't have been able to sustain my loyalty. Women were too beautiful, too alluring, for me to resist.

I laughed, mirthless and crazed.

Inanna could not have devised a more appropriate curse for me. Now I'd have no choice but to seek the pleasures of women. I didn't doubt for a moment the curse was a farce, I knew what the gods were capable of. As did Enkidu, which is why he tried to warn me...

My heart stopped as Enlil's dark promise resounded.

"For that, I take from you the one thing that your silly, human heart holds dearest."

"Enkidu..."

I broke into a run.

The palace was dark. Shadows loomed like a curtain across the walls.

As I neared Enkidu's chambers, my heart pounded painfully. Enlil had not spoken Enkidu's name, so he might still be safe. I could live with Inanna's curse so long as I had my dear brother by my side. Perhaps, in time, Inanna would make him immortal as well. Perhaps she could be convinced of my penance and allow me this one gift.

"Please let him be okay," I prayed, entering his chambers.

Two servant girls sat on either side of his bed. For a fleeting moment, glee shot through me—until I realized they were mopping his fevered brow, grave concern carved into their youthful faces.

"Thank you," I said to the women with a gesture towards the door. Their very presence summoned a painful urge from my manhood—Inanna's curse in full swing.

Once they'd gone, I rushed to Enkidu's side. Heat poured from his body like a wave. He coughed, fighting for the next breath. Beneath the blankets, his chest rose too slow and fell too fast.

Hot tears spilled down my cheeks. Sobbing, I buried my face against him. With herculean effort, Enkidu lifted an arm around my shoulder.

"Do not...cry, my...friend," he said, breathless. "I...do not belong... here."

I lifted my head. "What do you mean? Of course you belong here... with me."

"No, I was only here..." Through his gruff beard, he smiled. "...for *you*. I am a...wild man. I belong...in the forest. Now, I will go...home."

"No!" Like a petulant child, I pounded the mattress with my fists. "You cannot leave me! Not now!"

He stroked my hair and I calmed.

You were right," I said. "Inanna found out—she has cursed me. I am...*immortal.*"

The wild man smiled a peaceful sort of smile.

"I am happy to...go," he said, "...knowing my brother will live... forever."

"No! You don't understand! I don't want to live forever without you! I cannot do this alone!"

Enkidu cradled my chin within his massive palm, tears shining in his eyes. "You will make me proud, Gilgamesh. This...is your destiny..."

No sooner had the words passed through his lips, the light vanished from his eyes.

My brother, my Enkidu, was gone.

24

Resurrection

"*S*o you see, Solomon," Gilgamesh said with a weary smile. "There's a great deal more to this curse than you once thought. And now, you and I are in this together. I'm guessing we're stuck with one another for a very, *very* long time—unless she's cursed others like ourselves, that is.

"Listen, I have to go, you'll be resurrecting soon and I don't want to be around when *they* get here." He shuddered. "Give her my regards, will you…

"I need a brothel, but find me later and we'll talk. I'm sure you're going to have plenty of questions." At the door, Gilgamesh paused, his profile silhouetted by the dawn. "Just so you know, you *will* live through it, Solomon—but it's *horrible.*"

And he left.

'*I don't want to be here when* they *get here…*'

Paranoid, I tried in vain to move my dead eyes around the room.

Minutes moved like days. My consciousness writhed inside my corpse. Though I could somehow see and hear, I longed to blink, to breathe, to wet my lips—anything to feel alive again.

Outside, chickadees greeted one another in song. Insects droned, busy with chores. A golden glow coloured the morning, pouring light over the threshold. As the sun touched my deadness, something changed.

A *quickening.*

The resurrection had begun.

Sunlight, I'd come to discover, was the catalyst of life, even in death. If I perished in the night, my body would reawaken with the rays of a new dawn. The duration it took to regenerate, however, depended on the severity of my wounds. Life and death was a natural process. Resurrection too, it would seem, adhered to such biological laws.

But a resurrected body without a soul is just a shell. Unbeknownst to me, my soul was no longer my own. Once dead, I had pay for my body and soul to be reunited…and Death didn't come cheap.

In my peripheral, a shadow darted past the doorway.

On any other day, it might have been an animal, a wild dog or curious cat. But this creature, black as ebony and pulsing of pure evil, moved with purpose—*intention.* Amorphous, the anomaly entered the tomb, ghostly black tendrils questing. One shadowy finger slid over my foot. If alive, I'd have felt it lick my skin like a tongue.

Before me, it began to contort, to assume a shape.

Curvaceous, seductive, dark as sin.

A woman.

Slowly, sinuously, she manifested from the monstrous and into human form. Hidden beneath a black cowl, she lifted her chin and opened her eyes.

Within my sarcophagus of lifeless flesh, I gasped.

Inanna.

As if intuiting my shock, her vermillion lips curved into a sneer.

"No, Sumerian," she said, her voice surprisingly soft. "I am not my sister…"

'Twins,' Gilgamesh's revelation echoed.

Predatorily, Ereshkigal prowled the space before me. Paced like a cat toying with her injured prey—savouring my fear. My very being sensed her unnaturalness, and I withered before the anti-creator. Where my soul was made of light, she was forged of darkness.

Helpless, frozen by death, I could only observe and listen.

"We've been watching you for a long while, Solomon," she said, her face shadowed by a black cowl. "You've been the subject of many a debate in our realm."

I yearned to ask why I was of interest to the world of the dead.

Ereshkigal turned her violet eyes onto me. "You really don't know, do you? Interesting…"

Hollow and haunting, her voice slithered about the crypt. Each word seemed to die upon her lips, caught as a disembodied whisper. Phantom voices, inhuman and guttural, responded to their mistress's every utterance. Although the Goddess of Death and I were the only two in the room, I sensed invisible eyes watching, listening, from the shadows.

The goddess drifted closer and leaned in to further inspect my eyes. Hers, like lilac fire, stared deep into my being. "You, I can understand Inanna's interest—the other, however, is a cad and coward—a *mistake.*" Her entourage of obscurity thickened, grew louder and more menacing at mention of her former lover. "Regardless…" she said with a dismissive wave and the encroaching darkness ebbed away. "Despite my sister's curse, your soul belongs to me. For every death, you owe me a piece of your soul."

"There's more than one piece?"

"Yes," she replied. "There are many pieces to a soul."

I realized then that, somehow, she was able to hear me.

"Fragments, shattered by pain and loss," she continued. "How many depends on the man. Not all souls are destroyed equally. Those who did not dare to love, did not sacrifice or were shallow and cruel—their souls have not fractured at all. The souls left whole at the end of their lives are blackest of all. Those left broken, who have loved and lived through the greatest of sorrows—those are the souls I crave most. Like yours, Solomon.

"Each time you die, I will take another piece, one at a time until you are no more—and then you will belong to me…" She regarded me with sad, amethyst eyes. "You will suffer, of course. There's no other way to usher a soul into the Underworld. You will diminish a little more each time, becoming less and less of who you were—a soul cannot dwell in darkness unless it has surrendered all hope of the light."

Suffer.

A word I knew well. Some words burrow beneath the skin, resonate so deeply they no longer exist a word—but as an emotion.

Ereshkigal knelt before me, leaned into my ear. If I were alive, I'd have felt her icy breath as she spoke. "But, dear Solomon, should you ever wish to end this torturous forever," she whispered, drawing a pale fingertip over my lips. "You only have to offer yourself to me, join my army, and I can free you from this nightmare."

She stood. "Of course, the realm of the dead is a curse all its own—but at least you'd be free from *Inanna*." Ereshkigal winced as if her sister's very name was poison upon her tongue.

"I hate to do this to you—but even I am little more than a slave to my own creation...*mythosofaray*," she muttered, pointing a long, ivory finger at me.

My chest cracked open and an orb of shimmering blue escaped. I watched it abandon me, a piece of myself lost forever to the Queen of the Dead. Silent, graceful, it drifted through the space between us. A tiny glimpse of heaven. The instant it landed on her palm, the sphere was devoured by shadows.

With a sad smile, Ereshkigal took her prize and vanished in a plume of ebony mist.

Then the pain began.

Electricity fired inside every cell. Sharp and relentless, invisible needles began stitching my soul back into every fibre of my being. My organs screamed as they shuddered to life. Every muscle, every nerve, every inch of skin—I had no idea I could experience such excruciating sensations.

After an eternity, my heart thudded once, then twice, and then continuously, though weak and sporadic. My lungs begged for their first taste of air and I dragged in a wheezing breath, gasping as it entered too slowly. The smell of my spoiled flesh gagged me, but I greedily forced in one after another, hungry to live once more. My eyes burned and I willed my lids to shut, grit scraping the tender whites. With no saliva yet to swallow, I choked on my dry and wizened tongue. An insect crawled out of my ear and skittered down my neck. I tried to slap it away, but my hand only flopped clumsily.

My throat ached where Gilgamesh had sliced it open, the flesh not fully mended. My legs and feet, mottled purple and grey, swelled with fresh blood. Half the day was lost before I could bring myself to a stand. Reborn anew, yet imprisoned within a body caught between life and death, I could only wait.

When I can walk, I will find a stream, quench my thirst, and wash my body of the blood...and then, oh precious then, I will find Gilgamesh...and make him pay.

I stumbled over the pebbled paths towards Knossos. Emptier inside, Ereshkigal had warned I'd be lesser each time I resurrected. A reluctant part of me sympathized with Gilgamesh. How much of himself had he lost over the centuries? I loathed to empathize with his madness, but I could now understand how one could be driven to inhumanity. Gilgamesh was a mortal man cursed for defying the same spiteful goddess. That alone made him my ally—whether I liked it or not.

With only a handful of brothels on the island, he was not hard to find. Sweet incense and quieted moans wafted from the windows. Perched on a patio railing, the former king was eating a peach and gazing out over the roiling ocean. The deep lines carved into his face only hours before were smooth once more; the silver streaks in his hair were again dark and luxuriant.

I strolled up to him and drove my fist into his jaw, the peach sent flying from his hand.

"Solomon..." Gilgamesh chuckled, rubbing his chin. "I've been expecting you, my friend."

"You are *no* friend to me." I trembled with rage. "You're *never* to betray me like that again, do you understand? Or I will devote my eternity to killing you over and over every day until Ereshkigal has claimed every remnant of your soul."

Mouth twitching with amusement, he offered me a respectful nod. "I like you, Solomon. I've been threatened thousands of times over my many lives—but you, you sound as though you really mean it." He spat a crimson-tinged wad onto the flagstone patio and caressed his cheek. "Good punch."

Once my blood had cooled, I asked, "How many times have you died since...being cursed?"

"I've lost count over seven hundred years....dozens, I'm sure. It gets harder—and more painful—every time."

My eyes widened with horror. I couldn't stomach enduring the pain of resurrection ever again let alone dozens of times. A small part of me, however, was shocked he had so many fragments of his soul to spare.

"Why so many times?"

"If you haven't noticed..." He gave me a sardonic look. "I'm a bit of an ass."

"Oh, I definitely noticed." I laughed, but then a sad realization dawned. "People...*murdered* you?"

Gilgamesh drew a deep breath. "Some of my deaths were caused by people wanting revenge or saw that I'd not aged over many years and they grew suspicious—for which I was pronounced a demon and hunted down to be torn to pieces. That's an unpleasant resurrection, I can tell you."

A cold chill moved through me, Father's screams echoing.

"I've died in every way you could imagine, but strangely enough, the most common is plague. I believed once I was immortal, I'd be impervious to such nonsense, but for every illness that swept through a village, I was as susceptible as any mortal man."

"So you must sleep with women to remain young? What happens if you cannot...find a woman to be with?"

"I age rapidly, grow very weak and frail...and a bit mad. In the beginning, I made certain I was within reach of a new maiden each day. Over time, I realized I wouldn't die if I missed a few days, but I'd age a decade or more. That in itself caused more issue than finding sex."

"Why?"

"I couldn't hide my condition from the townspeople. They'd become frightened. Mortal men carry with them an instinct for the unnatural. They'll not listen to reason—I've tried many a time."

"My eyes," I said under my breath.

"Man fears what they do not understand, that is known, but why they seek to destroy those things they find curious, I'll never understand. And so, as to not run out of women, I often take lengthy leaves of absence to allow the young girls to mature—not to mention, to let the elders of the community pass on, thus giving me a whole new city to dwell within."

I sucked in a sharp breath. "The Storyteller!"

Gilgamesh gave a side-eyed glance. "I was wondering if you'd remember that..."

"You told us, Father and me, about this place—I knew I'd seen you before!"

He laughed. "Yes, I'd been living in Ur for a few years at that time. I was on my way back to Knossos when I came across you and your father."

A sudden breeze stirred the palms into frenzied whispers, violet clouds stalking the horizon.

"Come," Gilgamesh said, eyeing the looming storm. "There's something I need to show you—we're running out of time."

25
Macabre

*O*verhead, the tempest growled. Steel-black clouds churned, wind pressing at our backs. Copper-scented rain cascaded from the heavens. I found the island's pendulous moods unnerving, so a paradox to the slow and indifferent demeanour of the desert.

Gilgamesh led me down a path dense with foliage, into the shadows, civilization waning far behind. Muscles clenched, I remained on high alert. I didn't trust him, not after what he'd done.

"Where are you taking me?" I asked, my voice taut.

Ahead, Gilgamesh wrestled with a large carob frond blocking the path. He glanced back with a wide grin. "Don't worry, Solomon. I won't kill you again."

Unconvinced, I narrowed my eyes at him.

"I promise. Besides, I need your help."

"With what?"

"You'll see," he said, turning onto a game trail obscured by fallen leaves. "It's not far now."

An icy raindrop trickled down my back like the cold fingertip of intuition counting the bones of my spine. All warnings telling me to turn and run, I'm sure.

Finally, we broke through into a small clearing. In the centre, blanketed by lichen and spattered with bird droppings, stood the ruins of a stone building.

"What is this place?"

"It's the remains of a temple, but that's not what I wish to show you," Gilgamesh explained. "Come."

He knelt and pulled open a hatch door covered with dirt, exposing a stone stairwell that descended into darkness.

Without hesitation, I declared, "I am *not* going down there."

"I don't blame you." He chuckled. "Wait here."

He vanished into the opaque. Upon his return, he cradled a bundle of cloth within his hands. Carefully, he unfurled the corners. Inside was a pile of fragmented bones.

I met his grave expression. "W-What are these?"

Without reply, he plucked a bone from the pile and set it onto my palm. "Look closer."

Bulbous growths knobbed the ends of a smooth, pallid shaft. Interspersed along the shaft were tiny demarkations.

I frowned, confused.

"These are *human* bones, Solomon—and those," he pointed, "...are *teeth marks*."

I gasped and dropped the bone. Gilgamesh retrieved it, returning it gently to the pile.

I took a step back. "I-I don't understand."

Gilgamesh regarded me with dark eyes. "What's the *one* thing you've never seen in Knossos? Think Solomon! In all this sprawling kingdom, on every island, in every village—amongst the *thousands* of people—what have you *never* seen? What's missing?"

"I-I don't...know."

Gilgamesh grabbed me by the collar. "Before Theseus arrived, Solomon...what was *not* here?"

I raked my memory, searching—then horror sliced through me. "*Children...*"

Fog wreathed the island. From a distance, Knossos seemed a castle set in the sky. A heaven. Only it was just an illusion. Terrible truths lingered beneath the facade of enlightenment.

A chill embedded itself inside my bones. What kind of people *sacrificed* children?

Ahead of me, Gilgamesh stormed through the forest, slashing at wayward branches with his bare hands. Rage radiated from him. As much as I wanted to balk at his accusation that these beautiful, sophisticated Minoans—and my precious Ariadne—could be part of such a sinister deed, I sensed now was not the time.

This man, who claimed to be the wise and powerful king of my people had placed before me a heinous charge, an act so vile my mind could not conceive of it. I thought of Father, of how he'd sought to shelter me from the evils of the world—and how I wished I could return to those safe arms once again.

Gilgamesh paused before the threshold of the city, his anger somewhat abated.

"What are we going to do?"

He cast a dark eye at me. "We're going to stop them."

"How?"

"I don't know yet...but now that I have you, it'll be easier."

"Why do you need me?"

"Because *two* immortal heroes can do so much more than just *one*..." His gaze hardened as he panned the sprawling palace. "Look, there's a lot more to this than you know. I've been here for many years trying to unravel the secrets. But what I do know is it all leads back to one source—*Inanna*."

"Inanna? But she's so far away...in Uruk."

"Yes, but her reach is far, Solomon...so very far. Do you remember what I told you about her father ripping the Mes from her back? Well, after he removed them, he magically cast them out into the world—to hide them."

"Where?"

He gave me a bewildered shrug. "I've spent centuries trying to answer that question. What I strongly suspect is, because of his actions that day, Inanna is somehow linked to the Mes through her blood. Somehow, she's able to...*channel* herself to the location of the other Mes. They're somehow hidden inside various cultures, inside their myths. Inanna is able to merge her essence with those who come into contact with the Mes and she uses that individual to perform certain...rituals."

"*Use* them?"

"She possesses them," Gilgamesh said grimly. "But there must be a pact or something. A covenant of sorts. In all my travels, I've found her influence in many civilizations, in many different ways. She desires the blood and suffering of the innocent—through sacrifice and sexual acts. In some cases, it was through rituals of blood and cannibalism. Others, it was through forced prostitution—using young women, mostly virgins—sending them to brothels and keeping them prisoner as sex slaves. They call it the Cult of the Courtesan."

I sucked in a breath. "Indra..."

Gilgamesh frowned.

"My...wife."

"You're married?" he asked quietly.

"I *was* married. Inanna killed her..." After a few calming breaths, I asked, "How do you know so much about the Cult?"

Mirthlessly, he laughed. "I've spent many a day in a brothel. Too many. You can come by a great deal of knowledge—and many secrets—whilst between the legs of a lady, you know."

"How can you...be with them then? Knowing you're *catering* to Inanna?"

"Ahh, but one must know the enemy in order to defeat them, no?" Gilgamesh offered a sad smile. "Besides, the only way the cult will free the women is if a man pays for her services—and I pay *every* time. Many women are there for years, servicing hundreds of men before they're released or given to a bride auction. I have freed more prostitutes than I can count." He put a hand on my shoulder. "The point is —Inanna *must* be stopped...and I think I know how."

"How?"

"First things first. The Games are scheduled in two days' time—and we have a massacre to prevent."

26
Labyrinth

*B*eneath the midnight sky, a sea of people waited for the event to begin. Countless torches bathed the arena in an eerie, golden glow. Crimson swags flowed like blood waterfalls, puddling onto the smooth sandy floor. Excited Minoans packed the stands. Rhythmic drums announced the arrival of the royal entourage, stirring the audience into a susurrus of anticipation.

In a gown of white linen, hair laced with bellflower and tiny cochlear shells, Ariadne drifted phantom-like behind her mother, Theseus, and three other women who I presumed were her older sisters, the three dancers from the Bull Leaping event. Ariadne's lovely face was sullen, her petal-pink lips downturned. Pain scored my heart. How could she be part of such an abhorrent scheme? Even if she didn't have a hand in the actual sacrifices, she condoned it by not stopping it.

Ariadne lifted her chin, noticing my gaze. Her eyes lit up and she pushed past her escorts to get to me.

"Ariadne," Pasiphae said, her voice taut with disapproval. "We're about to begin."

Beside the Queen, Theseus shot me a murderous glare.

"Solomon! I couldn't find you on the pier afterward," Ariadne said with a warm smile.

"I had to leave." I feigned indifference. "And you were *busy* entertaining *Theseus*."

Her eyes lowered in shame. "You know then."

"I know you lied to me."

She placed a soft hand on my arm. "I wanted to tell you…"

"But you didn't, did you?" I jerked from her touch. "You should go back to your *husband*."

Ariadne's eyes filled with hurt and she backed away, returning to Theseus' side, arms wrapped around herself. Fists clenched, I drew a calming breath. My thoughts and emotions warred with one another. My mind told me she was a murderer, a child killer, a sadist—but my heart said I was wrong.

Gilgamesh touched my shoulder. "Calm down, friend—there're more important matters to attend to."

Introductory music blared and we settled into our seats.

Queen Pasiphae waved to the crowd. Daedalus handed her a cylindrical object, narrow at one end and wide at the other. She put it to her mouth and began to speak, her voice amplified.

"Welcome People of Crete! And welcome Prince Theseus of Greece, son of King Aegean." The crowd roared. "For too long, we've lost our children to a terrible fate. As your queen, I vow to right the wrongs of our king, who lied to Poseidon, allowing me to be raped and impregnated by the sacred white bull, and then imprisoned me within the labyrinth where I gave birth to…a monster—a monster who demands the lifeblood of our children.

"But, my subjects, I offer wonderful news! We are to offer the Minotaur a mass tribute, whereas he will feast and fall asleep for nine years and a day! Crete will be safe for our children once more! And so," she continued over cries of joy. "Theseus has brought us a priceless gift from his homeland, a gift that will end our long suffering!"

At her command, a massive set of doors opened on the other side of the pavilion. Two bulls pulled an enormous chariot, inside which were the fourteen boys and girls I'd seen arrive on Theseus's boat. Dressed in white gowns, like tiny angels, they clung to one another. The bulls lumbered to a stop in the centre of the stadium. One by one, the children were assisted off the gilded wagon and ushered onto a red carpet.

My blood froze—the *children* were going to be sacrificed!

Pasiphae brought the amplifier to her mouth. "Now, The Daughters of the Labyrinth, your princesses, Acalle, Xenodice, Phaedra, and Ariadne, will unlock the gate and send the children on their way!"

The crowd screamed with delight.

Ariadne rose, her expression made of stone, cold and dutiful. She and her sisters made their way down to the children. One at a time, Ariadne presented each child with a crown of poppies and a kiss. Two of her sisters blindfolded the children. The last princess followed with a bowl of rising smoke, blowing fumes into each child's face. Moments later, the children began to sway, drugged.

The children were then led to the large drawbridge at the end of the pavilion. Ariadne stepped up to the gate and a soldier knelt before her, holding a black box. She lifted the lid, retrieving a golden key, which she then guided into the lock.

With her hand still on the key, Ariadne paused.

The crowd of thousands held their breath.

"What is she waiting for?" Pasiphae glared at her daughter.

Ariadne lifted her eyes to the audience—to me—and I saw a single tear roll down her cheek. Then, she turned the key and backed away. The heavy drawbridge groaned, metal chains rattling as it lowered and landed with a resounding thud. The black mouth of a cave was revealed: stone walls wrought with lichen, silky threads of aged spiderwebs, stalactites like snarling teeth.

The guards corralled the children, prodding them forward. Boys in one line and girls in the other, they took hold of each other's hand—and entered the labyrinth.

The crowd surged onto the field, towards the labyrinth's entrance, for a better vantage should the Minotaur make a personal appearance. Amid the sea of people, faces blurred before me. I could no longer see Ariadne, the Queen nor Theseus.

"Quickly, let's go." Gilgamesh nudged me.

We hurried down a corridor.

"Do you really believe there's a monster in there?" I asked, my heart pounding.

"I know there is," Gilgamesh said cryptically.

"Have you seen it?"

"No, but they've sent hundreds of children into the labyrinth—and none have ever returned. So something must be in there, something that kills children."

"Those...little bones, they were in an old temple. If the monster is in the maze here, why were the bones so far away?"

Gilgamesh was quiet, then replied, "Their parents left them there."

My blood ran cold.

"The labyrinth," he continued, "runs everywhere under Knossos, under the temples—and further, I imagine. This is a cult, Solomon. The Minoans have been conditioned for many years to believe they must appease the Minotaur by sacrificing their young."

"What could make a parent kill their own child?"

Gilgamesh stopped, staring me in the eye. "Fear."

"Fear of what?"

"There's no time to explain." Gilgamesh descended a set of stairs. "We must find the children! Whatever is in the centre of the labyrinth must be stopped—permanently."

Concern for the children weighed on my soul. I couldn't allow them to come to harm. I wouldn't fail them—like I'd failed Miri.

"The secret entrance is down here," he said. "The door is locked so we'll have to break it down."

When we reached the bottom, I stopped in my tracks.

"I know this place," I said, recognizing it as the stairwell where Ariadne and I shared our first passionate kisses.

Gilgamesh looked surprised. "How?"

"Because *I* showed it to him," a voice said.

I spun around to see the figure in black at the top of the stairs. She yanked off her mask, dark locks spilling over her shoulders.

"Ariadne?" I gaped at her.

She had a satchel slung over her shoulder and long dagger belted to her hip. In her hand, she held the same key she'd used to open the drawbridge.

"What are *you* doing here?" Gilgamesh asked, scowling.

"I'm here to save the children—what the hell are *you* doing here?"

Gilgamesh looked taken aback. "Save them—but I thought you were one of those....barbarians."

"Of course not," she said, glaring at him. "*Some* of us can control our *primitive* urges."

I cleared my throat. "We're here to save the children too."

"Fine. If you're coming, let's go," Ariadne said coldly, taking over the mission. "We must hurry. Follow closely or you'll be lost."

Gilgamesh gave me a bewildered shrug. Ariadne retrieved three torches from her pack, each crackling to life as she lit them.

"I've spent many months wandering the labyrinth, trying to find the centre," Ariadne explained as she pushed the key into the lock. "But so far, I haven't been able to."

The door unlocked with a metallic *clunk*, hinges creaking as it swung open. I stared into the gaping abyss, pitch blackness stared back. Freed from its confines, cool, musty breath escaped the cave.

Fearless, Ariadne stepped inside. Gilgamesh ducked through the entrance first, and I followed. Anchored to the rocky floor was line after line of golden string, each webbing into a different cavern.

"These caves run for miles in every direction," Ariadne explained. "Some go on forever and then just end abruptly at a wall of rock— some just lead to traps."

"Traps?" I swallowed.

"There are chasms, deep ones—so be careful where you step. I've been laying down twine so I'd know where I've already explored. Last night, I think I found the way to the centre...but I can't get there alone."

"So, you're saying you need our help," Gilgamesh said, a smile in his voice.

Ariadne ignored him. "There's only one route that leads directly to the Minotaur's lair—the one they sent the children into, but my mother has that one heavily guarded. There are several hidden entrances, like this one. I've searched as many as I could, but..." her voice trailed off as a distant scream reverberated through the cavern.

"Time to go," Ariadne ordered. "Try to keep up."

The torches illumined little more than a dim sphere around us. Sweat stung my eyes, blurring my already limited vision. Dizzy, I clung to the wall. My heart fluttered. The world closed in, panic rising. As if buried alive, I could almost feel the dirt filling my mouth, my nose...

"I...can't b-breathe!" I fell to my knees.

Ariadne returned to my side, her face sheen with perspiration. "Solomon, I know it's hard to breathe, but we'll come to a cavern soon. One with an opening to the sky—bringing in fresh air. It's just a little further, I promise."

She took my hand, threading us through the pitch labyrinth. Sharp walls scraped my chest, stalactites reached as if to carve out my eyes. I thought of the children, lost and wandering this dark Hell. How frightened they must be.

"The Minotaur," I said, catching my breath. "Have you seen it?"

Ariadne was quiet.

Gilgamesh piped up. "Yes, Princess, do tell our young Sumerian about the *monster* who eats children."

She shot him a lethal glare and my stomach dropped as I realized there was even more to this macabre secret.

She sighed. "There is no Minotaur."

"What!"

"Before me," Ariadne began, "my mother became pregnant with another man's child. Enraged by her infidelity, my father told his people the story of the white bull and how a vengeful god had made Pasiphae lust for the sacred beast—thus becoming impregnated by it. As punishment, Father locked her inside the labyrinth beneath the city. Until then, he'd kept knowledge of the caverns a secret, using them to horde gold and ancient artifacts. My mother claims that while imprisoned within the maze, she came upon one of those items. She wouldn't tell me what this item was, only that it was...*unique*. She said when she held this object, a beautiful woman suddenly appeared, claiming to be a powerful goddess. The goddess offered my mother a number of magical gifts if she'd do as she asked. Of course, my mother accepted."

"What gifts did she offer her?" Gilgamesh asked.

"Riches, power, eternal youth, but also—" She swallowed. "The throne to Knossos. The goddess inflicted some kind of...*spell* onto my father, making him unfit to rule. My mother then went along with my father's lie about the baby being born half-human, half-bull and that it now lived in the labyrinth—and that's when the children started disappearing." Ariadne's eyes filled with sadness.

"Only a few went missing in the first year or two, not enough to cause suspicion—then dozens began disappearing. After a decade, there were hardly any children left and those who'd survived were kept hidden by their parents or sent to live across the water. There was nothing to feed this supposed Minotaur. Then we were struck by earthquakes and a volcanic eruption that killed thousands, ruining our crops, our land, our homes. The people were terrified, starving and desperate. They believed it was a punishment from the Minotaur. The Minoans began having babies simply to offer them up to the Minotaur, leaving them in the temples—the only thing found left were their tiny bones.

"And then there were none. Which is why when our people started trading overseas, my mother discovered there were others willing to bargain. These fourteen children aren't the first from other cultures, but they are the first in a long and horrific plot of mass sacrifice that I cannot see an end to—unless I stop her."

My heart hurt. All those children; all the lies, fear, and *death*.

"Solomon, I need you to believe me." Her eyes pleaded with mine. "My mother left me no choice but to marry Theseus. She told me the truth about the Minotaur, but she also lied to me. She said she wanted to make amends, and that we were uniting our cultures so the Minoans could move away and begin anew in Greece. I would never have agreed to such a thing had I known the real reason—that she traded my hand in marriage for...children."

"I believe you," I said, tracing her jaw. "I'm sorry I doubted you."

"I don't want to be with Theseus, Solomon. I want to be with—"

"*Excuse* me," Gilgamesh uttered around a bored sigh. "Sorry to disrupt this little...romantic interlude, but we have some lives to save. And I have to get back for a, um, midnight snack, if you catch my meaning—unless the Princess is feeling up to a little *charity*." He stroked the front of his pants and waggled his brows at Ariadne.

Her face twisted in disgust.

206

I shot him a disapproving glare. "Never mind him, let's go."

Minutes later, fresh air breathed onto my face, the tunnel opening up in to a massive cavern. The universe peered through an opening at the top and into a subterranean spring that filled the cave from wall to wall. Beyond, an arched doorway beckoned, aglow with distant illumination.

"That's the entrance to the lair, I'm certain of it." Ariadne stood at the edge of the water.

Gilgamesh started to remove his tunic. "Then let's swim across."

Ariadne didn't move.

I touched her arm. "Ariadne?"

"I-I can't swim."

I now understood why she needed our help.

"You can scale the outside walls of a building like a spider, but you can't swim?" I teased.

She pinked. "Well, I…"

"I can swim very well, I'll take you across." It was my turn to blush. "But you may want to…disrobe."

Wide-eyed, she stared at me.

"Clothes get very heavy when they're wet," I explained. "Makes it difficult to swim."

"Oh," she said quietly, peeling off her shirt.

"We'll roll up our clothes and put them in the sack. We can hold them above the surface to keep them dry."

Gilgamesh, now naked, slid into the water while holding his clothes over his head. With one arm, he pulled himself to the other side.

I turned away to give her some privacy as she stripped off the rest of her clothes. My body, however, was less than cooperative in my gentlemanly pursuit.

"Okay, done."

It took everything not to spin around and look at her.

"Climb into the water and hold tight to the edge," I said. "I'll be there in a minute."

After a calming breath, I removed my tunic and placed it in the sack. I turned around, expecting Ariadne to be politely looking elsewhere, but found her staring right at me—at my chest.

"Why do you and Gillis have the same mark?"

I froze. I'd forgotten about Inanna's symbol.

"It's…a Sumerian tradition," I lied.

She nodded, eyes suspicious.

At the water's edge, I handed Ariadne the sack of clothes. Ghostly mists curled atop the glassy surface. I lowered myself into the naturally heated pool, my skin tingling.

"Okay—come here." I wrapped my arm around her waist and drew her to me. Ariadne's body was warm, skin smooth and slick with the spring's melted minerals. Her bronze skin glittered in the faint glow, like diamond dust on her face and chest. The entire moment was becoming far too erotic. I could scarcely recall why we were there, let alone the urgency of our mission.

Using one arm, I dragged us across the water. With every stroke, I tried to fill my mind with mundane, even revolting things, like the smell of goat dung on a hot Sumerian summer day when I used to have to clean the pen—but even that wasn't helping.

Then a question flashed through my mind.

"Who was the man who impregnated your mother?" I blurted.

Ariadne drew a long breath. "Daedalus—he's my real father, too."

"And the baby? If there's no Minotaur, what happened to Pasiphae's baby?"

"My brother?" Ariadne said, her voice tightened. "He was the first sacrifice."

"Hurry!" Gilgamesh hissed, peering through the rocky archway. "It's the centre of the labyrinth!"

Ariadne and I threw our clothes on and rushed to his side. Beyond the doorway was a large cavern gilded with candlelight. Stalagmite spears rose from the floor, quartz glittering like diamonds in the stone. Tunnel entrances honeycombed the chamber. A massive limestone altar dominated the centre, crimson dribbling over the edges; and standing behind it, naked and drenched in blood—was Pasiphae.

My heart sunk.

The blood is fresh.

Ariadne gasped. "We're too late!"

I scanned for a tiny, motionless body, but could see nothing near the shrine except the Queen.

Arms raised to the heavens, a writhing serpent in each hand, Pasiphae chanted, *"Akiris masii e comredas mithon!"*

I turned to Gilgamesh for translation.

"I offer this child to you…"

"Sanda keiros ouya careesa."

"To fulfill the promise."

Pasiphae's final words ricocheted off the rocky walls, *"Assir cannos ekrita—en avanta mne morf!"*

Beside me, Gilgamesh paled.

"What did she say?" I shook his arm.

"Pasiphae has offered the Snake Goddess to inhabit her body permanently, thus making the Queen immortal." He leaned over, his voice low in my ear. "And freeing Inanna…"

Pasiphae turned her back to us. On her shoulder was a deeply engraved, circular tattoo.

The Mes.

Despite the heat, I shivered. Just the idea of something that had been in contact with Inanna sent chills of terror through me.

Suddenly, a great roar thundered from the tunnels, followed by the high-pitched scream of a child. A little girl emerged from one of the passageways; the white blindfold hung like a scarf around her neck. Horrified, sobbing, she stumbled into the cavern.

Pasiphae knelt before the trembling child, opening her arms in a motherly gesture. Despite Pasiphae being naked and covered in blood, the girl ran into the Queen's embrace. Whatever had chased her through the tunnels had to have been even scarier.

Animalistic growls echoed, growing louder—closer.

208

Eyes wide, we watched as a creature materialized from the darkness. Its body was that of a man: lean, strong torso, rounded shoulders, sweat glistening on his muscular stomach. The head, however, was a beast's—a bull. Coarse, black hair covered his face, snout dripping. Sharp horns protruded from his head, bone-white with bloodied tips.

I gaped at Ariadne. "I though you said the Minotaur wasn't real!"

"I-I don't understand—it's not! It *can't* be real!"

The Minotaur bellowed and the little girl shrieked, burying her face into Pasiphae's bosom. The Queen waved the monster away and it immediately obeyed, lumbering back into the tunnels.

Pasiphae cradled the child, muttering in soft tones as she laid her atop the altar.

"There now," Pasiphae said, lifting a chalice to the child's lips. "Drink this…" Within moments, the girl quieted, her eyes hooded and heavy.

More screams sounded from the tunnels—the Minotaur had found another.

"Okay, time to end this. You take care of the Minotaur," Gilgamesh told me, drawing a blade from his belt. "I'll stop Pasiphae."

Back against the wall, he crept through the shadows. I took the other side of the cavern. Ariadne, however, walked straight into the middle, in plain view of her mother. Not yet seeing her daughter, Pasiphae's eyes glittered with dark excitement as she launched into another round of chants. At the altar, Pasiphae produced a knife, poising it over the young girl's heart…

"Mother, no!" Ariadne screamed.

Pasiphae stopped, the crazed glow in her eyes clearing. "Ariadne?"

"Mother, please don't." Ariadne approached the altar. "You're not in control of yourself. Something *terrible* has taken over you."

Pasiphae's face twisted as she resisted the force within.

"You have to fight it! I know you, Mother. You're kind. You're wise. You're greater than this evil inside of you!"

The energy inside Pasiphae seemed strengthened by this, the Queen's brown eyes taking on a gleaming, lavender hue.

My mouth went dry. It was true. Inanna had found a way to reach out from her temple prison and influence the world from afar.

Ariadne took careful steps towards her mother "Why are you doing this?"

Pasiphae's eyes flickered with cognizance. "I-I only wanted for Minos to pay for…what he'd done to me."

"What Father did was wrong," Ariadne conceded, climbing the stone steps up to the altar. "But you can't murder children in the name of revenge."

"The Goddess promised me the throne to…to…" Pasiphae clutched her stomach, screaming as she doubled over in pain.

"She promised you the throne to Crete?"

"No…*everywhere*. She said we we'd rule a new world together—forever."

Ariadne shook with rage. "In exchange for the blood of *children*!"

At this, Inanna's voice thundered from Pasiphae. "How dare you question me! I am a god! *I own you!*"

"*No one* owns me," Ariadne's voice was dangerous. "Not even the gods."

Inanna laughed. "Someday you'll see just how insignificant you are, how worthless and diminutive your pathetic existence. You owe your life to me, all of you, and you have the audacity to defy me? Me!" her voice boomed, stones raining from the ceiling. "There were no humans before I made you. With these very hands, I molded you from clay, shaped you and gave you the gift of life using the blood of my own kind—and you disobey me? I am your creator. Your one, *true* god?"

I scanned the cavern for Gilgamesh. Crouched in the shadow of a great boulder, he too watched on in horror.

"If you are truly our creator, why harm us?" Ariadne climbed the last stair, resting her hand on the unconscious child's arm. "If you made us, was it not out of love? Are you not Mother to us all?"

"Foolish girl." Inanna rolled her eyes. "I wonder, do you feel the same of your pottery? If one is dropped, shattering to pieces, do you mourn your vase? Your cup? Your plate? No, they are...*disposable*. You toss it aside, make another, never thinking of it again."

Ariadne looked hurt. "You see us as nothing more than *pottery*? You don't care for us?"

Inanna sneered. "Care for you? I didn't create you for me to love... you were created to love *me*."

"And what of the other gods. Surely they had something to say of your little...project."

Inanna's face twisted in anger, taking hold of the knife again and moving around the altar towards Ariadne, who took slow steps in the opposite direction.

"I was punished for creating you," Inanna spat. "Stripped of my powers—we all were. My father didn't want any one god to behold such power again. And now my family despises me—but I've found a way to restore my powers." She eyed the blood on her hands with an evil smile. "And harness even more."

"But why does it have to be the blood of children?" Ariadne glanced at the girl on the altar.

Inanna tilted her head around a playful smile. "*It doesn't.*"

She lunged, thrusting the blade into Ariadne's stomach.

Ariadne!" I rushed from the shadows. "

Realizing what she'd just done to her daughter, Pasiphae awakened from Inanna's spell with a scream. She crumpled beside the altar, wailing.

I clambered up the crude steps, catching Ariadne as she fell.

"Solomon..." she whispered, pressing her hands to her abdomen.

"Don't move," I said, assessing the wound—blood gushed from a deep entry point.

She met my eyes, her lovely face ashen. "Go...save the children. Please..."

"I won't leave you."

"You must. For the children..." She moaned, breathing hard.

An ear-shattering roar shook the cavern, followed by shrieks and cries of terror. From the main passageway, the rest of the children flooded into the chamber—followed closely by the Minotaur.

Gilgamesh uttered a fierce battle cry as he leapt from the shadows and tackled the beast, knocking the creature off his feet. The children herded together, hugging one another and weeping.

"Please, go!" Ariadne pushed me, tears in her eyes.

Torn, I bent over and kissed her tenderly. She whimpered as my affections left blisters on her lips. As I stood, however, I felt the tip of a blade enter my shoulder. I yelled and spun around, coming face to face with Pasiphae—her eyes blazing purple.

"Well, well," Inanna's voice emanated. "If it isn't my blue-eyed Sumerian. How are you enjoying your *loveless* forever?"

I gritted my teeth against the pain, hot blood running down my chest.

"About the same as you, I would imagine," I fired back.

Furious, she lunged, slashing at me with the dagger. Backing away, I hedged around the altar. Inanna circled, crazed and bloodthirsty. As I stepped behind the shrine, my foot struck something solid. I glanced down to find Daedalus, his throat slit from ear to ear, eyes rheumy with death.

That's where all the blood came from, I thought, saddened.

On the other side of the cave, Gilgamesh wrestled with the Minotaur. He managed to straddle the beast, positioning his blade over its heart. The Minotaur roared and shoved Gilgamesh off. The beast lunged at the former king, who rolled out of the way, but swung his leg back and tripped the monster. The Minotaur slammed headfirst into a boulder. Stunned, he lumbered to a stand—his hideous head *askew*.

Gilgamesh watched on, amused; then sauntered up to the monster, took hold of a horn and yanked—*and the head came off.*

"Theseus!" I hissed.

Face stained with cow's blood, the Greek prince had the wherewithal to look ashamed before darting into an adjacent tunnel. Ariadne was right, there was no Minotaur. Only an ass wearing the hollowed out, decapitated head of a bull to frighten children into Inanna's lair.

Gilgamesh tossed the macabre mask aside, glancing my direction with a cocky grin. But his smile swiftly melted into alarm. "Solomon! Behind you!"

I whirled to find a wild-eyed, possessed Pasiphae standing over the altar, blade poised to plunge into the little girl's chest. She hissed and brought the dagger down. Instinctively, I knocked the weapon from her hands before it could pierce the child. Enraged, Pasiphae charged me, fingertips curled like claws. Without thinking, I pushed her, so hard that she tumbled off the edge of the stairs. Airborne for a breath, the lavender glow of Inanna's presence abandoned Pasiphae the moment she landed, impaled through the chest by a sharp stalagmite.

"No!" Gilgamesh raged. "*I* was supposed to kill her!"

I frowned, wondering why it mattered, when a searing pain shot though my back. Falling to my knees, I reached around to feel for what had hurt me. My fingertips traced a pattern carving itself into my skin.

I gasped.

It was Pasiphae's tattoo—*the Mes.*

211

An angry, supernatural wind tore through the cavern and extinguished the myriad of candles, enshrouding us in shadow. Only the pale glow of moonlight found its way from the hole over the hot spring. The ground rocked and the ceiling trembled, raining pebbles.

"We have to get out of here! The tunnels are going to collapse!" Gilgamesh rushed up the steps and gathered the unconscious child into his arms. I followed suit, lifting Ariadne's lifeless body from the floor. She uttered a pained moan and a flicker of hope ignited in my chest.

"This way, children!" Gilgamesh hollered to the boys and girls huddled in a far corner.

They scampered after us as we raced towards the main tunnel leading out to the pavilion. As we neared, the entire chamber shuddered. Disembodied laughter echoed from somewhere inside the mountain. Gilgamesh and I exchanged a grave look. Suddenly, the cave heaved and a massive crack split the stone floor into two. A landslide of boulders tumbled from the roof, burying the exit. Knocked off balance, I fell to my knees, Ariadne rolling from my arms.

The children shrieked as Gilgamesh herded them from the collapse, dust and debris drifting like a dark curtain.

"Gilgamesh!" I hollered, peering through the haze. "Where are you?"

"Head for the pool!" I heard him call out. He was leading the children back the way we'd come.

I patted the ground, searching for Ariadne. But before I could, a blinding blow struck me upside the head. Warmth trickled over my brow. I staggered and then dropped to my knees. Amidst the veil of dust, I saw a figure throw Ariadne over his shoulder—*Theseus*. I tried to get up, but my body wouldn't comply. Helpless, I watched as he disappeared into one of the tunnels.

Bloodied fingers outstretched, I reached for my stolen Ariadne—then fell into blackness.

"You could cooperate…a little," Gilgamesh grumbled, pulling me to a stand. "Come now, on your feet. We do have to hurry, you know."

"A-Ariadne. We have to save her." I leaned towards the tunnel entrance I'd watched Theseus escape through, but Gilgamesh redirected me toward the hot spring.

"Yes, yes," he said, wrapping my arm over his shoulder. "But first we must save *you*."

The mountain rocked again, pitching us side to side.

"Hurry!" Gilgamesh pushed me to go faster. We arrived at the pool, clambering in as another tremor shook the cavern. "Get in, swim across!"

Fully awake now, I jumped into the water and dragged myself across, Gilgamesh right behind me. Suddenly a massive jolt crackled through the rocks and the water around us began to recede.

"What's happening?" I floundered as the water started to swirl, eddying tighter into an abyss beneath us.

"She's trying to bury us under the mountain! We'll live forever beneath the stones if we don't get out of here!" Gilgamesh yelled. "Solomon! Over there! Ariadne's twine! Catch hold of it!'

I followed his line of sight to the sturdy, golden twine Ariadne had used to find her way through the labyrinth. With all my strength, I fought the dizzying current and reached for the thin rope. The pull of the water was too strong, yanking me away each time I neared.

"I can't reach it!"

Gilgamesh also tried to reach the twine, uttering a frustrated growl each time he grazed it with his fingertips.

"We're not going...to make it!" I shouted, struggling to keep my head above the surface.

Inanna's laughter boomed, the cave trembling. I looked up to see a large boulder loosening from the ceiling.

My chest tightened.

She's going to drop it on us...seal us in.

Gilgamesh and I met in the eye of the whorl, spinning faster and faster.

"Well," he sputtered through a mouthful of water. "This isn't...how I imagined my day going, how about...you?"

Saddened, I shook my head. Perhaps Ereshkigal would take mercy on us and let us die in peace rather than rot for all eternity under the mountain.

As the water rose above our chins, I stretched my neck up.

"Th...thank you...for coming...back...for me..."

Gilgamesh winked, then vanished as we were both pulled under.

A hush enveloped me as the water filled my ears. A curtain of bubbles swirled, drawing me down into a dark world. I wondered what it would be like to be conscious for eternity, trapped inside a body that would never let me go. Would I just die again and again?

Futilely, I reached up, as if in a last effort to touch the air. I had just closed my eyes, allowing myself to be carried away, when I felt a hand wrap around my wrist. I assumed it was Gilgamesh searching for comfort, so I returned the grip. Then the hand yanked, hard, nearly dislocating my arm. I was being pulled from the water! With my other hand, I swept the fathoms for Gilgamesh. I found him and grabbed hold of his tunic. Strong hands fought to drag us from swirling vortex.

Cool air kissed my face as I surfaced, and I drew long, ragged breaths. Beside me, Gilgamesh coughed and sputtered. I looked up to our saviours, seeing Rhadamanthys' determined face as he strained with all his might. Holding onto him, was Bansabira. Both men grunted, teeth gritted as they fought to save us.

Rhadamanthys looked past me, at Gilgamesh. "Is that Gillis? Ugh, throw him back, I was only saving *you!*"

With a final, heroic pull, the two men brought us up to safety. We all lay sprawled on the cave floor, panting. I rested against Bansabira's large chest.

"I am happy you are not dead, Solo-man," he said, patting my head.

"Well," Gilgamesh said between gulps of air. "That was unpleasant. If there was ever...a time for...a beer and a lovely pair of tits, it's now."

"Later," Rhadamanthys said, standing. "We have to get as far away from the island as we can. The volcano is angry, it may erupt at any moment."

"The children!" I exclaimed.

"They're safe," Rhadamanthys replied. "Duripi is sailing them to Tyre, we have friends there who'll care for them."

"How did you know where to find us?"

"Ariadne," Rhadamanthys said. "She told us to meet her in the palace basement, and to have the boats readied for the children—one of the little girls told us of the blue-eyed man who was hurt trying to save the children—now let's go!"

We rushed through the tunnel.

"We need to go after Theseus...he has Ariadne," I said, breathless.

"She's for dead, Solomon," Gilgamesh stated. "She was stabbed in the stomach, I do not believe she would survive that."

Upon his utterance, I noticed an odd, wordless exchange between Rhadamanthys and Bansabira.

"We don't know that! We have to try..."

We cannot, Solomon," Rhadamanthys said. "We'll be lucky to get out of here alive ourselves—" As if the mountain heard him, it shuddered, the floor heaving. "Let's go! My ship is waiting at the pier."

We scrambled down the white, pebbled path, tremors rippling over the island. Minoans raced past, making their way to a fleet of waiting boats.

As we reached the dock, Rhadamanthys began shouting orders, "Board the ramp! Lift the anchor! Free the sails!"

We rushed to comply, getting the boat out onto the water as fast as possible. As we bobbed away from the shoreline, a great explosion boomed. High atop the hill, amidst the shaking, the Knossos palace crumbled.

"Get the oars!" Rhadamanthys yelled.

We each grabbed an oar and began paddling out to sea. Behind us, amid the roiling smoke, a face appeared in the miasma—a face with glowing, lavender eyes.

The earth heaved, sending a powerful jolt through to the ocean floor. A wave rose from the depths, tossing our ship like a toy.

"Row! Row harder!" Rhadamanthys' dark eyes were fierce.

We pulled the oars, harder, faster. The boat began to pick up speed.

A tsunami of water slammed into the stern, with hopes of drowning us, but instead, it thrust the boat out into the safe, waiting arms of the open ocean.

27

In The Absence

*L*ured from sleep by the drone of the private jet, Petra blinked herself awake. Through the small, oval window, a newborn sun balanced on the horizon. It was twilight when they'd left Vancouver, now it was morning. How far had they travelled while she slept? She reached for her phone to check the time, but remembered Solomon had forced her to hand it over after boarding the plane.

"This can be tracked anytime you use it," he'd explained, turning off the smartphone and pocketing it. "We don't need to give them an advantage—they'll find us soon enough…"

When she'd tried to press the issue, inquiring as to who was after them and why, he merely shook his head and retreated to a far corner of the plane where he brooded alongside the darkening sky. She glanced back at his seat, now empty, with a wave of disappointment.

It's not like he just up and left, Petra—we're at 35,000 feet.

She rolled her eyes at herself, then yawned and moved to stretch her aching back. She cried out as fresh tattoos split open, feeling warm blood trickle down her spine.

There are so many now. I can feel them…

Fear settled on her soul. She thought of Pasiphae, how the queen had been compromised by the Mes—by Inanna. The reality of this mysterious affliction was becoming clear: Inanna was inside her.

Somewhere, burrowed inside Petra's own body, a vengeful malignancy had germinated, growing stronger, more powerful. Like a parasite, Inanna hid somewhere within Petra's psyche, waiting for a moment of weakness to wholly consume its host. Now, as she thought back, Petra realized she'd sensed this invasion since the moment she cut her finger on the urn. The erotic, frightening dreams of a woman with lavender eyes, the uncharacteristic sexual longing—the fantasies of Solomon.

"Hungry?" Solomon appeared at her side with an artfully arranged platter of sliced mango and passionfruit. Petra accepted with a smile, though her stomach churned at the thought of eating.

Solomon settled into the seat beside her. "We'll be landing soon."

"Where are we?" She glanced out the porthole, seeing only mile after mile of blue ocean.

"I have an island off the coast of Fiji, we should be safe there—for now." He gazed out the window, his azure eyes a mirror to the fathomless landscape.

"A whole island, huh?" Petra raised a playful brow.

His cheeks coloured. "One does not live four millennium without amassing a wealth of knowledge—and the knowledge to amass wealth."

Petra started to reply, but could only groan as she was assaulted by a wave of pain.

Solomon held her hand. "We're almost there, Petra. Hold on."

During their descent, Petra's stomach swooped and her ears pressurized. Moments later, the landing gear bumped along the runway.

"Okay, let's get you inside," Solomon said, scooping her into his arms.

"I can walk," she protested, squirming.

Solomon shot her a look that suggested it wasn't an option as he carried her out of the plane and towards a massive, modern beach house constructed almost entirely of windows and white limestone bricks. Three stories high, each level had a wraparound deck accented with Roman-influenced balustrades.

Solomon climbed the stairs and stood before a small, black box beside the door. After a quiet beep, the front door opened.

Biometric face scanner...impressive.

The dustless house smelled of freshly-waxed floors and wood polish, along with sterile traces of bleach.

Someone keeps it clean, she thought with a twinge of jealousy. Perhaps he didn't live alone. After all, he'd never conveyed he was single. She'd only assumed so—or rather, hoped. But was it truly herself who desired him? Or was it Inanna's pathological obsession for Solomon poisoning her?

He carried Petra into a sunken living room, placing her gently into the corner of a leather sectional.

"I've got some pain reliever in the other room, I'll be right back." Solomon grabbed a throw from the back of the couch and covered her before leaving.

Petra scanned the room, absorbing Solomon's decorative tastes and clues to his less apparent traits. For all the grandeur on the outside, the inside was modestly decorated, humble even. Other than the massive couch, there was only a couple of tall, black reading lamps, a side table with handmade sculptures of elephants and giraffes, and hanging on the adjacent wall, a reproduction oil painting of da Vinci's, *Virgin of the Rocks.*

From her vantage, there were no flouncy sheers, no tasseled accent pillows or coordinated colour palette—no real evidence of a female influence.

It reeked of a bachelor's pad.

Petra felt herself smile—though not of her own volition.

Solomon returned with a handful of items: gauze bandages, rubbing alcohol, and, surprisingly, a bottle of plain, old acetaminophen tablets.

"What, no willow bark to chew on? Or opium enema?" Petra joked. "I thought you might have some kind of ancient remedy in place of modern medicine."

He chuckled. "Sorry, but no. I, too, must keep up with the times. Though I admit, I often long for the days when things were simpler. Um, lift your shirt please."

She blushed, exposing her back. She'd foregone wearing a bra since the start of the affliction as the straps rubbed against the fresh wounds.

"This is going to sting...I'm sorry." Solomon dabbed each tattoo with an alcohol-laden piece of gauze. Petra reluctantly kept a tally as he cleansed each one in succession.

*There must be dozens...*she thought after the count reached twenty, tears gathering in her eyes. *How many am I going to get?*

In Solomon's rendition of Gilgamesh's story, even Inanna didn't know how many Mes there were. Her father, Enlil, kept that a carefully guarded secret in order to prevent any one god from obtaining all of the mysterious emblems.

Finally, Solomon applied a clean square of gauze and expertly taped down the edges. His touch was so gentle, yet professional, she almost felt like a patient in a hospital.

"You have the bedside manner of a doctor, you know," she said, wincing as she pulled down her shirt.

"That's because I am a doctor."

"Seriously?"

"Immortality can be very tedious at times," he said with a sigh. "After travelling the world a thousand times over, life can...lose purpose. I have often lost my way." His eyes darkened. "But when I found myself again, it was always through knowledge, thus learning became my passion—my purpose."

"Learning what?"

"Anything and everything." He sat beside her. "I crave all knowledge, all manners of education. When I want to learn something, I seek a master to teach me. When I cannot find a master, I immerse myself in the art and persevere until I perfect it. It's the only way to survive."

"Survive?"

"I don't believe the human mind was designed to process beyond a single lifetime. It has, I suppose what you'd call, an expiration date. When I met Gilgamesh, he'd already been alive for over seven hundred years, hence his frequent lack of civility—and often, sanity. Just like the seasons or cycles of the sun around the earth, everything in nature has a rhythm—an intelligent design, if you will. Gilgamesh and I, by our *unnatural* existence, violated these laws of nature, which is why we, at times, were driven to madness."

Petra nodded, but still thought it would be fascinating to live forever. "So, you're a medical doctor...what other professions have you acquired?"

"I have been all things," he said with stone-cold sincerity.

"Like what?"

Solomon's eyes widened as if she'd asked him to recite every star in the Northern Hemisphere. "Oh my, too many to name: A priest, a pirate...an *archaeologist*..." he winked at her, "...a Templar Knight...a painter..." He gestured to da Vinci's painting.

"Y-You painted that!" Petra eyed him, he couldn't be serious. "But, Leonardo...that's his, is it not?" She knew her art and that was most certainly a famous piece by the heralded genius of the 16th century.

"Yes, I reproduced it from memory. I was his understudy."

Petra gaped at the painting.

"Come...I want to show you something." A rare glow of excitement kindled behind his eyes.

Solomon led her through the expansive home. Just beyond the kitchen, hidden within a dark hallway, was a huge iron door sealed by vertical bars, further sequestered by an iris recognition scanner and keypad.

"What do you keep in there, King Kong?" she asked with a chuckle.

He returned a forced laugh, his blue eyes sliding surreptitiously from her to the massive portal. "Something like that..."

They entered a corridor with wall after wall of glass display cases. Locked behind the encasements were thousands of priceless artifacts unlike anything she'd ever seen. Relics originating from every century known to man: An onyx cameo dating back to the Roman era, the first known camera, various antiquated timepieces, a collection of rare swords and weapons, 14th century manuscripts with furling handwritten pages, a statuette of the goddess Athena, an astrolabe made of solid gold—everything one could imagine, yet not believe, existed in a single place.

"What *is* all this?" Petra ogled like a kid before the world's largest toy store, but only allowed to look, not touch.

Solomon shrugged. "Just my garbage collection."

She rolled her eyes, grinning. "I knew you were a relic junkie like me."

"Yes, well, these aren't your average historical relics." He regarded the pieces with a wistful eye. "They're more like...photographs. A memorial to those who sacrificed everything for The Cause."

"The Cause?"

He didn't reply, only nodded and led her out of the hall of memories and to a set of French doors filmed with fog. As the doors opened, humid air wrapped around her. Mist swirled through languid sunbeams emanating from a glass ceiling. A white-pebbled path led beneath a row of elder willows, arching boughs a gateway into paradise. As big as house and tall as a watchtower, the greenhouse was abound with life. Uncaged birds twittered, often spiriting from their hidden perches, only to vanish into another tangle of branches. Variegated butterflies flitted over beds of jasmine, occasionally alighting upon a flower. A stone path meandered around a pond with lily pads and lime-green algae. Every so often, she caught a glimpse of copper, koi gliding beneath the floating islands. Water trickled over rocky falls. Violet-headed clematis climbed the walls. Fruit trees—peach, apple, and plum—pregnant with ripened produce. Ivy dangled from the ceiling as if Tarzan was going to swing in at any moment.

It was heaven—*Eden*.

"Who takes care of this while you're away?" Petra asked, in awe.

"It's a self-sustaining ecosystem, I've designed it to behave as a natural environment would."

"So you're a botanist too?"

"Not quite," he said. "But I had a hand in building King Nebuchadnezzar's garden."

Petra searched her memory, then gasped. "*The Hanging Gardens of Babylon!*"

He gave a humble shrug. "His Queen, Amytis, missed her home in the forested Medes mountains, so the King commissioned me to design a garden inside the palace walls—in the middle of the desert. No easy feat, I tell you. It was the water that was the problem. At first, we tried to transport the water from the river outside the palace, carrying hundreds of vessels per day up a thousand steps—but it wasn't efficient. So I designed a method of moving the water upward from the river."

"How?" There were times, like now, that Petra wondered if she actually believed Solomon's tall tales of the past or if she just desperately wanted them to be true. Regardless, she stood before him like a child meeting Santa, eyes wide with wonder.

"Let's just say, Archimedes didn't invent the screw, he simply adapted it." Solomon spoke of an ancient irrigation system which transferred water from a ground-level body of water to a higher elevation.

"So…*you* invented it?"

He shook his head. "I, too, simply borrowed it. I'd seen it used in Egypt years before—though on a smaller scale. Much of the ancient technologies took decades to perfect. No one really knew who invented any machine or technique, only that it worked. Then we would tweak it, make it better. Back then, life was about improving survival, not necessarily gaining notoriety.

"This is my favourite area, come on." Solomon gestured for her to follow him into a shady corner.

A shadow of exhaustion moved over her, back aching and head dizzy; but she complied, trailing after him.

"Over here," he whispered, pulling back a drape of fronds to reveal a dark flower bed aglow with bioluminescent plants.

Petra ducked under his arm, feeling his body heat as she passed. She caught a whiff of his pheromones, his signature scent—earthy, as if the desert wind was embedded in his skin. Caught in a web of lust, a groan spilled from her lips. Heat radiated from her core. She slid her palms over his chest, lifted her face, mouth parted for a kiss.

"*Solomon,*" she uttered, pressing against him. "Take me…please. I *need* you."

His large frame stiffened. Petra gazed at him, soaking in the beauty of his face, his hair—his *eyes.*

For a moment, he watched her, as if undecided. Her hands roamed his hard body, exploring. Slowly, he returned her affections. His warm, soft mouth moved over hers. He kneaded her breasts, growling in her ear as she rubbed his hardening sex.

He paused, giving her a long, hard look. "Come with me," he said, leading her out of the garden and back through the house.

"Where are we going?" Petra muttered, wanting him now, her voice low and husky, foreign.

"In here," he said as they entered the master bedroom.

Long charcoal drapes further impeded a waning afternoon sun, pooling onto dark hardwood floors. Across the room, a large, four-poster bed beckoned, evoking notions of tying his wrists to the columns so she could ride him, tease him…

Solomon stood before her, an unreadable look on his beautiful face. He hesitated and she wondered with amusement if he was shy. Her body pulsated with desire, skin tingling in anticipation of touch. She felt feverish, yet free, wild and unencumbered.

He closed the space between them, bringing his face to hers, warm lips grazing her skin. Guiding her to the bed, he laid her down where he lifted her shirt and nuzzled her abdomen, making slow, wet, teasing circles with his tongue on her hip as he moved lower…and lower. She almost wept with pleasure, running her hands through his hair.

Petra clutched his face, forcing him to look at her. "Let me see you…I need to see your *eyes* when you enter me."

Solomon suddenly stopped.

Cradling her chin within a warm palm, he stared at her—into her soul. He then kissed her so tenderly, it brought a lump to her throat.

"W-What's the matter?" she asked, breathless.

He blushed. "I'll be right back, okay? I need some…protection."

Petra forced a smile, annoyed by his suggestion for condoms.

"Of course," she said tightly.

Solomon walked towards the door. She watched his ass, his strong, muscular back as he moved, a hot need throbbing between her legs. The tattoos on his back looked different somehow…

"*Hurry,*" she heard herself say, her voice a growl.

He crossed the threshold, but instead of heading down the hall, he slowly turned around—his expression dark. Without breaking eye contact, he shifted his face to the right—and she heard a beep.

Her stomach dropped.

The biometric scanner.

Petra lunged off the bed, running for the doorway as a series of thick, steel bars slid horizontally from one side of the doorjamb to the other—sealing her inside.

"No! What the hell are you doing!" she shrieked, reaching through the bars. "Let me out of here, you bastard!'

Solomon took a step back as she clawed at the air in front of him.

"I'm so sorry, Petra," he said, blue eyes fraught with guilt. "I know you don't understand, but…go look in the mirror."

Petra sobbed, hugging herself as she walked to the bureau. She kept her eyes averted, too afraid of what she might see.

Slowly, she dared to look at her reflection—and uttered a cry of horror.

Her eyes.

They were glowing purple.

Petra yanked back the heavy drapes, unsurprised to see bars on the windows. Outside, a fractured moon was rising, the island awash in silver. The ocean was just a black mass in the distance, wavering shadows of palm trees like claws raking the beach.

She bit her lip as yet another segment of skin separated—a fresh tattoo. Tears burned behind her eyes. How had it come to this? How had she gone from happily digging treasures in the ancient sands of Iraq to imprisoned in an immortal madman's bedroom with some weird curse slicing emblems into her back?

Somewhere inside, Inanna writhed. Petra shuddered at the sickening sensation.

Someone is inside me…a goddess.

Images from a movie, The Exorcist, flashed to the forefront of her mind. Of the little girl's mottled face, demonic amber eyes, and her inhuman growls.

Is that my fate? Am I…possessed?

If she was, why did she still feel so much of herself inside? Petra gazed in the mirror, her eyes casting an eerie lavender glow. How much of herself was left—and how much was Inanna? Petra wondered if—or *when*—Inanna fully consumed her, would she become some kind of silent witness?

Petra heard footsteps approaching. She knew it was Solomon, but didn't turn to greet him.

"I…brought you something to eat," Solomon said quietly. The tray clattered as he slid it under the bars.

She didn't reply.

"I know you're angry with me, and I completely understand, but… you have to eat, Petra."

At mention of her name, tears gathered in her eyes. It was so hard to think she was losing herself, that soon she might not exist.

She heard him sigh, and then as his footsteps retreated.

"Wait!" she called out.

Silence.

Solomon reappeared in the doorway, his handsome face drawn and sad.

"Can you get *her*…out of me?" Desperation strangled her voice.

She heard his breath many times before he spoke, "I-I don't know."

A tear slid down her cheek.

"I am doing everything I can, I promise," he said. "If I can fix this… I will."

"How?" Petra sobbed as she curled up on the bed.

"Help is coming, Petra."

She said nothing, but heard the sound of a chair being set before the barred door.

"Until then, let me finish the story, then…you will understand everything."

221

Part Four

The Egyptian

"With the Minoan culture crumbling behind us, their future shrouded in falling ash, we sailed into our own uncertain destinies. I mourned Ariadne, not only for her death, but that she could never have been mine to love. I'd come to terms with my curse and now, more than ever, believed it to be true. Love was to be a stranger to me from then on, as I realized I was a danger to any woman I grew to care about.

"So once again, I left my life behind. As we navigated the dark waters, towards a new shore, I hoped I might find a cure for my dis-ease amid the ancient culture of Egypt—in the mysterious Land of the Lotus."

28
Wrath

*T*he midnight sky over Crete bled crimson until morning when sunlight doused the island, transforming the flames into pillars of black smoke. Despite the Minoans recent slide into a barbaric mindset, my heart ached for the enlightened culture and their hardships as they rebuilt their devastated world.

My back stung as the Mes cut deeper into my flesh. Feverish and sick with dread, I felt the wedges engraved onto my skin, blood coating my fingertips. What was this thing? Like Pasiphae, was I now possessed by Inanna's evil essence?

Perched beside the mast, sewing a torn sail, Bansabira glanced up and offered me a warm, gold-toothed smile. My fears waned and for a moment I was reminded of home: huddled around the hearth, Father reciting stories of old. Perhaps these wayward men were my new family. With their culture in ruins and my life in limbo, maybe we could come together as brothers?

Then I looked over at Gilgamesh—and my hopes disintegrated.

Wrapped in a blanket, curled into himself, he glowered at me—at my back—with hatred in his eyes.

"No! I was supposed to kill her!" Gilgamesh's voice resounded from the moment I'd killed Pasiphae.

I hadn't understood his anger at the time, but now it was clear. He'd wanted the Mes for himself—but why? Hadn't he witnessed what it did to Pasiphae?

Not ready to deal with Gilgamesh's wrath, I moved to the back of the boat and joined Rhadamanthys at the balustrade. His dark gaze panned the blue landscape ahead, avoiding the catastrophe behind us. I empathized with his incredible loss, and understood he was grieving for more than just Ariadne and his family—he was mourning his entire world.

"We tried for so long, Ariadne and I," Rhadamanthys spoke, eyes hard with bitterness. "We fought for what was right, despite it making a traitor of us both. The evil, it was so much bigger than us. I did not fully realize the influence the goddess had over the queen. Ariadne understood though, in that uncanny way women do." He chuckled sadly. "She was the one who came to me, asking my help to stop her mother—to begin The Cause."

I raised a curious brow. "The Cause?"

"At first, we thought we were alone in this horror, in this...slaughter of the innocent," he said, bowing his head. "But after the trade routes began, we realized the bloodshed and inhumanities had landed upon many other shores."

"*...her reach is far, Solomon...so very far,*" Gilgamesh had warned of Inanna's influence just days before, when he showed me the bones of the dead children.

"For many years, Ariadne and I—along with many others—have been secretly fighting this curse. Ariadne would often accompany us on trade missions, searching for cultures afflicted with this ailment—as well as the origin of it. We thought perhaps if we could find the source, we might be able to stop it."

I swallowed hard. "So, there are children being sacrificed in other lands, far from here?"

"Not just that, but other atrocities as well. Human sacrifice, sins performed with beasts, women and children being kept as sex slaves...and that's just the beginning..."

Denial churned inside. I couldn't come to terms with the reality that Inanna, Uruk's Goddess of *Love*, could be the source of countless suffering. I felt somehow responsible for her behaviour, as if being a Sumerian myself held me accountable for my deity's actions.

'*I made you, you know....*' Inanna's claim echoed.

If she was speaking the truth, that she created us humans, then she was Mother to us all. And if so, how could treat her children in such a despicable way?

Rhadamanthys regarded the blossoming horizon—the shores of Egypt.

"How far is it?" I asked, eager to change the topic.

"Three days, four if she's disagreeable," he said of the ocean.

"What are the people like?" My imagination summoned images of a wild and primitive people. Nerves fluttered in my stomach as I wondered how they'd respond to my eyes. I'd had mixed reactions thus far, always unable to prepare myself for how a world with brown eyes was going to see me.

"The Egyptians are...unique." He patted my back, yawning. "I'm going to try to rest before we arrive."

After Rhadamanthys retired below deck, I took a deep breath and approached Gilgamesh. The skin on his face had weathered since the dawn, his hair silver and coarse. Even his physique had changed: back hunched, shoulders drooped, hands gnarled and arthritic. To my knowledge, it had been more than a day since he'd been with a woman. I surmised his mind was equally as frail, poisoned by the pervasive need for sexual nourishment.

I sat beside him. "How are you feeling?"

He turned a cold, deranged eye on me. "Wonderful. Can't you tell?"

"You fought well for the children. You saved them."

"Oh yes," he mumbled around a glare. "And how am I rewarded? Trapped on a boat with you and Captain Ridiculous."

Bansabira glanced over, looking mildly offended he'd been excluded, even if it was an insult.

225

I kept a cool head. "Rhadamanthys says we will arrive in Egypt within days…"

"*Days!*" Madness brimmed in his eyes. "Do you see what I've become in just a matter of hours! I see no one thought to bring a woman along on this damned journey! There's not even a goddamn goat to deflower!"

I stifled a gag.

"Gilgamesh," I spoke his true name quietly, certain Bansabira didn't know the king's real identity yet—though I wasn't sure we could keep it a secret much longer. He'd already aged several years in a matter of hours. "I empathize with your pain and I'm here for you…but you must try to contain yourself long enough for us to figure out how we can keep this from the others…unless…we tell them."

He shot me a wide-eyed look. "Tell them! Are you *crazy*? They'll throw us over the side of this wooden bucket since they can't burn us as the demons they'll think we are!"

"They'll do no such thing. They've seen the dreadful power Inanna is capable of and will sympathize with our afflictions."

I stood with the intention of going below deck and confessing everything to Rhadamanthys. I knew he would understand—in fact, I had no doubt.

Gilgamesh bolted to his feet and dug his nails into my arm. "You cannot tell them!" he hissed. "They'll kill us!"

I wrenched myself from his death-like grip. "We cannot die, Gil…"

"There are worse things than death!" He trembled, grabbing me by the shoulders. "You will see, Solomon! There are monsters on the other side. They're waiting for us. They lay in wait…"

After abandoning Gilgamesh to wallow in his own misery, I settled between two barrels and succumbed to bone-weary exhaustion. Within moments, a vivid dream began. In it, we were rescuing the children again, reenacted exactly as it had happened: the falling rocks, Theseus scooping Ariadne into his arms and disappearing into the tunnels, Pasiphae's lifeless body impaled near the altar, Gilgamesh helping me to the hot spring where we were to swim across. The water smelled of rotten eggs, as it often does with heated sulphur; only this time, it reeked of something else, something fetid and decaying—the smell of death.

My dream self turned to Gilgamesh, asking, "What is that awful stench!"

The answer was immediately clear.

Gilgamesh's flesh was mottled black and green with rot. Great fissures oozed with thick, soured blood. Pallid maggots writhed in the wounds, the white of his cheekbone peeking through ragged tears in his skin, purple tongue waggling between decomposed lips. He reached for me with terror in his bloodied eyes, begging for help. I backed away, horrified.

His gruesome lips parted, ebony blood spilled down his chin. "*They lay in wait…the monsters…they're waiting for us, Solomon…*"

I started awake, beaded sweat on my brow chilled by the waning sun. I took a deep breath, shaking off the nightmare, but realized the dis-

226

gusting odour remained. Gilgamesh was still huddled under a blanket at the stern, looking just as I'd seen him before falling asleep: old and cranky. Beside me, I noticed a barrel with the lid askew. I peered in: a school of dead, rheumy-eyed fish floated atop the surface, the smell utterly rancid. Revolted, I lifted the barrel over the edge of the boat and dumped the contents into the ocean. As I set the container down, the Mes on my back split open again and I hissed in pain.

Gilgamesh chuckled. "Serves you right, you know, stealing it from me."

I stormed over to him. "Stealing it from you? I had no idea you wanted it let alone you were going to *kill* Pasiphae for it!"

He turned an icy eye on me, his voice low and dangerous. "I told you *I* was to kill her. Besides, I need it more than you do. You stole the only one I've been able to find in *seven hundred years*."

"Why do you *need* it?"

"Doesn't matter anymore. You have it and I don't." He huddled tighter into himself.

"If you'd just tell me why, maybe I could…"

"Just leave me be!" Gilgamesh bolted to his feet. He elbowed past me and lifted the trap door leading into the hold, where he descended and disappeared from sight.

Bansabira peered around the mast. "Be careful with dat Gillis, Soloman, he is not right in da head."

"You have that right, my friend." I chuckled, not worried about what Bansabira may or may not have heard. I fully intended to tell him and Rhadamanthys everything as soon as we reached Egypt.

Somehow, Gilgamesh and I avoided one another for the next three days. He stayed below deck and I remained above. I was reluctantly concerned for his physical and mental state, wondering how old he would look after so long without satiating his needs and how much of his mind would be left intact. If he was too far gone, it would be impossible to find a women willing to serve his needs in order to return him to his usual self. Frankly, I wasn't sure I wanted him back at all considering his surly demeanour, but he'd saved me from the labyrinth and for that I felt obliged to return the favour—but little more.

Then my concerns turned to Ariadne.

"She's for dead, Solomon," Gilgamesh had said. *"She was stabbed in the stomach, I do not believe she'd survive that…"*

My greatest fear was that she'd lived and awakened in the arms of the enemy, despising me for abandoning her. I knew then I must go to Greece, home of Theseus, and hunt him down. Whether or not she'd survived, Theseus had to be punished for his crimes against the children.

My thoughts were silenced as a colossal land mass brimmed on the horizon. Like some primordial mountain borne of the deep, Egypt rose from the ocean. A long blue ribbon of water ushered us into an oasis of floating hyacinth, tall marsh grasses, and feathery papyrus plants. Long-legged herons strolled the shoreline, each keeping a watchful eye for any disturbances beneath the dark river. Just as they were fishing for lunch, so too were they a meal for a stealthy crocodile.

"Where are we headed?" I asked Rhadamanthys.

"Thebes. I have friends there—others who work for The Cause."

I nodded, reality settling on my shoulders. We still had a job to do—we had to stop Inanna. I sidled next to Rhadamanthys, taking a deep breath, knowing I had to divulge not just my secret, but Gilgamesh's as well. There was no other way to reasonably explain his aged appearance once we arrived in Thebes. I was certain both men already suspected something odd was amiss with Gilgamesh—still Gillis in their eyes.

"Rhadamanthys, I have to tell you something about Gil…"

"What a beautiful morning!" Gilgamesh flung open the hatch door and emerged from the hold.

He was vital and handsome and…*young*! Even his clothes were revived—clean and like new.

"H-How?" I blinked in disbelief. I'd avoided descent into the barracks, certain I'd find Gilgamesh a wizened and senile old man drawing his last ragged breath.

He twisted the tip of his lengthy moustache, further elongating his smirk. "Come, come, Solomon, don't look so surprised. A few days' rest does wonders to restore a man, no? I may not have my youth as you do…" He leaned into my ear and whispered, "But I do have a few tricks left."

Gilgamesh yanked off the lids of nearby barrels, peering into each. "I'm hungry! What means of suitable sustenance do you have on this pathetic vessel! Ah, beer! I'll start with that…"

Bansabira called me over, a glint in his eye. "Solo-man, come see."

Curious, I joined him.

"Look," he said, pointing southeast.

There, nestled between a break in the palms, sat three perfectly shaped mountain peaks. No jagged edges. Smooth on all sides and descending in size from massive to medium.

"What are those? Surely those mountains are not…natural."

Rhadamanthys chuckled. "Those are the Pyramids of Giza—the tombs of the gods. Welcome, Solomon…to Egypt."

29
Land of the Lotus

The moment we docked, Gilgamesh clambered over the rail, waded through the shallow water, and disappeared into a jungle of palm fronds. Rhadamanthys shook his head, but I knew he was just as relieved as myself to have some space from the demanding former king. While I was grateful for Gilgamesh saving my life, I still didn't relish his company.

I started down the ramp, eager to set foot on solid ground. Rhadamanthys joined me.

"Bansabira will stay with the boat," he said "There's not much of value aboard, but the ship itself is a fine prize for any thief."

"Is that a concern here?" In Sumer, the port masters kept a close eye on visiting ships. It was a miracle I'd been able to sneak aboard the Minoan vessel at all, truth be told.

"It's a concern everywhere. It's good practice to be cautious wherever one lands. They are accepting of strangers here—sometimes too much," he added cryptically.

As we neared city centre, massive monuments and buildings grew like mountains from the sand. Everything appeared designed for giants, larger than life. Articulate pictographs were etched onto every imaginable surface, their language as elaborate as the structures.

"How amazing…" I traced the carved image of an eye on an *obelisk*. "Is this their cuneiform?"

"*Mdju netjer*," Rhadamanthys said in Egyptian. "The 'words of the gods'."

As we walked by the necropolis, in the shadow of massive statues, I felt as though I was wandering through history. Sumer had a similar ambiance, but this place had lived far longer than even my own humble society. Power had been carved into these stones, inherited knowledge burned into the aged sands. Something else—something preternatural—also dwelled within the city. Lingered throughout the millenniums. I couldn't name it, this looming sensation of being watched. As if the veil between the living and the dead was thinner.

The marketplace was crowded, but not bustling. A sedating miasma of sweet-smelling frankincense hovered like a storm cloud. I studied the Egyptians, entranced by their regal features. Far from the primitive civilization I'd concocted inside my imagination, the people of Egypt were sophisticated, elegant, yet dark and exotic; their complexion closer to my own Sumerian skin. Both men and women wore makeup, their eyes outlined in kohl to dissuade the sand and bright sun.

Rhadamanthys touched my elbow. "I have some business to attend to, you will be okay alone, no? I'll meet you back at the boat in an hour or so," he said, then: "Be careful, Solomon—everything is not always as it appears."

I watched him vanish into the crowd, wondering where he was going and why he hadn't invited me to come along.

The sun had settled overhead, diminishing the shade. Midday heat soon sweltered and my mouth was parched. I glanced around for a beer vender, painfully aware of my lack of currency. I thought perhaps I could offer assistance in some way in exchange for a drink. In Sumer, such trade was acceptable, often preferable, to money.

Spotting a man standing beside several large barrels, I started towards him, my attention fixed on his wares. As I cut across the wide street, I accidentally bumped into a small figure and she dropped the many parcels she'd been carrying.

"*Khidae alkhuraqa!*" she exclaimed, her tone angry.

I knelt to help her pick up the items. "I'm so sorry," I said, wishing I spoke Egyptian.

Veiled beneath a brilliant jade *hijab*, she inspected me with dark eyes. Her irises were so brown I could scarcely distinguish the black of her pupils; her nose had an elegant curve at the bridge, a slight hook at the tip. She was dainty, yet womanly beneath the ivory linens.

Her gaze softened as she stared at me—at my eyes.

"*Azraq?*" she uttered.

"Blue," I said in Sumerian, surmising her meaning.

With her fingertip, she traced around my right eye. "Blue."

From across the street, I heard shouting. I turned to see two armed soldiers shoving their way through the busy marketplace towards us.

The woman gasped. Alarm registered in her beautiful eyes. She drew the green veil across her face, clutched the parcels to her chest, and hurried away. I tracked her as she slipped through the crowd and turned down a narrow alley before disappearing. Moments later, the soldiers shouldered past me. I considered stalling them, giving her time to escape, but what if she'd stolen those things?

Somehow, I sensed she wasn't a thief—and I had to help her if I could.

The narrow alley was cool and quiet in comparison to the market. Overhead, dark linens draped from one building to another, creating a multicoloured canopy that blocked out the sun. Threadbare clothes hung from various balconies, billowing as they dried in the breeze. A baby's cry drifted from behind a blanketed window, summoning painful memories of Miri—followed closely by Indra and Father. I'd not forgotten them, and pathetic as it was, I had tried. I told myself eventually the pain would fade, that time heals all wounds—but it was a lie.

Ahead, the soldiers were interrogating a vagrant, likely asking if he'd seen the veiled woman. My chest tightened, hoping she'd found a safe place to hide. Keeping to the shadows, I watched as the soldiers questioned a few more citizens, then with frustrated growls, they stormed down another dark corridor and out of sight. I crept down the alleyway, scanning each doorway in hopes of spotting her hiding behind a curtain.

One entrance stood out from the others. Windowless, cobbled of weathered limestone blocks, strange symbols carved over its arched doorway. An onyx blanket hung sentinel before its entrance, uninviting.

An ominous shiver grazed my spine and I backed away.

Realizing there was no way to find the woman in the green veil without getting lost, I headed back to the marketplace with renewed aspirations to charm the beer vender. Upon my return, however, I spotted a familiar figure standing beside the barrels of ale, fighting with the vender. I rolled my eyes and considered returning to the dark alleyway—but I was spied before I could sneak away.

"Solomon!" Gilgamesh shouted, pointing at the angry, knife-wielding vender. "Tell him I'm an honest man and will repay him for the beer! Tell him I have lots of money on the boat—I just need to go get it!"

Gilgamesh pulled me close, whispering into my ear with boozy breath. "Help me out here, friend, I used all my money for the ladies…"

"I have no Egyptian money, Gil," I said, patting my pockets. "In fact, I have no money at all."

The vender glowered at me.

"Run back to the boat, ask Rhadamanthys to spare some."

"Rhadamanthys is not at the boat, he went on an errand," I explained. "Why not offer the man a trade instead—see if he'll give you an hour's work in exchange?"

Gilgamesh eyed me as if I were crazy.

The vender shouted at Gilgamesh, slashing the air threateningly. Gilgamesh raised his hands in submission, placating the man with a string of foreign words. The man suddenly stopped and gaped at me— *at my eyes*—and paled. He dropped the knife and fell to his knees, bowing and praying at my feet.

"What did you say to him?" I frowned at Gilgamesh.

"I *may* have suggested you were a bit more than a regular man…"

"What!"

A crowd began to gather around the vender. All listened to his wild ramblings and then inspected me with wide, frightened stares. Two more fell to their knees, kowtowing. Soon, there were dozens.

"We need to get out of here." Gilgamesh's head was craned in the direction of the alley. "Now!"

The soldiers who'd been chasing the woman had returned—and they'd caught her! Only, she walked ahead of them, unrestrained.

"Wait," I whispered. "I know her."

She approached us, removing her veil. She was even more lovely than I'd imagined. I noticed her hands were no longer encumbered with parcels.

"*Ma maenaa hdha?*" she said in a commanding tone.

231

Anyone who remained standing in the crowd now gasped and fell at *her* feet in prostration.

Gilgamesh slid in front of me, twirling his moustache. He then launched into a lengthy dialogue with her in Egyptian. Never before had I felt such jealousy, wishing I too could converse with anyone, anywhere. Back in Crete, a frustrated Rhadamanthys had told me that Gilgamesh could speak every language—and I now understood the annoyance. He and the woman spoke rapidly, her dark eyes darting often at me.

Finally, the woman turned to the vender and offered him several pieces of silver. She then marched ahead while the guards took Gilgamesh and me roughly by the arms and compelled us to follow.

"W-What did you say?" I was afraid of the answer. "Where are we going?"

Gilgamesh slapped me on the shoulder through a nervous laugh. "Don't worry, friend, I have everything under control."

The soldiers escorted us to a great structure with thick sandstone walls that fortified a complex of buildings. A massive rectangular gateway yawned at the entrance, bordered by two obelisks. The veiled woman approached the gate and simply lifted her face to the sentries. They immediately lowered their weapons and bowed, allowing us to pass.

It was obvious she was not a thief at all, and I was now certain the guards had not been pursuing her for any crime. In fact, they now treated her as royalty. If she wasn't a thief or commoner, who was she? And why had she taken such precautions to hide from her own guards? I suspected it had to do with the mysterious packages she was carrying. I couldn't help but wonder what was in them and who they were for.

"Just let me do the talking," Gilgamesh whispered.

"As if I have a choice." My lips curled in disdain. "Where are we going?"

"To see King Mentuhotep III—or Pharaoh as he is called here," he said, nonchalant.

The blood drain from my face as I looked ahead to the veiled woman. "W-Who is she?"

"His queen—well, *one* of them. He has seven wives, apparently. Lucky man." He grinned.

"What did you tell her about me? And the vender?"

"I merely suggested that your eyes were not of...human origin." He shrugged.

"What!" I stopped short. "What else would they be?"

"Why, a gift from the gods, of course."

My chest tightened, Father's warnings flooding my thoughts.

"They cannot see your eyes, maru. Your eyes—they are different. There are people who will find your blue eyes beautiful...But others will think your eyes a curse and in their fear, they may want to harm you for it."

I took Gilgamesh by the shoulders. "I can't go in there! I've let too many see my eyes already—we have to leave!"

"Calm down, friend, I'm sure they just want a closer look, then we'll be on our way." He patted my arm.

232

We were led into a tall, white-stoned building with floors of polished marble. Ahead, the woman waited as a set of ornate doors were opened. She muttered something to the guards and they promptly stepped in front, barring us entry.

The twin doors were then closed—leaving us to contemplate our fate.

"What do you think they want with us—with me?" My stomach swarmed with fluttering nerves.

"I cannot say," he said, feigning indifference. "The Egyptians have, shall we say, an *affinity* for rare and exotic things. Perhaps they merely want to ogle your eyes and send us on our way."

"And…if they don't?"

"Well, best be prepared for the worst."

"Which would be?" I couldn't imagine what the worst could be, especially from Gilgamesh.

He met my gaze with cold resolve.

"Resurrection."

I paced the hall. We'd been kept waiting for hours. Out a nearby window, the sun blazed amber on the darkening horizon. Each time I approached the guards to question why we were being detained, they merely pointed with their spears to a far corner, telling me to 'be seated'—or so Gilgamesh translated.

My thoughts turned to Rhadamanthys and how concerned he'd be for my wellbeing. Or perhaps he would be angry and impatient, thinking I'd gone off with Gilgamesh (still Gillis in his eyes) for a night of drinks and pleasure in a brothel. I hoped he and Bansabira wouldn't set sail, stranding me in this foreign land.

No. Rhadamanthys would wait for me. Perhaps not Gilgamesh, but he would search for me. I knew what kind of man he was. Ariadne had trusted him, so I knew I could too.

Ariadne.

The mere thought of my Minoan princess summoned images of her lying beside Pasiphae's macabre altar of blood. Just like everyone else I'd lost, I couldn't believe she was truly dead. Anger replaced my sorrow. Why had everyone I'd ever cared for been taken from me?

"You will obey me—lest you pay the price." Inanna's vow haunted me.

"Inanna," I cursed her name.

Gilgamesh, who'd been napping against a pillar, snapped to attention. "Inanna? Where?" He glanced nervously about.

I glared out at the darkening night. The monuments stood as silent sentinels amid the shadows, golden halos arced over flaming pyres, soon to be the only source of illumination.

"All of this," I said with a weary exhale. "Everything that has happened. All the pain, the suffering—the death, it was because of Inanna."

Gilgamesh stood with a groan. "Ah yes, chaos and destruction often follows a strong, beautiful woman."

I gaped at him. "Strong? *Beautiful?* She's a monster! She killed my father, my wife, my *daughter.*"

"Yes, perhaps she can be…a bit out of control."

"*Out of control!?*" Rage simmered. "How can you condone what she's done? Not just to me, but to the Minoans, to Ariadne—to *you!*"

All too casually, he joined me at the window and regarded the stars as they blinked awake. He drew a long breath, tasting the cool night air.

"I was a normal man once," he said, voice rich with reverence. "I loved life, I loved beer—and, most of all, women. I was a great king with an even greater responsibility to my kingdom. I cared for my people. I cared if they were happy, sad, hungry, or poor. I ensured their safety by building a mighty wall around the city. They were, in a way, my children...and I, their father. I loved them, you see. Not many are given such an opportunity. To reign over thousands—a god among men."

I listened, though impatiently.

"After Inanna cursed me, I abandoned Uruk in search of a cure. The stories say I was so devastated by Enkidu's loss that I went on a quest for immortality, but that's not entirely true. I left because people were growing suspicious. I would age before their very eyes, only to return to youth after bedding a maiden." Gilgamesh exhaled. "Truth was, I was a coward. I no longer knew who I was and where I belonged—so I left. Not long after, the kingdom was attacked by wild nomads and nearly destroyed. It was decades before Uruk recovered. After the damage was done, I returned and tried to rebuild my life. Being that I had plenty of time to reflect upon my misdeeds, I wondered, 'If a king is capable of such offences, why not the gods?' The gods are not perfect, Solomon. They are so alike us, flawed and imperfect, even fragile. I met Inanna before her descent into madness—and I saw what she'd become afterwards," he said, wincing. "I feel to blame for her undoing. She was still grieving for her husband when I betrayed her. She wasn't the same afterwards..."

"So that excuses her behaviour?" I interjected angrily.

"Excuse, no...but perhaps, it might explain it. After hundreds of years of immortality, I understand her better than I did before. Living with one's self and the hardships of existence for a mere forty years is one thing, but tolerating life for hundreds—or *thousands* of years—is quite another. Man is not designed to live forever, you see. It can make one not quite right in the head." He tapped his temple.

"But Inanna is not human," I countered. "She's a goddess. She was designed to live forever, wasn't she?"

"So it would seem, but we're all tested, are we not?" He leaned on the railing. "Perhaps as we were created by the gods, so too were they."

"What do you mean? That the gods...have gods?"

"As I've come to see it, life itself has an inherent hierarchy. There's always something greater—more powerful—than yourself. So why wouldn't that apply to the gods themselves?"

I shook my head. "Regardless, Inanna is hurting people and she needs to be stopped."

"I agree." Gilgamesh's brown eyes met mine. "And I think I know a way."

"How?"

"We need to..." he began, but was interrupted by the doors opening.

From the threshold, a tall, stern man looked down his nose at us—at me, muttering something in Egyptian.

"This man is the royal vizier, Amenemhet," Gilgamesh translated. "He says Pharaoh Mentuhotep will see the blue-eyed man now."

"Wait, *me*? Not you? I-I need you to tell me what they're saying." Panic swelled with the thought of facing the Egyptian King alone. I'd met two kings in my life thus far—Gilgamesh and Minos—and neither had left me feeling particularly confident in the way of noble sanity.

Gilgamesh relayed my concern.

Visibly annoyed, the vizier gave a curt nod and gestured for us to follow him.

As the doors closed behind us, I felt Gilgamesh's hand on my arm. "Just let me do the talking and everything will be fine—*Trust me*."

30

The Seven Flowers of Thebes

A lyre lilted from a dark corner, married to the rhythmic tapping of a goblet drum. Lit only by tallow candles, the room was suspended in an unearthly glow. As my eyes adjusted to the low light, I saw a man seated on a gold throne. He wore a white, conical headpiece adorned with a gilded band, dark eyes outlined in kohl, lids glittering jade, and shorn brows penned into a thin arch. Hairless, his elderly chest sagged; flaccid stomach folding over a white cotton tunic. This was quite literally the oldest man I'd ever seen. He must have been in his seventies; which for the time, was unheard of.

The dour-looking vizier spoke, Gilgamesh translated, "His divine Kingship, Mentuhotep the Third."

Before the king, a harem of five young women lounged on decorative silk pillows. An older woman stood at the pharaoh's side, concern haunting her dark eyes. Behind the throne, a fierce-looking man wearing a blood-red sash across his chest glowered at us—at me.

Countless cats roamed freely about the room, haughty and aloof. To one side, a miniature man dressed in colourful clothing bounced about a red carpet, tethered to a pole by a collar and long leash. He giggled and danced, playing about the pharaoh's women who seemed taken by his impish charm. They smiled and tossed him bits of bread as a reward for his performance.

"A dwarf," Gilgamesh whispered, nudging me. I'd stopped walking and was gaping at the half-sized man. "He's kept as entertainment for the pharaoh—a favoured pet among the nobles of Egypt."

My insides curdled as I envisioned a gold collar placed around my neck, the Egyptians gathering to gawk at my rare eye colour. Would they keep me as a pet too? Despite the little man's glee, I couldn't help but feel irritated at the indignity of it all.

A veiled woman entered just then, taking her place next to the pharaoh in an equally grand golden throne. Naked beneath a gown of gold netting, a dazzling crown inset with a large ruby sparkled amid her ebony hair.

The vizier muttered in Egyptian, rolling his eyes at what he appeared to think was a profound inconvenience.

"Primary wife, Queen Neteraphare," Gilgamesh reiterated the vizier's introduction, then muttered, "*Bow...*"

Simultaneously, we bowed low to the queen. She nodded, lifting her veil—it was the woman from the market! She locked gazes with me, quietly pleading for my discretion. I gave her an imperceptible nod, hoping we'd eventually get a chance to speak alone. I longed to ask her about why she was dressed as a commoner, what was in the mysterious packages, and why was she evading her own guards?

The queen spoke to Gilgamesh, her voice soft but commanding.

"She wishes for you to approach the pharaoh—to show him your eyes," Gilgamesh relayed.

I forced myself forward, combatting my instinct to turn and run. Father's endless warnings against allowing the world to see my eyes ricocheted inside my skull. For all his attempts to keep me from harm, however, in that moment I felt I'd failed him. The pharaoh's cold gaze scrutinized me from head to toe, measuring me as a man before he paused upon my eyes. A flash of surprise registered behind his dark stare.

A flurry of unfamiliar words spilled from his mouth.

"He asks if you are a god," Gilgamesh translated.

I shook my head.

The pharaoh pondered this, then spoke again.

"He asks then, how it is you have blue eyes?"

I swallowed, uncertain how to answer. I thought it best to stick to the truth. "My father told me they were a gift from the Water God, Enki."

Gilgamesh communicated in their tongue. Everyone in the room gasped and began speaking feverishly to one another.

"What are they saying?"

Gilgamesh listened, brow bent, then: "They're talking too fast for me to follow…"

Suddenly the pharaoh pounded his fist and the room felt silent. Rising, he approached me. Shorter than myself, he had to look up as I looked down. Eyes narrowed, suspicious, he held my chin and turned my face side to side, examining my eyes.

He released me abruptly, uttering a command. The harem of queens gasped. Beside me, Gilgamesh paled.

The man with the red sash punched a wall, storming from the room. Sobbing, the older queen followed him. Shortly afterward, the pharaoh and his harem of women exited, which left only the dwarf alone, tethered, petting one of the cats.

Panicked, I grabbed Gilgamesh's arm. "What did he say?"

He brushed me aside. "I-I need some air."

I chased after him, heart thrumming.

I found him against a bannister, drawing deep breaths. "Before the pharaoh's father, Mentuhotep the *Second*, died, he united the two opposing sects of Egypt, called Upper and Lower, thus making Egypt a world power once more."

Confused by the spontaneous history lesson, I uttered, "Okay…how does this involve me?"

"While the current Mentuhotep has a son—the angry man with the red sash—he was sired by one of the secondary wives, Imi, but she's not Egyptian, meaning his son is only half-Egyptian. The king believes when he dies, his critics will refuse his son's reign and Egypt will be torn apart again. He believes you have been sent as a gift from Isis… their *Goddess of Love*."

237

My blood ran cold.

Inanna.

"And...?" I winced, knowing the worst was yet to come.

"It would seem...the pharaoh wishes for you make love to *all* seven of his wives to sire him a son with *blue* eyes, making the people believe the pharaoh is of *divine* blood and solidifying his child as heir. And apparently, you're not allowed to leave the palace until you do."

My heart weighed like iron. I should never have left Sumer. Father was right, people didn't understand my eyes. While the Minoans were merely enamoured by the rare colour, the Egyptians thought them an advantageous treasure they could exploit.

How could something as ordinary as *colour* define the measure of a man?

Soldiers led us down a long hallway and ushered us into a lavish apartment. Despite the frivolous decor, I knew we were not guests of this kingdom, but prisoners.

Gilgamesh rubbed his unshaven face, preternatural aging stalking him once again. "This isn't good—we don't have time for this."

"What do you mean?"

"After Inanna cursed me, I tried to live a normal life. It wasn't so terrible in the beginning. It was, of course, a wonderful excuse to indulge in the company of a new and beautiful woman every night of the week. I went from brothel to brothel, woman to woman, feeding the curse. Then, when those wells inevitably went dry, I would travel to the next city and satiate my needs. I learned a great deal in that time, of the cultures, the people, and their various languages. It was almost...thrilling. I even thought my curse a blessing....for a while." His grin faded to misery. "Then, as the decades went on, I found myself growing tired of sex, of the constant companionship of a stranger. Most never even asked my name. I paid for their services, pleasured them if I could—and then walked away. I never saw them again—and not a one came in search of me. I began to feel...empty, wondering how I was going to tolerate this...this...*loneliness*...for all eternity."

"So, after few centuries, I went back to Uruk to beg Inanna's forgiveness. To ask her to release me from the curse."

"What happened?" I asked, selfishly wondering if there was truly a way to be freed from her bondage.

His eyes hardened as he peered into the past...

"I wasn't certain when I entered the temple that I'd ever come out again," he began, "but by then, I was so broken, so...tired, I didn't care what happened to me. I'd wandered the world for over three hundred years and I only desired peace.

"I entered her lair with no delusions she'd have a change of heart, nor did I expect her to be pleased to see me. My only goal was to plead for mercy, and if that didn't work—I planned to anger her in hopes she'd destroy me in a fit of rage.

"Though I couldn't see her, I knew she was there. I could feel the narrow gaze of her hatred upon me.

"'Gilgamesh, my love,' she said smugly, 'I always knew, someday, you would return.'

238

"I fell to my knees. 'What choice did I have?'

"She emerged from her tent, her body firm and perfect. Her face utterly angelic. But even with her divine beauty, I couldn't bring myself to desire her. I realized then, that despite my immortal body, I'd died long ago.

"'I've come…to ask your forgiveness,' I told her. 'I cannot live like this anymore…please, Inanna, if you ever loved me…free me from this wretchedness.'

"She threw her head back and laughed. 'Oh, my love, but you haven't even begun this existence, why would you wish it to be over?' Her gaze hardened. 'I have lived since before time was invented, before man or beast walked this earth. I have stared into the eons; all the while, drowning in my loneliness, with only my formless family of gods to keep me company. I've gone thousands of years without whispering a word—and you come to me now, asking me to release you of this suffering after only *three hundred years?*' She laughed again. 'It wasn't until we, the gods, decided to dwell inside the flesh that life became tolerable. To feel, to taste, to smell…to make love. That's why we descended from the Heavens, leaving the safety of the cosmos to experience what it was to exist. It was truly wonderful…for a time.' Her eyes darkened. 'Then, we became bored. Our earthly pleasures no longer placated us.'

"She turned to me, her expression unnervingly innocent. 'It was my idea, you know, to create man. I wanted to be a mother. I am, after all, the Goddess of Love. I wanted something to hold, to nurture and love —and to have something love me—unconditionally. *Children.*'

"She smiled, smoothing her hands over her womb. 'I created children. I molded you in our likeness, bestowed you a spark of the divine. Consciousness. Immortality. Everything we were. Everything you needed to love and belong to me…*forever.*' Her lips curled. 'But my father disapproved. When he discovered what I'd done, what I'd made, he cursed man with mortality, with limited awareness, and worst of all…*free will.*'

"You did not wish us to think for ourselves?" I asked, bewildered.

"'Free will gave man the ability to decide their own fate, to believe or not believe in the gods, thus disobeying me. With free will, man has run amuck, they've become greedy, violent, and aggressive. Far from the loving, subservient creatures *I* created. So I have made a decision. When I'm free from my father's imprisonment to this vile basement, I will find every one of the hidden Mes…making myself the one, true god over all things. More powerful than any god in the Heavens. Then, I will change this world, I will make it peaceful and beautiful. A place without war, without hunger and disharmony…'

"'How is that possible?'"

"She gave me a terrible smile. 'Oh my dear Gilgamesh, by destroying it, of course. By destroying free will…*and beginning again.*'"

Gilgamesh's face was ashen. "So you see, we need to get out of here, Solomon. We have to get back to Sumer—to stop Inanna."

Enlil's punishment resounded, *'You are banished, Inanna, Ishtar, Isis, Goddess of Love—Lilitu, my first born child, to the temple basement for three full turns of your sun.'*

239

"Daedalus told me…" I recalled the inventor's exact words. "That the next alignment was Venus—at the start of the next equinox."

Gilgamesh nodded gravely. "Venus—Inanna's sun."

I roughly calculated the days since Daedalus's fateful estimation. "That's less than a month's time from now."

"Twenty-one days, to be exact," Gilgamesh corrected. "Twenty-one days to escape from Egypt, return to Sumer, and save the world."

"How long to travel from here to Uruk?"

"On foot, across the desert…two weeks at best."

"Two weeks! We only have *five days* to figure out how to get out of here!" I cried. "Why…why didn't you do it *before*?"

Taken aback, he frowned.

"If you knew how to stop her," I continued, "why didn't you do it years ago?"

"Because of *that*!" he pointed at the Mes on my back. "I've spent hundreds of years searching for a single Mes, and when I finally find one, you come along and steal it from me!"

"You had plenty of time to take it before I arrived…"

"I didn't know it was Pasiphae who had it until recently. She was *very* careful to keep it hidden. I almost had it—" Gilgamesh's eyes glittered with a familiar demon. "Then you and that…that…*frigid* little princess ruined my plans!"

We circled one another, primed to attack.

"Why do you want it so badly?" I knew him now. Everything with Gilgamesh was about ulterior motives.

He gritted his teeth, as if debating whether to tell me. "The Mes has the power to stop Inanna, without it, we are nothing but mice to a cat. Do you remember the story I told you about Humbaba?"

"Vaguely, I was busy being murdered by you, so…" I mumbled.

"Enkidu and I had to trap the demon inside the vessel by whispering its name into the vase. Inanna is like that demon, but far more powerful. She requires a…a…magical *seal* of sorts, to keep her locked inside. The *Mes* is that seal."

"You want to…trap Inanna inside a vessel?" A shudder crawled up my spine. "But that means…we have to *kill* Inanna!"

Gilgamesh shrugged. "Just look at the lives she's ruined. Do you think she's concerned with the many children sacrificed in her name? The countless courtesans forced to their knees to suck the cocks of enemy soldiers? Do you think the so-called 'Goddess of Love' has lost a single night's sleep for the way she has treated her beloved *creations*?" He put a hand on my shoulder. "Solomon, if we stop Inanna—the source of all this sorrow—her energy will be severed from the rest of the Mes…and her influence will be no more. We'll be free. Free from her power. Free from her tyranny. *Free from the curse.*"

"From…the curse?" I was suddenly breathless with hope.

We had to stop Inanna—no matter what.

Gilgamesh paced the room, stroking his goatee with dark consternation. The telltale signs of his curse were growing more evident by the hour: hair greying at his temples; wild, dangerous shadows gathering behind his eyes. "It'll take us no less than two weeks to travel to Sumer by boat—and that's if the weather stays on our side—we need to get out of here as soon as possible. You will simply have to make love to these women."

"I-I can't...they'll die!"

Gilgamesh smirked. "Of course, I'd be happy to take your place in this matter. Perhaps if we keep it very dark and I slip in at the opportune moment..."

"This is no time for your perverse jokes!"

"Who's joking?" Gilgamesh mumbled. "Look, Inanna's curse, as you've said, specified you were not to *love* another woman, correct?"

I nodded, chewing the side of my thumb.

"Maybe the curse only applies to women you truly love—like Indra."

A wave of dark images drowned me. Her lovely face, skin fissured, oozing blackened lifeblood. Then her screams, the sound of excruciating pain; dissolving into ash.

"Solomon?"

When I found my voice, it was a whisper, "I-I *can't*, Gilgamesh. What if...I bed these women and...they end up like *her*? I couldn't live with myself if I knew I'd caused another such agony—on purpose! It's... hard enough knowing I'm responsible for causing that kind of pain to someone I love." I sat on the bed, my limbs weighted with guilt. "We'll simply have to find a way out of this without me having sex with these women."

"How I wish I had the choice," Gilgamesh muttered. Then he turned to me, sighing as if compelled to spill a secret. "There's something else you should know about possessing a Mes..."

"What?" Fresh anxiety churned inside.

"It *can* temper the effects of a curse. So you may be able to sleep with these women now and not kill them."

"That's why you wanted it, isn't it? This has nothing to do with saving the world! You wanted it simply to quell your needs—and you were willing to kill Pasiphae for it!"

He gave a guilty shrug. "There were a few benefits, I will admit, but ultimately, I wanted it to entrap Inanna."

"I won't sleep with them on the *hunch* they will be left unharmed. We'll have to think of another way out," I said hotly.

"Okay then, what other options do we have?"

"What about Rhadamanthys? Perhaps he could get his friends from the Cause to break us out of here?"

"That's a possibility..." Gilgamesh gave me a malevolent grin. "Or maybe, there's another way."

31

The Face of Death

"*N*o!" I yelled. "Out of the question!'

"It's either that," Gilgamesh said, "or take your chances having sex with seven women—which I'd do anyway, escape or no escape."

I rubbed my forehead. "*If* I do this, how will you get out...afterwards?"

"If we do it right, they won't see any further need for me. I'll just walk out the front door."

"And if you can't?"

"You don't need my help to stop Inanna, you have the Mes." His eyes darkened. "Only you have the power now."

Fear snaked up my spine. "I...I don't think I can kill her, Gilgamesh."

"You have to," he said, dead serious. "Remember what she's done to you. To Indra. To your father. What she'll do to the world. You're the only one who can stop her, Solomon..."

Just then the doors swung open and Queen Neteraphare glided in. One of the younger queens trailed behind, head bowed and eyes averted, naked beneath a sheer gown.

Neteraphare spoke through Gilgamesh.

"This is Safiya, second wife to Mentuhotep," Gilgamesh said, circling Safiya like a hungry hyena. "She says you have one hour."

My heart stopped—the first of my sexual partners had arrived.

Neteraphare turned to leave.

"Wait!" I blurted. "Ask her what she was doing in the market. Why was she evading her guards?"

Neteraphare spun around and shot me a venomous look.

Gilgamesh relayed the question, but was preoccupied with seducing Safiya, running a fingertip down her arm. The young woman giggled, surprisingly interested in his advances—until she heard Gilgamesh translate my query. She paused and frowned at Neteraphare.

Neteraphare's lovely face twisted in anger.

"You..." she pointed at me, "Come," she ordered—*in Sumerian.*

I followed her out of the room and caught up with her halfway down the hall.

242

"How is it you speak Sumerian?" I eyed her, bewildered.

"Because I *am* Sumerian, you fool!" Neteraphare's dark eyes raged. "But no one here is supposed to know that!"

"I-I'm sorry, I didn't mean to..."

"Never mind," she said coldly and started to leave. "It's none of your concern."

"It is now." I took hold of her arm "Besides, you're partially to blame for getting me into this mess. You owe me an explanation, don't you think?"

She drew a breath, calming herself. We started down a secluded hallway, observed only by the larger than life anthropomorphic statues.

"What I tell you now could have me and my loved ones put to death...you understand?" She implored with desperate eyes.

"I would never say anything that would bring you harm, I swear."

She sighed, her shoulders relaxing. "The pharaoh thinks I am of pure royal blood, a Hittite," she confessed. "But I'm no more than a runaway slave girl from Sumer. Shortly after my escape, however, I was captured by a band of Hittites. They are a brutal and savage people. I was kept prisoner in their village for many years, until the Hittites went to war against the Egyptians. When the Hittites lost, they were ordered to send their beloved royal daughter to marry the Egyptian King. Instead of sending the real princess, whom the Egyptians had never seen, the Hittites tricked Mentuhotep—and sent me."

"Are you...happy here?" I asked, treading carefully.

"I've had few complaints. I was made a queen, and treated as such. A slave's dream. Mentuhotep is a great king. He's good to the people and is trying to keep Egypt united, to make the country stronger and more powerful again."

"But..." I nudged.

"But he's very old and...*unable* to make love. Most of the younger queens are still...untouched" She moved to the balcony, lifting her bronze face to the stars. "I was just girl when I came here, young and naive. I didn't understand the importance of love and romance and... passion. I thought I could live without it. After so many years as a slave, cold and starving, beaten and treated less than a dog, I thought I'd be happy here. I have everything I could ever ask for—well, *almost* everything.

"The other queens feel as I do. They're often sad and lonely. I suspect several have taken secret lovers. I'm certain you're not an unwelcome suitor—except for Imi, of course. She's utterly devoted to the pharaoh."

"The older queen who was crying?"

Neteraphare nodded. "Her son, Mentuhotep the IV, is the rightful heir to the throne."

"The angry man with the red sash," I surmised.

"Unlike me, Imi is known to have been born a commoner, therefore her son may not be respected by the people."

"But I am a commoner—wouldn't my status be a hinderance in the eyes of the Egyptian people?"

"The pharaoh intends on claiming your blue-eyed offspring as his own. Egyptians are very devout. They don't question the gifts from the gods. You're merely a surrogate. With any luck, you'll simply be allowed to leave once you've fulfilled his wishes…"

"*Allowed* to leave?" Anxiety prickled through my veins, visions of the shackled miniature man resurfacing.

'*He's kept as entertainment for the pharaoh,*" Gilgamesh's words reverberated. '*A favoured pet ..*'

I swallowed hard. I had to tell her the truth—or at least part of it.

"I-I cannot…lay with you or any of the other queens…"

She put a warm palm on my chest. "I do not wish to be with you either, Solomon."

Feeling strangely slighted, I said, "But I thought you agreed with the pharaoh."

"You may choose to be with another of the queens but…I'm in love with another man," she said with a smile, draping her hands over her womb. "And you cannot make a child with me…when there is already one growing within."

Relief swept through me.

"The timing of the Pharaoh's demands couldn't have been better," she said plainly.

"You're going to tell the pharaoh this baby…is mine?"

"It's the only way. If Mentuhotep was ever to discover my betrayal…" Neteraphare's expression turned fierce, as if just realizing the consequences of relinquishing her dangerous secrets. "If you tell *anyone* what I've told you, even that hairy, perverted friend of yours, I'll have you thrown to the hippos!"

"*Hairy*, perverted friend," I said around a chuckle. "I promise I'll tell no one. Though I am curious as to why a queen would be dressed as a commoner and running from her own soldiers in a dirty marketplace?"

She relaxed, cradling her stomach. "I was going to see *him*, the father of my baby. He has been…unwell."

"The packages were medicine?"

She nodded sadly. "We've tried everything…but he's not getting better."

"If there's anything I can do to help, I will."

"I-I am so sorry I got you into this." Neteraphare eyes brimmed with guilt. "It was the only thing I could think of at the time to distract the guards. I never would've dreamed the pharaoh would…force you to…" She covered her mouth.

"I understand, but now I need your help to escape. There's something very important I need to do…and soon." My insides knotted at the thought of facing Inanna.

Neteraphare's thin brows pulled together. "At the moment, you're the pharaoh's most prized possession. He'll have ordered hundreds of soldiers to stand guard at every entrance. To keep watch over your every move. The only way Mentuhotep will allow you to leave is if you are… *dead.*"

"Apparently," I said under my breath. "That's the plan."

A spectacular orgasm crescendoed the moment I re-entered the apartment. On the bed, Gilgamesh rolled off the young queen, a sheen of sweat around her smile.

244

"Took care of that one for you," he said, grinning, his face youthful once again.

I turned a wary eye toward the guards just outside the door. "You best be careful, you don't want the pharaoh to hear of your...antics."

He laughed, naked as he strolled across the room to get a cup of water. I shut my eyes, but not before the offensive image was seared into my mind. The young queen followed suit, but was dignified enough to wrap a blanket around herself. After a wet-sounding kiss with Gilgamesh, she headed towards a large, colourful tapestry hanging on the wall. Safiya drew aside the blanket to reveal a hidden doorway, which she pushed open, and then vanished down a dark passageway.

"Gilgamesh!" I said, wide-eyed. "Did you see that?"

He nodded around a postcoital yawn.

"Maybe it can lead us out of the palace?"

"Perhaps..." he said, uninterested. "But I suspect it leads straight to the king's chamber. Trust me, I've snuck out of more bedrooms than I can count."

I pulled back the curtain, examining the narrow passageway. "We have to at least *try* to get out of here."

"I suppose," he said with a shrug. "I like my plan better though."

"That's because *you* aren't the one who has to die," I growled.

"I'm not the one with the pretty eyes that got us into this mess, now am I?"

"Actually, it is. If you hadn't told them my eyes were a gift from the gods..."

"Yes, yes, I'll admit my little plan went awry...but if I walk out that door, I doubt anyone will notice. I'm only here to help *you*, Solomon."

"I'm sorry. You're right. I just...don't cherish the idea of resurrecting again. I don't want to lose another piece of my soul. And it's...horrible."

"Yes, it is." Gilgamesh shuddered. "But there's also another reason you have to die."

I abandoned the hidden door, crossing the room. "What?"

"We need to know Inanna's true name—or else it'll be *your* soul that's sucked into the urn instead of hers."

"I-I thought you knew that already."

"No." Gilgamesh crawled back into bed.

"Then who does?"

He closed his eyes, his breath slowing.

"Gilgamesh!" I demanded. "Who?"

Through his feigned nap, he muttered, "Ereshkigal."

The problem then was *how* to die.

I'd come to terms with the idea that I had to kill myself to escape the clutches of the pharaoh, as well as knowing it was imperative I speak with Ereshkigal. There was no way around it. I had to die—again. Only this time, I wanted it to be peaceful.

Painless.

If that was at all possible.

Macabre scenarios filled my thoughts, each less appealing than the last. From jumping into the Nile and drowning myself to tying a long sash around my throat and hanging from the balcony—none struck me as particularly humane. My stomach curdled with the memory of resurrection, the slow, agonizing reconstruction of my broken body. Every cell breathing to life, screaming as they bled from mortal wounds not meant to be mended.

"There are many pieces to a soul...how many depends on the man." Ereshkigal's words haunted me. *"Each time you die, I will take another piece, one at a time until you are no more—and then you will belong to me."*

A chill crawled up my spine. How many pieces did I have left?

I stole a glance at Gilgamesh, recalling the goddess's words as she spoke to me while trapped inside my dead body, awaiting resurrection:

'Fragments, shattered by pain and loss...How many depends on the man. Not all souls are destroyed equally. Those who did not dare to love too deep, did not sacrifice or were shallow and cruel—their souls have not fractured at all...The man left most broken in the end...those are the souls I crave most.'

If Gilgamesh was still here, seven hundred years later, having paid Ereshkigal for his soul time and again, surely I'd earned hundreds more fragments with which to pay. He himself admitted to a shallow and coarse existence whereas I'd loved with all my heart, and lost everything, thus destroying every ounce of my being.

But as I considered another resurrection, Ereshkigal's offer haunted me.

"But, dear Solomon, should you ever wish to end this torturous forever...You only have to offer yourself to me, join my army, and I can free you from this nightmare."

The next morning, we were escorted to the breakfast room.

Beyond the ornate, arching windows, the Egyptian sun poured hot rays across an awakening city. The palace overlooked thousands of rooftops, each blending seamlessly into one another as they stretched over the landscape, shoring up the Nile. I thought of Rhadamanthys and Bansabira, who were surely concerned of my whereabouts. I was certain they didn't care where Gilgamesh was.

In the breakfast room, Gilgamesh had found a seat between two of the lesser queens, rubbing his hands together like a miner who'd struck gold. The women giggled, seemingly charmed by the former king. I had to admit, watching him, Gilgamesh possessed a rare atmosphere all his own. His salacious grin, shadowed by his long, thick moustache and goatee; that mischievous twinkle in his eyes; an infectious laugh. It wasn't hard to see what made women flock to him. He had a magnetism. But like gravity, his amassing pull was inescapable, only recognizable after he had you in his grasp—but by then, you were powerless to free yourself.

I couldn't help but notice that the Pharaoh and Neteraphare had not joined us. Queen Imi and her scowling son had not made an appearance either.

I considered all I'd learned of Neteraphare—of her secrets. It was dangerous of her to confide in me, leaving me to wonder exactly why she did. If I told anyone she was Sumerian, or that she was pregnant with another man's child, she'd probably be put to death along with her unborn baby. With her glaring absence, I worried for her welfare.

I cleared my throat. "Will the Pharaoh and Queen Neteraphare be joining us?"

Queen Safiya answered, using Gilgamesh to translate. "The pharaoh was summoned to the temple early this morning to oversee an execution. Neteraphare has recently begun taking breakfast in her room..."

The young queens exchanged telling glances and my chest tightened. Perhaps Neteraphare's secret was not a secret at all.

After breakfast, Gilgamesh and I were allowed to wander the gardens outside the palace. Again I thought of Rhadamanthys, anxiously awaiting my return, fearing demise. I eyed the heavily guarded exit to the palace, trying to find an unmanned escape route.

"There's no way out," Gilgamesh said, noticing my constant scanning. "You need to speak to Ereshkigal anyway..."

"Then you do it!" My temper flared.

He sighed. "I...can't."

"Why not?"

"I used up all my resurrections a long time ago. Over five hundred years ago, to be accurate." He gave a mirthless chuckle.

"Then how have you resurrected since?"

"I owe Ereshkigal...something else...in lieu of my soul."

"What?"

Through a shaky breath, he said, "You need to understand, Solomon; there are other realms all around us, ruled by ancient and powerful beings. Each of them wants to be the one true god over everything. There's a war going on—a war amongst the deities." He lowered his voice, that crazed look festering in his eyes. "If you were a god waging an epic war against a dozen other gods, what's the one thing you would need?"

I shrugged despite a chill rising in my skin.

"An army, Solomon. A damn big one. Ereshkigal is using me to build her an army..."

"How?"

Gilgamesh paced a tight circle. "Ereshkigal cursed me too...I'd only died four times when I used up my own soul fragments. Each time she resurrected, I owed her *a thousand souls*. Any woman I...impregnated," he said slowly. "Ereshkigal...*owns* the baby's soul."

A sharp breath escaped me.

"She...collects them after they are born. Sometimes just the soul. Sometimes the whole body. Those she turns into these...these...*creatures*. She said something about owning their soul while they're still pure..." he rambled on, but I was no longer listening.

...she collects them after they are born...

My blood turned to ice.

Trembling violently, I asked, "Gilgamesh, I'm only going to ask you this one time...please don't lie to me. When Father and I met you outside Ur last spring...and..." I forced the words through my lips. "... had you ever *visited* the Cult of the Courtesan?"

Gilgamesh bowed his head.

"Yes, Solomon," he said. "I was with Indra. Her child...was probably mine."

247

Before I realized what I was doing, I was on him, pummelling, my vision black with rage. My fists swung again and again, spattered blood raining to the ground. Gilgamesh didn't fight back, he only covered his face with his arms and took the blows.

"Solomon!" I vaguely heard Neteraphare.

Two guards were suddenly on either side of me, wrenching me from a near-unconscious Gilgamesh.

"What is wrong with you!" Neteraphare whispered in Sumerian.

Angry tears wet my face. "He…is a monster. A *child killer*."

Neteraphare gasped, draping her womb. "Is this true?" she asked Gilgamesh.

Through a pained groan, Gilgamesh sat up. "A monster, yes—a child killer, no."

"Close enough." I glowered. "Is that what really happened to the Minoan children? They were stolen by Ereshkigal? Or were they sacrifices to Inanna?"

"Both." He offered a pathetic chuckle. "The sisters fight over them."

"Sisters?" Neteraphare gave me a confused look.

"Inanna and Ereshkigal. Goddesses of Love and Death," I explained. "Apparently they compete for the souls of the innocent by stealing or sacrificing children—among other atrocities." Inanna's sex cults leapt to mind.

Neteraphare's brows pinched in dark realization. "Here in Egypt, we too have macabre mysteries which cannot be explained…though not with missing babies."

"What do you mean?" I asked.

"Thousands of years ago, before the great pyramids were made," she began, "it's said the Egyptians were told to begin preserving the bodies of the dead—mummies. In order for them to someday…*resurrect*."

A chill sliced my spine.

"Over time, the reasoning for this ritual has been reinterpreted to mean the gods will reward us with a rich afterlife inside our original bodies," Neteraphare explained. "But I've seen the ancient texts…and that's not what they say."

"Ancient texts?" I leaned in.

"Yes," she said quietly, sweeping the garden with furtive eyes. "In The Book of the Dead."

"This way," Neteraphare whispered as she stole a lit torch from the wall, her willowy silhouette guiding us down a shadowed hall.

Behind me, Gilgamesh moaned. "I think you broke my ribs."

Ignoring him, I addressed Neteraphare. "What are these tunnels used for?"

"The previous pharaoh desired to oversee the construction of his secret funerary chambers without leading thieves to his future place of rest. He had this passageway dug so he could wander freely. It also leads directly to the temple, so the king could worship alone."

Ahead, the darkened hallway led into a vast room awash with candlelight, empty save for a large, wooden chest. Neteraphare knelt before the box and lifted the lid. Inside were several sheets of papyrus, each elegantly penned with row after row of hieroglyphics.

"The Book of the Dead..." I utterly, reverent as I fingered the delicate, timeworn pages. Hieroglyphic and hieratic scripts in charcoal swept across the pages in precise, almost musical strokes. Compared to the sturdy stone tablets my culture utilized, papyrus seemed a fragile, ephemeral form on which to document history.

"This is a manual of sorts?" I asked.

Neteraphare nodded. "They began as Coffin Texts, thousands of years ago. A pharaoh would have the incantations painted on the inside of his sarcophagus and on the walls of his tomb to help his *ka* navigate the afterlife—past the obstacles and monsters—in hopes of reuniting with his *ba*."

When I looked confused, she explained further.

"The Egyptians believe when we die, our two souls—the *ka* and the *ba*—are separated from one another. If the souls survive judgement and are reunited with the mummified body, it becomes the *akh*. A supreme being. A god."

She scanned the papyrus, reading through the hundreds of ciphers. Finally, she pointed. "Here, this one, within the Twenty-First Pylon, never made sense...*'Knife which cutteth when its name is uttered, slayer of those who approach thy flame is thy name. She possesseth hidden plans.'*"

"The mummies," I said in a whisper. "Ereshkigal could be reuniting the souls with the bodies, using them for her army."

Neteraphare frowned. "Ereshkigal? The Sumerian goddess? She's not in the Egyptian beliefs, here they worship the God of the Dead, Anubis. Besides the bodies are still in the tombs and crypts. I've seen many of them with my own eyes."

"She could be waiting..." Gilgamesh offered, a suspicious look in his eye. "For the war of wars—the apocalypse."

Neteraphare and I fell silent, uneasy as we turned our attentions back to the papyrus. Colourful images of figures painted in bold crimsons, whites, and blues reenacted the various challenges the deceased must overcome to succeed in navigating the afterlife. In one elaborate drawing, a man awaited judgement as a black-headed jackal with a human body weighed his heart against a feather. Behind the man sat a snarling beast with a crocodile head, the torso of a lion, and the backside of a hippopotamus.

"What does this mean?" I asked.

"That is the Judgment of Osiris," Neteraphare said. "The deceased is brought before the God of the Afterlife in order to deem him worthy. His heart," she pointed to the scales of justice, "must be lighter than that of a feather, proving him to have lived a moral existence on earth. He cannot enter the next world with a 'heavy heart'."

"And this monster?" I indicated the waiting beast.

Neteraphare swallowed. "She's Ahemait, a demoness. The Devourer of the Dead. If a man's heart is heavy with sin, she devours it and the soul will not cross over. He becomes a restless ghost for all eternity. But if his heart is pure, he'll continue on to the Underworld."

"She said something about owning their soul while they're still pure..." Gilgamesh's comment about Ereshkigal collecting the soul's of babies played inside my head. I felt myself pale.

I turned to Gilgamesh. "Pure. The souls have to be pure."

"Ereshkigal wants her souls to be free from sin..." His forehead creased. "And Inanna is trying to corrupt the innocent."

Distant footsteps sounded in the tunnels.

"We have to leave!" Neteraphare placed the papyrus back inside the wooden chest and closed the lid. "Come!"

She led us out another tunnel, engulfing us in pitch darkness. Once we'd reached the safety of open air again, I turned to Neteraphare.

"What else is in the Book of the Dead?" Nothing I'd seen could aid us in stopping Inanna.

"Much of the rest is love potions and charms," she said. "And, of course, summoning spells."

"Summoning spells?" I parroted, daring to hope. "Who can it summon?" If there was another way to speak to Ereshkigal without dying again, I was in.

"I don't know, but..." Neteraphare paused, a flicker of something unreadable in her eyes. "There's only one man who knows the secrets of The Book of the Dead."

"Who?" I leaned in.

"The Mummifier."

32
The Book of the Dead

*E*ven in mid-morning, the tunnels beneath the palace were pitch as midnight. Threading through the darkness, Neteraphare led me from the secret passage in my room, past the King's chamber, and into the underground maze.

"You *must* be back by nightfall," Neteraphare whispered, the welcoming light of a doorway ahead. "Mentuhotep cannot know you're gone. He is away for the day, meeting with the leaders of the Indus Valley to discuss trade agreements. The guards believe you to be in your room servicing the queens..."

A lie, of course, but Gilgamesh was delighted to stay behind and pleasure the women in my absence. The neglected royal ladies, it would seem, were eager to accept his offer.

I, however, was only too glad to be far away from Gilgamesh.

He'd marked Miri to be stolen by Ereshkigal and transformed into... a *monster*. Even worse, he'd *been* with Indra. He was one of the men she'd so vehemently despised. Angry tears burned behind my eyes, but I had to suppress the pain and continue the mission as if Gilgamesh had not played a part in destroying my life.

Disguised in a commoner's clothes once more, Neteraphare guided me past the same marketplace where I'd first bumped into her, turning down the alleyway in which I'd seen her flee from the soldiers.

I knew where we were going before we even arrived.

My stomach clenched as she paused before the strange abode.

Amid a wary sweep up and down the alley, Neteraphare pushed the curtain aside and ducked into the dark den. I drew a consolatory breath and followed her into the mummifier's lair.

There was little, if any, natural light. Shadows ebbed in dark corners, reaching and receding by whim of candlelight. Potent aromas lingered in a vain attempt to mask the scent of death. Ivory canopic jars and obsidian blades of various lengths littered a long work table. Dozen of barrels, heaping with a fine white substance, lined the rounded walls. A corpse rested on a table in a far corner. Gratefully, it was covered from head to toe with a thick linen shroud.

"Where is the mummifier?" I asked.

"I'll see if he's resting." Neteraphare vanished through a blanket-covered doorway. Hushed whispers soon emanated, followed a barking cough.

"The father of my baby. He is...unwell," Neteraphare's confession resounded.

The mummifier is her lover, I realized.

Neteraphare reemerged from behind the curtain, followed by a tall, elegant man with eyes that gleamed onyx in the low light and a regal Egyptian nose curved like the beak of eagle. His presence bespoke of centuries, yet he looked no older than thirty. A telltale sheen of fever glistened on his shorn head, his movements slow and weak. Neteraphare kept a constant hand upon his back as he made his way to me.

"This is Master Zevadyah...or Zev," Neteraphare said reverently.

"I am Solomon," I said with a respectful nod.

"I'm happy to meet you," Zev replied in my native tongue.

"You speak Sumerian?"

He smiled alongside an intimate glance at Neteraphare. "Yes, it's...a long story."

The candles flickered ominously, as if an exhale, and my gaze slid to the dead body in the corner.

Seeing my discomfort, Zev said, "He was a friend of mine—he was executed this morning."

"Why?"

His lips pursed. "The pharaoh claims he was a traitor to our city, bringing death and destruction but he was a good man, fighting against an evil that threatens to consume Egypt. I will mummify him at no cost, out of respect. He deserves..." His words were cut short by a violent coughing fit.

"Zev," Neteraphare said once he'd calmed. "Solomon wishes to ask you about a spell."

The wise man stiffened slightly. "As I told you, my Queen, only a mummifier may know the secrets of The Book of the Dead. I cannot betray my vow to those who passed the knowledge onto me. It's an... ancient oath."

"I-I'll take the oath!" The words sprang from my lips, surprising even myself. "Teach me, please."

A thrill chased my pulse with the thought of obtaining ancient, clandestine information.

The mummifier chewed his lip, measuring me with a scrupulous eye, deciding if he should allow me into his secret world.

"Perhaps," he said with a smile.

Once Neteraphare had left, returning to the palace to ensure the guards hadn't discovered my absence, Zev turned to me. "Follow me—there is much to do."

Down a set of roughly-hewn steps, I descended into yet another maze. The deeper we ventured, the more the shadows oozed with the ubiquitous presence I'd sensed on the first day of my arrival.

For an ill man, Zev meandered the dark tunnels with little effort. I struggled to keep pace, terrified I'd lose sight of his pale robes. Before long, an odd smell permeated the passageways, seeping from a honey-comb of shallow recesses.

"What are all these…rooms?" I asked.

"They are the temporary tombs."

Curious, I peeked my head into one—and I immediately understood.

A mummy.

Wrapped in long strips of linen, a feminine figure lay upon a plat-form of blocks, arms crossed over her chest. Another human form rested near her, smaller and scarcely recognizable beneath a thick layer of salt. Atop a tiny pallet in the corner was the unmistakable shape of a mummifying cat. Beside that, a bird. Each appeared in the midst of their own stage of embalmment.

"Are all of these tombs…occupied?" I swallowed hard.

"Mostly." Zev chuckled around a cough. "I'm the only mummifier left in Thebes. Since the unification, many have left the city. They disagree with the king. There were only three mummifiers in Upper Egypt as it was, and now two have gone."

"Don't you have an apprentice? In case…" I didn't want to imply he could expire soon, but he sounded terribly ill.

He glanced back, his face half in shadow. "I do now."

A part of me was thrilled, but I didn't have the heart to tell him I couldn't stay in Thebes for more than few days, just long enough to learn the spell to summon Ereshkigal and ask her about Inanna's true name.

"Ah, here we are," Zev said, entering a narrow niche where the bloated corpse of a middle-aged man rested on slatted planks. "This one died just yesterday."

I suppressed a gag.

After a short blessing from the Book of the Dead and a recitation of the Embalmer's Oath, I was officially sworn into a secret brotherhood that dated back to an era when the measurement of time had scarcely been conceived. Despite the vow being merely words rendered from an antiquated papyrus scroll, I felt changed inside.

Worthy.

A keeper of sacred knowledge.

Now, the mummification could begin.

Zev retrieved two small pouches and poured the contents into clay bowls. The first satchel contained tiny golden pellets that laced the air with a sweet fragrance. The second pouch was a jumble of amber stones that added a perfume of lemon and pine.

"Frankincense and myrrh—helps with the smell," he said, matter-of-fact.

He then moved to the body. Eyes closed, hands manipulating the space over the man's chest, Master Zev muttered an ancient Egyptian incantation:

"O my divine father Osiris! I come to embalm thee. Come then, strengthen my breath, O Lord of the winds. Grant thou that I may enter into the land of everlastingness.

And when the soul hath departed, a man seeth corruption, and the bones of his body crumble away and become stinking things, and the members decay one after the other, the bones crumble into a helpless mass, and the flesh turneth into foetid liquid.

Let life rise out of death. I shall live, I shall flourish. I shall wake up in peace. I shall not putrefy, my intestines shall not perish, I shall not suffer injury. My eyes shall not decay. The form of my face shall not disappear. My ear shall not become deaf. My head shall not be separated from my neck. My tongue shall not be removed. My hair shall not be cut off. My eyebrows shall not be shaved away, and no evil defect shall assail me.

It shall neither become a ruin, nor be destroyed on this earth."

Zev anointed the body with palm oil to cleanse it of impurities, both carnal and of spirit. "A soul is born of nine fragments—but six are most important for mummification," he said. "The *Ba* is who you are, your personality. *Ka* is the eternal life force. *Khat* is the physical, the unique shell in which we all reside. Each night, in dream, the three are reunited in the immortal body—the *Akh*. And again when a man dies."

A coldness passed right through me.

Nine.

Only nine fragments.

I prayed Master Zev was wrong. For if he was correct, I only had eight fragments of my soul left. Eight deaths and resurrections before I, like Gilgamesh, would owe a debt to Ereshkigal or become a monstrous slave in her Underworld.

Zev set his palms against the the dead man's temples. "Then there is the Shadow, *Shuyet*, the silhouette of self who stands guard against the waiting evil should you be caught unaware—blinded by the light of life or lost in darkness. And last, there is the Name, the *Ren*...a man is nothing without his Name. Without it, he ceases to exist or to ever have existed. An Egyptian is given many an alias at birth, as to protect the one *true* Name."

My ears perked. That's what I was here for. As much as I yearned to stay in this place forever, with Zev, amassing ancient knowledges and practices, I had to glean from him the summoning spell so I could speak to Ereshkigal and ask her for Inanna's true name.

"Why is that?" I asked.

"Words have power, Solomon," Zev said, his tone somber "One's true name, should it be spoken, holds more power than any spell. Many a king has been erased from history because his name was chiseled from the stone monuments, the papyrus texts which bore his likeness, burned—but his soul lives on in the afterlife if he still has his secret Name.

"In order to become immortal," Zev continued, "all parts of the soul must be reunited in the afterlife. The body, then, must be preserved in such a way so it can be recognized by the soul. If the soul cannot find its body, *resurrection cannot occur*—the worst fate for an Egyptian." He regarded me with dark eyes, ensuring my complete attention.

"The salt of the Nile, called *natron*, draws the lifeblood from the body, saving it from decay." He retrieved a long iron tool from the work table and positioned himself over the man's face. "All organs are removed, except the heart."

After peeling back the shroud to expose the man's mouth and nose, he shoved the rod up a nostril and gave it a firm tap. A sickening crack echoed inside the tiny alcove. "We must break through the bone which acts as a wall to protect the thoughts. Then, we break up the mind." He pushed the tool into the man's skull and gave it a swift whisk. "The *Khat* mind is no longer needed, only the thoughts of the *Ka* and *Ba*. Once the brain is broken into small pieces, we pour in the warm resin —mostly to lubricate and purify the cavity." Around a pained cough, he pointed to a copper basin filled with a viscous amber substance. Through narrow tubes of reed inserted into his nostrils, we funnelled tree sap into the man's head.

"We must allow the resin to rest awhile, and then we will sit him up and drain the contents from his nose. After which, we stuff the head with strips of linen and swab the cavity clean. We may have to do this many times."

I nodded, swallowing the bile that burned the back of my throat. While I was fascinated by the whole procedure, the image of a dark, soupy syrup chunked with brain matter oozing out a dead man's nose churned my stomach.

Zev continued, "There are many tasks to complete while we wait for the resin."

He stepped to the body's side and, with a shard of obsidian, sliced a clean, three-inch slit into the torso. I was surprised the cut did not bleed, but immediately after, the fetid stench of putrefying meat intensified. Zev pinched his fingers together, making his hand smaller, and slid it into the gap. After a moment of slow exploration, he latched onto something, twisted his forearm once, and then extracted a slimy maroon glob from the incision.

"This is a bag of blood," he said, examining the spleen with quiet interest. "I've often wondered what this organ was for..." He set the sac onto the work table, and then proceeded to disentangle yard after yard of mottled intestine, a pair of lungs and kidneys, and an impressive-sized liver. Soon all the essentials which had once given this man life were aligned in a moist macabre pile across the table. Zev instructed me to bury each organ in a heap of natron, thus dehydrating them before their permanent entombment in the canopic jars.

"The heart," Zev explained, "remains in the body so it can be presented to Anubis who will weigh it against a feather from the winged goddess, Ma'at. If the heart is as light as the feather—meaning the man led a good and honest life—he'll move on to the Next World. If his heart is heavy with sin, however, he will not pass into the afterlife, but be consumed by a terrible monster."

I tensed. "A monster?"

"*They lay in wait...the monsters...they are waiting for us, Solomon...*" Gilgamesh's dream warning whispered.

Zev looked grave. "There are many monsters in the Next World. Those who wish to become a part of this one."

"How?"

The mummifier furrowed his brow. "There's no need for us to worry about it in this realm. Let us continue."

255

Deflated, I wished I could confess everything I already knew of the afterlife. I felt certain Zev would believe me, having been perpetually surrounded by death so often, and the mythology that haunted it.

"There's so much to remember," I said, hours later after taking stock of all we'd done and what we had yet to do.

"The Art of Mummification," Zev began, "takes a lifetime to study. There's not enough time for you to learn all you must to become a master."

I fought the urge to laugh. If only he knew how much time I actually had.

Instead, I said, "I am a fast learner."

"What I mean is," he uttered around a wheeze. "I may not live long enough to teach you everything you need to…"

His last words were strangled as he doubled over in a violent coughing fit.

"Master Zev!" I ran for a cup of water.

"Thank you," he said, sipping between ragged breaths.

"When did you become sick?"

"Last moon. I travelled by boat to collect natron from a man in Dendera. The river became unruly and my boat capsized. I swam to shore and when I didn't return home for several days, Neteraphare came looking for me." He chuckled. "But ever since, I've fought this sickness…"

An idea dawned on me.

"Master, where is the nearest healer's hut?"

"Just a few doors down—the one with the red sash," he said, followed by a shake of his head. "But I've gone to see him many times and his remedies haven't helped."

"Let me help you back to your bed," I said. "I need to talk to the healer."

"Wait, you…don't understand…he's…" Zev tried to speak but was overtaken by a frenzy of whooping coughs.

I patted him on the shoulder. "I'll be back as soon as I can."

A tenacious late afternoon sun seared my vision the instant I set foot outside Zev's cavernous hut. Bloodthirsty black flies dove at my face, probing for an unguarded moment to steal a mouthful of flesh. Up and down the block, people littered the alleyway.

Amid my search for the healer's hut, the sun dipped ever closer to the horizon. With little time to spare, I scanned the buildings for the telltale wave of crimson. Each blanketed doorway mirrored the last, threadbare, pendulous in the stagnant breeze. Then, the alleyway ended. As I backtracked, I wondered if I'd made a mistake in wandering these foreign streets alone. Even if I did find the healer's hut, I didn't speak Egyptian, how was I to ask for the supplies I needed?

'You must be back by nightfall,' Neteraphare's urgent warning resounded. *'Mentuhotep cannot know you are gone.'*

Anxiety writhed beneath my skin.

Then defiance.

What if I simply didn't return to the palace? To the barren queens awaiting my *exotic* seed? What if I just followed this dusty path out to

256

the river, rejoined Rhadamanthys and Bansabira on their Minoan ship, and sailed far, far away from Egypt?

Gilgamesh.

Still at the palace, entertaining the women in my absence, I considered what would happen to him should I run away. Perhaps the Egyptians would simply keep him as a royal pet, a perverse lover for the lonely empresses. Knowing him, he'd likely adore the idea—until his inevitable dark side emerged. Then what would they do to him?

And did I care?

Perhaps he deserved to suffer for all the women he'd exploited over the centuries. All the children he'd delivered into Ereshkigal's waiting hands. My insides churned with disgust. I closed my eyes, warring with a legion of inner demons...

"Solomon?"

I spun around. Neteraphare had returned from the palace. She stood before me with an expression of pure concern.

"Solomon, are you all right? You're trembling..."

"I-I'm fine," I stammered. "I'm...lost."

Quickly, I explained to her the ailment I experienced in my youth after I'd swum in the river; how Father had taken me to a healer in Uruk and of the strange treatment the old woman had concocted to cure my cough.

"Zev told me there was a healer only a few doors down, but I couldn't find it..." I said, exasperated.

An unreadable look crossed Neteraphare's lovely face as she led me down the alleyway and around a dark corner I'd not noticed. "This way, it's hard to find—for good reason."

I expected the same dark, mystic hut from my youth—but the Egyptian healer's hut was nothing of the sort.

Closer to a brothel than an apothecary, men lazed on enormous, cushy pillows, heads lolled to one side, blue lotus flowers pressed to their noses, inhaling with euphoric smiles. After an orgasmic sigh, one man plucked a petal and stuffed it into his mouth, chewing slowly, erotically.

"They're the Lotus Eaters," Neteraphare whispered into my ear. "They invoke the tranquility of the gods through the nectar of the flower in order to commune directly with the spirit world."

Viscous drool trickled over one man's chin, his eyes glazed, irises eclipsed by his pupils.

"Oh," I said, cringing.

Sickeningly sweet poppy smoke curled about the room. My eyes stung and my stomach turned; the memory of the Minoan brothel swam inside my head. Crete. The Minoans. Opium filled my nostrils and the line between worlds started to blur.

A waking nightmare began.

Father's screams. The pieces of his broken body thudding to the temple floor.

Terror in Indra's eyes. Blackened blood oozing from the fissures on her beautiful face.

Inanna...no, Ereshkigal...stealing Miri.

...she collects them after they are born...

I gasped in sudden realization.

"Solomon?" Neteraphare touched my forehead. Her eyes were hooded as though the drug-laden air was affecting her as well.

"She took Miri."

Neteraphare frowned. "Who's Miri?"

I fell to my knees, clutching my chest.

"Navi!" Neteraphare shouted to someone across the room.

Blackness swirled around my vision. I thrashed, heart pounding too hard in my chest as I relived the nightmare. Running...running to the temple.

"She was sacrificed at dawn."

Enusat's words resounded, his malicious smile transparent.

"He lied...it wasn't Inanna," I heard myself mutter. "It was never Inanna. Ereshkigal...Ereshkigal took her...turned her into a...*monster*..."

"You're not making sense, Solomon..."

"Miri," I sputtered. "She's...*alive*."

"There now," a distant voice said. "Just breathe this in..."

Softness tickled my nose. A delicate perfume. Within seconds, every worry I had drifted away. I floated on a cloud, carried, carried away...

"Solomon?" Neteraphare's voice called.

I blinked back to reality.

A man hovered over me, dressed in shiny purple robes. He held a large lotus flower in his hand; the antidote to my anxiety, I presumed. The little man gave a sharp inhale when he looked into my eyes, and then spoke rapidly in Egyptian, running in small circles.

"W-What's wrong with him?" I said, groaning as I sat up.

Neteraphare gave a little laugh. "Nevi thinks your blue eyes are a sign that you died moments ago and your body has been re-inhabited by the spirits."

"Let's just get Zev's medicine and get out of here," I said. "Can you translate for me?"

I described the various ingredients I needed and she interpreted them to Nevi, who nodded but only stared at me. Afterwards, he ran to the back of his shop and returned with a bundle of ingredients, including a mortar and pestle so I could grind everything into a paste. As I reached for the items, however, he clutched them to his chest, giggling as he spoke to Neteraphare. Blood rushed to the queen's face and she replied in an angry tone.

"What's wrong?" I asked.

She huffed, crossing her arms. "He requests payment."

"That's understandable..."

"He does not want money, Solomon."

"W-What does he want?"

The little healer tittered excitedly, retrieving a small dagger from his pocket and polishing it with the hem of his robe. *"Euyun."*

Neteraphare glowered. "He wants your eyes."

"I tried to...tell you," Zev said through a raspy cough. "The healer... he is crazy."

"Because of all the lotus flowers he eats, I am certain," Neteraphare added, brows drawn in annoyance.

Still reeling, I turned to the queen. "Thank you for paying him...and so much." The healer had demanded thousands of shekels and Neteraphare's gold necklace in lieu of my eyes.

"I would've paid twice that," she replied with a loving glance at Zev. "Anything..."

I set the ingredients onto a worktable, raking my memory for the correct amounts and procedure. I was only twelve when Father took me to the healer and I'd been so afraid of the old crone, I wasn't exactly paying attention to her macabre recipe. Despite this, I summoned what I could recall, drawing forth any sights, smells or impressions that still lingered.

"Thyme, myrrh, oxen hair...ground turtle shell and the inner lining of a pig's stomach," I mumbled, adding each to the mortar. "And a dollop of pulverized pear."

Beside me, learning as to recreate the remedy afterwards, Neteraphare cringed at some of the less than appetizing ingredients. "He doesn't have to...eat this, does he?"

I chuckled, shaking my head.

With the pestle, I ground the mixture into a thick, rancid-smelling paste until it resembled the concoction I'd witnessed in my youth. I prayed as I dipped my finger into the muck and painted a triangle onto Zev's wheezing chest, and then another overtop, inverted. A star.

Beneath a sweat-laden brow, Zev frowned at the symbol. "W-Where did you learn that?"

"The healer, she claimed it represented the opposing forces of nature. The good—and the evil. She said it brings balance to the body... or something like that. I even made it into a ring..." I displayed Indra's wedding band on my smallest finger.

"It does a great deal more than that..." Zev said cryptically. "How... can I repay your kindness?"

I sighed, wishing there was nothing I needed in return, but replied, "I...need to learn a summoning spell."

Zev's eyes widened. "Who, or rather *what*, do you dare summon?"

"Ereshkigal—the Goddess of Death."

Gasping, poor Zev was assaulted by series of whooping coughs. "But...why?"

"I cannot tell you—I've already hurt too many I care about...please, you have to trust me."

"It will take time...and preparations," Zev said, mistrust gathering behind his eyes.

"Solomon, we must return to the palace," Neteraphare warned. "The pharaoh will be on his way back by now..."

At the door, I turned to look back at Zev, his marked chest labouring for every breath. "I will try to return tomorrow."

He smiled weakly. "I will try...to still be here."

33

Silence of the Dead

We wended through the Theban streets, obelisks casting long shadows across the bronze sands. Gold brimmed on the horizon, gilding the black soils and the ocean of desert beyond. Magic, ancient and sage, seemed borne of the very land itself. While Sumer beheld a sense of aged mysticism, Egypt exuded an older genesis, the very garden of creation. Rich with gods and goddesses, mythology and lore, I found myself wondering not *if* but *how many* Mes had guided this civilization into its current magnificence.

In sync with my thoughts, the Mes on my back hummed painfully and the pervasive presence I'd felt since my arrival intensified. It pressed upon me—watching.

Overwhelmed by the unseen eyes, I asked Neteraphare, "Do you feel that?"

She glanced back, confused. "Feel what?"

"It's like a *power* of some kind…a humming. You don't feel it? "

"No." She panned the dark surroundings, paranoid. "When did you first notice it?"

I shrugged, feeling awkward. "Ever since I arrived, three days ago."

"I'm sorry, Solomon, I don't feel anything."

Ahead, a pair of soldiers marched by. We backed into the cover of darkness amidst a legion of massive stone pillars adorned from base to top with hieroglyphs.

"This way," Neteraphare whispered, leading me into a candlelit temple. "Commoners are forbidden here—but it's faster."

In the heart of the inner sanctum, we passed a number of priests and priestesses. Heads shorn to a shine, they quietly dressed and fed the various statues of the gods. Obviously recognizing the queen, they merely pursed their ochre-painted lips in disapproval of my presence. Down a shady stairwell, Neteraphare wove through the narrow corridor and up a ramp leading into yet another back entrance to the palace. Finally, we reached the hidden door to the room Gilgamesh and I shared.

"I must leave you now," Neteraphare said with a glance over her shoulder. "I have to greet the pharaoh when he arrives, to avoid suspicion, but I'll check on Zev in the morning." She smiled before vanishing down yet another dark corridor.

I swept a cautious eye around the room before entering. Not surprisingly, I discovered Gilgamesh in the bed, with not one, but two of the younger queens curled lovingly at his sides. Uneasiness stirred within, considering the unborn children who might be quickening inside the women. Not the blue-eyed offspring the pharaoh so desired, but spawns of something far more sinister.

'Miri...she's...alive,' my own words echoed.

In the midst of my drug-induced madness, I'd come to a profound disturbing realization. Miri could still be alive. But if she was, what was she? Had Ereshkigal transformed Miri into a monster? Some horrific creature—half-man, half-beast?

Amidst my dark anxieties, Gilgamesh yawned like a lion, waking the women beside him. Out of respect for the undressed ladies, I averted my eyes and hid behind a divider woven of thick papyrus reeds. Once I heard the women leave, I slipped out from my hiding spot.

Gilgamesh grinned when he saw me. "Did you get the summoning spell?"

"Not yet, the mummifier is very sick. But he promised to tell me tomorrow, if he's better."

"I hope so," he said, wincing. "We only have a day or two before we *must* leave this place or we'll never make to it Sumer in time..."

Before I could respond, a guard entered, a cloaked figure trailing behind him. "Her Highness, Queen Imi."

Imi lifted her chin, her expression as sharp as chiseled obsidian beneath the dark hood. Once the guard left, Imi drifted wraith-like into the centre of the room, scrutinizing the space with a look of distaste.

Gilgamesh translated as they spoke.

"You must feel very privileged," she said, her voice icy, taking slow, predatory steps towards me. "Little more than a slave, yet here you are in the palace of the pharaoh—bedding his wives. You're undeserving of this task. A commoner. A *low-born*."

Gilgamesh's expression mirrored my thoughts. It was obvious the elder queen wasn't here to fulfill the pharaoh's wish to make a blue-eyed baby, but for some other, more personal, agenda.

"*My* son is the next in line for pharaoh," she hissed.

"That doesn't seem to be what your husband wishes..." Gilgamesh started.

"I do not care about my *husband's* wishes!" Imi's stony demeanour ignited into fury. "I only care for my son's future...and I will let *nothing* stand in his way!"

From beneath her cloak, Queen Imi withdrew a *khopesh*, a deadly sword shaped like a sickle, and sliced the air in front of me. I recoiled, the tip barely missing my abdomen. Furious, the queen shrieked and attacked again. I lunged right, avoiding her, but tripped, landing hard on the floor. As I tried to stand, Imi was already upon me, sword raised, aimed to impale. She raised her weapon as to lop off my head. I shut my eyes, anticipating the pain, fearing the resurrection...

But nothing happened.

Instead, I felt the full weight of a body land on me.

261

Opening my eyes, I realized Gilgamesh had jumped in front of the blade—saving me. Having heard the commotion, the guard re-entered, bringing three more with him. They took hold of Imi, disarmed her, and dragged her screaming from the room.

Dark blood pooled beneath Gilgamesh. A long, deep slice ran from his shoulder to his groin, his intestines bulging.

He was dying.

Tears burned in my eyes. After all the horrible things this man had said and done, after all his crude behaviour, his betrayals—even murdering me—he was all I had now in this long forever.

"Why did you do that!" I asked, cradling his head in my lap. "I would've resurrected!"

"But not...in time..." he said, then chuckled, adding, "Besides, no one's allowed to kill you...except me." He coughed, crimson droplets glistened like dew on his lips.

"I'll wait for you to resurrect..."

He shook his head. "That time on the boat...Ereshkigal was angry with me...she vowed that was the...last time she would help me. There won't be any more resurrections..."

I swallowed the lump in my throat. "She...won't let you come back this time..."

"Go get the summoning spell," he said, struggling to breathe. "Get Inanna's real name from Ereshkigal—and then go. Go to Sumer. Get there as fast as you can. Stop her, Solomon. You...*must* stop Inanna..."

And then, there was silence.

Coated in Gilgamesh's blood, I escaped.

Heart thundering, I plunged through the secret passageway, down pitch-black corridors, past the tombs, and found my way to freedom. While sad I couldn't say goodbye to Neteraphare or give Gilgamesh a proper burial, I couldn't waste a single moment. The guards were sure to return and take away Gilgamesh's dead body. Then, I surmised, Imi would lie and I'd be punished for a crime I didn't commit; or worse, I'd be forced to continue the sexual plight to provide Mentuhotep a child with blue eyes.

Neither premise intrigued me.

Now past midnight, the sacred temple was quiet. I darted out the open entrance, the streets eerily empty. Silent as the dead.

Sheer instinct led me right to Zev's door.

Praying over the shrouded body of the executed man, the mummifier drew a sharp breath when I entered. I'm sure I was a horrifying sight to behold.

"Solomon!" he cried out. "What happened?"

"I...was attacked..." I gasped for air. "...by the older queen, Imi... my friend was...killed."

Sympathy swept his face, but swiftly melted into terror. "Neteraphare? Was she hurt?"

"No, she wasn't there."

He exhaled with palpable relief. "Come, let's get you cleaned up. I have fresh robes in the back."

Keen to rid myself of the stained tunic and hide within the dark tunnels of Zev's lair, I followed. Along the way, I noticed his breathing was easier, his cough loosened.

"Are you feeling better?" I asked.

"Very much," he said with a smile in his voice. "You're quite the healer."

Zev turned into a larger chamber where a host of fresh robes sat folded on a bench. "I will return shortly with a basin of water."

After he left, I began the sticky process of peeling off the blood-soaked tunic. Grief stung my heart as I eyed the crimson essence that once flowed through Gilgamesh's veins.

'There won't be any more resurrections…'

Apparently, whatever agreement they might've had in the past was no longer. Perhaps he'd angered her—which wouldn't be a surprise. Or maybe he'd paid his dues and she was disinclined to offer anything more.

Naked, I shivered, waiting for Zev to bring the water so I could clean off the blood. Hearing him return, I turned around—and Zev paled. The basin slipped from his hands and shattered against the stone floor, water splashing the sandy walls.

He stared, horrified, at the tattoo on my chest.

"W-Who are you?" Zev sputtered, backing away.

I snatched a clean robe from the pile, wrapping it around myself. "Zev, please listen to me…"

"You must leave…*now!*" he shouted, grabbing a sharp implement from his work table. "You've brought evil into this house. That is the mark of the Cult. You are a creature of darkness…a *demon!*"

"Please," I begged. "You don't understand!"

"Leave!" Zev pointed towards the exit.

Heartbroken, hands raised in submission, I did as I was told. Weapon raised, Zev marched me through the honeycomb of tombs. At the main door leading out into the dark alley, I turned around in a last effort to plead my innocence.

"Zev, if you'll just listen to me, I promise I'll leave after."

His expression faltered. "Fine, speak."

"I'm cursed," I blurted. "A goddess put this mark on my chest. She killed my father, my wife—she's taken everything from me."

The mummifier scrutinized me, unmoved, as if the tattoo on my chest was a symbol of irrefutable guilt.

"Because you healed me, I will spare your life." He trembled with rage, sidestepping towards the shrouded corpse I'd seen earlier. "This man was my friend. He was put to death because he fought against everything that mark stands for. He and others like him, me included, have dedicated our lives to seeking those with the mark of the Cult— the very mark on your chest—and *destroying* them. He was a brave man, an honourable man who sacrificed his life—for The Cause."

Zev clutched a corner of the death sheet and yanked. The shroud floated to the floor, exposing the dead man for who he was—and my knees weakened beneath me.

Rhadamanthys.

263

Egyptian soldiers stormed past the mummifier's lair, the alley a cacophony of angry words.

"Why are they yelling?" I asked Zev, my voice trembling. "Who are they looking for?"

Strangely calmed, he gave me a wry look. "You—come, there's another way out. Follow me."

Given his recent suspicions, I feared he might betray me, deliver me into the hands of the pharaoh, returning me to a purgatory of sexual slavery. But as the tunnels stretched on, snaking through an endless darkness, I believed he was steering me towards freedom.

Soon, fresh evening air, perfumed with cool river water, graced my senses. Through a narrow crevice cloaked by an olive tree, the passageway opened up into a veritable jungle. Not only had he led me out of danger, he set me onto the path where I'd begun this journey—on the shores of the Nile. The Minoan boat was only minutes away. Hope blossomed at the thought of finding Bansabira still aboard the ship, awaiting my return. I swiftly quashed the idea. I could not bear the devastation should he, too, be dead, killed by the Egyptians for treasonous activities. I'd rather find the boat gone and delude myself with the fantasy that Bansabira had escaped persecution and was sailing to some exotic island on a wide, blue ocean.

"Thank you," I told Zev, wishing he'd not seen the tattoo marring my chest. My spirits were crushed that I'd lost the mentorship of this wise man.

He exhaled. "You're welcome...and I am sorry I grew angry with you."

My heart lifted.

"Perhaps I was in error," he admitted. "Your face...when you saw Rhadamanthys...I don't believe that kind of anguish can be faked. I believe he was your friend, and that you cared for him as I did."

I could only offer a sad nod. The world was truly a lesser place without Rhadamanthys.

Zev patted my shoulder. "May the gods be ever merciful."

"Thank you," I said, my throat tight with emotion as I started down the dark path towards the river. "For everything..."

The soft whisper of the Nile carried me along the banks, eyes peeled for any sign of the Minoan boat. Soon, a large shadow came into focus, bobbing atop the water. My heart soared and I started to run.

"Bansabira?" I nearly shouted. "Are you here?"

The hull creaked with the rippling current.

"Bansabira?" I said, quieter, my hopes fading.

Trepidatious, I climbed aboard. The boat shifted slightly with my weight, weathered floorboards groaning alongside my every step.

Amid the gloom, the little door to the captain's quarters crept open. "Solo-man?"

"Bansabira!" I swept the large man into an embrace.

He held me like a parent clutching a long, lost child. I might have stayed there forever had he not spoken.

"I waited for so many days...but none of you returned," Bansabira's strong, baritone voice was taut. "Solo-man, Rhadamanthys has not returned..."

264

Tears pinched my eyes. "He is…dead, my friend. T-The pharaoh had him executed."

An odd silence followed.

"The Captain is…dead?"

In the darkness, I nodded. "I saw his body…in the mummifier's lair."

"And Gillis?"

With the shock of Rhadamanthys' death and the joy of finding Bansabira, I'd forgotten about Gilgamesh.

"He was killed by one of the Egyptian queens," I replied, a bitter-sweet aftertaste coated every word.

Bansabira bowed his head. "I must retrieve da Captain's body and take him home to Crete…"

I drew a breath of courage. "I need to ask a great favour of you. Before you return home, will you…take me back to Sumer? There is something very important I must do there…and soon."

"Of course," Bansabira replied. "But know it is harder to sail across da waters with just the two of us to man da boat."

My chest tightened, dread coiling around my heart. What if I didn't make it in time and Inanna was freed from her banishment before I could stop her?

Bansabira disembarked, promising to set sail as soon as he returned with Rhadamanthys' remains. Brokenhearted, I stared up at the sky, into the fathomless expanse of forever, wondering what fate could possibly want for me. One star amid the thousands flickered, as if in warning—the star Daedalus had shown me. *Inanna's Sun.*

Like a lighthouse across a dark ocean, steering me from the jagged coastline, to the safety of land. More radiant than all the rest, the star glittered, reminding me of things greater than myself, of my responsibility—of my purpose.

As if standing beside me, Father's loving voice reached through my memories and whispered to my soul…

'The gods made you this way, maru. They gave you this heart and this mind—and one day, you will understand why.'

265

34

The Hero Returns

*T*he shores of Sumer felt unsteady beneath my feet. Once so familiar, now felt foreign. Had I changed so much I couldn't remember
who I was or who I'd been?

As the Minoan ship vanished into the twilit horizon, a fresh scar
opened in my soul. Bansabira promised to return for me after he'd
delivered Rhadamanthys' body to Crete. I hadn't the heart to tell him I
might not be here when he came back. Not because I didn't want to
see him again, but because I may not live beyond this night.

'There are worse things than death…'

I was no longer afraid of dying. In fact, after all I'd experienced as an
immortal, I was more frightened by what might become of my soul
when my body permanently expired—if it ever did.

After a deep breath, I willed myself forward. One step, and then another. Away from the looming city of Uruk. With a glance over my
shoulder, at the shadow of the ziggurat like a mountain amidst pebbles,
I embarked on a journey I dreaded as much as facing off with Inanna—going home.

The tiny hut looked even smaller than I remembered. Empty of life.
Void of warmth, as if it realized those who'd once dwelt within its
walls, those it had promised to shelter, were gone forever. Never to
come home again. Its inner glow seemed extinguished with the loss of
future memories, the people, and the love. There, amid the gathering
shadows of an impending midnight, the place I once called home, I
realized, had died alongside us.

As I crossed the threshold, memories drowned me in an undertow of
nostalgia. Haunting voices whispered, conversations from a past not so
long ago. My heart pounded with illogical expectation. As if it were all
a nightmare and I'd finally awakened. As though I'd find Father there.
That he'd been there all along, eagerly awaiting my return. I could
almost see him as he sat at the dinner table sharpening his skinning
dagger, his activity of choice to soothe an unquiet mind. Needless to
say, the blade was kept razor-sharp. I imagined his bronze face lifting
as I entered, brown eyes brimmed with tears of relief.

266

"*Maru!*" he would exclaim. "Where have you been?"

I could almost feel the warmth of his arms as he drew me in, held me tight. I could almost smell him, hear him, see him. The pain was unbearable. My chest threatened to split open with the amassing sorrow.

Familiar scents lingered, assaulting me without mercy. Barrels of honey beer fermented in the corner—Father's favourite. Our lumpy reed cots loitered in the corners where we'd slept. One cot, witness to my first and only intimacy with Indra, still bore the grey discolouration of her ashes. The other cradled the blankets that once swaddled our little Miri.

I shut my eyes, wishing I'd not come back. After a few steeling breaths, I turned with cold resolve towards the corner where Father and I had stored the cured tablets, goddess statuettes—and *death jars*. All I needed was one. One, perfect and unbroken. As I reached the corner, however, my heart sunk. Everything was shattered. Every single clay urn was smashed or cracked, useless to imprison the soul of an all-powerful goddess. Recall flashed through my thoughts. Of the wraith-like figure hovering over Miri, of my attack, and of my body hurled magically into the wall of shelves which held the pottery.

Where was I going to find another vase? There was no time to make one. The morning market was still hours away and by then it could be too late...

As I stared at the clay shards in my palms, realization chilled my blood.

I knew exactly where I'd find one. It was buried beneath the sands of my secret oasis.

The one that held my love.

The one that held Indra's ashes.

On my hands and knees, amidst the pewter glow of a slivered moon, I burrowed into the cool desert sand; ever deeper, grit gathering beneath my fingernails. With each stroke, I anticipated the touch of hard clay, the smooth surface of the urn. Irrational thoughts, of not being able to locate it, plagued me.

Finally, my fingertips struck something solid and my heart hesitated. Being this close to her again, despite her insubstantial state, I was taken aback by the desperation I felt. The raw emotion entangled alongside this seemingly innocuous object was overwhelming.

Pulse racing, I slowly unearthed the body of the urn, sweeping aside the sands to uncover what remained of my love. I cradled the pottery within my hands, carrying it to the water's edge. The river was a sussurus of ripples, stirred by a midnight breeze.

Removing the seal, I released her ashes onto the gentle current, freeing her soul to the waters. The mighty Euphrates carried her away to the Otherworld, where someday we might meet again...

I regarded the dark horizon, towards Uruk. The apex of all my fears. I took a step, then another. To confront my past.

To journey's end.

Silhouetted by starlight, Inanna's temple loomed in the darkness. The moon had slipped behind a cover of cloud. I regarded the night sky, the stars scintillating without the obstruction of earthly lights.

'It's home to the Snake Goddess,' Daedalus pointed to a bright star on the horizon. 'When it is in alignment with the centre of the sky, we will know the exact day to celebrate her time in the heavens...'

High overhead, Inanna's sun, Venus, blazed amid the navel of the firmament, exactly where Daedalus predicted it would be when it was her turn to rule over the world. Trembling, I stood before the colossal structure, knowing who I'd find within the basement. Tears blurred my vision, vengeance amassing within. If I didn't end this now, before she was freed from her imprisonment, no one would be able to stop her. This was my burden alone to bear.

On my smallest finger, Indra's ring glinted, offering me a spark of hope. With the urn tucked under my arm and Father's skinning dagger gripped tight inside my sweaty fist, I crept through the entrance. It hadn't escaped me that I'd never learned Inanna's true name. Even if I managed to kill her, I had no idea what I was to whisper into the urn to capture her soul. No matter the odds against my success, I had to try to stop her from destroying the world. And perhaps, if I was lucky, the curse she'd placed upon me would be lifted.

Wracked with trepidation, I wondered where the secret door was that Gilgamesh had so often used to slip in undetected, and if perhaps it would give me an advantage in the way of ambush.

Too late now...

It was darker than the night Father and I had descended the same steps to meet our terrible fates. The shuddering torches which had previously shone the way remained unlit. Instead of the den of a goddess, I felt I was entering into an ancient, long-forgotten crypt where the dead lie moldering, dreaming of a life long since gone. It occurred to me then that the omnipresent pulse, the one I'd sensed in Egypt, had returned. I was vaguely aware of its absence as Bansabira and I sailed away from Thebes, but it had faded so incrementally, and I was so distraught with the death of my friends, that I scarcely noticed when the mysterious sensation had vanished completely.

Until we arrived in Sumer.

The Mes on my back had once again started to sing a song all its own. A hum, a soundless requiem only I seemed able to hear. Strangely, as I braved entrance into the lair of the beast, the lurking presence allowed me a sense of comfort. Of not being entirely alone on this dark journey.

Down and down, I tread into the belly of the ziggurat. Finally, as I rounded the last spiral of the stairwell, a single candle greeted me. When my vision adjusted, I gasped. Inanna's chamber was in shambles. As though a mighty earthquake had shaken the stones from its very foundation. It was a wonder the ziggurat above remained intact at all. Inanna's once lavish Bedouin tent lay in a haphazard pile on the floor, the silken drapes shredded. The alcoves which once held the nine alabaster busts of her and her fellow deities now sat empty, their precious contents in fragments on the floor. Everything had been destroyed in a fit of rage.

Cautious, I stepped through the arched doorway, navigating the labyrinth of fallen stones. Save for my ragged breath and the blood quickening in my veins, the room embraced a terrible silence.

Where is she?

I scoured the goddess's lair. Was I too late? Had she already been freed?

I searched for any hint of movement, a glimpse of her pearlescent skin, of her violet glare. Eyes peeled, I took slow steps further into the room. Past the fallen tent, beyond the stern-eyed remnants of the godly busts, and towards a dark corner. Across from me, the single candle quivered as if disturbed by a phantom breeze.

I felt her before I saw her.

My knees weakened as she emerged from the shadows. Graceful and statuesque, her profound beauty betrayed her true nature. Though stoic, her violaceous cat-like eyes narrowed at the urn and dagger in my possession.

"*You,*" Inanna's said, prowling ever closer, her voice like an icy fingertip tracing my spine, "are the *last* person I thought I'd see coming to celebrate the final moments of my imprisonment." She cast a long arm over her den. "I've been redecorating. What do you think?"

I shrugged stupidly.

"How nice of you to bring me a gift..." she said, eyeing me seductively.

"G-Gift?" A shot of terror raced through me. Did she think I was here to surrender myself? To become her sexual pet?

She sneered and casually opened her palm. Immediately, as if summoned by its true master, the Mes on my back began to burn, lacerating itself from the layers of my body. I cried out as my skin cracked open.

She was taking the Mes.

Inanna's long-ago confession to Gilgamesh resounded: *'When I am free from this punishment, free from my father's banishment...I will acquire each of the hidden Mes...making myself the one, true god...Then I will change this world...by destroying free will...and beginning again.'*

The Mes, however, remained firmly affixed to my body.

"Stubborn little thing, isn't it?" Inanna tapped her chin, feigning confusion. "Oh yes, silly me, how could I forget—it will only come off *when you are dead.*" She lowered her gaze, wolf-like, a sadistic smirk marring her lips. With that ubiquitous flick of her finger, she lifted me magically into the air, and at once, unimaginable pain ripped through my body. I screamed as my shoulder tore open. A long, jagged gash exposed the white of my bones beneath a mess of blood and pulp.

She's tearing me in two!

Like my father and mother before me, I would be ripped into two. If not for the pain, I almost relished the idea of the end. I closed my eyes, ready, waiting for the torment to subside, waiting to see my loved ones again, waiting for my afterlife to begin.

In the midst of my agony, I could hear Inanna's vindictive laughter.

Laughing at my pain.

At my suffering.

At all I'd lost...

Suddenly her laughter turned to screams.

I fell, landing hard on the stone. Sparks flashed behind my eyes, consciousness threatening to abandon me. My left arm, limp at my side, had nearly been severed. Confused, I looked for Inanna. Slumped on the floor, the goddess panted, gasping for breath. The tip of a long, silver blade protruded from her stomach. She'd been impaled straight through from the back. Resplendent pewter blood ebbed like pooling mercury beneath her.

She was dying.

And there—holding her, rocking her, weeping for what he'd done—was Gilgamesh.

Shocked by both his impossible presence and what he'd just done, I could only stand there, gaping.

Tears rolled down Gilgamesh's aging face. Quiet sobs wracked his chest as he stroked her hair. She gazed up at him, the lavender glow within her eyes dimming to pale lilac.

"Gilgamesh," she said, her voice frail as a snowflake. Silver tears trailed past her temples. "You…came back."

"Always." His face contorted with pain. "I'm so sorry… for everything. I did this, all of this. I hurt you, your sister—even what happened to Solomon…I was a selfish, arrogant ass…"

Inanna glanced at the sword protruding from her abdomen and then looked at Gilgamesh with unimaginable hurt. "Then why…would you…do *this*?"

"I cannot not allow you to harm this world—no matter how much I…love you."

A pewter teardrop slipped down her cheek. "You…love me?"

"Gods yes, woman," Gilgamesh said, stroking her cheek. "I always have."

"I lov…" she tried to say but amid a final, shuddering exhale, the radiance in her eyes extinguished.

Gilgamesh released a pained cry, clutching her lifeless body to his chest.

Moments later, Inanna's soul lifted up out of her corporeal body. A shimmering cloud of illumination, ethereal, it twisted midair. Pale rose, her spirit embodied what a goddess truly was—divine. Spellbound, I couldn't tear my gaze from the beauty of it—until I felt a sudden pressure on my good arm. Gilgamesh was beside me now, a fevered look beneath his bent brow.

"Solomon," he hissed. "Whisper her name into the urn, now!"

Confused by the urgency, I regarded the essence of Inanna once more, horrified to see it had shifted from a pale pink mist to that of a violet storm cloud. It brewed, furious and seething, pulsating with power. Freed from her earthly shell, she was pure energy. Raw, uninhibited vengeance.

Across the room, Inanna's corpse transformed to ash.

"We have to hurry," he said, trembling as he took the urn and wrenched out the plug. He thrust the vessel into my hands. "Here, now say her real name into it…"

"But I-I don't know her *real* name!"

270

"I do," he said, raising his voice against the howling winds. "Ereshkigal told me, right before she resurrected me."

I wanted to ask him why Ereshkigal had changed her mind, why she'd allowed him live once again, but now was not the time. Unsure if I trusted either him or Ereshkigal with my soul, I offered him the urn. He could say Inanna's true name into it as far as I was concerned.

He held up his palm. "It has to be you!"

"Why!"

He pointed to the Mes on my back.

"Fine!" I held the mouth of the urn to my lips. "What's her true name?"

He uttered it into my ear.

I frowned. "Are you certain?"

"Hurry! Before she possesses one our bodies!"

This was it.

This was the moment.

Sweat rolling over my brow, I brought the mouth of the death jar to my lips and took a deep breath.

"Do it!" Gilgamesh shouted. "Hurry, Solomon! Hurry!"

Enlil's words echoed: *'You are banished, Inanna, Ishtar, Isis, Goddess of Love —Lilitu…'*

I closed my eyes, praying to the very gods who'd forsaken me.

"*Lilitu…*"

Breath locked in my chest, I squeezed my eyes shut, and waited…

I creaked an eyelid open.

Nothing had changed.

It didn't work.

I gave Gilgamesh a bewildered stare, but his expression mirrored my own. She was a goddess, not a mere demon. I'd been a fool to think something so banal could contain the cosmic power of a god.

Debris hurtled around us, harder and faster. A strengthening hurricane eddied into the centre where we stood. Instead of the diabolic storm weakening, it grew stronger. Amidst it, I could hear Inanna's laughter.

"Are you sure it was the right name?" I shouted over the cacophony.

Before Gilgamesh could answer, an arm of the wind reached across the room and intentionally knocked over the single candle, somehow untouched by the preternatural gale. Thrown atop the heap of fallen bed linen, a great fire blazed to life. Hot tendrils licked at our skin, black smoke filling the small chamber.

Forced to back up, I glanced at the nearby exit only a few feet away. Instinct told me it was time to run. As if reading my thoughts, however, the chamber rumbled, sending a cascade of stones to bury the doorway, entombing us. Gilgamesh looked from me to the exit, and offered a remorseful grimace. The only way out was his secret one—somewhere on the other side of the storm.

Despair pooled my soul. All of this was for nothing. All the deaths, the lives destroyed. Father, Indra, Ariadne, Rhadamanthys and the Minoans, little Miri—all would remain unavenged.

I had failed them.

Then, from the mouth of the jar came a faint sound.

Ghostly, the voice whispered again, and again, *"Lilitu…Lilitu…"*

Inanna's soul screeched and fought against the gravitational pull of the urn. Her energy, a writhing serpent of violet smoke, was being drawn towards the mouth of the jar. Inch by inch, she resisted, but she was no match for the power of the urn.

In a final howl of fury, she was gone. The room fell eerily silent. Quickly, Gilgamesh shoved the plug into the urn. But almost immediately, the urn grew warm—then hot. Soon, it was so hot my fingertips were scorched. Even the clay was softening.

"It's not strong enough to hold her!" Gilgamesh said, wild-eyed.

An idea flashed.

I glanced at Indra's ring on my smallest finger, the hexagram signet glimmered amber in the fiery light.

"This symbol," the healer's whisper reached through the arc of time, *"represents the opposing forces of nature. The light and the dark. The good—and the evil. United, they form an unbreakable bond, a seal, which nothing can tear apart.'*

A seal.

With my good arm, I turned the urn onto its side. Red hot in my hands, I moaned as my palms blistered. Intuiting my plan, Gilgamesh helped me lift my wounded arm up to the base of the death jar. Together, we pressed, stamping the star onto the bottom. Inside, Inanna relinquished one last whimper as an image took form on the surface of the urn. On one side, an image of Inanna as the Goddess of Love, receiving offerings from her people. The other side, however, depicted her wrath, her demands for blood and sacrifice. An exhibit of her fickle, dual nature.

A moment later, the urn hardened, cool to the touch.

Bloodied and exhausted, we laid upon the floor. Unlikely heroes, the former king and the farm boy with blue eyes, we stared up at the buckled ceiling of the crumbling ziggurat. Faint traces of early morning sunlight bled through the cracks.

It was finally over.

We had defeated a goddess. We'd reclaimed our fate, our future. Our destinies were now unwritten. Emotion swept through me. Relief and sorrow, but mostly, closure. Misty-eyed, I glanced at Gilgamesh, this mighty King of Uruk, wondering if he too was embroiled in deep and introspective thoughts.

After a long sigh, Gilgamesh said, "I wonder if the brothel is open yet…"

"What are we going to do with…her?" I glanced uneasily at the urn on the table.

After escaping through the secret door, hidden inside Inanna's fireplace, we returned to the hut so Gilgamesh could stitch up my shoulder.

"We could drop her into the ocean, I guess…" He gave a casual shrug. "Don't worry, I'll deal with it…"

My mind hummed with everything that had transpired. Inanna, the curse, the adventure—I couldn't believe it was over.

Still, something niggled at me.

"How did you get Ereshkigal to resurrect you again?" I asked.

He frowned, focused on suturing my wound. "Hmm?"

"Did she make you promise her more souls in exchange for resurrection?" I shuddered at the image of Ereshkigal lingering over more cradles, abducting children for her hellish army.

"Um, no, she asked for...something else." His eyes betrayed him as they flicked towards the urn.

My stomach did a flip. "What?"

"Don't worry." I winced as he knotted the suture. "I've got it under control."

He turned his back to me, cleaning his hands—and my heart stopped. Dark crimson, fresh from a weeping wound, soaked the back of his shirt.

Then I looked down at my chest.

Sick with realization, I breathed deeply, pretending I didn't suspect anything.

"So, after Imi killed you, then you resurrected...how did you travel so fast from Egypt to Sumer?"

He glanced over his shoulder, that telltale smirk on his lips. "Oh, I hid aboard one of the Indus merchant ships. They're renowned for their swift travel across the waters."

"Oh?" I feigned interest, scanning the room for a weapon. The closest thing I could see was the larger remnant of a broken tablet. Ironically, the Epic of Gilgamesh. Inconspicuous, I leaned over, my new stitches stretching painfully with the movement.

"Hey, there's a lot of blood on the back of your shirt," I said. "You sure you're okay?"

He examined his soiled tunic. "Oh, uh, I'm fine. Must be your blood."

With the stone tablet behind my back, I rose and took stealthy steps towards him, placing myself firmly between him and the urn.

"We're still cursed, aren't we?" I pointed to the tattoo on my chest.

He chuckled. "Yeah, seems so."

"You said it would end when she died! What else did you lie about? Did you really talk to Ereshkigal? Do you owe her a favour for Inanna's name?"

Gilgamesh had the decency to blush. "Um, actually, Ereshkigal wouldn't tell me Inanna's real name—I just guessed."

"What if you were wrong! Then *my* soul would have been trapped in the urn..." I stopped short, disgusted.

I didn't give him a chance to smirk, I just swung the tablet. A loud crack ricocheted inside the little hut as the clay smashed against his head and fractured into a dozen pieces.

Gilgamesh landed with a hard thud. While he was unconscious, I lifted his shirt. Sure enough, there was a Mes manifesting on his back. Inanna's Mes. That's why he was so desperate to return and kill her. It wasn't about saving the world or the children, or even ending the curse. It was about obtaining the only *other* Mes he'd seen in seven hundred years. He knew he wouldn't be able to kill her alone.

This had been his plan all along.

Seething, I stood and grabbed the urn from the table.

He may have gotten the Mes, but he was *never* going to find the urn.

35

Return of the Goddess

*V*oices.

"Petra?"

Whispers of clarity, almost heard. Memories, not her own.

Trapped.

No—*Imprisoned.*

Time utterly endless. Watching the millenniums crawl by.

So alone.

Lavender and crimson.

Shadows dancing, writhing, erotic.

Serpentine.

"*Petraaa….*"

Laughter.

"You're mine…"

"Petra?" Solomon called to her from beyond. "Can you hear me?"

Her eyelids were so very heavy.

"She doesn't look too good…" a new voice commented. "Are you sure this is going to work?"

"Shh!" Solomon hissed. "She might already be here."

Petra forced her eyes open. Her back still wept with fresh blood, the Mes cutting like teeth on her skin. The bedroom spun as though she'd drunk an entire bottle of champagne. The last thing she recalled was laying on Solomon's bed, listening to the conclusion his epic tale.

Then, darkness.

"Solomon?" her voice sounded gritty.

He cupped her face within his hands. So warm. So safe.

"Stay with me, Petra, it's almost over."

She blinked back tears. Something was coming, growing inside her—she could feel it pulsating, slithering alongside her soul.

A tendril of her blonde hair fell across her eye. Petra started to lift her hand, to brush it away, but realized she couldn't move. A jolt of fear raced through her as she realized she was immobilized, bound to a chair with long strips of fabric.

"Solomon? Why am I tied up! Let me go! Please!"

"It's for your own good," Solomon said calmly. "*Trust me…*"

Petra started to cry. "Why is this happening?"

Solomon knelt before her, guilt in his beautiful blue stare. "When you found the urn and cut yourself on it, your blood…it *fed* her. It gave her enough strength to transfer her soul from the urn…and into you."

Confused, Petra shook her head. "Fed…who?"

She'd suspected the truth all along, of course, but was afraid to say it aloud.

"Inanna," came the second voice, from somewhere behind Solomon.

Petra willed her eyes to focus on the stranger—then grimaced as she recognized him.

"G-Gabriel?"

Amusement danced in his dark brown eyes.

"Good day, Newfie," he said, twisting the tip of his moustache. "Nice to see you again. And may I say, your legs are as lovely as ever."

Solomon sighed. "Petra, his name is not Gabriel. This is Gilgamesh…"

Gilgamesh gave a dramatic bow. "*King* Gilgamesh—but *you* can call me Gil."

"You two are…*friends?*" Petra asked, bewildered.

The men exchanged an awkward glance.

Gil raised his hand, wobbling it side to side. "Depends on which century you refer to…"

Solomon rolled his eyes, standing. "Let's just get this over with."

Petra watched as the two men placed themselves strategically before her. Solomon withdrew a knife from his belt.

"W-What…are you doing?" Petra's body shivered uncontrollably, yet something inside remained calm. Cold as ice. And it was expanding—*stretching*.

Gil held a decorative clay vase. *A death jar.* At this, the thing inside her hissed and recoiled in horror.

'*Prison*,' it whispered.

"It's time, Solomon," Gil said, his expression grave.

"I'm so sorry, Petra," Solomon said, tears in his eyes as he pressed the cold blade to her throat. "It'll be quick…I promise."

Gil brought the mouth of the urn to his lips, ready to whisper *her* true name once more…

The entity inside Petra thrashed. She screamed as the inhuman being exploded from within. The *other* surged forth, devouring, consuming everything that was once Petra in its wake; rising as though from the fathoms of the ocean and breaking through the surface for its first breath of air. Petra felt her own soul being pulled under the water, dragged beneath the cold black depths and slowly drowned.

Swallowed.

Inanna opened her violet eyes.

Overjoyed to be free, she was also enraged to once again be confronted by the mere mortals who'd so heartlessly destroyed her beautiful body and locked her soul away for thousands of years.

"So, here we are again," she said, her voice smooth as velvet, eyeing the blade at her neck. "If you kill me, you kill Petra too. You can't save her *and* capture my soul at the same time."

"I know." Solomon nodded sadly. "I…have no choice."

She uttered a mirthless laugh.

"I do…" she said with a flick her finger, hurtling Solomon across the room and into a wall, his blade sliding into a dark corner. Inanna closed her eyes and effortlessly *pushed* the power seething within. The fabric binding her to the chair turned to ash.

She stretched catlike. "That's *much* better."

"Inanna?" Gilgamesh took a cautious step forward, his expression filled with hope. "My Love, is it really you?"

An unbidden ache swelled inside her chest.

'I cannot not allow you to harm this world—no matter how much I…love you,' his long-ago confession resounded.

The ache evolved to a slow burn—then rage.

"You *killed* me."

"I know, I know…" He raised his hands. "You were going to destroy the world and I had to stop you…but I've missed you. I should never have killed you. These thousands of years without you have been torture…but now we can truly be together. Soon you'll have all the Mes. You can make me a god, like you, and we can live as one. *Forever.*"

She prowled a few steps towards him, a mocking smile on her lips. "And what, pray tell, on this pitiful plane of existence makes you think I still want *you*?"

His face fell.

"You are nothing to me, Gilgamesh. *Nothing.* Why would I desire to spend eternity with a pathetic being such as yourself? You were created, all of you, out of sheer boredom. An experiment, if you will. A passing amusement…a mere plaything." She ran a satin white fingertip down his cheek. "And I've grown tired of you—*all of you.*"

She made a dismissive gesture and Gil was flung across the room.

On the other side of the room, Solomon groaned, bringing himself to a stand.

"Inanna, stop!" he dared to shout at her. "Enough of this! You've hurt so many people. Don't you care about the pain you've inflicted?"

"Of course not," she scoffed. "Do you care about the ants when an anthill is washed away by a flood? No. I am a god. An overseer of *lesser* creatures. Humans are little more than intelligent monkeys. *I* designed you that way. Submissive, obedient, utterly devoted to me and my kind —until my father intervened, that is," she added darkly. "Enough of this—it's nearly time."

The combined power of the Mes pulsed through her veins. She didn't possess them all, she realized, but she'd be able to find where her father hid them with little effort as they called to one another. If not for the wretched limited human form, she'd be able to bend the very fabric of the universe. Once she obtained them all, however, she would be more powerful than any god—even her own maker.

Bloodied and out of breath, both Solomon and Gil stood bravely before her.

Inanna laughed at their sad attempt at heroics. "Really, boys? Do you think you can defeat *me*? Oh, and I'll be needing those," she said, indicating the Mes on both men's backs. "But, of course, for that you must die…" She lifted her hand to rip their fleshy bodies to shreds.

"Inanna, wait!" Gilgamesh shouted. "You can't kill me…"

She raised a barely interested brow. "Oh, why is that?"

"I, and I alone, know where the last of the Mes are," he said with a confident smirk.

Inanna gritted her teeth. "Fine, you can live—for now."

She turned to Solomon, raising her hand to remove the curse she'd bestowed on him so long ago, to send his soul to a hellish eternity. "But you, my pretty, blue-eyed boy, it's time to die…"

An odd expression crossed his handsome face—relief.

"Or…" Gil offered her a sly smile, holding up the urn. "You could return the favour?"

"What!" Horrified, Solomon gaped at his *so-called* friend. "You…traitor! I always knew you couldn't be trusted! From the first time I met you, you've been nothing but a liar and a fraud! You could never have been a hero, Gilgamesh. You've only ever proven yourself a waste. A waste of time. A waste of a man. And especially, a waste of a king!"

From a hidden holster under his shirt, Gil withdrew a sleek black gun and turned it onto Solomon. The former king's hands trembled with rage.

"For *thousands* of years I have tolerated your whining, your snivelling and, frankly, nauseating mission to save the world. I saved you and this…world, and for what? I lost the only woman I've ever truly loved." He turned a tearful gaze towards Inanna. "Please forgive me. I searched for you, my love. I scoured the world to find you. To free you. But no no matter how devoted a friend I pretended to be to him, he would never tell me where he'd hidden the urn. I'm so very sorry I ever helped him kill you. I love you. I've always loved you, Inanna. And I want to be with you…forever."

Solomon's eyes filled with hate. "You're nothing but a useless coward!"

"You're making this easy…" Gilgamesh sneered, sauntering up to Inanna and handing her the urn.

Solomon swallowed. "What are you doing?"

"Sorry, old friend…" Gilgamesh aimed the gun at Solomon's chest—and fired.

Solomon fell to his knees, clutching his heart with an expression of confusion and betrayal. Thick scarlet blossomed, spilling down his torso.

Amid his last breath, like an exhale in an ice storm, Solomon's soul drifted from his mortal shell.

With a smile, Inanna brought the urn to her lips. She would imprison Solomon as he had her. Then, she would bury him the desert or drop him into the deepest part of the ocean where he could contemplate the endless moments, for all the ages.

In a whisper, she uttered his name, "*Solomon.*"

A hush fell over the bedroom.

"*Solomon…Solomon…*" the urn whispered, beckoning his essence.

Inanna watched as Solomon's soul drifted closer to the urn, towards its eternal prison. Unlike her entrapment, he didn't struggle against the gravitational pull of the tide. Graceful, it probed the mouth of the urn with ghostly fingers…then stopped and began drifting away.

Inanna frowned.

278

Across the room, a bead of sweat slipped from Gilgamesh's brow. The urn whispered again, *"Lilitu…"*

"Your mother loved the water," Father began the story of my birth. *"One day, she asked to go swimming. She said her back hurt and the water helped her. So I took her. She swam a while, but she was quieter than usual.*

" 'I think he is coming, nga arammu,' she told me, rubbing her belly. Then after much pain in the belly and many hours, she cried out and you came from her. There in the water! Our son! Our little maru!

"She named you Shelomoh, which means 'peaceful' in her native tongue. In Sumerian, it translated to Solomon…"

Petra felt her leave.

It was a swift but painful process as the goddess's soul was forcibly jerked from Petra's body and stuffed back into the urn. Petra ached as if Inanna had clawed her from the inside out. For the first time in weeks, she finally felt alone.

With a tentative touch to her back, she was relieved to find every single Mes now gone. Vanquished like the demon-goddess who'd haunted her every moment since she'd cut herself on the urn.

Petra rose on unsteady legs and made her way to Solomon. Kneeling, she touched his arm and gasped. His skin was already cold. She'd seen everything that happened. Every moment. She could observe through Inanna's eyes, but was unable to control her own body. Though silenced, she'd screamed when Gil shot Solomon. Horrified, she watched him slump to the floor, dead.

Amidst it all, she noticed Gil's face turn ashen as Inanna whispered the wrong name into the urn.

With the urn clutched protectively to his chest, Gil lay on the floor, catching his breath. Petra noticed the star symbol already stamped into the bottom.

"The urn already had the seal," she said. "You guys *planned* all of this, didn't you?"

"He was determined to save you," Gil said with a reverent glance at his dead friend. "So we had to make Inanna believe I was betraying him."

"How did you know she would say the wrong name?"

"We didn't, we just hoped like hell she didn't know he had another name." He offered a tired grin.

"So you…don't love her?"

His eyes widened. "Are you crazy? After four thousand years of being damned by her twisted sex curse, I'd rather run naked through bear country covered in honey than spend another minute with that woman!"

Petra started to laugh, but stopped short when a black mist rose in the centre of the room. All around her, the shadows darkened, as if the midmorning sun outside had been shrouded. A sussurus of voices, low and hissing, emanated from the gathering darkness.

"It's not over yet, I'm afraid," Gil said under his breath. "Time to pay the reaper…"

"What do you mean?" Petra trembled. "What does Ereshkigal want?"

Gil held up the urn. "It's what she's always wanted, scoured the earth and killed for—her sister's soul."

"The deal…" Petra uttered in dark realization. "That's the deal you made with Ereshkigal after the Egyptian Queen killed you, isn't it? In exchange for your resurrection?"

"Among other things…" He chuckled sadly. "Only Solomon messed up my plans and buried the urn where no one, not even me, could find it—that part was true enough. It all worked out for the best, of course, until you dug her up and let her crazy ass out."

Ereshkigal manifested from the mist. But for her dark hair, she was a replica of her sister.

"You have something for me, I presume," she said coldly, forgoing formal introduction, but Petra recognized her as the woman she'd seen in the museum back in Vancouver.

Gil nodded, cradling the urn. "On one condition."

Ereshkigal's violet eyes flashed with impatience. "You ran out of favours a very long time ago, human…"

"Heal Solomon first…please."

The Goddess of Death pursed her lips and sighed. "Fine, I've always had a soft spot for him anyway." She waved her hand over Solomon's corpse and a brilliant white mist appeared before him, entering through his pale lips.

"Thank you." Gil started to offer the urn to Ereshkigal with his right hand, but at the same time straightened his left arm. Petra saw something slide out from within his sleeve and into his palm.

Her heart stopped.

It was Solomon's knife.

"Take care of the old man for me, will you?" Gil said to Petra. "He's not as strong as he thinks. And tell him to hurry—he'll know what I mean."

Gil withdrew the blade and sliced a long gash into his palm—and then placed it against the urn.

"Fool! You'll set her free!" Ereshkigal screamed.

"I figured it would be a good for me to experience life from a woman's point of view for once, don't you think?" Gil said with a wink.

She growled, and then seemed to reconsider, a nightmare smile on her lips. "Fine, have it your way…"

With a wave of her hand, the shadows lunged from every corner and took hold of Gil. He screamed once before being consumed by the black mists and vanishing through the floor.

Petra cracked open an eyelid, a soft smile on her lips as she remembered where she was. A balmy island breeze brushed the ivory drapes, lifting them into a slow billow. Outside, exotic birds gossiped over the whisper of palm trees. Sea-salt laced her every inhale.

The night before, after an angst-ridden eight hour wait for Solomon to resurrect, she had a long, hot shower and then fell into the king-sized bed. Around a satisfying stretch, she cautiously revisited the wild experiences over the last few weeks. Some memories made her cringe, many made her tremble, but most made her smile. The latter, coincidentally, carried a common theme—Solomon.

With Inanna's soul now exorcised, Petra could feel all her own feelings again. She could trust her thoughts and emotions without the toxic influence of the obsessive goddess. Gone were the lustful, desperate, power-hungry desires. All replaced by a sense of...peace.

Rising, she dressed and headed down the hall to Solomon's bedroom. He too, for obvious reasons, was exhausted and fell asleep almost instantly after coming back to life. As she peeked into his room, she was struck with dark surreality.

This was where it had all happened.

'Take care of the old man for me, will you?' Gilgamesh's last words echoed. *'...tell him to hurry—he'll know what I mean.''*

After Solomon had resurrected, she was so weary, she'd forgotten to tell him Gil message before he was stolen by Ereshkigal.

With no sign of Solomon upstairs, she headed to the kitchen. Redolent of fried eggs and toast, she surmised he'd been here recently. As if to catch her attention, a breeze exhaled on her arm, originating from the adjacent hallway—the one with the big door heavily guarded by a biometric scanner and steal bars.

'What do you keep in there, King Kong?'' she'd asked him.

His eyes darkened. 'Something like that...'

Petra started down the dark corridor—towards the now open door.

Inside, a dozen candelabras illuminated a large windowless room. Thousands of little alcoves lined the walls from ceiling to floor, each housing an ornately decorated urn. In the centre, shirtless, Solomon sat cross-legged, mediating before a large shrine shrouded by ten curtains of fine woven linen, elaborately designed with blue, purple, and scarlet thread.

Petra admired the well-defined muscles beneath Solomon's dark-brown skin—then spied a single tattoo on his lower back.

A Mes.

Petra gasped.

Startled, Solomon quickly stood.

"I'm sorry, I didn't mean to intrude, but..." she stammered. "Why do you still have a Mes? I thought it was all over..."

He sighed. "I'm afraid not. In fact, it's only just begun. This war has been a longtime coming, Petra. You don't have to help," Solomon said intuitively. "You've done more than enough."

"I want to help," she said, then remembered her mission. "Gilgamesh—he told me to tell you to hurry. Why?"

"We need to find the remaining Mes before Ereshkigal—or any of the others," he said cryptically. "They'll be hunting for them..."

"But Gil said he knew where the rest were," Petra said.

"No, he lied to buy time—only one person knows where they are. *Me.*"

A thread of fear tightened around her soul.

Solomon swept a wayward blonde strand from her face, his fingertips grazing her cheek. With a sharp inhale, Petra brought her hand to her face, feeling the start of an angry welt on her skin. With a tortured expression, Solomon turned away.

"The Mes," he said sadly, "they...lessen the effects of the curse. But with just one left..."

She looked at him, and for the first time, really saw him for who he was. A man, an ancient man, who'd lost everyone he'd ever loved, enduring centuries of loneliness and despair.

She touched his back, feeling the warmth of his skin.

"Careful Petra..." he whispered, moving just out of her reach. "I can't lose you too."

An ache gathered inside her chest. Tears building in her eyes, she glanced about the room to distract herself from the sorrow—and something within the shrine caught her eye.

Hidden just beyond the thick curtains, atop a podium exalted by more candles, statues, and tasselled banners, was a massive gold box adorned with two winged cherubim. Long poles extended from sides as to be carried...

Petra's knees went weak and she reached for something to steady her, finding Solomon's warm hand.

"Is that...what I think it is?"

"Do you remember when Father asked me what I dreamed of becoming?" he asked quietly.

Breath caught in her throat, she nodded mutely.

"I dreamed of making a difference in the world, like the great kings of old," he said. "But to wield great influence, one must obtain great power..."

She felt herself pale.

Petra swallowed, eyeing the Ark. "W-What's inside?"

Solomon just smiled.

Epilogue

Pictures littered the walls of his office, captured images of the various adventures he'd embarked upon over the many years; excavations in exotic locations in and around Iraq, Egypt, and Crete. One in particular, buried amid the lot, was an aged black and white photo showing a youthful version of himself standing beside the infamous Howard Carter after he'd discovered the tomb of King Tut —nearly one hundred years ago.

He smiled at the photo.

Searching, always searching…and finally found.

With a click, he switched off the lights and started down the hallway.

The janitor gave a friendly smile and wave. "Good night, Professor."

"Good night, Jerome," Emmett replied, plopping his tweed hat onto his head.

As he exited the university and entered into the cool Vancouver night, he drew a long breath, the air felt crisp and clean in his lungs. Winter was on its way once more. Overhead, the gleaming eye of a pendulous moon lit the way home.

A few blocks later, he walked up the stairs to his small apartment. Upon entry, he removed his shoes and hung up his tweed hat and jacket. After fingering through the new mail, Emmett crossed the room and stood before a closet door where he removed the rest of his clothing, folding them neatly into a pile. Moonlight traced the black tattoo on his chest as he whispered a prayer in a language not spoken in over four thousand years.

With the flare of a match strike and a plume of sulphurous smoke, the old professor lit a black candle. A halo of gold imbued the tiny closet with light. As he knelt before a shrine, candlelight trembled across the face of Petra's urn. He loathed to kill the driver, but sacrifices had to be made.

Darkness ebbed. Shadows crawled across the walls. Disembodied whispers breathed all around him.

She was here.

Drawn forth from the abyss, she manifested before him.

He bowed low. "My Goddess."

"The plan has changed," she said with a hint of annoyance. "I will send you new orders when I decide how to proceed."

"I will await your instructions."

The goddess turned to leave, but paused. "Did Solomon recognize you?"

"No—our secret is safe."

She smiled darkly.

"For now…"

Acknowledgments

I would like to thank everyone who read The Ancient during the writing and editing process, in particular: Sandra (my partner in crime), Karen, Pat, Crystal, Phil, Stephanie, and so many more. I appreciate your help more than you know.

And a special thanks to my husband, Chris. None of this would have been possible without your endless support and patience.

Thank you for believing in me when I found it hard to believe in myself.

And now for a sneak peek at Book Two...

The Ancient

&

The Ark of Time
Book Two in The Ancient Chronicles

1
Zemblanity

"*I'll meet you in Vancouver,*" Solomon promised, a storm gathering behind his ancient blue eyes. "*There's a few things I have to take care of first…*"

Petra traced her lips with a slow fingertip, Solomon's parting kiss lingered like a burn. Literally.

Outside the porthole of the private jet, Petra could almost see the ocean of people on the ground, noise and chaos polluting the air even more than the exhaust. Taxis honking, frustrated drivers shaking their fists; ambulances shrilling as they raced through narrow, crowded streets to resuscitate an ever-dying junkie; endless streams of commuters, hippies, panhandlers, solicitors of porn and prayer alongside an Armani army en route to the same job they did yesterday.

She remembered a time, not so long ago, when she wished her life had some semblance to those nameless souls below. So-called *normal*. No ancient curses. No preternatural symbols carving themselves into her back. No parasitic evil goddess invading her thoughts and dreams from within—but if she wished all those away, there would be no Solomon, either.

Now Petra wasn't sure what she wanted. While happy to be free from Inanna's possession, she noticed a gaping absence left behind. An emptiness. A black hole, swirling and hungry, threatened to consume what remained.

Of course, Petra realized it couldn't be the unstable goddess who'd branded her with longing, but a certain brooding, blue-eyed Sumerian.

Memories of the warm, quiet arms of Solomon's island held her tight, unwilling to let go. Turquoise waters scalloped ivory sandbars. Verdant-plumed palm trees sighed, wavering to the whim of a salty breeze. The susurrus of the foamy white breakers as they lapped the shoreline.

It was Heaven.

Edin.

Petra smiled.

Despite Gilgamesh's urgent message to 'hurry' amidst an attack by Ereshkigal's terrifying shadowy demons, sucking him through the floor into some ancient hellhole, Petra and Solomon had spent two whole days wandering his remote island off the coast of Fiji, spelunking dark caves and collecting seashells as they strolled the long, warm beaches.

While not unwelcome, the miniature—and utterly chaste—holiday was not by choice. Solomon told her he was waiting for a call and could do nothing until he received it. He wouldn't tell her who it was from, nor any details concerning Gilgamesh's fate. Forced to trust him, Petra resigned to enjoying herself and, most of all, just being alone with Solomon.

It would've been all too easy let this new existence to simply sweep her up and carry her away into some modern fairytale. While she'd always cringed at the cliche stories of women falling head over heels for some dark and gorgeous stranger, abandoning their lives and freedom, their singularity in the universe, and joining the fleecy cult of 'love at first sighters', Petra suddenly understood the allure. But Solomon wasn't an ordinary man. He was an ancient man. A wise and gentle soul who'd suffered the ages as no other. He'd witnessed the rise and fall of empires, the birth and destruction of civilizations—the evolution of mankind over the last *four thousand years*.

Her thoughts drifted to the box, hidden amongst his many secrets within the mansion on the island. Made of acacia wood, plated with solid gold, two winged cherubim gazing at one another from across the mercy seat—*the very seat of God*. Sweat pearled on her brow. She could hardly speak its name aloud. For to utter its true name meant she had to admit who Solomon claimed to be.

'*King...*' her treasonous thoughts whispered.

If he was who she surmised him to be, then the box had to be the *Ark of the Covenant*.

"What's inside?" Petra had implored him, eyes wide with wonder; but Solomon had only smiled, the clandestine contents remaining sealed within. Her imagination couldn't even guess what it contained. Whatever it was, it was as old as time itself, brimming with power of epic, no, *biblical* proportions.

Then the mysterious call arrived. Solomon's eyes darkened the instant the phone rang, vanishing into the makeshift temple and closing the biometric-controlled steel door behind him. When he finally re-emerged, Petra was told it was time for her to go.

"It's not safe for you to be around me right now," Solomon said as he led her out to the landing strip where his personal plane waited to take her home.

"Not safe from who—or what?" she replied, knowing too well the bizarre nature of his world.

Regret filled his eyes. "I-I can't tell you."

She nodded but overwhelming sadness stung her heart.

Tenderly, he kissed her. Though his lips had scarcely grazed hers, pain seared her skin. She stifled the whimper, but he knew he'd hurt her. After guiding her aboard the airplane, he turned away in shame.

Now, with stomach swooping and ears popping, the plane started its descent. Reality was closing in, and fast. Petra winced, afraid if she returned to her old life, her old routine, that the unbelievable adventure she'd experienced would dissipate, and she'd eventually convince herself it was all just a dream. That none of it had ever happened.

That Solomon didn't exist.

As if in a gentle nudge, her swollen lips tingled, reminding her of his kiss.

'You shall not love another woman so long as you live—lest you pay the price...' Inanna's fateful curse resounded.

No, he was real, as were his feelings for Petra. Of that she could not deny.

Petra withdrew the phone from her purse and touched it awake. Still in airplane mode, she hesitated. Once she flipped that switch, she'd be surrendering to reality. If she ignored it, and perhaps conveniently 'lost' the phone before landing, she could continue pretending her former life didn't really exist. University, student loans, bills, responsibilities...none of it was appealing. Even her dream of becoming an archaeologist was waning, incomparable to the fantastical world she'd been immersed within for the last few weeks.

"I'll call you when I'm on my way..." Solomon said with fierce conviction in his ocean-blue stare as he handed Petra her phone, and then watched as she entered the plane.

Petra sighed. She had no choice. For Solomon to be able to call her, she had to switch it on. With a grimace, Petra flipped the switch and watched as the phone connected to the outside world. After several minutes, praying all the while her inbox would be empty or some cataclysmic technological event had occurred in her absence and destroyed her messages, the devil-red notifications started popping up.

Petra's eyes widened.

167 unread texts.

145 missed calls—and almost as many voice messages.

She didn't have to guess from who.

Since she'd been exorcized of the crazed goddess and, subsequently, the sought-after Mes, Solomon assured Petra that her apartment was likely safe for return. Despite his confidence, Petra eyed every corner and shadow with abject paranoia. As she entered into the main corridor, the door to her left swung open and her landlady, Sue, came running out and swept Petra into a bear hug.

"Petra!" Sue examined her tenant with wide eyes, over-botoxed brows further accentuating the shocked expression. "Where on earth have you been?"

Flustered, Petra withdrew from the embrace and pretended to search for her keys inside her purse, but realized they were already in her hand. "I, um, just went on a little holiday…why?"

Sue took Petra by the shoulders and shook her a little too hard. "Your mother—she's been frantic! She even filed a missing person report!"

"What!" Petra dropped her purse, a few items, including her phone, clattered across the tiled floor. With a sigh, Petra bent to retrieve her things. Sue's knees crackled at she knelt to help pick up the mess.

"I guess I should call her before she declares a national emergency," Petra mumbled, reaching for the phone last.

"No need." Sue stood, re-adjusting her too-tight jeans beneath a prominent roll. "She's been staying in your apartment—waiting for you."

The elevator doors slid open, betraying her covert arrival with a loud ding. Petra peered out and down the hall, at her apartment door, as if returning to the scene of a murder or a poltergeist infestation. Either of which she would gladly have chosen over what was really behind door number one.

Wild and daring escape plans flooded her thoughts, most requiring the services of a hot air balloon or ninjas; followed by even crazier excuses as to why she'd vanished without a trace, no note, no phone calls. From amnesia caused by a benign brain tumour to being kidnapped by an Arabian prince (which, ironically, wasn't far from the truth), she resigned to the least inventive, and most cliche, of explanations—*love*.

Petra stood outside her apartment door and drew a few deep breaths before entering. Her mother, Vera, took her role as matriarch of the family, ruler of the Monroe clan, very seriously. And since her husband's death over two years ago, Vera appeared to relish her elevated status as sole parent of their trio of adult girls.

A little too much, Petra thought.

Being the youngest of the three siblings, Petra bore the brunt of her mother's vendetta to right the wrongs she felt had been inflicted upon the children by their father's lack of discipline. Her father was the 'fun' one, the one the girls had turned to for advice, a hug, and a soft place to fall. When he died, the world felt hardened around her; everything was duller, lacklustre by comparison.

It was only recently that her world appeared brighter again, safer— after she met Solomon.

Petra summoned courage and placed her hand on the doorknob, but before she could turn it, it swung open with the force of an atomic blast.

"Petra Magdalene Monroe!" Her mother's eyes blazed like polished jade. "Where the *hell* have you been!"

Petra sighed. "Fiji."

Vera gave her a bug-eyed, disbelieving glare. "What, they don't have phones in Fiji?" Without waiting for an answer, she added, nose crinkled as if she smelled something rotten. "What did you do to your hair? It's so…short."

"I-I cut it," Petra stammered, running her fingers self-consciously through her blonde pixie. "It was hot in Iraq."

Glowering, her mother resumed her rant. "You can't just go traipsing off with some strange man without telling anyone—" She stopped short. "It is a man, right? I mean, it's completely fine if it's a woman—in fact, that would explain *a lot*—and there are plenty of ways you can still have a baby as a lesbian. Why just the other day I read an article that the scientists have successfully conceived a baby using *three* sets of DNA..." With clawed hands, her mother molded an imaginary, biologically-modified child midair.

"It *is* a man, Mother," Petra managed to get the words in edgewise. Why couldn't she have one of those mothers who gave her the silent treatment when she was angry?

"I know," Vera huffed, tossing her silk-soft locks over her shoulder. "Joe told us."

"Joe? You talked to Joe—from my ancient mythologies class? How did you—"

"Professor Emmett told us where to find him," Vera said, lifting her chin haughtily.

Petra gaped at her mother. "You talked to Emmett too! Mother, I'm a grown-up, you can't go around..."

Vera took a threatening step into her daughter's personal space. "Then act like it, Petra! Do you even care how worried I was? Did you even think what it must be like to not know where my daughter is or who she's with? Did you even consider how frightened I might be for you? I've already lost my husband, Petra, I don't need to lose anyone else." Her mother's voice tightened at the latter, tears brimming in her eyes.

Petra's heart cracked. "Mother, I—I'm so sorry...I didn't think..."

"No, you didn't think." Her mother sniffled, dabbing at her eyes with a monogrammed linen hanky she'd retrieved from her purse. With a final shuddering breath, Vera made her way to the door, pausing before the mirror to correct the line of her burgundy lipstick. "Now go get ready, and dress nice, I'll make the dinner reservations for six o'clock."

Left raw inside, Petra reeled from her mother's harsh interrogation. Her emotions swung, pendulous, from guilt to that of profound regret. She never should have gotten on that plane. Never should have turned on her phone—and never, ever should have left Solomon.

A seed of darkness germinated within, a weed, one that had been thriving amidst the garden of doubt. Already, Solomon and the supernatural adventure had fallen into that dreaded crack between memory and imagination. Psychological limbo. Where it was easier to believe it was all just a dream. Just a flight of fancy that never really happened.

Petra glanced at her phone and an ache gathered in her bones.

"I'll call you as soon as I can...I promise," Solomon had whispered into her ear, hugging her one last time before ushering swiftly her onto the plane.

With her thumb, Petra scrolled through the long list of missed calls, but only her mother and sisters' numbers appeared, and was further disheartened when she realized she didn't even have Solomon's number.

Her stomach did an uncomfortable flip—there was no way to contact him. She didn't even know the precise location of his private island nor anyone who knew him personally. She had no pictures of him, no proof he even existed...

"Get a grip, Petra!" she said aloud, rolling her eyes. "It hasn't even been a whole day yet."

With a glance at the clock, she started to hurry. Her mother was sending a car to take her to the restaurant in just half an hour. The last thing Petra wanted to do right now was spend time with her mother in a public place. She wanted to stay in, have a long hot bath, a glass of wine, perhaps pine and mope a little more.

Sighing, she slipped on a sapphire camisole and draped an ivory shawl around her shoulders. As she studied the finished product in the mirror, she couldn't help but think how the blue of her shirt reminded her of Solomon's eyes.

Steely clouds barred the evening sky from view, behind which, logic told her, the stars still sparkled. As a perpetual test of faith, each day the sun plunged into a mysterious borderland; in its place, we are given the moon, the stars, and an infinite blackness with which to scry our universal purpose, to dream inside a fast of consciousness.

We don't question the renaissance of the day, just as we don't fret with the onset of night. Somehow, deep within every one of us, we *know* each are there on the other side, hidden from sight, but that, in due time, they *will* return.

Why then did she not have such faith in Solomon? In anyone?

Because sometimes people leave and don't come back, Petra thought with a pang of loss. Like Solomon with Father, her own father had been her world too. Her hero. In retrospect, idolizing anyone was risky. They were either bound to disappoint you or fated to abandon you. In a kinder world, she realized her father would not have chosen to die when he did, or how, but he left right when she'd needed him the most.

En route to the Le Crocodile, her mother's favourite French restaurant, streetlights washed Burrard Street in an eerie amber hue. Darker and cooler than it should've been for early autumn, Petra shuddered and drew her shawl tighter, wishing she'd worn something a little more substantial.

Suddenly, the car slowed to a stop. The driver's head obscured her view, but from what she could see, a crowd had gathered in the street. The car edged forward, negotiating the throng of people, who seemed both curious and horrified. An ambulance screamed past her window, arriving on the scene.

The masses parted for the medics, revealing what remained of a woman who'd apparently fallen, or jumped, from the upper levels of a nearby building. Petra tracked the length of the skyscraper, spying an open window near the top where red curtains billowed flag-like. She followed the impossible drop to the pavement where the woman now laid, crimson spattered like a gruesome halo around her dark hair.

Petra squeezed her eyes shut, wishing the image away.

What would drive a person to leap to their death? Did fear and regret plague them the entire trip down?

Or was she pushed? Petra shuddered, grateful as the crowd and chaos grew smaller behind them.

A few blocks later, the car turned onto a narrow, one-way street and pulled up to the curb.

"Ma'am." The driver opened the door and she climbed out, still shaking.

Upon entering the posh restaurant, embraced by aromatics of garlic, olive oil, and savoury pasta dishes, it would've been easy for Petra to merely sweep aside the gory scene she'd just witnessed, filing it in her memory banks as 'unpleasant, please delete'. Instead, she made a mental note to follow up on the accident later that night, curious if there'd be a news story on the woman.

"Reservation?" the host inquired, his voice scarcely above a whisper. Petra always wondered why the employees of fancy restaurants felt compelled, or were trained, to speak at nearly inaudible levels. Did that somehow make the dining experience more lofty? She had no idea.

"Monroe," she said, scanning the lounge but not locating her mother. Petra guessed she'd been seated in the main dining room, beyond a long dark hallway.

The host perused the reservation book with a long finger. "Ah, table for four. Follow me."

Four? Who else is coming? Petra frowned as she trailed the host through a hallway laden with racks of aged wines. Then she nodded to herself, surmising the extras were probably her sisters, Sistine and Vienna.

Great. She cringed inwardly.

Quaint and intimate with a modern decor, Le Crocodile exuded elegance. An ivory runner led them into the main dining room, passed an oval wall decor shaped like a porthole. Inadvertently, it made her remember the plane ride, then the island—then Solomon. Which, in turn, made her itch to check her phone for the nine-hundredth time.

Pathetic, Petra, she thought. *You used to be the cool chick who didn't need a man, remember? Didn't* want *a man—and especially didn't chase a man! It's not like Solomon is* that *good-looking. Okay, he is, but that's not the reason I'm in love with him...*

The restaurant suddenly spun. Breathing heavily, Petra stopped short and took hold of a patron's chair for support. Amid a forkful of grilled asparagus headed for his mouth, the elderly man turned and regarded her with an expression between confusion and annoyance.

Reeling, she blinked in disbelief.

"Oh no," Petra said under her breath. "I *am* in love with Solomon..."

This was not like her. Pining over a guy like a lovesick teenager? What the hell was going on? She drew a sharp breath.

"Inanna," she uttered. "Is she still inside of me?"

That had to be the answer. There was no other explanation as to why Petra would feel such...longing. Such desperate desire. She must still be cursed. Still inhabited by the maniacal, power-hungry Sumerian goddess. That had to be it—she hoped. She didn't want to be in love or have to deal with relationships or dating...or men in general!

"Petra," she heard her mother call. "We're over here."

291

Petra glanced to her left to find her mother and sister, Sistine, seated at a table in the far corner. The third person at the table wasn't her younger sister, Vienna, however.

It was Joe.